REACTIVE MAGIC

The Complete Series

Helen Vivienne Fletcher

First published in this format by HVF Publishing in 2023
Copyright © Helen Vivienne Fletcher, 2023
Edited by Jess Senior

ISBN:
978-1-9911980-1-3 (paperback)
978-1-9911980-2-0 (epub)

REACTIVE

Helen Vivienne Fletcher

Chapter One

Toby

It was growing, that was for sure. Small green points crept up through the soil, spreading across the surface like a deformed octopus unfurling its tentacles. It was a succulent, but there was something different about it, something more sinister, like it had been crossed with a fungus, oozing poisonous sap.

Zo popped her head over my shoulder. "That is definitely not a sunflower." She laughed, sending brightly coloured sparks shooting out over me.

"Stop it!" I slapped my shoulder, as my jersey started to singe. That just made Zo laugh harder, spraying another round of red and gold embers.

"That's enough, Zoe. Back to your own work." Miss Trager's tone indicated this was non-negotiable.

Zo made a face at being called "Zoe" then turned back to her own plant spell. Naturally, she'd managed to grow a perfect yellow flower. In fact, looking around the classroom, I was the only one who hadn't produced something pretty and floral.

Miss Trager picked up my flowerpot. The stems were twisting now, turning a reddish-brown as they did. Miss

Trager watched it, her lip curling in disgust. Her eyes didn't match the rest of her expression, though. The intensity of her stare and the way her breathing had deepened, she almost seemed excited... eager... Eager to use this to get me out of her class, probably.

Zo and Julianna's flowers were leaning out of their pots, their stalks curling around each other until the plants became one beautiful, exotic, living floral arrangement. I glanced down at my abhorrent creation and swallowed, my stomach churning. The leaves were starting to wilt, letting off an unpleasant smell.

"Oof, Toby let one rip!" Elijah yelled, causing an explosion of laughter from Asher and Julianna.

Fortunately, Zo kept a straight face. I wasn't sure I could take another fire. Miss Trager had told us Zo would probably start to develop magical manifestations – magistations as Zo called them – of all her emotions as time went on. We didn't know what they were going to look like, but let's just say I was planning to avoid getting her angry at all costs.

Miss Trager cleared her throat and the laughter stopped instantly. I wasn't sure if that was her using magic on us or just our fear of her severe gaze. Either way, the effect was impressive.

"Very... interesting, Toby." She craned her head to look up at me, still intimidating despite being a foot shorter than me. "I think Mr Grandace will want to see the direction your magic is taking."

The churning in my stomach went into double-time. Even after six months in this school, the headmaster's name still caused a knot of dread to form inside me, especially now Miss Trager wanted to show him my failure. She seemed to be waiting for a response, so I forced myself to nod, then shoved my hands in my pockets, and broke eye contact as soon as I could.

Miss Trager gestured for us to return to our desks. Like always, we clustered into the five desks in the centre of the room, finding security in being close to each other. It was weird. The classroom was set up for forty, but it had just been the five of us since the beginning. The whole school was like that – corridor after corridor but only our small group moving through them. Everything was really old too. Outside, ivy creepers wound over the school walls; inside, there were inkwells built into our wooden desks, and layers of names and other graffiti carved into the tops. I traced my finger over a pair of initials, surrounded by a heart. UT & AG, whoever they were, had left their mark. The staff claimed we were a pilot programme – the first class of our kind – but if that were true, the school had been here for sixty years waiting for us.

I leaned my chin on my hand, as Miss Trager began a lecture on the theory of botanical magic. I wasn't sure anything about my magic could be called botanical. The putrid stench still wafted from my flowerpot. Somehow, it managed to smell like both decomposing leaves and rotting meat.

I stared out the window over the school grounds and the rolling hills beyond them. Back home, I would have been furiously making notes every time a teacher opened their mouth, scared of failing a test if I missed something. Here, the tests were all magical, and I was pretty sure I was going to fail either way.

My gaze drifted to the open classroom door as someone walked past. My stomach dropped as I locked eyes with Mr Grandace, his black devil-beard and long flowing cloak as intimidating as ever. He held my eye for a moment then swept on. Two other staff members followed in his wake, quickening their pace to keep up with him.

There was a girl walking between them. She turned as she passed our room, her eyes meeting mine too. She had a wild look to her – her long dark hair loose and messy around her face, and she clutched a book to her chest, her fingers biting deep into it, as if it was by sheer force of will that she didn't implode.

She seemed to hold my stare for minutes, her gaze somehow both pleading and aggressive. Then she was whipped away.

I turned back to Miss Trager.

She frowned at me, the seriousness taking her well beyond her thirty years. "As you may have seen, you will have a new student joining you from tomorrow."

Elijah whispered something. I wasn't close enough to hear, but it sent up giggles from Julianna and Asher, and yet another round of embers from Zo.

"You will meet Calliope this evening after classes, for now please take out your grimoires."

We all groaned but pulled out our textbooks nonetheless, Elijah and Asher levitating theirs out, just to show off.

Zo leaned over to me. "You see her?"

I nodded. "Looked terrified."

Zo shrugged. "We probably all looked like that on our first day. She'll settle in."

Zo turned her attention back to Miss Trager, and I tried to follow suit. Something about the girl's stare haunted me though. I felt a crawling over my skin and I desperately didn't want to be sitting still.

* * * *

A FAMILIAR TUG IN MY stomach told me when it was the end of classes for the day. Zo told me she saw the calls to move as streams of colours she had to follow, and Julianna had said something about a scent. For me, it was like a hand pulling at

4

my belly button as if it would rip the remnants of my umbilical cord from my body if I didn't get up and go the way it wanted. The girls' versions sounded more pleasant, but either way, none of us were in any doubt when the school expected us to do something.

I walked back to the dorm room with Zo. She was trying to explain a spell to me, but all I could think about was my failed plant. Was it bad enough for me to get kicked out of the magic programme? The thought played on a loop in my head.

"Ow!" Zo jumped as she crossed one of the rune lines painted on the corridor floor, and a buzz of magic shot through her. "Dammit!" A clap of thunder sounded above us, and a rain of silver sparks fell over us.

I jolted too, stubbing my toe. "Ow, Zo!" I shielded my head as the deluge continued.

She laughed, and the sparks turned red and gold, before fizzling out. "Sorry, I got a fright."

I rolled my eyes. I guess that answered the question of what her scared-magistation looked like. I still wasn't looking forward to angry.

"Six months of crossing these things, and they still make you jump?" I kicked the rune line, feeling the magic tingle through my toes.

Zo poked her tongue out at me. "You jumped too."

I couldn't argue with that. We crossed over the next one and headed back to the dorm.

The new girl was already inside. She stood in the middle of the room still clutching her book. The wild look I'd seen in her had intensified, and I wondered if she'd heard Zo's thunder-clap echoing through the halls. Her whole body was tight and alert, primed as if ready to run.

For a moment, we stared at her, then Zo took charge.

"Hey, I'm Zo."

The girl just stared back at us. She met Zo's eye, and her gaze was sharp, seeming to cut straight through. Zo hesitated, a flash of something that almost looked like fear crossing her face, then she pulled herself up taller.

"This is Toby." Zo jabbed me in the ribs, pushing me forward.

"H-hey." I wasn't sure whether it was the pain in my side from Zo's jab, or the girl's intense stare that made me stutter.

I reached out my hand to greet Calliope, but she looked at me as if she had no idea what I was doing. I froze, my hand still stretched out, then eventually, I dropped it to my side, stepping back. Fortunately, the others walked in at that moment, saving me from my own social incompetence.

Actually, it wasn't quite that simple. Julianna ran into the room, her eyes welling with unshed tears, and Asher followed after her, as if trying to scoop up and comfort a bolting toddler.

Elijah ambled in after them, smirking. I had no idea what was going on, but I was pretty sure I was already on Julianna's side. All three stopped dead as they saw us, a glance passing between them that seemed to be drawing up a contract of silence.

"This is Julianna," I mumbled. "And Elijah and Asher."

They muttered hellos, each more awkward than the last. Elijah disengaged quickly, moving to his bunk, but Julianna and Asher hung back, at least trying to look interested in the new girl. Not that Calliope looked interested in us. Her expression was still a cross between pissed off and terrified.

Zo sat down on the floor, perhaps trying to make herself look non-threatening. I took her lead, stepping back and leaning against the wall on the other side of the room.

"What's your name?" Zo asked.

The girl eyed us, then swallowed. "Calliope." Her voice was tight, but it was progress that we'd got her to speak.

"That's pretty." Zo smiled.

I just prayed Zo's rapport-building wouldn't result in laughter. Red and gold sparks were hardly going to put anyone at ease.

Zo pointed to the book in Calliope's hands. "I haven't read that one. Is it good?"

Calliope glanced down at the book, as if she'd forgotten it was there, though how she could while gripping it so tightly, I don't know.

She shrugged. "I just started. I was reading it for school."

Her hand was over the title, but the cover seemed vaguely familiar. I had a feeling the story had something to do with magic, not that it would help her here. Five minutes after learning magic was real, I learned everything I'd ever read about it was not.

"This will be your bunk." Zo pointed to the bed under mine. "If you ask nicely, Toby'll probably even let you have the top." Zo grinned at me.

Julianna had fought Zo desperately for the top bunk. Not that it really mattered. Each of the beds came with tent-like sides, so we could have our own space despite the fact that we were all sharing a single room.

Now that I thought about it, it was kind of weird we were in just the one room. The school was huge, but they'd crammed us all in here. Easier to keep an eye on us, I suppose.

Calliope crept forward, her eyes exploring the bed and the room. She pulled on the zip around her bed, experimenting with closing the sides.

"And you can put your stuff in here." Julianna indicated the chest of drawers at the end of our bunk. "I borrowed your drawers." She blushed. "But I'll clear them—"

"I don't have any stuff." Calliope cut Julianna off.

I frowned, suddenly noticing how little she was wearing.

Not in a pervy way, just it wasn't warm, and the rest of us were all bundled up in two or three layers. Calliope wore a singlet, which was grubby around the neck, and a pair of ripped jeans. Goosebumps rose on her bare arms as I watched, as if to highlight how cold she must be.

"You don't have any other clothes with you?" Asher asked.

"What did I just say?" Calliope's voice was the loudest it had been since she got here, and the fear in her eyes was replaced by irritation.

"Sorry, I just meant–"

"Hey, don't worry about it," Julianna interrupted Asher's apology. "We can lend you some stuff, right, Zo?"

"Yeah, sure, of course." Zo gave a smile.

Calliope eyed them, seemingly wavering between suspicion and gratitude at the idea. "One of the teachers said they'd bring me some things," she said finally.

I was surprised Julianna had even made the offer. She was particular about her appearance, and I hadn't taken her for the sharing type. To be fair, I hadn't really taken much time to get to know her. Zo and I had become friends easily, but I always felt on the out with the others.

Julianna shrugged. "Well the offer stands if you need it."

There was something really off about this. Why had Calliope brought a book she was reading for school, but not bothered to pack anything else? The rest of us had arrived with a couple of suitcases each – admittedly, mine had been packed by my mum – but even Zo, who didn't seem to feel the cold and couldn't care less what she looked like, had brought a fair bit from home.

"I like your bracelets." Julianna reached out to touch Calliope's wrist.

Calliope jerked away. She clutched at one of the silver bands around her wrist, though it looked more like she was trying to pull it off than protect it. She had one on each wrist, and I saw the glint of another around her ankle through the rip in the hem of her jeans.

Julianna raised her hands, as if in surrender. "I'm sorry, I didn't mean to–"

Calliope shook her head, violently. "Is this a big joke to you people?!"

Julianna blinked, as lost as the rest of us. "What? I just said I liked–"

"Screw you!"

Julianna's cheeks flushed red. "What is your problem?!"

Calliope made a noise in her throat, looking away.

"I was just trying to be nice." Julianna shook her head. "You don't need to be such a–"

I stepped between her and Calliope automatically. Not that I really thought they were going to fight, but you could never be too careful with magic. Sometimes emotions running high led to some "interesting" accidents.

For a moment we all just stood there, Julianna glaring and Calliope looking determinedly in the other direction, then Calliope climbed into her bunk, pulling the zip closed, and shutting herself away.

There was an awkward pause, during which I realised Elijah had been watching the whole thing from his bunk, a stupid grin on his face.

"Well, that was weird." Zo cracked up, but Julianna still looked like she couldn't decide whether to yell or cry.

"It was certainly that." I lowered my voice, not wanting Calliope to hear and re-emerge to yell at us again.

Asher had crept forward and was standing awkwardly next to Julianna. I felt for the guy. With everyone else, he was Mr Confident, but around her, he got an attack of the shys. It didn't take a genius to work out why.

He cleared his throat and touched her back. "We should head down for dinner..."

"Yeah, I guess." Julianna's voice held on to the hurt, and she was still glaring at Calliope's closed sleeping pod.

Asher shifted his weight, perhaps trying to get Julianna to look at him. "You want to walk with me, Jules?"

Julianna blinked a couple of times, then nodded, a smile hinting at the corners of her mouth. I couldn't help it, but I smiled too. Call it cheesy, but deep down I had a soft spot for people falling for each other.

Elijah made a gagging noise. "Dude, do we have to watch this cutesy crap? Just jump her and get it over with."

Julianna and Asher's faces both flushed, and weirdly, so did Zo's. Her eyes flicked between Julianna and Asher, lingering more on Jules than him. I got the sense Zo's feelings for her weren't entirely platonic. I also knew her well enough to know she wouldn't want to talk about it.

"Yes. Food. Now," I said, trying to keep my tone light.

The others didn't need any more prompting. Zo and I both held back, letting them disappear down the corridor to the dining room. I fell into pace with her, then rubbed the top of her head, ruffling up her spiky hair.

"Don't!"

She squirmed away, then jumped, reaching up to try do the same to my hair. Being tall had its benefits.

"Ew, gel!" she said, as her hand finally connected with my head.

I laughed, smoothing my hair back into place. She unconsciously did the same, then nodded towards the dorm room, now we were out of earshot. "That came out of nowhere."

"Which bit?"

She gave a half-laugh, fortunately not enough to cause

any fire hazards. "I meant the new girl. Good luck sleeping with her underneath you!"

I was tempted to make a dirty joke, but the truth was, the way Calliope had overreacted, I was a bit nervous about us sharing a bunk. Would she go off at me if I snored?

"She's new. She'll settle down." I wanted to believe that, but the way she'd looked at me when I first saw her in the corridor – the way she was clutching that book – she seemed scared more than anything else. I couldn't help wondering what of.

Chapter Two

Calliope did eventually join us for dinner, but only in that she came and sat down at the table with us. She didn't speak to anyone, and her hunched shoulders and prickly glare told us it wasn't because she was waiting for us to introduce the topic of conversation. Not that any of us were game to try now anyway. The air between her and Julianna was tense, and I was pretty sure we were expected to choose sides.

Things were still uncomfortable in the morning. I'd never been one for confrontation, so I skipped breakfast, heading down to the classroom early to avoid ending up in the middle of it.

Unfortunately, a bigger problem greeted me when I got there. My desk had been swallowed, a tangle of poisonous-looking foliage twisting its way around the metal and wood. It took me a moment to recognise the plant as my failed sunflower. The leaves had spread out, encompassing the pot and the tabletop, and tendrils cascaded to the floor. The whole thing was oozing, a red sticky liquid seeping down to a puddle on the Lino.

I stepped forward, torn between wanting to throw the whole thing out the window and a strange pride at having created something so impressively awful.

Weirdly, it didn't smell bad anymore. In fact, the sticky red liquid had a sweet, fruity smell. I was struck with an urge to touch it – to lick it. It reminded me of something... some food I'd tasted long ago and was suddenly desperate to try again. I found myself moving closer, reaching out a finger to...

I felt a little ping in my stomach, like an elastic band. It wasn't like the call from the school, it was something else. A warning, maybe. I took a step back, moving away from the sap.

"You won't be saying that when you see it!"

I ducked down behind the desk, as I heard Miss Trager's voice in the corridor. It was stupid, I was allowed to be in the classroom, but I still felt like I'd be in trouble for being in here alone.

Miss Trager and Mr Grandace's assistant, Miss Caraway, came into the room. I hid under the table, the creepers from my plant blocking me from view.

"Mr Grandace isn't convinced it's Toby."

My stomach lurched at the mention of my name.

"You're telling me this doesn't give you pause?" Miss Trager's voice was more animated than I'd ever heard it.

"Of course it does! But you know what the prophecy said: we keep them all safe, or we save none of them."

Save us? What were we in danger from? Things started to grind into place. We'd been brought here to learn, sought out and hand-picked for our latent magical ability... or so we'd been told. If we were really here because of a prophecy, it would explain why there were only six of us, and why my magical ability was hardly anything to write home about.

"But if the rest of it is true, if they really are a danger to humanity, then surely removing him would—"

"These are children, Ursula! One siren plant doesn't warrant 'removing' him."

I swallowed, squeezing myself in even tighter under the desk. It was pretty obvious "removing" me didn't mean sending me home. And what on earth was a siren plant? I edged away from the delicious-smelling sap, hoping the movement wouldn't alert the adults to my presence. The scent still tempted the back of my throat. I bit down on my lip, resisting the urge.

"I knew it was a mistake to bring them here. How do we know we haven't created a self-fulfilling prophecy by putting them together? They could have gone for years without meeting."

"Mr Grandace thought it was better to trigger them under our guidance."

Miss Trager made a noise in her throat. They both came closer, examining the plant above me.

"We'll have to move to another classroom," she said. "We can't expose them to this."

I felt a tug at my belly button, the magical pull telling me to move to the new room. I had to figure out how to get out from under here before I was discovered, or worse yet, got locked in here with my awful creation.

"I just... I don't want any more deaths on my hands." Miss Trager's voice was choked with emotion, and Miss Caraway was silent for a moment. She was the older of the two women, by decades, not just years, yet somehow Miss Trager was the one in authority. I wondered if my teacher was using magic to achieve that, compensation for her small stature and seemingly sweet face. She'd always scared the crap out of me, topped only by Mr Grandace.

"Please just promise me you won't act on this until we see how she influences him?" Miss Caraway said finally.

I guessed they must mean Calliope, but if she was our best bet for saving my magic, I wasn't sure there was much hope.

"I know the balance has been off, but she may be what we need to right this..." Miss Caraway trailed off at the sound of voices out in the corridor, the rest of my class following the magical call. She and Miss Trager stepped away from my plant, moving to the classroom door. I ducked out from under the table, scrambling across the room behind their backs.

I caught Zo's eye through the gap in the door and made a desperate face at her. She frowned, but quickly caught my meaning.

"Miss Trager," she said, darting forward and drawing both women's eyelines. "I was wondering if you could–"

Zo misjudged her leap forward and crashed into Calliope.

"What the hell?" Calliope glared at Zo.

It wasn't the distraction she'd intended, but it was the one I needed. I slipped through the still open door, joining the group as if I'd been walking with them the whole time.

"I'm so sorry!" Zo scrambled to pick up Calliope's books. "I really didn't mean to do that."

Calliope looked from Zo to me, and I could tell she'd seen exactly what happened. Her eyes narrowed, and for a moment, I thought she was going to blow everything. Then she shrugged.

"Look where you're walking, next time."

Zo widened her eyes at me, and I'm pretty sure that meant "you owe me". I made a face back that I hoped she knew meant "will explain later". At any rate, by the time Miss Trager glanced towards me, the classroom door was shut, and she had no idea I'd overheard anything.

Chapter Three

I paid very little attention in any of my classes that day, doing even worse than normal. All I wanted was to talk to Zo. I was sure she would be able to help me make sense of it all.

In our last class of the day, Miss Trager said something that made me pay attention.

"All of you were especially chosen to come here…"

She avoided looking at me as she spoke, but I swore she was keeping an eye on me in her peripheral vision. Was she going to tell us about the prophecy?

"Each of you has a very special type of magic. You may have noticed your abilities have gotten stronger since you've been here."

That was hard to gauge, in my case. I hadn't known magic existed until Mr Grandace showed up at my home and insisted I needed to be trained in it. Perhaps that insistence should have been a warning sign.

"The six of you are each what we call geminus magic-wielders. That means your magic is twinned with another person's. Alone, you may struggle to control it – either it will fade completely as you grow older, or..." Miss Trager trailed off, swallowing as if unable to face what she'd been about to say.

Despite her fearful look, I allowed myself to feel a small amount of relief. Perhaps this is what she and Miss Caraway had meant about saving us. Alone, our magic could become dangerous, *a threat to humanity*. But when we were together, we would be able to gain control.

I'd seen the way Zo and Julianna's magic seemed to complement each other's; the way their work was stronger, more luminous, when they worked on spells together. Elijah and Asher weren't the working together type, but they were much further along in their magic than the rest of us and spent a fair bit of their time one-upping each other, in good-natured competition. It made them both work harder, and their magic had been gaining power because of it.

"This evening, I'd like you to explore working with your geminus pair. Julianna and Zoe, Asher and Elijah, I want you to work on finding the similarities in your magic. See where you can add strength to each other's spells, or correct areas where your partner's magic is going off course."

I could see where this was going. I made a face at Zo, and she shot me a sympathetic one back.

"Toby and Calliope..." Miss Trager paused again, her breath audible as she struggled with what to say next. "Just spend today learning more about each other."

So far, all I knew about Calliope was that she was weird and had anger issues. Well, that and she was apparently supposed to stop me becoming a threat to humanity. Probably not something I should lead with, but it sure sounded like us spending more time together was going to be worth everyone's while.

Miss Trager dismissed us, and I followed after Calliope, determined to start as soon as possible.

She didn't acknowledge me at first, keeping her head down and hiding behind her long hair. She was holding herself so tightly, she was almost vibrating. I fell into pace beside her, and stooped my head, trying to see if I could catch her eye. I couldn't.

"Can we try this again? I'm Toby." I held out my hand, but she didn't take it, nor did she break her stride.

"Callie," she said.

A nickname, that was something at least. I waited, but it became clear that was all she was going to give me.

"So, apparently our magic complements each other. Pretty crazy, huh?"

"I don't have any magic." Callie's voice was flat.

I let out a half laugh. "Well, you might be the lucky one then."

She frowned, and I realised she was serious. I cleared my throat. Laughing at her probably hadn't been my smoothest move.

"I thought that too when I first arrived." It had taken me and my parents a long time to believe that magic was even real, let alone that I had any. Mr Grandace had visited us six times before Dad finally let him in the door. Honestly, it was lucky Dad hadn't called the cops.

Callie shifted a little, looking up at me through her hair. I took that as encouragement and carried on.

"I'm not like these guys." I gestured to the empty corridor, indicating my absent classmates. "They all knew they had powers and could control them. Me? My magic was more... accidental."

"I don't have any magic," she repeated.

"Yeah, see you might think that, but sometimes it's kind of subtle. I mean, you wouldn't be here if you really had *no* magic, right?"

This time she just stared straight ahead. I felt my smile falter. Was I being patronising? I guess she would know better than anyone if she really didn't have any abilities.

"Sorry," I mumbled. The silence hung between us for a few minutes.

She sighed and stopped walking, turning towards me. "So, what does your magic look like then?" She fiddled with the bracelet around her wrist, not looking up at me, but her tone seemed genuinely interested, if a little reluctant.

"Like I said, it's always been mostly accidental. Things like, if I was scared, something would go flying off the table, or once, when I was excited, this tube of paint exploded all over the classroom at school." I guess I could see why Miss Trager was worried. I could probably do a lot of damage if my magic really went awry.

Callie's eyes flickered, and I could tell she was remembering something. No doubt she'd had something similar – an accident or strange occurrence she couldn't explain. It would make sense if our magic was supposed to be twinned.

I moved forward a bit, encouraged. "There was this one time where I got angry and all the electronics in the house turned on. We thought it was a power surge."

"Wow," Callie said – the biggest reaction I'd gotten from her about anything.

I relaxed a little at that. Strangely, I could tell that wasn't what she really wanted to say. It wasn't like I could read her thoughts – that had never been one of my magical abilities – but it was like I *knew*. She wanted to ask me why I was angry that day. Somehow, I was also certain that *she* knew I didn't

want her to ask. Was this what the geminus connection was all about? I wasn't sure, but I decided to risk it.

"Anything like that ever happen to you?" I asked.

I held my breath as I waited for her to answer. She studied my face, her eyes flicking through a range of emotions. Then she turned away.

"No."

"Callie, please! This is important." Without thinking, I grabbed her arm.

She jerked away from me. "Don't touch me!"

"We need to control our magic. I need YOU to help control my magic. The fate of humanity could depend on it!"

Even as I said it, I knew it sounded insane. From the look on Callie's face, she was thinking exactly that.

She stepped back a pace, still staring at me. "I told you," she said, her voice low. "I don't have any magic."

For all I knew, I *was* crazy. I'd overheard half a conversation, and now I was trying to persuade a girl I barely knew she had to stop me from endangering humankind.

Callie turned and walked away, leaving me alone in the corridor.

Chapter Four

Callie avoided me for the rest of the day, and honestly, I didn't blame her. I kept my distance, but I felt like I always knew where she was. I snuck looks at her, and every so often, I caught her looking back. It really seemed like she was feeling exactly the same thing I was.

I finally got to talk to Zo that night after the others had gone to bed. She climbed up onto my bunk, and I told her about the conversation I'd overheard.

"Woah," she said when I'd finished.

I didn't tell her what I'd said to Callie. I was too embarrassed, and I didn't want Zo waking everyone up by laughing too hard.

I'd been thinking about Miss Trager's words all day, but I still couldn't wrap my head around it. I wasn't even sure Zo would believe me, but she was my best shot. I could see it all running through her mind, but she didn't say anything else straight away. I waited as patiently as I could.

Finally, she took a breath. "What makes you so sure you're the danger?"

"What do you mean?"

"It sounds like they don't really know what this prophecy means. If one of us really is a *danger to humanity* – and that by itself is a big if – what makes you so sure it's you?"

I stared at her. Despite the time I'd spent puzzling over it all, it hadn't occurred to me to question that. "Well... Miss Trager seemed to think it's me."

"Yeah, but she doesn't *know*, right? I mean, my sparks are as likely to cause damage as your plant."

"No way. You'd never do something like that." I shook my head at the image of my vegetarian best friend hurting anyone.

Zo shrugged. "Not on purpose. But neither would you."

I couldn't fault her logic, but that seemed too simple an answer. She sighed, obviously realising I wasn't convinced.

"Take Asher, then. His magic is way stronger than both of ours put together. And Callie – we don't have a clue what's going on with her, and let's not forget Elijah. If anyone's likely to cause damage, it's that sociopath."

I frowned. "Sociopath? What?" Elijah was hardly the nicest guy, but did she really think he was that bad?

"Didn't you hear what happened yesterday? *His* plant – he grew these pretty flowers, then gave them to Jules. She was stoked until she broke out in a rash and started having trouble breathing. Turns out they're some poisonous, tropical thing. He did it for a laugh, called it a 'prank'. Didn't even care about how sick it made her."

"Wow." No wonder Julianna was crying when she came back to the dorm yesterday. That was a pretty awful – and dangerous – thing to do to someone.

"I mean, she's fine," Zo continued. "Asher healed her, no big deal, but Elijah's a jerk."

"Understatement." He was clearly a creep, though it still seemed a big leap from a nasty prank to causing danger to the entire world. Then again, it was an even bigger leap from my accidentally making a scary plant.

"I just mean, don't worry about it too much. If we really are in some kind of danger – whichever one of us is the cause – seems like we're in the right place for it, don't you think?"

It kind of freaked me out how calm she was being about it all. Normally, I loved how chilled out Zo was, but right now I felt like I needed more of a reaction. Knowing we'd been brought here under false pretences made me want to run. I mean, what else were they lying about? If it wasn't for the fact that it seemed like I'd be a bigger danger on my own, I would have been calling Mum and asking her to come get me. As it was, I just had to keep working on Callie, and hoping like anything I didn't kill us all in the meantime.

Zo yawned, and stretched, moving towards the ladder to climb down from my bunk. "It'll be okay, Toby. You'll see."

I wished I could be so sure. I watched her shuffle off to her bed, then I lay down – not that I really thought I was going to sleep.

A few minutes later, I felt a shift below me – Callie turning over in her sleep... or maybe not in her sleep. Was she awake? Had she been listening to everything we'd said?

It wasn't the end of the world if she had. Her taking the geminus thing a bit more seriously might work in my favour, but this wasn't exactly the best way for her to find out.

"Callie?" I whispered.

The sound of Elijah snoring from across the room was the only answer I got.

* * * *

THINGS CONTINUED IN much the same way for the next week. Miss Trager treated me like normal, though since she hadn't liked me to begin with, that didn't say much. I didn't hear anything else about the prophecy, and I made no progress on getting Callie to work with me.

One strange thing I did discover was that Callie was getting up in the night. I never saw her do it, but twice I woke up to her creeping back into the room. The rational part of my brain told me she was just going to the bathroom, but if I'd learnt anything in the last few days, it was that rational didn't mean anything here.

Thursday night, I was lying awake, unable to sleep, when I felt the bed shift as Callie moved. I held my breath, not wanting her to realise I was awake. After a moment, I heard the soft sound of her feet padding across the floor, then there was a brief flash of light, as she cracked open the door and slipped out.

Again, the rational part of my mind told me not to follow. She already thought I was a creep. Stalking after her was hardly going to change her mind about that, but somehow, I couldn't leave it. I waited until I was sure she'd moved away from the doorway and then climbed down the ladder.

I padded down the corridors, looking for her. I quickly established she was not in the bathroom. But where was she?

I turned a corner, and there she was in front of me. I ducked back into a doorway, before she saw me, and hid in the shadows as she walked past.

She was muttering to herself, too softly for me to hear the words, and fiddling with her bracelet. I waited until she was a decent distance ahead, then crept after her.

She turned down another corridor. I wasn't sure where this one led. The school had so many twists and turns, it was hard to keep track of them all. But Callie was walking as if she knew exactly where she was going.

Suddenly, she stopped, staring down at something on the ground. She paused for a moment then did an about turn, heading back the way she'd come. I hid again, narrowly missing being seen, then watched as she turned down yet another corridor.

I crept to the corner, watching as she strode purposefully forward, only to stop abruptly after a few paces and turn back. Was it possible she was sleep walking? She looked wide awake, but her path made no sense.

I ducked back into a doorway as she came closer, but I wasn't quick enough this time. She rounded on me, glaring.

"What are you doing here?" She hissed.

"What are *you* doing here?" It wasn't my best comeback, but I thought the question was valid. She had no right to get angry at me for following her when she had no right to be here in the first place.

She glared at me, then turned away, continuing her purposeful, striding walk. I followed after her.

"Where are you going?"

She shook her head. "None of your business. Go back to bed." Suddenly, she stopped again, her eyes wide.

"What is it?"

Her fingers were spread, palms raised slightly, as if she'd seen something that frightened her. She swallowed slowly, then stepped backwards.

"Callie, what's wrong?"

She was shaking, staring at the floor. I followed her gaze, trying to work out what had frightened her. There was nothing there, except one of the painted rune lines which ran all over the castle.

I let out a breath as I realised that was it. "Hey, it's okay. You don't need to be scared of the runes. I know it feels weird when you cross them, but it's just protection magic."

She looked up at me, her face scrunching up. "Protection magic? Are you serious?" She spat the words at me

"Well... yeah." I stared at her, too baffled to know how else to respond.

She shook her head, the movement coming out jerky with anger. "You call that protection? What is the matter with you people?!" She turned, stalking back down the corridor.

"What on earth are you–?"

"Leave me alone!" she yelled over her shoulder.

At that point, that's exactly what I wanted to do – the girl had some serious issues – but then she turned the wrong way, heading towards the restricted staff area.

"Callie, wait, you can't go down there!"

I raced after her, expecting to have to chase her all the way down the corridor, but instead she was stopped at another rune line. She was teetering on her toes, as if she'd frozen suddenly, only seeing it at the last minute. I slowed my pace, walking towards her cautiously.

She let out a bitter laugh. "I bet you think this is really funny, don't you?" She sniffed, and I realised she was crying.

I reached out to touch her arm, but she flinched away.

"Honestly? I have no idea what to think about this. Why don't you go home if you hate it so much here?"

That wasn't what I wanted, of course it wasn't. She was the best hope I had of controlling my magic, but I was sick of having to act like a stalker just to get her to talk to me.

She took a sharp breath in. "Go home?!" Her face screwed up. "You're a jerk." She shoved past me, walking back towards the dorms.

I followed after her. "Jesus, Callie! I was just trying to help."

She rounded on me. "Help? You think trying to get me to cross those things is helping?"

She flung her hand out, gesturing back at the rune line.

"So, it buzzes a little when you cross them? Why do you have to make such a big deal out of every little—"

"Buzzes?"

I shrugged. "Buzzes, tingles... I'm not sure what else to call it."

The anger had fallen from her face and now she was staring at me, a frown creeping down her forehead. She turned back, looking at the line. She shook her head, slowly. "You actually don't know, do you?"

I sighed, my patience with her well and truly gone. "Know what?"

"I can't..." She swallowed, audibly clearing her throat. "I can't cross the line, Toby."

"Huh?" It was the first time she'd used my name – the first time she'd used anyone's name as far as I could tell. I wasn't sure if that meant something, or if I was reading too much into it, but it felt significant.

She met my eye, holding it. She seemed so vulnerable, all of the bristle from the last few days dropping away. "I thought you all knew," she whispered.

"Knew what?" I repeated.

She stared at me. Everything seemed to slow down. I watched her blink, it seeming to take minutes for her eyelids to meet, then her lips parted, letting out a breath. She walked slowly back to the runes, stopping and looking at me as she reached them.

"I can't cross the line because of this..."

She took another step towards the rune line. Something pinged in my stomach. It was the sensation I'd felt when I was standing next to my plant. The sensation that had saved me from tasting the sap and from being caught by Miss Trager.

I grabbed Callie's arm, pulling her back.

"What are you–?"

"Shhh!" I clapped my hand over her mouth.

She moved as if to pull away, then her eyes went wide. I heard it too – footsteps, coming towards us. I pulled Callie towards the dorm, but she shook her head. There wasn't time. She grabbed my shoulders, forcing me down into a crouch behind a cupboard.

Miss Trager and Miss Caraway turned into our corridor. "Mr Grandace still says–"

"I don't care what he says! You've seen the oracles – there needs to be a sacrifice. I'm sure it's the boy." Miss Trager's voice was high and sharp, bordering on hysterical.

Callie glanced at me, and I pressed my finger to my lips.

"It's still not clear, Ursula. We can't–"

"We have to! As far as I can see, it's a given that he will die if his magic progresses. It's just a matter of how many others he takes with him."

I felt sick. Was it really that bad? My only options were to take myself out now, or kill god knows how many other people before dying myself anyway.

Callie was staring at me, but her face wasn't full of the horror I would have expected. Instead her expression was soft, sympathetic. She reached out, grasping my hand.

"Mr Grandace wants to give him and Calliope more time. He's sure she'll balance his magic."

Miss Trager made a noise in her throat. "Arthur doesn't know what he's talking about. That girl barely has enough magic to light a birthday candle." She sighed. "It's too late. We need to remove Toby, now."

I closed my eyes.

"We'll tell the other students he went home," she continued. "Don't worry about Arthur, I can handle him."

There was a pause, during which I swore I could hear Miss

Caraway's conflicted thoughts battling it out.

"All right," she said finally. "But please promise me you'll make it painless."

Their footsteps continued towards us. In a second, they would be upon us, and I had no doubt us sneaking around at night would be exactly what Miss Trager needed to convince Miss Caraway neither of us were worth saving.

Callie squeezed my hand. I looked up as she stood. She gave me a half-smile, then stepped backwards, dropping my hand. I opened my mouth to tell her to stop, not to do whatever it was she was planning on doing, but she pressed a finger to her lips.

"Miss Trager!" she called, then she turned around, running straight across the rune line.

"Calliope, what are you doing?" Miss Trager yelled, but Callie didn't stop.

She turned back to look at me, for once the anger gone completely from her face. Instead she just looked sad, and at the same time kind of... proud.

The bracelets around her wrists snapped together forming shackles which bound her in place. A second pair around her ankles did the same.

I stifled a gasp. Miss Trager and Miss Caraway rushed towards her. A loud pop sounded, and suddenly the headmaster was in the corridor, standing next to them.

"What are you doing out of bed?" Miss Caraway asked.

Callie just stared at her. The two women were flustered, clearly wondering what, if anything, she had heard. Callie gave nothing away staring them down. It made sense now, why she'd got so mad when Julianna mentioned her bracelets, and why she'd spent so much time fidgeting with them.

Mr Grandace took hold of Callie's arm. "I think we'd better have a little chat." His tone was calm, but the deepness of his voice made me nervous. A flash of fear crossed Callie's face, then in another pop, they all disappeared.

I couldn't stop shaking. Callie was a prisoner here... Callie was a prisoner here, in this school, where two of the staff were trying to kill me, and she had just sacrificed herself to save me.

I leant back against the wall and covered my face with my hands. I'd asked Callie why she didn't go home if she didn't like it here, but I hadn't realised she didn't have the option of leaving. For the first time, I wondered if any of us did.

*　*　*　*

I SAT ON THE FLOOR for a long time. When Callie didn't re-appear, I got up and made my way back to the dorm. I thought about waking Zo, but I wanted to talk to Callie before I brought another person into this. More than anything else, I wanted to know she was okay.

I could have gone looking for her, but where would I start? Besides, I had a feeling the rune lines were going to be difficult for me to cross now, even if I didn't have bracelets. Miss Trager had made it pretty clear she wanted me dead, so there was no way she was going to let me go wandering the school freely.

I lay awake listening to the others breathing. Elijah had a tendency to snore, and Zo sometimes let off sparks from her dreams, but otherwise it was usually pretty quiet in the dorm. Tonight, I was hearing every little creak and shuffle, wonder-ing if it was Callie coming back, or worse, Miss Trager coming to "remove" me.

Finally, the dorm room door creaked open. Light flooded in from the corridor, but the others didn't wake. I froze, listening to the hushed voices outside the room, then Callie slipped inside.

I could see the silhouette of one of the teachers outside the door, so I didn't move, pretending to be asleep. Callie climbed into the bed below me, and the door closed, leaving us in darkness again.

I'd been desperate to talk to her, but now she was here, I felt nervous. Would she blame me for what happened? I still wasn't sure what *had* happened, let alone why.

"Toby?"

I let out a breath at her whisper. "Yeah, I'm awake."

I hung my head over the side of the bunk. She was sitting on her mattress, the blanket wrapped loosely around her. She looked really small in the middle of that space. The pyjamas she was wearing were too big for her, like half of the clothes they'd given her. Suddenly, it made sense why she'd arrived here with nothing but that book.

She bit her lip. "Can I come up?"

I'm embarrassed to admit, I blushed. This was not exactly what I pictured as the first time I had a girl in my bed. I nodded, awkwardly, and moved over to the wall. There was a rustling, then I heard her climbing up the ladder.

She brought the blanket with her, wearing it like a cape. She sat down cross-legged and wrapped it around herself.

"I'm sorry," I said. "I had no idea—"

She shook her head, brushing away the apology. "I couldn't let Miss Trager do that to you. I knew the headmaster would be called if I crossed the line. It seemed the simplest way to..." She shrugged.

The simplest way to stop them killing me. I reached out, touching her arm. "Thank you." I held her eye, wanting her to know exactly how seriously I meant that. She had quite literally saved my life.

She nodded, and I felt she did know. Just like when we'd

talked earlier and I knew what she wanted to ask me, it felt like we were in sync.

"This is so stupid. Neither of us even have any magic!" I surprised myself saying that, but it was true. Since coming here, I'd only been able to produce the weakest of spells, or ones that went wrong, and I hadn't seen Callie do anything whatsoever.

Zo stirred in her sleep as my voice rose. Callie and I both froze as we waited for her breathing to return to normal.

"I know but try telling them that!" Callie whispered. She didn't specify who, but it was pretty clear she meant our murderous teachers. "We've got to get out of here."

"But how?"

"I have no idea. I've been trying since I arrived."

The madness of the situation really settled on me then. I had been here for six months, my biggest worry that I was going to fail exams. Meanwhile, Callie had been a prisoner.

"What happened to you?" I gestured to her wrists – to the bracelets bound around them. "How did you end up here?"

Callie shook her head. "Same as you, I'm guessing. Weird guy with a goatee kept showing up, telling my foster mum I have magical powers and that he was going to teach me. She thought he was high."

I gave a half laugh. "Yeah, my dad thought the same."

"But you eventually gave in?"

I nodded. I felt stupid about it now. I should have trusted my instincts. Something had seemed wrong about Mr Grandace from the start, but I'd gotten caught up in the idea of magic. We all had. Except Callie.

"I'm guessing you didn't?"

Callie shook her head. "No. We kept telling him to go away, but he kept coming back. He got more and more insistent, then eventually he grabbed me from school." Callie looked close to tears. "And my foster mum probably thinks I've run away. She's the nicest person I've ever lived with, but now..."

I wanted to tell her we would get her home, but I didn't know if I could promise that. I wanted to anyway – to force myself to make it true.

Callie sniffed, staving off the tears. "I've been here for three weeks. They kept me isolated at first, then they put the bracelets on me before I joined the rest of you. Mr Grandace kept saying I was important – that the fate of humanity might depend on me being here."

I swallowed. "The prophecy."

Callie nodded. "I heard you and Zo talking about that. Honestly, I thought it was a trick to make me stay. I really thought you were all in on this."

I shook my head. "I'm sorry that happened to you." It seemed like such an inadequate response, but I didn't know what else to say.

"It's happening to all of us, Toby."

I wanted to look away – pretend I wasn't a prisoner here too – but I couldn't. Either our teachers were crazy, and we were all trapped here until someone figured that out, or... Callie squeezed my hand as if urging me on, though I hadn't spoken aloud.

Or we really were some magical threat to humanity.

"Either way, we have to stop it," Callie whispered, responding to my unspoken thoughts.

"We will," I said. "I promise."

Chapter Five

Callie slept in my bed that night. Or rather, we both lay awake all night in my pod. We were too scared to be alone, but I'm not sure we were really any safer together. My magic would make a pretty useless defence if Miss Trager did come after us.

Callie climbed down before any of the others were up. I didn't think anyone had seen, until later that morning when Zo raised her eyebrows at me then glanced pointedly towards Callie. I wanted to tell her what had happened, but Julianna was having some kind of meltdown, and Zo was caught up in looking after her. Besides, Callie and I had agreed to try and act normal. If Miss Trager knew what was going on, we were sure she'd be even more determined to "remove" me.

Mr Grandace had told Callie he would be observing our classes for a few days, which seemed like it might offer us some protection, but I still felt uneasy as we walked down to our lessons. The call was pulling us outside, rather than into a classroom.

"Hey!" Zo prodded me in the back when I got to the sports field.

I jumped, more startled than I cared to admit.

She grinned. "What's going on with you and Callie?"

I stared at her, wondering where I could possibly start.

Her expression fell at my silence. "Are you okay, Tobes?"

I shook my head. "No, I don't think I am. I don't think any of us are."

Zo frowned. "Seriously, what's going on?"

I wanted to clue her in, but we needed to find somewhere private to do it. Miss Trager and Mr Grandace stood at the edge of the field. They were far enough away that they shouldn't have been able to hear, but I didn't doubt that they'd be listening in magically.

"Later," I said.

Miss Trager called us to attention and held up what looked like a normal dodgeball. "Being physically fit is just as important to your magical training as spells are."

I swallowed. She was staring at me, her gaze hard and intense. Normal dodgeball had been dangerous enough back home, let alone adding magic and a teacher who wanted me dead.

"You need to be able to focus your magic, even when under physical strain or mortal danger."

I frowned. This sounded more serious than dodgeball. I looked at Callie, but her eyes were fixed on the ball. She held herself tightly, as apprehensive as I was. I glanced around at the rest of the group. Julianna was hidden under a hoodie and sunglasses, still sulking about whatever happened this morning, though the rest were smiling, their eyes lit with excitement.

Miss Trager gave a sharp jerk of her hand and the ball burst into flame. Julianna gasped, but the others were laughing. Asher gave a whoop and high-fived Elijah.

Callie did meet my eye this time, and she looked like she was about to throw up.

"Make no mistake, children – this is real fire you are dealing with here," Miss Trager said.

There was something so perverse about her telling us it was real fire while calling us children. She tossed the ball lightly between her hands. It floated just above her skin, not burning her, but I could see her palms were red with the heat.

"Use whatever magic you have to keep the ball in the air and away from yourselves. Keep passing it, no matter what."

So, we were playing an extreme – potentially deadly – game of hot potato. I reached automatically for Callie, putting my arm around her. All I ended up doing was squeezing her, seeking the reassurance I couldn't give.

"She's going to kill us right now," she whispered.

I shook my head, but I couldn't quite find words to disagree with her. *We need to remove Toby...* Miss Trager's words repeated in my head. Callie stared over to where Mr Grandace was still watching. Would he help us if we told him? Would he even believe us?

"We need to run," I whispered.

Callie shook her head. "I can't. There are rune lines."

She was right – they were painted all around the field.

She squeezed my hand. "But you can. Go now, Toby."

"No." I was fairly certain I wouldn't be able to cross the lines either, but more than that, I couldn't leave her and Zo to deal with this alone. I was the reason for Miss Trager's anger, I couldn't let my friends get hurt because of it.

"All right." Miss Trager tossed the ball up in the air. It hung there, suspended like an artificial sun. "Everyone spread out. Zoe and Callie over this side, Toby and Julianna to the right."

Callie looked between me and Miss Trager. She was intentionally separating us. I felt a tug in my stomach, pulling me to move where Miss Trager had directed me to. Callie said she never felt the pull, but she was leaning away from me, the magic having its effect anyway.

"It will be okay," I said. It didn't sound comforting.

Callie nodded, releasing my hand like she was saying goodbye. She started walking away, hunching herself smaller as she did.

"Look after her, Zo." I stared at Zo, trying to make her understand the gravity of what was happening.

Zo frowned, as if she were about to protest.

"Please, Zo, she doesn't have any magic!"

Zo nodded. "True." Her confusion was obvious, but I trusted her to keep her word. "I'll do my best." She headed across the grass to join Callie.

Once we were all in position, the ball dropped. Asher dove forward, forgetting for a moment he couldn't touch it. Elijah shoved him out the way, pushing the ball up with magic instead.

They both laughed as it shot up, carving a golden arc across the sky. I held my breath. It was swooping down towards me. I raised my hands and widened my stance, hoping by some miracle I would be able to produce enough magic to send it flying away from me.

At the last second, the ball veered away, flying towards Julianna instead. She flicked her hand, raising a wind which sent the ball flying back at Elijah. She giggled, clearly pleased with herself.

Elijah sent it towards Callie this time. He was hitting it hard, sending the passes faster than they needed to be. Callie dropped back, and true to her word, Zo moved in front of her, keeping her safe. Zo was struggling with the force of Elijah's magic, though. She sent the ball away, but it wobbled, resisting her magic and still trying to follow the course Elijah had sent it on.

"Come on, Callie, at least try for the ball!" Miss Trager called.

I swear I could hear Callie swallow from across the field. She nodded, making an effort to look like she was getting ready to play.

Elijah had the ball again. He was spinning it above his head, showing off before passing it, then he shot it sideways, straight at Callie.

She threw her hand out, as if she was going to produce some magic, but at the last second she folded, ducking as the ball whizzed over her head. Even from where I stood, I could smell it had singed her hair.

Elijah cracked up, but he was the only one.

Asher shook his head. "Dude, chill. She hasn't got any magic."

Elijah's face darkened at Asher telling him off. Asher tossed the ball to Julianna. Zo was helping Callie to her feet, so Jules sent it back towards Elijah.

I could see it was a mistake before the ball left her hands. Elijah was pissed off, angry at us for spoiling his fun.

He swiped his hand in a sharp, striking blow. The ball flew off the field, towards Miss Trager and Mr Grandace.

Miss Trager shot the ball back at me. I dropped my stance, ready to fling it away but something was wrong. It was moving slowly, growing as it did.

"Toby!" Zo screamed, but it was too late.

The ball burst in mid-air, flames exploding over me. I saw Callie take two steps, running across the field, then she disappeared. Everything erupted in pain. I screamed, feeling myself burn.

"Oh my god, oh my god, oh my god."

Someone was repeating that, but I couldn't be sure who. Callie reappeared beside me and water blasted over us, drenching the flames. But I was still burning. I couldn't breathe. I stared up at Callie, gasping for air.

She stared back at me with panic written all over her face. Then she grabbed me, her fingers biting into my arms. She closed her eyes, scrunching them up. She started to glow, a warm light enveloping both of us. I closed my eyes too, letting it wash over me. The light tasted like honey, the sweetness filling my mouth and nose. There was nothing, nothing except the glow. And then slowly, it faded to black.

*   *   *   *

I WOKE, SUDDENLY. Everything was dark, and the pain had dulled to a throbbing ache. I shifted, trying to work out how badly I was injured.

"Shh, shh, shh."

I felt cool palms on my face, and I rested back against a pillow.

"Try not to move, you're still healing."

I opened my eyes. Zo sat next to my bed, her face pale in the dimly lit room.

"What happened?" My voice was croaky, and I tasted soot in my mouth.

Zo shifted, moving aside so I could see Callie asleep in the bed behind her. Callie's face and arms were bandaged. I tried to sit up, but Zo pushed me back.

"Hey... don't go undoing all her hard work."

I frowned at Zo, trying to piece together what I remembered.

She took pity on me. "She teleported across the field, conjured bucketloads of water, and healed your injuries. Pretty impressive for a girl with no magic."

"What happened to her?"

Zo sniffed. "She got burnt herself, before she put the fire out. Try as she might, she doesn't seem to be able to heal her own injuries."

She was hurt because of me. Was this what the prophecy had meant? Was this the type of harm I would cause to everyone around me? Maybe Miss Trager was right to try and get rid of me. I closed my eyes, letting the guilt wash over me.

I had pins and needles in my hand. I flexed it, trying to shake off the feeling. They continued, pricking at my fingertips. The sensation felt familiar, like the ping in my stomach. I sat up, reaching for Callie.

"What are you doing? You need to rest." Zo intercepted me, pushing me back.

"Please, Zo." I wasn't sure why it was so important, but I had to touch Callie's hand. I could feel the magic pulling at me, guiding me to reach over.

Zo stared at me. I could feel her confusion and doubt, but I also knew she trusted me. She gently lifted Callie's hand, without waking her, and placed it in mine.

I didn't know what I was doing, but I tried not to question it. The magic was flowing through me, running down my hand into hers. I watched as her wounds started to heal.

Zo gasped. "How did you...?"

I couldn't answer. Yesterday I could barely control my magic, and here I was healing Callie. It didn't make sense, but neither did any of what Callie had done to save me today.

Callie murmured, frowning in pain, then her eyes fluttered open. The magic moved between us, healing us. My pain eased, and colour came back into Callie's face.

"Woah," Zo whispered.

I wanted so much to explain it to her – warn her how much

danger we were in, especially now Miss Trager had burnt me. But I could feel my eyes closing. Callie's eyelids were drooping too. She squeezed my hand as we both fell back asleep.

41

Chapter Six

When I woke again, Zo had left, and Callie sat on the edge of my bed, watching me sleep. Her bandages were gone.

"Finally," she said, as I opened my eyes.

I gave her a weak smile. She didn't speak again, the worry on her face saying it all. She jumped at a noise in the corridor, and I had a feeling she'd been doing that every few minutes while I slept.

The door opened, and I felt sick as Mr Grandace walked in. He sat down beside the bed, and Callie shifted, moving between us. She wasn't worried about herself, I realised. She was trying to protect me.

"How are you both doing?" Mr Grandace's gravelly voice made him even more intimidating. Neither Callie nor I spoke.

"I'm very sorry this happened to you. Accidents like this should never occur."

An accident? I couldn't tell if he was lying or just deluded.

"But the one good thing to come from it is we now know how your powers work, Calliope." His voice had a syrupy quality to it, and I was sure he was using magic to influence us. He smiled at Callie, and from her expression it was taking everything in her not to slap him.

I made a noise in my throat, and his gaze fell on me.

"Something you wanted to say, Toby?" His tone was genial, but his expression was not.

I almost lost my nerve, under his penetrating stare, but I couldn't just sit back and say nothing. "If I hadn't agreed to come, would I be a prisoner here too?" I gestured toward Callie's bracelets, giving away that I knew exactly what was going on. There was no more time for games and secrets.

Mr Grandace raised his eyebrows, and for a moment the surprise seemed to silence him. Then he shook his head. "Toby... there are forces here that you can't understand."

"So, explain it to me."

Mr Grandace sighed and leaned back in his chair. He stared at me and scratched at his devil-beard. This was the first time I'd ever seen him look unsure of anything. "This is much more complex than just you and Callie."

I stayed silent. He wasn't going to get off that easy.

"There are prophecies. You are both more important than you realise."

He paused. I waited for more of an explanation, but the silence stretched out.

"Really? That's all you're going to give us? We already heard about the prophecy from Miss Trager. Before she tried to kill us."

Mr Grandace blinked, and in that moment, I could tell he'd really thought the fireball was an accident. It didn't make me trust him any more than I had a minute ago.

He cleared his throat. "You and Callie both have a very special type of magic," he said carefully.

Callie sighed. "We're geminus. We know."

Mr Grandace shook his head. "No, your classmates are

geminus pairs. The two of you, you're something... more." He stood, pacing the room in a forced way.

This was new, but how could we be sure he was telling the truth?

"Reciprocus magicae – reactive magic. Basically, your magic will respond to the situation – react to it – in whatever way it sees fit, with or without your approval."

Like Callie suddenly being able to teleport and me being able to heal her. I frowned. That didn't sound like such a bad thing, but Mr Grandace's tone implied it was.

"It's rare for magic users to be both twinned and reactive. It is a somewhat... volatile combination."

Callie and I glanced at each other. We had both shown magic well beyond our abilities in the last 24 hours, but I couldn't see how that justified trying to kill me.

"Now that your magic has activated, Callie, my hope is that your connection will allow you to influence each other's magic. The prophecy warned of very dire consequences if your magic is not controlled, so you can understand why we have gone to..." he gestured to Callie's bracelets, "such measures to keep the six of you here. But please know, I do not in any way condone Miss Trager's actions here today. Rest assured she will be reprimanded."

With a slap on the wrist, no doubt. Even if she did get what she deserved, that wouldn't solve anything. It was my fault Callie was being kept prisoner here. Mine, and our reactive magic.

"I do accept that this is hard for you both, and I'd like to try to make it a little easier. I understand you've been feeling confined, Callie." Mr Grandace was using that syrupy voice again, and a wave of turquoise floated out from him.

Callie blinked, slowly. I was struck by how restrained she'd been in dealing with the staff who were keeping her prisoner. The colour surrounded her until it seemed like she was breathing it. It had to be a spell, that much was obvious, but for what? I wanted to pull her away from the cloud, but I had a feeling I wasn't supposed to be able to see it.

"I'd like to give you some more freedom."

Hope flickered in her eyes, but she shut it down. I hated seeing that – the way she couldn't let herself feel happy.

"I realise you'd like to be able to explore a little more. From now on, you may cross the rune lines as long as Toby is with you." Mr Grandace let out another wave of colour – purple this time.

Callie's eyes took on a glazed look. He was trying to control her – make her think this was a good idea. I squeezed her hand, wanting to shake her free of it. Some of the colour dissipated as I did. She blinked, the influence seeming to clear, then frowned, and I felt my forehead pucker up too.

She looked from me to Mr Grandace. "So, basically you're making him my jailer?"

My stomach turned when she put it like that. It was sick enough that they were keeping her here, now they were making me a part of it. I dropped her hand, not wanting her to feel in any way restrained by me. How could the staff here possibly think this was okay? Without thinking, my hands were in fists, the anger rising in me, needing an outlet.

Mr Grandace raised his eyebrow and sniffed, his frustration obvious. "Our estimate is that the events mentioned in the prophecy will begin sometime in the next few days. One way or another, this will all be over very soon."

Callie looked away, blinking hard, then she took a breath and turned back to him. "Thank you. I'm sure Toby and I will make great use of the extra *freedom*."

I itched to get up and walk away – or better yet to punch

him square in the jaw – but Callie's face was calm, waiting patiently for him to leave.

He sighed. "With time I hope you will both come to understand this is the best thing for everyone." He stared at us for a moment, before turning away and leaving us.

I couldn't look at Callie. She must hate me for causing all this. I hated myself for it. But as soon as Mr Grandace was gone, she turned to me, leaning in close to whisper.

"Tonight, Toby. You and I are getting out of here."

Chapter Seven

There wasn't time to tell Zo we were leaving. Callie convinced me the safest thing would be to get ourselves out, and then send help for the others. She was right – if I really was a danger to everyone, then getting as far away as I could was the best course of action. It still felt like a betrayal to leave without Zo. Not to mention the fact that I was putting Callie in danger by staying with her. I'd already been the cause of her imprisonment and left her with burns. As soon as she and the others were somewhere safe, I would get myself as far away as possible from everyone.

We waited until curfew passed, the school's lights going out for the night, and then snuck out of the nurse's office. I just hoped Mr Grandace had been true to his word about letting Callie cross the rune lines if I was with her.

We paused when we reached the first one. I looked at her and she shrugged.

"Guess there's only one way to find out." She stepped across it.

I held my breath, but nothing happened. I grinned and followed her. "Come on, we better keep moving."

We raced down the hallway, towards the staircase, but the door to the stairwell was closed. This was a bad sign; it had never been shut before. I rattled the doorknob anyway, hoping against hope it would be unlocked, or that I could break it.

"We're trapped." Callie's eyes were wide, and I could feel mine mirroring hers. I half expected our reactive magic to appear then, showing us another way out, but no such luck. If we couldn't get to the stairs, we would be stuck here. Unless...

"This way," I whispered.

Miss Trager would have locked all the doors, but there was a chance the windows would be unlocked. The temporary classroom we'd used after my plant took over had an oak tree right outside. I grabbed Callie's hand, taking off at a run.

We crossed two more rune lines on the way to the classroom. They no longer shackled Callie, but I had no doubt they would be tipping someone off to our movements.

I opened the window in the classroom. The branches weren't as close as I'd imagined them. We would have to jump. I climbed up onto the sill.

"You can't be serious!" Callie stepped back from the window, her eyes wide. A wild wind blew, sweeping the limbs of the tree close to us, then violently away again.

"Do you have a better idea?"

She chewed on her lip, her fear obvious, then eventually shook her head.

I reached for a branch. It was just beyond my fingertips, the wind battering it back and forth. I waited until a gust threw it towards me, then jumped, letting myself fall. Callie screamed as I did, but the momentum flung me far enough to grasp the tree. I swung forward, finding my footing on a branch below.

"It's okay, Callie. I'm okay," I said as soon as I had enough breath.

She was shaking, her face pale. "I thought..." She shook her head.

"Your turn." I reached out my hands. She wouldn't have to fall; I could pull her across, but I could see how scared she was. "I won't drop you, I promise."

Her mouth pressed into a firm line, and she nodded, once. We reached out, our hands locking.

"Now jump," I said, but she already was. I pulled her across, aiming for the branch below me. Her feet found it, and she let go of my hands, dropping into a crouch to gain her balance. She looked up at me, sweat slicking her grinning face.

Then the branch snapped beneath her feet.

"Callie!" I lunged forward, grabbing for her as she screamed. My fingertips grazed her palm, but still she fell.

"No!" I threw my hand out again, clasping for her. She froze in the air. My hand was nowhere near her, my magic having caught her instead. She stared at me, her mouth and eyes wide, still caught in the feeling of falling. I kept my hand where it was, palm up, fingers spread, too scared of disrupting whatever it was that was holding her to move.

I let out a little nervous laugh, but the panic on Callie's face wasn't easing.

"Toby," she whispered.

It was then that I noticed there was no branch beneath my feet either. Callie's hand was spread out like mine. I had saved her, suspending her in the air, but now she was suspending me too, both of us dangling there dependent on each other.

I swallowed. "We need to get down."

Callie nodded, beads of sweat appearing on her forehead again. "How?"

That was the question, wasn't it? How did we set each

other down without dropping ourselves?

"Close your hand into a fist," I said. It might mean she dropped me, but maybe I'd be able to keep her afloat long enough as I fell.

Callie shook her head. "I'm not dropping you. *You* close *your* fist."

I laughed, not because it was funny but because we were as stubborn as each other. "Same time?"

Callie gave a single nod. We didn't need to count to three, I could sense her thoughts, our bodies moving in sync. We closed our hands, and both dropped to the ground with a whoosh.

Somehow, she landed on top of me, knocking the air out of me.

"Toby? Toby are you okay?" Callie shook me, but I didn't have the air to answer yet. We'd hit the ground hard, but it was soft and wet, the mud cushioning our fall. Apart from being winded, I was fine.

"Toby!" Callie's voice was high-pitched with panic, and I forced a spluttering cough out.

"I'm fine, I'm fine. Are you?"

She nodded, pulling me into a hug. "How did you do that?"

I hugged her back, though it hurt where she squeezed my chest. "Hey, you save me, I save you, right?"

I felt a ping in my stomach again, this time harder than the others had been. I pulled back to look at her. "You save me, I save you..." I repeated. That's what the prophecy meant. I don't know how I could possibly know that, especially as I'd never heard exactly what it said, but suddenly I was sure of it.

Callie stared at me blankly, unable to hear me over the wind.

"We have to go back," I shouted.

"What? No, we just got out of there." Callie stared at me

like she thought I'd hit my head.

The pings in my stomach grew, firing again and again, like fireflies were dancing around in there. I turned towards the school, and it became even more insistent.

"We can't! Miss Trager will..." Callie trailed off. Her eyes darted back and forth, her mouth dropping open. "Fireflies," she said.

It couldn't be a coincidence that she'd said that right after I'd been thinking about them.

"Where?"

Callie pointed. "A trail of them." She traced the pattern in the air, leading around the side of the school.

"We have to follow them."

"We can't," she whispered. She stared at me, her eyes filling, and her forehead broken by a frown.

This would be our only chance of escape; we both knew that. But we could feel the pull of our magic, asking us to return. It wasn't like the school's calls. We could resist it if we wanted to. But our magic was reacting to something, and it wanted us to follow.

Callie blinked, and the tears fell from her eyes. "Okay," she whispered. "Let's go." She linked her arm through mine, bracing us against the wind, and led me the way the fireflies indicated.

Chapter Eight

The trail led us back to our regular classroom, or rather, what had once been our classroom. The windows were blown out, the twisting tentacles of my plant forcing their way through.

"What the hell is that?" Callie yelled over the wind.

I shook my head. "It's me."

She frowned, not understanding, but there wasn't time to explain. Around the horrific monstrosity I'd created, I could see sparks flying, and there were screams coming from inside. Zo was in there.

"Come on."

Callie trailed after me. "How are we going to get back in?"

I slowed my pace. We were locked out. All of Miss Trager's attempts to keep us inside had failed but were now backfiring in a bizarre way. I turned back toward the classroom. The wall bulged with the weight of my plant, a large crack appearing in it. "I don't think it's going to be a problem."

The ground outside was soft, waterlogged, like the earth under the tree had been. Strange, as it hadn't been raining. We slipped as we made our way over to the wall, and we had to duck as more of Zo's sparks flew out at us.

"Cover your mouth and nose. Don't let the smell draw you in." I ripped the bottom off my shirt, wrapping it around my face. Callie did the same.

We squeezed through the crack in the wall, taking in the scene inside. My plant was huge, encompassing most of the room now. The sticky sap covered the floor, but water was rising, seeping up through the ground and creating a sweet-scented deluge. Even through the fabric, I could smell it, drawing me in.

I felt the ping in my stomach and stepped back.

"Ow!" Callie accidentally brushed against the plant, then flinched away. She raised her arm, inspecting the wound. There was a bright red rash appearing on her skin.

I glanced at the plant. Small, tropical flowers peeked out between the tentacles. My plant had mixed with Elijah's poisonous one.

"Toby!"

I recognised Julianna's voice coming from somewhere in the room. Callie and I edged our way around the side of the plant to reach her. We found her on the other side. She was clinging to Miss Caraway and Mr Grandace's wrists, desperately trying to hold them back. Asher had his arms wrapped around Elijah, struggling to keep control of him. Their eyes were glazed and they pulled away from Julianna and Asher, blindly trying to reach the plant.

"It swallowed Zo and Miss Trager already!" Asher yelled.

I looked up. The shooting sparks showed Zo was still alive but for how much longer? The sparks weren't just around her anymore, either. Leaves lit up with them, letting off charges of their own. Miss Caraway broke away from Julianna.

"No!" Julianna lunged to grab her again, but in the process lost control of Mr Grandace too.

I watched, horrified, as both of them disappeared into the tangle of plant limbs.

"Why didn't you stop them?!" Julianna screamed.

That was a good question. Why didn't I? I felt lightheaded. I glanced at Callie, and noticed she was swaying slightly, the siren sap pulling her in. The fabric covering our faces wasn't working. It took the edge off it, but we were still being drawn.

I shook my head to clear it. I grabbed a piece of broken glass and slashed at the plant, cutting off a stalk. The remaining tentacle drew back, as if avoiding my blade, but then layers of bark grew over it, instantly healing itself.

"No use," Asher yelled. "We've thrown everything at it, but it keeps healing and drawing more people in."

"Why isn't it affecting you two?"

"It can't." Asher sniffed. "I've got barely any sense of smell."

Julianna made a noise in her throat and pulled her hoodie back from her face. Her skin was warped, extra layers growing across her nose and one of her eyes. "Your healing spell worked too well," she said to Asher. "The skin won't stop re-growing."

I stared, horrified, and so did Asher. That was awful, but it worked in our favour right now. Callie swayed towards the plant again, and Julianna grabbed her, holding her back.

"I'm fine, it's okay." Callie slapped herself across the face, trying to regain control, but her eyes were still glazed, and Julianna's grip on her was waning.

"Find something to tie yourselves together," I yelled to Julianna.

My eye landed on Callie's bracelets. Before the thought even fully formed in my mind, our magic was reacting. The bracelets twisted, shackling Julianna and Callie together. That would hold her back at least.

Elijah was mumbling now, talking about how hungry he was and needing to taste the sap.

"Dude, help me!" Asher called.

I grabbed Elijah's arms, helping Asher force him back. It was hard with the wet floor; my feet slid underneath me. A gust of wind rushed through the room, swooshing through the branches of the plant, making them claw over us like reaching hands. My back burned as it connected with poisonous flowers and sparking leaves.

Wind... Like Julianna used during the fireball game. I looked around at everything that was happening. The plant was mine, but it had parts of the others in it – Elijah's poisonous flowers and Zo's sparks. It was healing itself excessively, like Asher's spell had done to Julianna, and I guessed the water was coming from when Callie had put the fire out. There was a piece of each of us in there.

"I save you, you save me," I whispered.

Suddenly, I could feel it, like I had when I first found the connection with Callie. The ping resounded six times inside me. Our magic wasn't twinned, it was the six of us – *all* of our magic linked. Without each of us controlling it, we would destroy everything.

The pings inside me were arrows. I knew what I had to do. I leaned back, spreading my arms wide, letting the magic flow from me. It shot out, spreading lines between us. I felt as each one hit one of my classmates.

Elijah resisted at first. I could sense his thoughts. How awkward and angry he felt all the time; how he just wanted to let go, let the plant take him. Suddenly, I could sense everyone's thoughts. They each sent their own call back, our magic linking and communicating between us.

"What the hell was that?" Callie asked.

The glazed look was gone from her eyes, and she glowed

with the magic flowing through her. We were all glowing.

"We're all reactive," I said. I didn't know if they would understand, but I felt it. We had to let the magic take over.

Julianna was the first to start. Her wind, which had been blowing the limbs of the plant around, allowing it further reach, changed direction, blowing the scent away from us. Elijah's thoughts cleared as soon as it did.

He drew out his poisonous flowers, directing them down into Callie's water. They poisoned my plant's and its own life source, the magic keeping itself in check. Meanwhile, Asher's healing turned to us, ridding the poison and siren sap from our bodies.

As the plant began to wither, Zo appeared at the top of it, standing strong as if the leaves had created a platform for her. Her and Callie's powers wrapped themselves around each other. The water cooled the sparks, and the sparks dried up the water, somehow both of them exactly in sync, both reducing each other, neither taking over.

And me? I remembered what Miss Trager had said. There had to be a sacrifice. I turned and walked straight into the centre of the plant.

*　*　*　*

MR GRANDACE, MISS CARAWAY and Miss Trager were all in the centre, limbs restrained by creepers, and a cage of branches surrounding them.

"I see now what you were trying to do," I said, though whether to my magic or my plant I wasn't sure. "You knew they were trying to hurt me".

Miss Trager shook her head, desperately trying to deny it, but it was no use. I knew it all now.

"The six of us are strong now. We are balanced."

Miss Trager and Miss Caraway stared at me, bug-eyed in panic. But Mr Grandace had taken on a calmness. He understood. They hadn't factored themselves into the prophecy. The six of us were never destined to be a danger. It had been their interference which had caused the problems, bringing us together before we were supposed to meet, and then trying to remove me from the group.

Our magic was strong, and it belonged to all six of us equally. One of us trying to use it would always fail. The sacrifice was not my death, but the deaths of all of us. There was no Toby now, nor Zo, Callie or any of the others. We were all one.

We smiled, a sudden peace rushing through all of us. We were terrifying, capable of destroying humanity, just as Miss Trager had predicted. We were also capable of saving it.

"Be a sunflower," I said to my plant, and I felt all five of my classmates repeat it softly with me. "Be a sunflower."

In an instant, my plant – Elijah's plant, the wind, sparks, water and all the rest of it – was gone. Instead, in Miss Trager's hands was the sunflower she had asked for.

MAGNETIC

REACTIVE MAGIC BOOK 2

Helen Vivienne Fletcher

Chapter One

Callie

"Be a sunflower."

Toby's words filled me with a warm peaceful feeling.

"Be a sunflower," I repeated, hearing all of my classmates echo it too.

Toby's plant – the one that had been terrorising us for the last hour – disappeared. Instead, he stood in the centre of the room, magic flowing from him so intensely even I could see it. Around us, the chaos stopped, the wind calming and Zo's sparks burning out.

"You did it," I whispered.

He stared down at Miss Trager and Mr Grandace. They had survived being pulled into the centre of the siren plant, and I couldn't say I was entirely happy about it. They should have faced consequences for causing all this.

Zo laughed, and new sparks danced around her, shimmering like drops of water in a spider's web. Asher held Julianna as she cried tears of relief into his shoulder, and Elijah lay on the floor, simply breathing being all he could manage right now.

And then there was Toby, standing in the centre of all of it. He glowed, magic flowing through him. I looked down at my hands.

The same magic ran through me – through all of us, tying our bodies and minds together.

Words whispered inside my head, too fast to catch. I stepped back, confused by the swirling mix of voices – my classmates' thoughts – echoing through my mind.

Toby turned to me, his face euphoric. "I save you, you save me, right?" he said.

"Yeah..." I couldn't keep the hesitancy from my voice.

The threads of magic he'd sent to join us pulled tight around me. I pulled back, but they drew me in again, growing taught. Elijah strained against them too, wearing at the magic.

Suddenly I was laughing. The sound bubbled up inside me, but it didn't come from me. Zo and Julianna laughed too, the fluttering sound spreading.

Toby moved toward me, pulling me into a hug and then cupping my face in his hands. I stared at him, everything swirling. Out of the corner of my eye, I saw Miss Trager stand. She held a sunflower, and the petals wilted, the plant decaying faster than seemed possible.

Toby's fingers brushed my face, drawing my attention back to him. But the moment fractured. I saw it through six pairs of eyes. My own and Toby's, and all four of my other classmates watching. I lost myself, dizziness taking over. Magic crept over our skin, winding and twisting around us, like the crawling vines of his siren plant. They tightened, making it hard to breathe. Elijah pulled against them, resisting like I was.

And then, a snap.

Toby drew back, his eyes widening, and I felt mine mirror his. The laughter died in my lungs. I reached for the threads of magic and found only frayed ends.

"Toby?" His name cracked on my lips, my mouth suddenly dry.

He went pale, his eyes widening. "We have to go back," he whispered.

MAGNETIC

*   *   *   *

I GASPED, OPENING MY eyes. For a moment, I had no idea where I was; my dream of the school overtaking everything else. Then I heard Zo snoring softly in the bed across from me, and my eyes finally adjusted to the gloom.

Light crept in at the window, giving the frilly pink curtains a halo. Darkness obscured the walls, but I pictured the pale purple flowered wallpaper, a remnant from Zo's childhood, and the eclectic mix of pictures she'd covered it with. The strangeness of waking up here – of living in someone else's bedroom – settled over me, but I was safe... far away from the school.

Zo let out a shimmer of little sparks – red and gold ones, so she must have been dreaming something nice. They fluttered through the air, burning out before they landed – thank goodness. She'd gotten better at controlling her emotional magical manifestations – magistations as she and Toby called them – but sometimes they still became unruly. Both our beds held scorch marks from when she'd had nightmares a few weeks ago.

I covered my face with my hands, willing my breath and heart rate to slow. If I kept quiet and calm, perhaps I could avoid dragging the others awake.

I'm safe, I said to myself. *It's okay.*

Zo stirred in her sleep, and I looked over at her. A selfish part of me wanted her to wake up. Her reassurance would probably take the form of an unimpressed shrug and sarcastic comment, but still... Funny how things had changed. It seemed strange now that I'd once seen Zo, and my other classmates, as the enemy.

I reached out, feeling for the magic. The thread connecting

me to Toby held strong, winding across my skin like swirling tattoos, but only torn edges remained of the one which had tied me to Elijah. The sensation of it snapping burned raw in my mind.

Zo's breathing fell back into the regular pattern of sleep, and the heaviness of my former classmates' dreams washed over me. I lay still, hoping the calmness would rub off on me, but instead my heart tap danced on the inside of my chest. Though I was only tied to Toby, he was also tied to Zo, and she to Julianna, and so on. If I wasn't careful, I would wake them, despite the miles between us, my emotions travelling down the line until all six of us were wide-eyed, staring at the clock. Every action was like a strange, long-distance game of dominos.

I slipped out of bed, grabbing a hoodie and my phone. I bundled the limp, sweaty coils of my hair up into a bun, and padded softly across the wooden floorboards in the hallway, making my way down the stairs. Classmates aside, Zo's parents would not be impressed if I woke them up crashing around at 3am.

I opened the front door, stopping at the threshold. I itched to be outside, to take a cold breath of night air and stare up at the sky, but even so, I found myself tensing at the thought of taking that last step.

I'm safe, I said to myself. *Nothing is blocking me from leaving.*

Still, I couldn't help but look down, inspecting the doorstep for rune lines. I imagined shackles appearing as soon as I stepped over it, and I had to touch my wrists to reassure myself that the bracelets the school had made me wear were gone. I wasn't a prisoner anymore. We'd left the school three months ago, but it still followed me into my dreams almost every night, and the echoes of my time there filled my days. I swallowed, then stepped through the doorway into the night.

The tension in my body eased as soon as I did. I looked up, breathing in. Being able to see the stars always helped. I sat down on the lawn, ignoring the dew creeping through my pyjamas, and closed my eyes. I cupped my palms in front of me and pictured starting a small fire in my hands – just enough to warm me. Zo would have been able to do it. Even Toby probably could have given it a shot. His magic had gotten stronger since he tied the six of us together, though it remained unpredictable. Mine hadn't. I could feel and see the magic in ways I hadn't been able to before, but I still didn't have control of it. My hands stayed determinedly empty.

I opened my eyes and blinked. Something orange caught my eye, and my stomach lurched – setting fire to the garden was the last thing I needed. But it was a sunflower, peeking up from between Zo's mum's roses. Once upon a time, I'd found them beautiful; now the sight of them reminded me of Miss Trager and filled me with a nauseating mix of anxiety and rage.

My phone beeped in my pocket. A message from Toby.

- YOU OKAY?

Of course he had woken with me, despite my efforts to avoid rousing him. YEAH, JUST A NIGHTMARE.

There was a pause, then my phone lit up again.

- I KNOW. IT BUMS ME OUT YOU KEEP HAVING NIGHT-MARES ABOUT ME HUGGING YOU.

He followed that up with "lol", but I cringed at the thought of him seeing that. Nothing was private, not even our dreams.

- THAT WASN'T THE SCARY PART! I wrote back.

I'm not sure why I kept dreaming about that last day at the school. Sure, it had been terrifying at the time, but we had survived it. Honestly, I couldn't even put my finger on exactly what about the dream unsettled me so much. I'd had much worse ones, and so had the others. Last night, Toby dreamt of the fireball Miss Trager had tried to kill him with, and we'd both woken to our skin burning with sweat. Still, something about the urgency in dream-Toby's voice... the sudden fear on his face... It all unnerved me in a way I couldn't quite explain.

It's okay, Callie. Toby's voice sounded in my head.

My breath caught, and I let it out slowly. I'd never get used to being able to read his mind.

You're safe, he thought. *We never have to go back.*

He moved his hand, gently folding his fingers down as if encompassing mine. I did the same, imagining we were next to each other, our fingers intertwined.

My phone lit up again.

– VISIT TOMORROW?

I smiled. He didn't need to message; I could hear his thoughts as naturally as my own. He did it because he knew it made me feel more normal – a pretence that I could actually control what I communicated and when.

My smile fell. CAN'T, I wrote back.

I could feel how much he missed me, the magical thread between us pulling tight every time he moved, despite him being over two hours' drive away. I missed him too, but tomorrow was Zo's little brother's birthday party and I'd promised I would help.

I didn't tell him it was my birthday too – my seventeenth. I hoped I'd buried that deep enough within myself that even the magic couldn't find it.

He sent back a sad face and I imagined squeezing his hand. I wished they were all there with me. It's not like I wanted to go back to the six of us sleeping in one room again, but after everything that happened, it was almost painful to be apart. Sometimes I could almost see the chain of magical ties stretching between me and my former classmates, even now with the miles between us. Then I would blink, and it would disappear, leaving me with just the taut, physical sensation of it pulling tight.

I sighed and opened my eyes, almost ready to go back inside. My breath caught. A man stood across the street staring at me. For a moment, I thought it was our former principal, and my muscles tensed, ready for an attack.

You okay? I heard Toby's voice, but it crackled like a bad phone connection.

The man wasn't Mr Grandace – his greying hair and superior height told me that – but he was still a stranger standing outside Zo's house, staring at me, in the middle of the night.

I forced a smile, raising my hand into a wave. The man didn't smile back, and unease crept over me. He took a step towards me. I scrambled up, backing towards the house.

Toby!

Static filled my head, blocking out his voice. My phone beeped, and I jumped, dropping it. I fumbled, but the phone fell to the ground. I left it there.

I looked up. The man was gone. I scanned the street, searching for him. Nothing. A dog barked further down, and I started again, spinning around to look for it.

A figure drifted towards the corner, a black Labrador pausing to sniff something beside him. I let out a breath, watching it crystalise in the air in front of me. Of course. He hadn't been staring at me, but at the dog hidden in the shadows. I started to laugh, and I felt Toby do the same.

Gave me a fright there, Reactive Girl. His voice came through clear, the static gone.

"I think I gave myself one," I said aloud.

I picked up my phone, checking it for damage, then opened the message – a group one from Elijah.

- ANY CHANCE YOU TWO WILL SHUT UP AND LET ME GET SOME SLEEP SOON?

Damn. Our conversation must be echoing all the way down the line if even Elijah had been woken by it.

- SORRY! I messaged the group.

My phone beeped with replies from Asher and Julianna, acknowledging my apology. They were too sleep-riddled to make much sense.

I glanced down the street again. The man had disappeared for real this time, taking the dog around the corner. Without meaning to, my hand had crept to my wrist, checking for the bracelets which had kept me prisoner.

Relax, I said to myself once more. *You're safe here.*

The front door behind me creaked, and Zo appeared in the entryway, rubbing her eyes.

"You okay?" she asked.

I nodded. "Sorry, I didn't mean to wake everyone."

She shrugged. "We've all done it before."

She reached out a hand to me. I hesitated, not quite ready to give up the peaceful feeling of being outside, though the dog walker had already ruined that. I wondered how long it would take for us all to start feeling normal again, or at least, normal apart from the magic.

I could feel Toby's eyes closing, slipping towards sleep. Beyond him, the others were on the verge of it too, only awake because my nightmare had set off the chain reaction.

Night, Toby, I said inside my head.

Dream well, Callie, he whispered back.

Chapter Two

Zo and I woke late the next morning. She hit the snooze button so many times it stopped ringing, and I'd turned my phone off after the first chime. Her mum eventually came in to wake us, and I dragged myself off to the shower. Zo lay on her back, getting only so far as to flop one foot out of bed.

I felt for her. Toby and the others were still asleep. Just as one of us waking suddenly could drag the others to consciousness, one being deeply asleep could pull us all back down again. The balance was not in our favour this morning. I only had the connection to Toby, and that made me feel like one of my limbs was still asleep. For Zo, being connected to Toby on one side and Julianna on the other, it would be like trying to wake from an anaesthetic.

I headed downstairs, giving up on trying to get Zo out of bed. Every so often, images from Toby's dreams flickered through my mind, and I'd have to pause, doing nothing but breathing until the real world came back into focus. I stepped off the last stair just as Josh ran down the hallway, looking back over his shoulder.

"Watch it, Josh!" I grabbed his shoulders, steadying both of us before he crashed into my hip. He backed away a pace, staring at me.

I forced my face into a smile. "Guess I should wish you a happy birthday?" It came out sounding sarcastic, which wasn't what I meant.

Josh went quiet, his eyes growing wide. He was like that around me. Fair enough – I wasn't his sister, just some strange girl Zo had brought home with her from school – but the stares made me nervous, and prickliness crept into my voice. Of course, that only made him shyer, and the cycle began again.

A frown appeared between his eyebrows, and he ran off. I sighed, closing my eyes. Hopefully the gift I'd got him would make it up to him.

I headed to the kitchen. Outside the window, a blackbird picked at the sunflower, pulling seeds from its centre. It was starting to wilt, turning brown and diseased looking, though the one next to it was still bright and cheerful. Strangely, I'd never noticed Zo's mum grew sunflowers. I guess the nightmare had me looking for them.

I poured bowls of cereal for me and Zo, then opened the fridge. The milk carton felt light. I weighed it in my hand, estimating how much was left. Had Zo's mum finished all the baking for the party? I decided not to risk it, eating my cereal dry instead.

Zo finally appeared, with one of her eyes scrunched up, letting in only the tiniest crack of light. "Morning..." she mumbled.

She picked up the bowl I'd left for her, then opened the fridge. My mouth was full of dry flakes, and she poured out the milk before I could stop her.

Zo's mum, Angela, popped her head around the kitchen

door. "I've got to run to the store for a few things. Can I leave you two to froof up the cupcakes?" She flapped her hand at a plate of naked cupcakes on the bench.

I nodded, shoving another spoonful of dry cereal into my mouth.

"Sure, Mum." Zo stifled another yawn. "Can you get milk? I used the last of it."

"And left Callie without any?" Angela frowned.

Zo glanced over at my bowl, but I shook my head. "It's fine. I like it this way."

Zo scoffed. "No, you don't. Here." She flicked her hand, and a bubble of milk rose out of her bowl, landing with a splash in mine.

I blinked. Even after being surrounded by it at the school, magic still had the power to leave me speechless. "Thanks…" I wiped drops of milk from my shirt. "Maybe next time just pour it, though?"

Zo gave me a sleepy grin.

Angela had gone still, and the frown on her forehead deepened. "You know there can't be any magic in front of the guests, right?" She lowered her voice as if discussing something distasteful.

Zo rolled her eyes. "Of course."

Angela's gaze flicked over to me, and I didn't like the feeling of challenge I saw there.

"You think I'm going to cause a scene with my weak-ass magic?"

She blinked, her lips pinching up. I dropped my gaze before I said something else snarky.

Awkward silence filled the room, then Angela cleared her throat. "Are you feeling all right, love?"

I looked up, but she pressed her palm to Zo's forehead, talking to her, not me.

"I'm fine, just tired," Zo mumbled.

That was a safe answer since her mum had to have noticed the dark circles under her eyes. Angela paused, clearly wanting to ask more, but she didn't. She squeezed Zo's shoulder, instead, then headed out. She'd stopped trying to get answers about what happened at the school. From what the others had said, their families had given up asking too. I can't imagine what it would have been like for them, arriving to find the school half destroyed, the teachers having fled, and all of us shivering in the flooded wreckage. I know it must have been bad because when Zo told her parents I had nowhere else to go, her mum just hugged me and ushered me into the car.

Zo shuffled over in her chair, wrapping her arm around me and leaning her cheek against my shoulder.

"Happy birthday," she mumbled. The spiky ends of her short hair tickled my neck.

"Thanks." *So much for that being buried deep in my thoughts.*

"Toby was cross you didn't tell him."

I let out a half-laugh. "He didn't take the hint that meant I didn't want anyone to know?"

Zo shrugged, then yawned again, which set me off too. "Just accept that we love you and want to celebrate your birth."

I didn't know what to say. It's not like I'd had a long list of people "celebrating my birth" before. My dad used to send a card every year, when I lived with my grandma, but that stopped once I went into foster care. Not surprising, since I don't think he even knew where I was.

I stood, putting my bowl in the dishwasher and splashing some water on my face. "So, how exactly does one 'froof' cake?" I asked over my shoulder.

Zo made a "who knows" noise in her throat. "Probably the same way you zhush-it-up?"

"Helpful." I rolled my eyes. "Do you at least know how to make icing?"

"It's just butter and powdered sugar, right?" Zo stifled another yawn.

I could see at least ten ways that could go wrong if we messed up the quantities. Zo gave a sudden snort, making me jump.

"Finally!" she said.

"Huh?" I glanced back at her.

"Asher's up."

Already, the bags under her eyes had lightened with one less magical tie pulling her towards slumber. It wouldn't take long for Elijah and Julianna to wake now, their ties with Asher strongest. Honestly, it was amazing Toby managed to sleep in with both me and Zo up and chatting. I guess my nightmares had tired him out.

Zo stood, her movements far more energetic now. She grabbed a few things from the cupboard and started adding ingredients to the mixer. I cringed as she turned on the beater, sending the powdery sugar flying. She flung out a hand, and it froze, sparkling around us like fairy dust.

"Woah..." I laughed, and Zo stuck out her tongue, tasting the sweet air.

This is what I'd imagined magic would be like, before the school. The word "magical" had taken on a sinister meaning for me now, creating visions of killer plants and deadly dodge-ball, but this is what it was supposed to be – sparkling sugar and fun.

Zo's breath hitched and she let out a massive sneeze, sending the sugar flying again. It scattered over the benches, landing as it would have if she'd never stopped it.

Zo rubbed her eyes and grinned. "Grab the vanilla for me, will you?" she said, as if nothing had happened.

I opened the cupboard, searching through the bottles of essences. Judging by the stickiness, they'd all been there a while. I checked the expiry dates.

Suddenly, everything swam in front of my eyes. I grabbed the shelf to keep myself upright.

Behind me, Zo stumbled too. "Callie!" She reached for me, and her fingers bit into my arm.

"It's okay, it's just Toby," I said.

Zo and I both blinked, clearing away the images of his bedroom, as he rubbed sleep from his eyes. Zo's hand relaxed on my arm, and I felt Toby smile as he found us waiting for him to wake up properly.

"Morning," I whispered.

Morning, came the reply in my head.

Zo rolled her eyes, but she laughed too, producing a few little sparks. "You two are so cute it makes me sick." She let off another round of giggle-sparks.

Of course, Zo's mum chose that moment to come back into the kitchen to grab her handbag. She dodged the sparks, and her frown deepened as she took in the scattered sugar. Her earlier words about not using magic echoed in my mind.

"You both look a lot more awake," she said, her voice tight.

Zo nodded. "Yeah, just like magic."

* * * *

JOSH'S PARTY WAS ABOUT as exciting as you'd expect a ten-year-old's birthday to be. There were tears early on, and one kid with a sprained ankle, but mostly it was just watching them eat way too much junk food and hit each other with stuff.

The most fun part was playing "guess which one throws up first" with Zo, though neither of us really wanted to win that particular game.

I reached out in my mind a couple of times, to see what Toby was doing, but he appeared to be singing the same song on repeat. Correction, he appeared to be singing the same three lines of a song on repeat. I did my best to block him out before it drove me nuts.

I was getting to the point of edging towards our bedroom, hoping Angela would consider my helping duties done, when I heard a car pull up outside.

"Finally!" Zo unfolded herself from the couch, getting up and stretching. "You have no idea how hard it's been to keep this a secret."

"Keep what a secret?"

She didn't answer, already making her way outside. I followed after her, mainly because I didn't want to be left in the house with 24 ten-year-olds, though I had to admit, she'd piqued my curiosity.

I stumbled in the corridor, as my vision swam. I saw the outside of the house through someone else's eyes. I blinked, trying to clear it. "Toby...?"

My heart started to flutter, and I picked up my pace, following after Zo. Before I knew it, I was running, a stupid grin spreading across my face.

Julianna stood on the lawn, leaning back into the car to get something. I dashed down the path, rushing straight into Toby's arms. He was only halfway out the car himself, and he stumbled back, not letting go of me.

"Oh my god, you're really here!"

Zo cracked up, letting off a ridiculous number of sparks. Julianna straightened up, and I reached out to her with my other arm. She and Zo piled on top, turning it into a teetering group hug.

"Ow, Zo!" Toby pushed her away and slapped a spark out of my hair before it caught flame. "Stop laughing, then you can hug us."

She laughed more in response. I pulled back to look at Toby, but I kept my hands on his arms, not ready to let go completely. His arms stayed resting around my waist.

I nodded to the car. "You got your license."

"Had to." Toby grinned. "How else was I going to get here for your birthday?"

My cheeks flushed, and delighted bubbles of warmth filled me.

He chuckled and gave me a little squeeze. "Happy birthday, Reactive Girl."

I'm sure my cheeks flamed at that. I ducked my head, letting my hair fall over my face.

"Elijah and Asher are on their way too," Zo told me.

Even though the two of them were the furthest away from me in the magical link chain, I could feel them coming closer, echoes of it passing through the minds of my classmates.

"It's so good to have you here," I told Julianna, though to be honest, of all my former classmates, she was probably the one I knew the least. My fault, since I'd yelled at her on my first day at the school. I mean, I *was* being kept prisoner at the time. That should give me at least a few free passes on angry behaviour.

She laughed. "And to think, you didn't want us to know when your birthday was!"

I frowned. "Yeah..."

Was it weird that she knew that? Sometimes I forgot the others were all much more interlinked than I was. Her connection with Zo probably meant she heard at least an echo of every conversation Zo and I had. I'd have to be careful what I said if everything got passed down the line like that.

Julianna's smile grew tense. I forced my frown into something more socially acceptable, trying to dispel the awkwardness, but I'm not sure I could ever entirely get away from resting-bitch-face. My default expressions were mild panic or surly scowl.

"Elijah and Asher might be a while," Zo said. "Let's head in. Mum's set up the basement for us."

Toby unwound his arms from around me. "Sounds good. As long as there's no possible-possums, right, Jules?"

Zo sent out another round of sparks, and Julianna's face went red. "It was dark!" She gave Toby's shoulder a playful shove.

"What's this?" I asked.

Toby shook his head. "Oh, nothing. Jules freaked everyone out last week, when she thought there was a possum in her neighbour's basement."

"It was their cat," Zo poked Julianna's shoulder, "which she's met."

"It. Was. Dark!" Julianna pouted, but a laugh broke through.

"Funny," I said, trying to keep my tone light.

Toby's eyes flicked to me, and his expression told me my attempt at playing it off hadn't landed. Apparently, my version of "light tone" was the vocal equivalent of resting-bitch-face. Not to mention he was probably reading my stupid jealousy in my thoughts.

Why did it bother me that they were all laughing about this? With their connections, of course there were going to be moments they'd all shared. Only some things filtered down to me, so I relied on Zo to tell me about it, or the glimpses I saw in Toby's head. I guess a silly story about a cat didn't rate as important enough to pass on.

I forced a laugh. "You should know, Zo's cat likes to attack feet. I've got the scratches on my toes to prove it."

"Oh god, not another one!" Julianna groaned melodramatically.

"That's how Loki shows affection," Zo said.

Toby scoffed. "What did you expect when you named your cat *Loki*?"

I let out a genuine laugh, this time, and Toby gave my shoulder another squeeze. His thoughts danced, pleased with himself at making me smile.

"Come on." Zo linked her arm through mine, then took Julianna's hand. "I promise I will protect you from all marsupials *and* felines."

I laughed, but it petered out as something caught my eye. A small sunflower had sprouted up in the middle of the lawn. I glanced at Toby, but he wasn't looking at me, still laughing with Zo and Julianna.

You're safe, I told myself. *We're all safe.*

But a little sunflower-shaped niggle made me have doubts.

Chapter Three

Elijah and Asher arrived not long after that. A strange hum began pulsing in the air, as soon as they did, probably a magistation from Zo. At least it was less noticeable than the sparks – her mum would be happy about that. But it made a similar pulse start up behind my eyes, and the basement swayed in front of me.

None of the others seemed bothered by it. Of course, Asher only had eyes for Julianna anyway – big surprise there – and Elijah followed him around like a puppy. Asher tried to be nice, but honestly, I think he just wanted him to go away so he could focus on Julianna.

I don't know what it was about Elijah, but he'd always got on my nerves. I could only read Toby's thoughts, but I got the feeling everyone else felt the same. I'd overheard Zo calling him a sociopath, and Julianna hated him after he gave her poisonous flowers. We'd all changed a lot after Toby linked us, though, so I supposed I should give him the benefit of the doubt. Really, I didn't care who else was here. I was just so happy to see Toby.

Zo's mum had set up the basement beautifully and gone to a lot of trouble with the food. She'd put as much effort into this as she had with Josh's party, which set a warm glow flickering in my stomach. I hadn't had a birthday party since I was a little kid.

"Good birthday surprise?" Asher asked me, finally dragging his eyes away from Julianna.

"The best."

Elijah scoffed. "Apparently you have low standards."

I frowned, and Asher rolled his eyes.

"Just be quiet, would you?" Julianna's tone was *almost* the same as the one she'd been using in teasing the rest of us, but there was an edge to it.

"What?" Elijah gave a stupid grin, which at the school had usually meant he was about to do something malicious. "You really think six people in a basement is anything other than lame? We're not even her friends, we're a bunch of losers she was held hostage with."

My stomach dropped. They were my friends, weren't they? Well, maybe not Elijah so much, or even really Julianna and Asher, but Toby and Zo definitely were... weren't they?

"Dude, shut up." Asher shook his head. "No more words, okay?" He grabbed a cupcake, shoving it in Elijah's mouth.

Julianna and Toby both laughed, but Elijah's face darkened. He glared at Julianna, wiping icing off his face, then he glanced down at the cupcake.

"This is pretty good," he said. He looked up, meeting Asher's eye. "Guess you did me a favour."

He always had this weird tone when he spoke, where I couldn't tell whether he was making a joke or a threat, no matter how innocuous his words were. He turned away, going to examine the food, and the rest of us let out a collective sigh of relief.

Though now the focus was off Elijah, it was back on me, and I didn't know what to do with myself. Toby took pity on me. He gave me a cupcake and pulled me over to the couch to sit down beside him.

"Thanks," I said, and I hoped he knew I meant not just for the cupcake, but for helping me behave like a normal human being in social situations.

"Sorry I couldn't get any of your old friends here," Zo said. "I had grand plans... but it kind of fell apart when I realised I had no idea how to contact them. I guess this *is* a bit lame."

I shook my head. "No, it's great. I love it." I didn't bother mentioning that *I* didn't have much idea how to contact my old friends. The school had gotten rid of my phone when they kidnapped me, so I didn't have anyone's numbers, and I couldn't exactly log on to my old social media without raising a whole bunch of questions about where I'd been for the last six months.

"She got the best people here, though, right?" Toby grinned. "Or should I say, best *person*."

Zo shoved his shoulder. He ruffled her hair up in response, and she let out an indignant squeal.

I felt awkward again. Was I supposed to join in the play-fighting? Basically the only fighting I'd done in my life was anything but play, though with Zo's magistations, even the lightest of roughhousing could quickly turn dangerous. I took a bite out of the cupcake instead.

Toby and Zo finally settled down. I couldn't tell who'd won; they both seemed to think they had. Zo glanced over at Julianna, and she went quiet, deflating. I followed her gaze. Elijah pestered Julianna and Asher again, and their patience was clearly wearing thin. There wasn't much we could do about that, though. There were only so many ways to tell the guy he was being a dick.

Zo frowned as she watched them. "I'm going to get some food," she said.

A light crackling filled the air, mixing with the pulsing hum – a magistation of her irritation at Elijah, I assumed. Not much we could do about that, either.

Toby flopped back on the couch next to me. Weirdly, now he was in front of me, I didn't know what to say. We'd been communicating in our heads for so long, it felt weird to speak aloud. Besides, the pulse drowned out my ability to think.

He stared at me for a moment, then his face broke into a grin. "I've missed you," he said.

I let out a breath. "Me too."

He wrapped his arm around me, and I settled against his shoulder. Zo put some music on, which instantly made things more comfortable. The beat hid her magistations and drowned out our conversation. Or it would have, if we'd ever started a conversation.

Something across the room drew Toby's attention. I glanced over. Julianna and Asher stood together, Julianna's head thrown back in laughter. They held hands, their fingers intertwining.

"So, they're properly together now?" I asked.

It wasn't a surprise. They'd been on the verge of it at the school, but with everything else going on, there hadn't exactly been time for a relationship to develop. I wondered if that might have been the only reason she was here – to get a chance to catch up with him.

"Yeah..."

Toby wasn't really listening to me. He frowned, his focus on Zo. She stood to the side of the room, chewing her lip. Her gaze kept travelling to Julianna and Asher, then she'd force it away, shaking her head as if chiding herself.

Elijah interrupted them, yet again, talking to Asher in an

animated way. Asher nodded along, but his focus was clearly still on Julianna.

"I'm going to..." Toby trailed off as Zo turned and walked upstairs. A much louder crackling of static electricity filled the air, and I felt my hair frizz. Toby sighed.

I touched his arm, drawing his attention back to me. "What's going on?" I tried to read his thoughts, but they were scattered... half-formed. I felt his worry but couldn't quite see what it was attached to.

"Hm?" Toby glanced back at me, almost like he'd forgotten I was there. "Oh, nothing, Zo's just having a hard time with Julianna and Asher dating."

I frowned. "Why?"

Toby glanced at me, blinking. "She likes Jules. She didn't tell you?"

I shook my head, a little pit forming in my stomach. It was strange. Zo and I shared a room, so it felt like we were close... but we never really did the deep and meaningful conversations. Maybe she didn't feel like she could share stuff like that with me.

Toby shrugged. "To be fair, she never actually told me; I guessed. Can't you hear it in her thoughts, though?"

"I can only hear yours."

Sometimes I could hear echoes of Zo in Toby's mind, but not clearly. He was basically connected to everyone, all of their thoughts trickling along the line to him.

A flicker of a smile crossed his face, and he squeezed my hand. "Mine are the best ones though, right?"

Another warm bubble grew in my stomach. He chuckled, brushing the hair back from my face. For a moment, I thought he might kiss me, then he looked away, his eyes searching for Zo.

"I better go find her," he said. "Check she's okay."

I nodded. "Yeah, of course."

He squeezed my arm, then let go. "I'll be back soon."

I watched him walk up the stairs, feeling something I was horrified to find must be jealousy growing in my stomach. I didn't like how possessive I felt. The thread of magic joining us made me want to attach myself to him, but I had to remember he had those same magical ties to Zo.

I could understand why she was upset. With their connection, there would be no way for Zo to hide anything from Julianna. I couldn't imagine not only having unreciprocated feelings but knowing that the other person could see it all play out in your head. No wonder she ran away to hide.

If I was honest, I also felt sidelined by Zo. Why hadn't she told me she liked Julianna? Did she think I'd judge her? I wasn't exactly warm-and-cuddly best friend material, but I'd thought we were getting closer. Was that all in my mind?

I closed my eyes. *Toby will be back. He's being a good friend*, I told myself. Even so, the taut feeling of the magic thread between us niggled at me. Somehow it was worse when I knew he was so close but still out of my reach.

Raised voices made me look up. Elijah's conversation with Asher had devolved into an argument. I got up, wondering if I should run and get Toby. Julianna stood between Asher and Elijah, and leaving her alone seemed like a bad idea.

"Grow up!" Asher yelled at Elijah. "Stop following me around like a puppy."

Funny, that's exactly what I'd thought earlier. Perhaps the words had passed down the line, without me realising. I moved to stand beside Julianna.

Elijah scoffed. "You want me to stop following you? Let me off this bloody leash!" He flicked his hand, and the thread of magic joining him to Asher snapped tight. Asher stumbled, and the ripple of power jerked Julianna off her feet too. The pulsing in the air had turned from a hum to a deep bass. I covered my ears, disorientated.

"Quit it!" Asher shoved Elijah.

"Make me!"

Elijah moved as if to shove Asher back, but something glowed in his hands. Julianna dived forward, flinging her hand up. A fireball rose in the air, like the one Miss Trager had thrown at Toby. I froze, my stomach curdling at the memories. It floated in the air.

Julianna held her palm up, suspending it there. "What the hell, Elijah? Didn't you learn last time why we don't play with fire?"

Elijah sneered. "How about wind, then?" He threw his hands forward, sending the fireball crashing against the ceiling. Flames spewed out, lighting the room up.

Julianna and I both screamed. She rushed to put the flames out, but there were too many. Asher charged Elijah, abandoning magic for brute force.

"Stop!" I yelled.

Toby and Zo ran back into the room, but Elijah and Asher took no notice, clawing at each other.

"What the hell?" Zo tried to help Julianna with the flames, but they wouldn't go out, the energy from the fight feeding them.

Toby got between Asher and Elijah, and Elijah punched him, sending him stumbling back.

"Enough!" I shoved Elijah and Asher apart. The two of them flew back, landing on opposite sides of the room with a crash. Julianna and Toby were knocked off their feet too, and even I stumbled backwards. The house shook, the pulse bouncing around the room.

"The fire," Zo whispered.

As if in answer, water rained down on us, quenching the

flames. I raised my face to it, letting it calm me. I had no idea if I caused the deluge, or if it came from one of the others. Either way, I welcomed it.

Stunned silence fell over the room, but the magic still bounced around us, sending plates and furniture crashing to the floor. I didn't know how to stop it. My heart raced, and I shook with the power of it, then suddenly Toby was beside me.

"It's okay, Callie, it's okay." He wrapped his arms around me.

"The kids," I whispered. A fire alarm screeched above us, and I could hear screams from upstairs. Adult voices shouted over the chaos, everything out of control.

Julianna ran to Asher's side, helping him up. Elijah laughed, his face plastered with that stupid grin. But I couldn't focus on either of them right now, not even to check whether they were all right. Zo's mum stood on the stairs. She took in the destruction, and I heard an echo of her earlier words in my mind. *You know there can't be any magic in front of the guests, right?*

Toby squeezed my shoulders, and I shivered as the cold water ran down my neck. I wanted to feel comfort in his hug, but all I could see was Zo's mum staring at me.

It wasn't my fault, I wanted to tell her. *I tried to stop them.* But she wouldn't believe me. Who would?

Finally, the rumbles of magic began to still, but the damage was already done. "I'm sorry, I'm so sorry," I said. "I didn't mean to do that."

"Sure you did." Elijah's voice sing-songed around his laughter. "Got a bit of a masochistic streak, haven't you?"

"Just shut up, Elijah!" Julianna screamed.

Elijah pulled himself to his feet. "Chill, Jules. Callie broke your boyfriend, not me."

She shook her head. "Just piss off."

Elijah smirked, though he walked stiffly from when I'd thrown him. "Can't with this around." He tugged on the magical thread, harder this time. I felt it ripple through the group, tugging from Asher, to Julianna, Zo, Toby then finally me. The world jolted with it. I wanted to jerk it back, flinging Elijah off his feet.

Julianna spun around, slamming her fists into Elijah's chest. "You ruin everything."

His face went dark. "By all means, blame everything on me. You always do."

Toby let go of me, moving in close in case he needed to step between Elijah and Julianna to protect her. But Elijah shook his head. He turned, pushing past Angela on the stairs and walking out.

For a moment, we just stood there, dripping in the water. It still rained down on us, and I didn't know how to make it stop.

"It's okay," Toby said, responding to my thoughts. He raised his hands, and the others all joined him, switching the water off with their magic.

Zo's mum cleared her throat. My eyes shot to her, and my heart gave a squeeze.

"I'll get a mop," she said, and turned, practically running up the stairs.

I sighed, sitting down on the damp couch and pulling my hands down my face. Toby joined me, wrapping his arm around my shoulder and saying comforting things. I ignored him. We didn't need a mop; we could easily clean up the water with magic. Or at least, my classmates could. Right now, though, we all just needed to breathe.

"Someone should go after him," Zo said. She made her way down the stairs, kicking through the puddles like she would start tap dancing.

We all waited for Asher to say he would, given he was the only one of us connected to Elijah. He stayed silent, his face flushed and jaw tightly clenched.

"I'll go," I said, surprising even myself. I stood up, before I could give myself a chance to back out.

Toby frowned. "You don't have to. It's your birth—"

"It's fine," I said, cutting him off. I followed Elijah's path up the stairs, not waiting for anyone to stop me.

Chapter Four

I wandered down the street, looking for Elijah. I probably should have run to catch up with him, or at the very least broken into a light jog, but I dawdled. It wasn't like I had a clue what I would say once I found him. Volunteering to go after him had mainly been an excuse for me to leave.

I caught sight of him around the corner. He hadn't run that far. Perhaps he hadn't expected anyone to follow.

"Elijah!" I called.

His head jerked at the sound of my voice. He swayed on the spot, as if he might turn and run, but then he stilled, waiting for me. I made my way over to him. The pulsing hum intensified as I got closer. Strange – that must mean it wasn't one of Zo's magistations.

"Are you all right?" I wasn't sure whether I meant emotionally or from where I'd thrown him. He could interpret it whichever way he wanted.

He shook his head, and his face twisted. "I can't do this, okay? I just…"

I didn't need to be able to read his thoughts to know they

were a swirling mix of anger and confusion.

"I hate this!" He tugged on the magical thread connecting him to the rest of us. The pull rippled through again, and I was jerked towards him, the force strong enough that I couldn't stop it.

I swallowed. I wasn't expecting this. He always behaved like such a cocky asshole; I didn't know what to do when I felt sorry for him.

His breathing slowed, and I found myself matching his inhales.

"All the time," he said quietly. "All the time, it's there, nagging at me. I want to be close to you all, but then I get here and…"

I reached out but stopped short of actually touching him. "I get it."

"Do you?" He sneered. "They all like you. Toby fucking loves you." He shook his head. "None of them like me. They're just bound to me, so they *have* to want me here."

"That's not true!" But even as I said it, I knew he would hear the waver in my voice. He'd behaved like a creep at the school – he'd given Julianna poisonous flowers and acted like it was funny, and thrown fireballs at me when I didn't have the magic to defend myself. I *did* want him here, but only because it eased the strain on the magical threads linking us. I didn't like him, and I couldn't tell him otherwise.

Elijah gave a half-laugh. "Yeah, exactly." He shrugged. "Don't worry, it's not like I give a shit about you either."

Strangely, that hurt more than I would have expected. I may not like him, but the bonds we'd all formed in saving each other's lives meant something to me. Clearly they didn't mean anything to him.

He must have read that on my face, because he shook his head. "See? I'm a jerk, you don't want me around."

I let the silence hang for a moment. I'd felt the same way for most of my life when I'd been in foster families. The families *wanted* to want me. They wanted to love me and be there for me, but it was always harder than they thought it would be. They'd found me prickly... too independent for them to bond with me.

I didn't know anything about Elijah's life before he came to the school. I didn't know much about his life now, for that matter. Maybe his situation hadn't been that different to mine, at least in the sense of feeling like an outsider.

I pulled gently on the magical thread and felt it ripple all the way through the others to Elijah, making him stumble a step towards me. He glared at me, but I shrugged.

"We're the ends, we've got to put up with being pulled around."

The hint of a smile played on his lips. "Maybe you get it a bit," he said quietly. He took another step towards me, watching my reaction.

The movement wasn't threatening, it was... something else. I wasn't used to people looking at me like that, and it sparked a little something inside me. He swallowed but didn't move away or break eye contact. Neither did I. His eyes were this really deep brown. On someone else they would have been warm, beautiful even. He took one more step towards me, and reached out, as if he would brush the hair back from my face.

The pulse grew stronger in the air between us, throbbing against my skull until I was sure my eardrums would burst. Heat flushed my cheeks, and I stepped back, wrapping my arms protectively around myself.

He frowned. "You feel that too, don't you?"

"Huh?" I forced myself to look back up at him.

"The magic pushes us away." He reached out again, and the pulse grew, vibrating until it hurt.

His hand stopped, hovering near my cheek, almost as if he couldn't get any closer.

"Can't you feel that?" he asked.

The air turned thick between us, pushing us both back. It wasn't quite solid – we could have broken through if we'd wanted to – but the resistance was like pressing against the surface tension on jelly.

So that's why he'd moved so close to me. I shook my head. "I don't know," I said. "I don't always feel the magic."

He raised his eyebrows. "Wouldn't that be something?" He dropped his hand and looked away.

I wasn't sure why I lied. Something about this felt danger-ous. I'd wanted so much to see everyone – I'd been so happy to have them all here, but was Elijah right? Was the magic trying to push us apart? I couldn't deny that something was happen-ing, but maybe it had always been that way, and my magic hadn't been strong enough for me to recognise it. Had I ever touched Elijah before? Embarrassment rose inside me at the thought, and I was glad he couldn't read it. Maybe back at the school when we were trying to save everyone from Toby's siren plant. Everything had been so chaotic; I couldn't be sure.

Not for the first time, I wished my magic was simpler to use. Sure, it protected me when I desperately needed it, but the rest of the time it had a flat battery.

"I need some space," Elijah said finally. "Just leave me alone, okay?" He stepped backwards a few paces, then turned, walking away properly.

"Okay..." I mumbled, not knowing what else to say. "I'll see you later."

He raised his hand into a wave, without looking back. I watched him until he turned the corner, then let myself relax. I'd been holding so much tension, my limbs tingled now I'd let it go.

I took a deep breath, enjoying the freedom of being alone for one final moment.

Space.

It's what Elijah said he wanted, and it's what I'd been craving too. Slipping outside at night to stare at the stars helped, but it didn't stop the claustrophobic feeling of constantly being linked to five other people. It was a strange thing being desperate to be close to them, but also feeling trapped by it. We couldn't even choose when to sleep without the others all being affected by it.

I made my way back to the house, but stopped a couple of metres down the road, staring at the yard. The flower in the middle of the lawn had sprouted up, like an ornate yellow fountain in a green sea. It reached my ankles now, and smaller ones poked up through the grass in a couple of other spots. The crow I'd seen earlier hacked at them, sending a spray of mutilated yellow petals flying across the grass.

Could flowers grow this fast? I wasn't kidding myself that this was normal, but where were we on the continuum of strange-but-benign-magic to terrifying-siren-plant-trying-to-kill us?

Toby came outside, as I walked up the driveway. He spotted the sunflowers before he saw me, and he knelt down to examine them, a frown on his face.

"Hey," I said.

He glanced up, forcing the frown into a smile. Worry flittered behind it. His gaze travelled back to the sunflower, and the smile slipped.

"Are you okay?" I asked him. "Did I hurt you?"

Toby blinked. "What? No, that was amazing. You stopped everything."

I shook my head. "I don't think Zo's mum will see it that way."

"Nah, don't worry about it. Zo will explain what happened."

How many times had I heard something like that in one of my foster homes, only to find myself packing my bags the next day?

Toby rubbed his jaw. "Elijah on the other hand... He hit me pretty hard, you know?"

"Let me see?" I touched his face, running my hand over his jaw.

He swallowed, trying not to flinch under my touch. The pain of it echoed through his mind, and I felt the brush of my own fingertips on his skin, the sensation both fascinating and unnerving. We'd healed each other, once before – him saving me, me saving him. But like always, I couldn't control it.

Toby swallowed. I almost pulled away, but then his eyes flicked up to meet mine, holding my gaze.

"I know how he feels," I said. I wasn't sure where that came from; it seemed to burst from my lips.

Toby frowned. "Elijah?"

Heat filled my cheeks again at his name. Just moments ago, I'd been standing this close to him, and a pang of guilt hit me. I wasn't sure what that was between me and Elijah, but I did know it shouldn't have happened. I shook my head to clear it.

"Me and him, we're on the edges," I said.

"What do you mean?" Toby ran his hand down the side of my face, mirroring the way I had traced his jaw. Again, I felt both the brush of his fingertips and the feel of my own skin under his hand. His thoughts, and my thoughts, simultaneously flicking through my mind.

"We talk about us all being connected, but we're not. You're joined to me, but also to Zo. Me and Elijah, we're the ends."

"But... we're all linked to each other," Toby said.

The way everyone's thoughts echoed down to him, I could almost have believed he was, but it was a horseshoe pattern. The missing link between me and Elijah broke the circle.

Toby had formed those connections to save us – to control our magic and stop it from destroying everything. And it had worked, we were safe. That didn't mean the magic was perfcct, though.

"Except we're not. The magic is unbalanced. It's..." I didn't finish that thought, but I could see it pained him anyway. I hadn't been able to articulate this to Elijah, and I'm not sure it would have helped him even if I had.

I wasn't sure why Elijah and I weren't drawn to each other in the same way the others were. Instead, the magic seemed to want to push us away.

Toby didn't answer. I could see he was still confused and maybe a little hurt. I'd believed I'd been able to understand his thoughts, even with the distance we'd had between us. But he didn't know what I meant. How much had we been missing over the last few months?

He shook his head. "Aren't you connected to Zo too? You live with her... The two of you are friends."

I forced a smile, though I could tell there wasn't much warmth behind it. "The friendship helps, sure, but it's not the same as this." I tugged on the string of magic between us.

It pulled tight, and he stepped towards me almost without thinking. I swallowed. I wanted him to be closer. The threads of magic spiralled around us as if to cocoon us together. I wanted to melt into him, letting the magic join us until we wouldn't ever be able to separate. He tilted his head as if he were going to kiss me. I raised my face, moving my lips towards his.

His eyes flicked away. "Callie," he hissed.

His voice hit me like cold water.

I stepped back. "I'm sorry, I–"

"No, look!" He grabbed my shoulders, turning me around.

One of the sunflowers had risen up, growing half a metre in the few minutes we'd been talking. It still grew now, giant petals writhing as they stretched out like the tongues of some godforsaken monster.

"It's like your siren plant, isn't it?" I covered my mouth, feeling ill at the memory. "I've created another one."

"No." Toby put his arm around me, rubbing my shoulder. "No... that was different. This is just..." He trailed off, unable to provide an explanation.

The leaves turned black, collapsing in on themselves as they began to wilt, and the stalk shrunk back down. It seemed to sigh as it shrivelled, its entire lifespan reduced to a single breath, until all that was left was a half-rotted pile of leaves and petals.

"I tried to create fire," I said, "and..." And then the man with the dog had scared me. None of that seemed like it should equate to this twisted mass of decomposing plant matter, but neither did anything Toby had done when he created the first one.

"Look." Toby released his arm from around me, to move towards the pile of mulch. He crouched down beside it. "It's dead now, see? It's not going to grow out of control."

I glanced around at the other flowers on the lawn. They withered in different stages of dying. Some, the petals were wilted, but others had dried out completely, becoming pot-pourri then crumpling and disintegrating to nothing.

Toby stood and took my hands. "You don't have to worry, Callie. The magic is safe now we're linked."

His expression was gentle and open. He genuinely

believed that, and perhaps it was partly true. Even so, I pulled away from him. His face fell, and I looked down, embarrassment filling me. I didn't know why I'd done that. I'd wanted him to kiss me a minute ago – at least I thought I had – so why had I pulled away?

The silence hung for a moment, then Toby gestured towards the house. "We should head inside, I guess."

I nodded. "Yeah."

He hesitated, glancing down the road. "Is Elijah coming back?"

There was more behind that question. He'd seen what happened.

I glanced down the street too, guilt filling me again. I knew Elijah wouldn't be there, but I stared as if he would appear. "He needed some time alone," I said, my voice tight. "Time to adjust to this. He's... confused."

I hoped Toby read the rest of that thought in my mind. I needed time too. Neither Elijah nor I were used to relying on other people.

"Okay... yeah, I can respect that." Toby stepped back a little, giving me space.

Suddenly, he seemed too far away, and I wanted to grab hold of him. His expression lightened, and I knew he'd read that in my mind. I shook my head, trying to clear it. I made myself take a step toward him, and he met me halfway. *This is okay,* I said to myself. *You're safe with Toby.* Another niggling doubt started in my mind though.

"The sunflowers..." I said.

He reached down, picking one of the plants which hadn't yet started collapsing in on itself. "They're just flowers, Callie, I promise."

He handed it to me, and I smiled at the yellow petals.

In that moment, sunflowers were a happy thing again.

"Come on." He took my hand, intertwining his fingers through mine. "Let's go find the others."

Chapter Five

I woke in the middle of the night. I wasn't aware of having a bad dream, but something had pulled me from the depths of sleep. Toby hadn't woken – I could feel the heaviness of his slumber from downstairs – and Julianna's slow breaths rumbled from the air mattress on the floor.

Zo had invited the others to stay the night. I think they'd all been ready to bail, but after getting some takeaways for dinner and watching a movie together, we all felt much more companionable.

Elijah came back halfway through the movie. A scowl twisted his face, of course, but we'd saved him some food and Asher caught him up on the movie. He'd seemed to soften after that.

The hum started up as soon as we were in the same room. I tried to ignore it, but I caught him staring at me a few times during the evening. He gave me a little smirk when I met his eye, and I was annoyed to find myself blushing again. Then I noticed Toby watching, and I'm sure I went from red to crimson under his gaze.

Finally, we'd all started to yawn, and decided to call it for the night. Zo's mum set the guys up to sleep in the basement, and Julianna joined me and Zo in our room. The gender divide was silly, given we'd all shared a room at the school, but I guess Angela was still trying to pretend we were normal teenagers. Honestly, I was relieved. Things felt complicated with both Toby and Elijah now, and I don't think I would have gotten any sleep lying next to either of them.

I rubbed my eyes and yawned. My jaw clicked with the stretch. It had been a long day, but broken nights seemed to be a given now, even without confusing interactions with my male classmates. I glanced around at the familiar room, reassuring myself.

Zo sat bolt upright, startling me.

"You okay?" I asked her.

She didn't answer, perhaps still making sense of where she was. She sat perfectly still and straight-backed, as if this were a late-night attempt at yoga. A knot of anxiety formed in my stomach.

"Zo?" I propped myself up on my elbow to look at her.

Her eyes were wide and blank. She stared straight ahead, but she didn't seem to see anything. I swallowed, trying to ignore the goosebumps crawling over the back of my neck.

She moved suddenly, making me jump. She slid out of the bed, but then just stood beside it, staring at me with those blank eyes.

"Zo?" My mouth felt thick. "What are you doing?"

She turned, walking towards the door.

"Zo!" I scrambled out of bed. Julianna's mattress lay between me and the door, and I clambered over it, somehow not waking her. Zo disappeared into the hallway. "Where are you going?" I caught up to her at the top of the stairs and grabbed her arm.

She stopped, but her face remained blank. Voices came from Zo's parents' room, and I froze.

"You mean she just... threw them back across the room?"

My stomach dropped. Brian, Zo's dad, was talking about me.

"You said you asked them not to use magic today. They both promised they wouldn't!"

"Come on, Zo," I whispered. I didn't want to hear this, but more than that, I didn't want to get caught eavesdropping.

Angela had loudly insisted it was an earthquake, which most of the guests seemed to believe, but she'd been uneasy around me all afternoon. Evidently, Brian felt the same. I couldn't blame them – my whole life was an earthquake with me at the centre.

"You know they can't always control it." Angela's voice projected calm, and I felt a surge of warmth towards her.

"That's the problem! We've got five of these kids in our home right now. That doesn't scare you?"

"Of course it worries me, but Zo needs this. Besides, Callie's never used her magic here before."

"That's exactly why I'm afraid. If that's what it looks like, are we really comfortable having her here?"

My throat burned, and heat pricked the backs of my eyes. They were dry, though. I was used to this. I hadn't understood why in the past, but I'd always created chaos when I felt threatened. My foster families never blamed me outright – how could they when none of us had known magic was real? But it was never long until I was moved on anyway.

Zo turned towards the stairs. I clutched her arm again, but she spun towards me, shoving me with both palms. I stumbled backward, tripping and landing on my butt. Zo's mum and dad went quiet, the silence of them listening palpable.

Zo stared down at me. Her pupils were small, tiny black

dots in the blue of her eyes. This wasn't sleepwalking. I hadn't seen her blink since she got up.

She turned away from me, making her way down the stairs to the front door. I heard someone get out of bed, though whether it was Angela or Brian, I wasn't sure. I dashed after Zo, not wanting to get caught by whoever it was.

Zo opened the front door and walked outside, in that same blank, almost robotic way. My heart danced against my rib-cage, skipping and thudding to its own scattered rhythm. I stumbled across the threshold, my legs wobbly underneath me.

The front yard was empty, aside from the mess of shred-ded sunflowers the crow had distributed across the lawn. I glanced left and right, but there was no sign of Zo.

Where would I go if Brian kicked me out? I couldn't get rid of the tight feeling in my throat. A fleeting thought of Toby's family taking me in crossed my mind, and I almost laughed. I bet *his* mum would love that idea.

I shook my head, trying to focus. As if in response, a string of fireflies lit up, like they had that last day at school. I took a tentative step towards them, but then stopped.

I wasn't like the others. They had all known, or at least suspected, they had magic before being brought to the school. I'd still been convinced I didn't have any, even once I got there. My magic was always in the moment – Reactive, the head-master had called it. It made it hard to trust – hard to be sure I was doing the right thing by following it. But right now, what other choice did I have? I broke into a run, following the path of lights.

The fireflies led around the corner, and I quickened my pace. My feet were bare, and I shivered in my pyjamas, but I kept moving. This felt like when Toby had followed me as I'd tried to find a way out of the school. It scared me to think that

Zo might be trying to escape something too.

I caught sight of Zo up ahead. Her walk was unhurried but brisk, her steps as easy as if walking on a beach. Gravel cut into the souls of my feet, and I wondered how she didn't feel it. She wasn't searching for anything; she barely seemed conscious. It was almost like she was being puppeted.

She stopped suddenly, and just stood there, staring blankly in the middle of the road.

"Zo?" I called.

I approached her, slowly. She didn't react, neither running from me nor pushing me away. I reached out, looping my fingers around her wrist. Her arm remained limp under my grip, and the chill of her skin worried me. I pulled her towards the pavement. Her feet stayed planted, my tug only causing her head to tip towards her shoulder lifelessly.

"Come on!" My voice came out high and cracked. "You can't stay in the middle of the road."

"She can't hear you."

I spun around. Mr Grandace stood behind me. My breath caught, and I stepped instinctively in front of Zo, raising my hands as if I would produce a defensive spell. She didn't react. Her head slumped forward in a parody of sleep, but her eyes still stared, nightmarishly.

"What did you do to her?"

Mr Grandace had ditched the long cloak, and his devil-beard had grown out, taking on a softened shagginess, but he was no less imposing than the last time I'd seen him.

He raised his palms. "Peace, Calliope. I mean no harm."

I tensed, waiting for signs of him using magic on me, but there was nothing – no persuasion or manipulation behind his words, as far as I could tell.

"Zo is fine. I just wanted to talk to you, and I knew you would follow. I'll send her back if it would make you more comfortable." As if to prove his point, Mr Grandace flicked his hand, and Zo raised her head. She began walking slowly back towards the house.

For a moment, I wanted to run after her. To grab her hand, and hold her here, so I wasn't alone. Instead, I watched until she turned the corner, heading back towards home.

I lowered my hands, letting him believe he was in control of the situation, but I didn't relax my stance. "What do you want?"

He smiled. "Just to talk. That's all."

He had ripped me from my home and placed me in a school where my teacher tried to kill me. He'd kept me prisoner and put all of us in danger. There was nothing this man could say that I wanted to hear.

I swallowed. *Toby*, I said in my mind. I wasn't sure if he heard, or if he was even awake. My phone was back at the house. Mr Grandace could kill me right now, and no one would be any the wiser.

"You have no reason to trust me, I know that." Mr Grandace backed away a few paces, moving to sit on a low wall at the edge of one of the neighbour's properties. If he was trying to make himself seem less threatening, it wasn't working.

"Come, Callie, you can't stay in the middle of the road."

He never called me Callie – always my full name, Calliope. His manner seemed genuine – pleasant even – but everything he did was calculated. He watched me, as if curious as to what I would do.

He was right, it was stupid to continue standing in the middle of the road. I picked my way over the stray gravel to the pavement, keeping some distance between us.

Mr Grandace leaned his head back, looking at the stars. "It's beautiful, isn't it? Being able to see the sky. It was unfair of me to deprive you of this while you were at the school. I'm sorry for that."

That's what he was sorry for? Depriving me of the sky?

"What do you want?" I said again. It came out as a hiss.

Mr Grandace lowered his gaze, blinking as his eyes adjusted. "I want to tell you a story."

A strangled laugh escaped my lips, and I shook my head, my patience gone. "I'm not interested." I turned to walk back to the house.

"You should be. This affects you – all of you. You're not the first, you know."

Something in his voice made me stop and look back. He stood, the smile gone. The streetlight fell across his face creating dark shadows, and he seemed to have aged years in the last few minutes.

"The first what?" I cursed myself for asking that – for getting drawn in by him.

He swallowed and closed his eyes for a moment. "Reciprocus magicae – reactive magic. I told you it was a volatile combination for magic wielders to be both reactive and geminus pairs."

"But we're not geminus pairs. The magic is linked between all six of us."

The corners of his lips curled, but the smile it formed was tired. "In a way, yes. The six of you have created a… field of magic, for want of a better word. Within it, you draw each other in, your powers attracting each other's and growing stronger when they combine. We call it Magicae Magnes – magnetic magic."

In a strange way, that made sense. The thread of magic between us constantly pulled me toward Toby, but it wasn't just him. I wasn't connected to any of my other classmates, but I still felt drawn to them, like the pull of a magnet. All except

Elijah. But even then, it fit. The magic pushed us apart, forcing us away from each other with that pulsing hum, like magnets of the wrong polarity repelling each other.

Mr Grandace studied my face. "In figuring out those links, you managed more than my six ever did."

I frowned. "Your six?"

"Like I said, you weren't the first, Calliope."

Toby had told me he'd thought there was something strange going on. The school said we were a pilot programme, but there was evidence the school had been around for a long time. We'd never considered that the headmaster might have been a part of that.

"What happened?"

"We were the first students of the school. Miss Trager and I are the survivors. The others..." Mr Grandace looked away, blinking slowly, the movement heavy. "They were destroyed by the magic."

Something jolted in my chest. I remembered the fearful way Miss Trager had introduced the subject of Geminus magic, the way she'd trailed off, barely able to bring herself to talk about it.

"Your magic is twinned with hers?" The two teachers seemed so different. But then again, my classmates and I had little in common outside of our magic. If the school hadn't brought us together, we may never have even met.

Mr Grandace shook his head. "Not me. Like your classmates, we were connected to others as well. We never understood that though. We thought we were three sets of geminus pairs."

I tried to imagine Miss Trager and Mr Grandace as teenagers, but I couldn't. They were both so imposing, it was hard to picture them as anything other than the adults who had terrified me the whole time I was at the school.

Mr Grandace cleared his throat. "When we realised the same pattern was going to happen again, we wanted to prevent... history repeating."

"Toby was the one who figured it out," I said.

Mr Grandace raised his eyebrows in question.

"*We* didn't figure it out. Toby did. He's the one who saved us."

Mr Grandace nodded. "That's true. Toby's connection to the rest of you is very strong."

"And Miss Trager tried to kill him."

Mr Grandace grimaced. "You have no idea how sorry I am about that."

I could almost believe him. I didn't think he had been a part of Miss Trager's plan – in fact, she had clearly done everything she could to keep him in the dark. It didn't absolve him. It was his fault we'd been trapped in the school in the first place.

He sighed. "Ursula... she lost more than the rest of us."

He didn't elaborate, but it didn't matter. He could make excuses for her all he wanted; I wasn't going to forgive her.

"Calliope, I understand why you're afraid to come back to the school, but–"

"No way." I moved away from him.

"You wouldn't be a prisoner this time, I promise." He took a step towards me. "It's not over, the magic is still unstable!"

"No!" I turned and walked away. I wanted to run, but I didn't want him to know I was afraid of him.

"Calliope!"

To his credit, he kept his distance. I knew this pattern, though; it's what he'd done when he first approached me about the school. He'd tried to convince me, tried to convince Lorna, my last foster mum, to send me to the school voluntarily. Then, when he hadn't got his way, he'd kidnapped me.

I could feel the others waking. It was amazing they'd slept through this far. Mr Grandace must have done something to them, in the same way he'd influenced Zo to sleepwalk.

I felt Toby making his way outside, searching for me.

"The magic is still unstable!" Mr Grandace called. "We thought things were normalising while you were apart, but the moment you came together–"

"Callie!" Toby's shout cut Mr Grandace off.

I couldn't see him in the dark, but I felt his magic pulling me in. I turned the corner, making my way towards it.

Pulling me in, just like a magnet. I shook the thought away.

Toby's arms wrapped around me. "What happened? Are you okay?"

"Let's get inside," I said.

Toby hesitated, glancing back towards where Mr Grandace had been. I saw it running through his mind – the idea of going after him, in some misguided belief that he could protect me. I grabbed his hand, pulling him towards the house.

Zo and Julianna stood in the doorway.

"What happened?" Zo asked.

I shook my head. Elijah and Asher watched us from the basement stairs. Five pairs of eyes stared at me now, but none of them had noticed Zo leave the house – Zo didn't even realise she'd been outside.

Toby locked the door behind us, and I leaned against him. He put his arms around me, and I could feel it; the pull of the magic, drawing me towards him.

We're safe. Mr Grandace is wrong. The magic is fine; it's stable. But even as I thought it, I felt a niggle of something... a pulsing hum – the push of Elijah's magic against mine. Four strands of magic were pulling me in, while one of them tried to drive me away.

* * * *

"WOW," ZO SAID, WHEN I finished telling them what had happened.

We'd congregated in the basement, hoping to avoid waking Zo's family. All was quiet upstairs when I got inside, and I didn't tell them what I'd overheard Brian saying. Still, his words circled around and around in my mind, fighting for precedence even over my conversation with Mr Grandace.

"UT and AG," Toby said quietly.

"Huh?"

He shook his head. "It's nothing, there was some graffiti on my desk at the school. The initials and a heart."

UT and AG – Ursula Trager and Arthur Grandace… it was strange to think about them like that.

"It's nonsense," Asher said. His jaw worked, making his words clipped and fast. "He just wants to get us back to the school. We're fine. Linking our magic fixed things."

Toby's hand found mine and squeezed it. I wanted to feel comfort in that gesture, but all I felt was the need to be closer to him. On the other side of him, Zo had shifted in tighter, and beside her, Julianna moved in too. All of us being drawn in together, exactly like a magnetic field. All of us, except for me and Elijah, the two ends, pushing each other away.

"It's not though, is it?" Julianna's voice was quiet, but we all dropped to silence as soon as she spoke. She glanced at Asher, and her lips twisted in a grimace. "We all felt it. Things started to go wrong as soon as we were together again."

Toby shifted uncomfortably. I could see it in his thoughts. He'd felt something wrong in the magic as soon as he'd arrived, but he hadn't wanted to acknowledge it. I looked around at the group and saw a similar discomfort on all of their faces. They'd all felt the same. It was so frustrating not being able to sense things in the same way they did. It was so hit and miss what magic I detected, and what went completely over my head.

Zo shook her head. "So, what's the solution? We never see each other again?"

Toby's hand tightened on mine, and Asher's arm around Julianna did the same. That couldn't be the answer, could it? Something squeezed in my chest. Never seeing Toby again felt like too great a punishment, not to mention the fact that I lived with Zo. Where would I go if I had to leave? Of course, I may not have a choice about that if Brian kicked me out.

"That can't be it," Toby said, his voice hoarse. "We made the magic better together."

Had we though? It's true we'd stopped our magic destroying everything by joining it, but it had only become dangerous because the six of us had come together in the first place.

Zo rested her head against Toby's shoulder, and Julianna touched Zo's arm. All of us drawing in yet again.

"Stop pussyfooting around it. We all know what the answer is." Elijah was the only one who didn't seem to be being pulled in tighter. He stood next to Asher, but they didn't make physical contact, Elijah's hands shoved deep in his pockets.

I frowned and he stared back at me, his face stony. My stomach started to tighten.

"Really, we don't," Toby said. I felt him glance at me, but I couldn't look at him. I squeezed his hand so hard, I was sure my nails must be biting into his flesh, but he returned my grip equally as tight.

"It's me and her," Elijah said, still staring at me. "We're the problem."

"We snapped the threads," I whispered. I remembered the feeling of it – the magic pulling tight, making it hard to breathe, and the pop as I broke them.

Elijah nodded. "And now we're the ones who need to leave."

Toby scoffed. "Don't be ridiculous, Callie doesn't need to go anywhere."

My throat felt clogged, but I forced myself to speak. "He's right."

The thought of leaving Toby hurt, but the thought of him and the others being destroyed by the magic because of me hurt even more.

"No. He's not." Toby stood, still not letting go of my hand. "Just shut up, Elijah. You don't know what you're talking about."

I noticed the others were silent. They could feel it too – the push of magic Elijah and I caused. The rest of them were connected to each other – two people to help stabilize the power, and it worked... at least until Elijah and I threw off the balance.

Elijah sneered. "What, you think because you're into her, it's going to stop her getting all of us killed?"

Toby's face flushed, and he stepped towards Elijah. Zo and Asher stood too, getting between them, and Julianna moved to me, trying to comfort me or just getting out of the way, I wasn't sure.

"Calm down!" Zo's voice was a whispered hiss.

Asher put his hand on Elijah's shoulder, but Elijah flinched away. "Dude, just chill," Asher said quietly. I couldn't tell if it calmed Elijah or made him angrier. Either way, he turned his back on us, taking a deep breath.

"Mr Grandace is gone, right Callie?" Asher asked me.

I nodded. "I think so."

"Okay." Asher rubbed his chin, thinking. "So, we don't need to decide this tonight. I reckon we try to get some sleep now, and we talk it over in the morning when we're all thinking clearer."

Julianna moved back towards him. "I agree. That's a good plan."

I had to stop myself from rolling my eyes, but I nodded anyway. "Yeah, all right. We can try and sleep."

Zo jerked her head, in something that could have been a nod or a shake. "Yeah, whatever. I'm still creeped out that he made me sleepwalk." She moved towards the basement door but then hovered without opening it.

I felt Toby's eyes on me. I didn't want to look at him.

"Perhaps we should all stay down here," Asher said.

A collective sigh seemed to fill the room, and the others all murmured in agreement. Elijah scowled at me from across the room. I tried to ignore him. Everyone began rearranging blankets and pillows, as if any of us really thought we would be getting much rest.

Toby brushed the hair back from my face. "Promise me you'll wake me if anything else happens?" he said.

I forced myself to meet his gaze. "If anyone else goes sleepwalking, I promise I'll wake you this time," I said.

He studied my face for a moment, then nodded. He settled down in his bed, making room for me to join him. We'd shared a bed before – at the school, when neither of us felt safe enough to be alone. It still felt odd... way too intimate when I wasn't sure what we were to each other. If I was honest, it felt nice too.

I could feel Elijah's eyes on me, but I didn't look up. I lay down next to Toby, guilt brewing in my stomach. Technically, I hadn't lied to him. I didn't plan to be asleep when I went walking.

Chapter Six

It took forever for the others to fall asleep. Asher was the first, pulling Julianna down with him. Zo stayed up a little longer, her mind whirring with everything that had happened, but finally she succumbed to slumber. I thought Toby wouldn't be too long after her, but he resisted. Every so often, his restless limbs would flail as he tried not to drop off.

He kept looking over at me, but I stayed still and silent, hoping I would fool him into believing I was already asleep. Fat chance of that working when we were connected to each other.

I hummed a song in my head, using his trick of repeating the same three lines over and over to block out any other thoughts. After a while, his foot started to jiggle in time with the beat, and I couldn't help but laugh. I would miss being this in sync with another person.

Finally, I heard his breathing slow, and the tension on the thread between us eased as he dozed off. I waited, not daring to move in case I disturbed him, while straining against the pull of sleep. A part of me wanted to curl up next to him and close my eyes, but a couple of hours' rest wouldn't change things. We'd still be a danger to each other when I woke up.

I slipped out of bed, moving carefully. There was something calming about listening to all of them breathe, their exhales heavy. Toby's lips parted as his jaw relaxed, the softness making him look younger. I brushed his fringe back from his face and leaned down to kiss his forehead.

"I'm sorry," I whispered.

And then I left, before I had a chance to change my mind.

I didn't really have a plan. *Get away from the others*, was about as far as I had gotten. The question of where I could go swum in my mind – not just where I could go tonight, but where I would live. Zo's family had taken me in when I had nowhere. Being alone again terrified me.

I got changed quickly, grabbing my phone and a few spare clothes from upstairs. I shoved them into a bag, then slipped out of the house.

I only made it a few steps before the smell of rotting plants made me reel back. Layers of decomposing sunflowers littered the lawn, and a few live ones poked up between the mess. They had to be multiplying by the minute. Toby could tell me this wasn't like his siren plant all he wanted, but he couldn't convince me this wasn't dangerous.

I shivered in the night air. The live sunflowers turned towards me, their faces watching as if they would grow legs and follow. I picked my way through the mulch and out onto the street.

* * * *

I SCANNED THE TIMETABLE fixed to the wall of the bus station. Even if I didn't know the destination, getting out of town seemed the best way to ensure my magic didn't hurt anyone, myself included. There was only one more bus leaving tonight, heading to Hamilton. I blinked at the name, wondering if it was a sign. Hamilton was where my foster mum lived, where *I'd* lived, until Mr Grandace had forced me away to the school.

The bus left in a few minutes. I made my way to the ticket office, but a sudden, horrible realisation hit me. I'd left my wallet at Zo's. An even worse realisation followed quickly after, that I probably didn't have enough cash in it for the fare anyway. Zo's parents had given me a credit card for emergencies, but I couldn't exactly use that while running away.

I sat down, laying my head in my hands. Dampness crept through my jeans from the bench, and that seemed about right for how this night was going. The thread between me and Toby strained with the distance, even though he hadn't woken. It brought with it the taut sensation that had pulled at me all the time we'd been apart. It would be so much easier to go back, even if we did get hurt because of it.

"Thought the idea was to get away from each other."

I jumped, scrambling up from my seat. Elijah stood in front of me, his face in a stupid smirk. His eyes travelled over me in a way that made me want to squirm.

I stared back at him, scowling. "What are you doing here?"

He shrugged. "Same thing you are, I'm guessing."

"Kind of defeats the purpose, if you're here." I shifted my weight, eyeing him.

He gave a half-laugh. "That it does."

He didn't walk away, though. Strangely, he seemed more relaxed around me now. The pulsing hum rose, but weaker this time, almost indistinguishable from my own heartbeat. Perhaps we didn't repel each other as much without the rest of our classmates pulling us in different directions. Or maybe we were getting used to the effect it had on us.

He nodded at the timetable. "You heading to Hamilton?" he asked.

"I was, but I forgot my wallet." I didn't mention the non-existent funds inside it.

He scoffed. "Ever heard of magic, Callie? Oh wait, that's right; you're useless at that."

I frowned. "Saved your ass from Toby's plant, didn't I?"

He smirked, then walked over to the ticket office. I followed him, more out of curiosity than anything else. The woman behind the counter looked tired, and I almost wanted to warn her that Elijah was doing something dodgy. Would she get in trouble later, if her supervisor found out she'd given us tickets without paying?

I watched what he was doing, intrigued, but knowing I wouldn't be able to replicate it myself. Elijah and Asher's powers had always been the strongest in the group, and I had to admit, it was fascinating to watch them in action.

In movies, characters always presented a napkin or old piece of paper in these situations, tricking the person into believing it was money. But as Toby had told me a few times, pretty much everything we'd ever seen or read about magic was wrong.

Instead, Elijah just talked to the woman. I'm sure if I'd been able to see things in the way that Toby did, I'd have seen clouds of colour spilling out from him, magical persuasion calming and confusing her. After a minute, her eyes glazed over, and she swayed on the spot. She took two tickets out of the drawer and handed them over.

Elijah grinned, but then stifled it. I glanced around at the other people at the station. Most of them were drunk or out of it – the usual crowd at this time of night – and none of them were in the best state to be noticing magical goings-on.

Elijah thanked the woman, then made his way over to me,

the grin morphing back into a smirk.

"Will she be all right?" I wondered if the woman would be handing out free tickets all night.

Elijah frowned. "She'll live."

I didn't need to be connected to him to feel his irritation at my lack of admiration and praise. To be fair, I probably should have at least said thank you, but I wasn't going to congratulate him for brainwashing some poor stranger.

He handed me the ticket. His fingers brushed mine, and his hand lingered longer than it needed to. The magnetic push built up, but for some reason, neither of us moved away.

I swallowed, stepping back. I stared at the woman behind the counter, then at the ticket, then the ground – anything to avoid looking at him.

Elijah studied my face for a moment, and the hum grew in the silence. He turned away, heading towards the bus. I let out a breath and shook my head.

"Wait up!" I broke into a jog, following after him.

He didn't look back, but he slowed his pace, letting me catch up.

*　*　*　*

"WHY HAMILTON?" I ASKED him, once we were on the road.

The pulsing hum pressed against us, intensifying the bouncing of the bus's wheels. Empty seats surrounded us, only half a dozen other passengers on board. Under different circumstances, I might have sat alone, but a creepy dude with long, greasy hair sat a couple of rows away, staring at me, and Elijah seemed like the safer option. Besides, after a while, the hum quieted down to a manageable level, as if growing bored with trying to force us apart when neither of us were listening.

He shrugged. "Last bus leaving tonight."

I didn't think that was the whole truth. I was certain he'd followed me here. Strangely though, I wasn't mad about it. We'd both decided we needed to get away from our classmates, only to find we weren't quite ready to fully leave each other.

"They're going to be pissed you left." Elijah's smirk returned.

"Yeah." More than pissed, Toby would be hurt. We'd survived the school by sticking together, but if our magic caused damage every time we got close...

"Don't worry about it. We're the type who do better on our own, anyway." Elijah settled back in his seat and closed his eyes.

The rhythm of the road underneath us jolted my head against the seat, this time countering the hum I felt from Elijah. I wasn't sure how I felt about him saying we were the same. Sure, we'd both been loners before we came to the school, but Elijah was the type of loner who poisoned his classmate as a joke. For me, it had always been part choice, part circumstance.

Something twisted in my stomach. I'd thought that in the past tense. I had been a loner, but Zo and Toby had become my best friends... maybe even something more in Toby's case. I cared about Zo's family, and Julianna and Asher were important to me too. Even Elijah had become like a weird cousin.

I shook my head. It didn't matter. In six hours, we'd get off this bus, and I'd never see any of them again.

I tried to relax back in the seat, but my muscles clung to the tension. I felt like a meerkat, constantly on alert, looking out for threats. Whether I thought they were going to come from the other oddball passengers, or from Mr Grandace, I wasn't sure. A part of me even expected Toby to appear, though how he would do that with the bus moving, I don't know. I resisted the urge to reach out to read his thoughts.

"I guess it won't be long before they realise we're gone," I said.

Elijah shook his head. "We'll be fine. I deepened their sleep. Won't work on Asher for long, but Toby and Zo are weak."

I stared at him. After what had happened with Mr Grandace, I didn't like the idea of him messing with our friends' sleep.

He rolled his eyes. "Don't look at me like that. I do it on myself all the time. How else would I get any rest with you losers talking all night?"

"Fair enough." I had to admit, it would make things easier. At the very least, it meant I could stop singing the same stupid song over and over. Of course, now it was stuck in my head.

"So why Hamilton for you?" Elijah asked.

"It's where I used to live. I thought maybe Lorna, my old foster mum, would take me in."

"Good luck with that." He smirked.

I rolled my eyes. "Thanks."

"Why were you in foster care?"

I looked up, surprised. It had been a long time since anyone asked me about that. I'd told Toby and Zo the whole thing a while back, but I didn't think the others would be interested. The way Elijah asked the question, it was like he hadn't known that was a part of my history. Why did he think I lived at Zo's?

He held my eye, his face neutral... no hint of the usual smirk or scowl. His expression wasn't exactly warm, but there was something soft about it when he wasn't pulling faces. It made me want to at least try to trust him.

"I lived with my grandma when I was a kid, but then she died. There wasn't anyone else."

A depressing story, but not the worst I'd heard by far. The

only really rough part was that I was old enough and surly enough that the chances of me being adopted had been slim to none.

He frowned. "What happened to your parents?"

"My mum died when I was born," I told him, keeping it simple. "My dad... I guess he wasn't very good at being a dad."

Elijah's expression was serious for a moment, then his lip quirked into something mean. "That's a lot of dead people around you. You sure you're not killing them off?"

"You're an ass." I turned my face away, staring out of the window. It was too dark to see anything, the light from inside the bus turning it into a mirror. I watched Elijah in the reflection. His eyes fluttered, regret filling his dark eyes. I didn't care. He could sit with that guilt. I would have changed seats, if it wasn't for the fact I'd have to climb over him to do it.

Elijah fell quiet, then he cleared his throat. "My sister's adopted," he volunteered. "Her birth parents died too."

"Good for you."

I waited for the joke – something about us both being killers, or both freaks... a cheap laugh where he could make me feel crap about myself. Instead, he settled back in his seat, closing his eyes again. This time he didn't reopen them.

*　*　*　*

I HALF WOKE AS THE bus pulled into the station. My head lay on Elijah's shoulder, the bare skin of his neck warm against mine.

"Cal?" he whispered. He touched my face gently, his thumb caressing my cheek.

I opened my eyes, startled. He held my gaze for a moment, his expression soft, then a wave of magic slammed into both of us, ricocheting around my head. I groaned, pulling away from him. The pulsing hum eased as I did.

He cleared his throat. "You were drooling on me," he said.

"Yeah?" I asked, but he was already on his feet. He didn't look back at me before disembarking and heading off into the night. I guess we weren't going to bother with any awkward goodbyes.

I watched him go. He was the resourceful type – too smart for his own good, Lorna would have said. Besides, he knew how to use his magic to his advantage. Still, I wondered where he planned on going. Did he even have a plan?

He was gone by the time I got off the bus. I stood for a moment, half waiting for him to reappear, then I made my way to the street. It had been a while, but I knew these roads better than anywhere else. Lorna lived about a 45-minute walk from the station, but that was fine. I set off at a steady pace.

The sun peeked over the hills in the distance, turning the sky a yellowy grey. I didn't want to wake Lorna – she'd be more amenable to hearing me out and letting me stay if she'd had enough sleep. Besides, I didn't know who she had with her now. She might have taken in another foster kid, if my disappearance hadn't put her off. My stomach twisted at the thought, but I shook my head. I would cross that bridge when I came to it.

I'd gotten soft living at Zo's, not having to walk anywhere. By the time I turned into Lorna's street, a raw, burst blister rubbed against the heel of my shoe, and my thighs ached.

I'd been intending to hang around outside until it got to a decent hour, but a yellow glow spilled out from Lorna's front windows onto the grass. Strange. Lorna normally struggled to get up early, sitting in the dark with her coffee for ages before she could open her eyes properly.

I hesitated, a tight feeling building in my stomach. Had

Zo's mum called her to say I was missing? No, that couldn't be it. I'd told Toby and Zo about Lorna, but they wouldn't know how to contact her.

I shook my head. I was being silly. It had been months since I'd seen her – perhaps she'd taken up a health kick, getting into early starts. I crossed the road, heading over to her house.

The lawn sprouted up in overgrown tufts, but the flower-beds sat in regimented rows, all neatly weeded. It made me laugh. Lorna would never admit it to anyone else, but the lawnmower terrified her. She was convinced one day she'd accidentally run over her foot and lose all her toes. I'd taken over the gardening after she told me, but I still teased her about it every week.

I took a breath, then knocked. A rustling came from inside, then Lorna opened the door. I wanted to explain straight off – give her the whole spiel about how I hadn't really run away; Mr Grandace had kidnapped me, and I'd never wanted to leave her.

The words died on my tongue. Her eyes widened as they fell on me, and she frowned, almost as if it took her a moment to place me.

"Callie," she whispered.

"I'm sorry," was all I managed to say.

She stepped forward, wrapping her arms around me. I started to cry, relief and exhaustion overwhelming me.

She turned her head, as if to kiss my cheek, but instead her lips moved to my ear. "Run!" she hissed.

I froze. Her hair covered my face, but I opened my eyes, sensing movement behind her.

"Go!" Lorna shoved me out of the house, and I stumbled back.

"Lorna..."

"Just run, Callie!" Lorna slammed the door in my face. Through the frosted glass panel, her blurry image turned to face someone – someone with long blonde hair. Miss Trager.

"No!" I clawed at the doorknob, then slammed my hand against the glass.

Both blurry figures turned towards me. Finally, my brain kicked in. If Miss Trager was here, it was for me not Lorna. I stumbled backward, breaking into a run. Behind me, the door opened but I didn't look back. What was she doing here? Had she known I would come?

It didn't matter; I had to get her away from Lorna. My head pounded, and my feet slapped against the pavement. I didn't dare look back. I might be able to outrun her, but her magic far outweighed mine.

"Calliope..."

Her voice whispered into a hiss, but it echoed around me. Underneath it, a slithering sound, like thousands of crawling insects crept across the ground towards me. And behind that, static, like a radio tuned to nothing.

Something wrapped around my ankle. I stumbled forward, somehow keeping my feet under me. I turned back, kicking, trying to free myself. Vines spread across the pavement, stretching out to grab me. I screamed and ripped the vine off my ankle. It disintegrated as soon as I touched it, but more reached out, sliding over each other like a pit of snakes. I scrambled away, then broke into a run. Were the plants real, or was Miss Trager manipulating me, making me see something she knew I would be afraid of?

Vines crept up from between cracks in the pavement in front of me. The slithering hissed in my ears, magic and reality blurring. I couldn't tell which way to run.

She appeared on the road in front of me, blonde hair strewn over her face, swirling in the wind as if alive. I turned, stumbling back towards the mess of creepers.

They parted, a gaping hole opening in the middle ready to swallow me. I froze, and the vines seemed to as well. Time slowed as they closed in on me. Feelers stretched out like forked tongues eager for a taste of my flesh.

A battered, rust-covered car pulled up in front of me. The door swung open.

"Get in!" Miss Trager sat in the driver's seat.

"Wh-what?" I turned. The blonde lady who'd chased me stood, still behind me, her hair falling over her shoulders now. She sneered at me, her face familiar but not. Not Miss Trager, at least.

Elijah's head appeared from the backseat. "Just get in the car, Callie!"

"Elijah? Why–?"

"We don't have time for this, get in!" Elijah grabbed my arm, pulling me into the car beside him. The tyres squealed as Miss Trager floored it.

The force flung me back against the seat. "I don't under-stand," I said. My head filled with the hum of being too close to Elijah.

We lurched around a corner, sending me crashing against him. He cursed under his breath, the pulse pounding in both our heads. He leaned over me to yank my seatbelt out. "Ex-planations later. Escape now."

I took the seatbelt from him, but didn't buckle myself in. "Seriously, what the hell?"

Miss Trager didn't glance back at me. Her eyes moved to the rear-view mirror, looking at the road behind us. She swore, hitting the accelerator.

I clutched my head as the slithering turned to a hiss. The vines were outside the car; it shouldn't have been this loud, but my ears rang with the noise.

Suddenly, she slammed on the brakes, throwing us forward. She spun the wheel to the right, sending me flying across the seat towards Elijah. He grabbed my arm, but the force of the magic between us threw me back. I gasped, trying to get air in my lungs.

My head rang, overloaded with the sounds of that pulsing hum, the static, and the slithering vines. "How is she still chasing us?"

Miss Trager shook her head. "No, it's not her." Her face paled, and her hands gripped the wheel so tight all the tendons popped up on the backs of her hands.

The car made a strange chugging sound, and our pace slowed to a crawl.

Miss Trager swore under her breath. I turned to Elijah, hoping to make an escape plan, but he stared horrified at the window beside me. Vines covered it, layer after layer of leaves slithering over each other. One crept through the gap in the window beside Elijah, reaching out to graze his cheek.

"Shut it! Shut the window!" I screamed.

Elijah scrambled for the switch, but the vine circled his neck. I wrenched it away. Heat pulsed through my palm and the leaves disintegrated. The car ground to a stop, and more vines crept up over us. Between them, a man walked towards us. It was him – the man I'd seen with the Labrador outside Zo's house. He held my eye, his pace unhurried as he stepped towards us.

"Callie!" Elijah yanked a vine away from me. "Snap out of it!"

The vine turned on him, wrapping around his wrist instead. Another tightened around my leg.

I blinked. The mess of leaves covering the car hid the man from view and blocked the light from outside. Elijah hit the overhead light switch, gifting us with a weak orange glow. The vines grew towards it, climbing up our bodies as if they would smother us.

Miss Trager rummaged in the dashboard compartment. She undid her seatbelt. "I'm sorry, Callie," she said.

"Wait, what?!"

She reached over the back of the seat, grabbing my wrist and shoving a silver bracelet onto it.

"No!"

She started to climb over the seat, reaching for Elijah, and I threw myself in front of him to block her. The force of the magic shoved me away. I crashed into Miss Trager, and she screamed as her back hit the dashboard.

I scrambled for the door handle, ready to face whatever was out there over becoming a prisoner again.

Miss Trager grabbed my other wrist, shackling it. "It's the only way, I'm sorry!"

Elijah yelled something, but his words crackled with static. Miss Trager opened the car door, squeezing her way out between the vines. They piled into the car, ignoring her. She walked towards the man, another pair of those silver bracelets in her hand, as the vines constricted around my chest.

I tried to scream, but my body disappeared beneath me. I reached for Elijah's hand, and I saw him reach for mine, but our fingers slipped straight through each other's.

Chapter Seven

I shivered. Cold floor pressed against my cheek, and darkness surrounded me. I eased myself up. My shoulder clicked, stiff from lying in an awkward position, and hot pain told me bruises lined my hip.

"Elijah?!" I called. My voice bounced back to me.

I scanned the room. The narrow width indicated it was a corridor, but other than a few framed photographs, the white walls and wooden floors were plain, nondescript. It didn't matter – I knew I'd been sent back to the school. I'd known the moment Miss Trager slapped those bracelets on my wrists.

A vine clung to my arm, tiny burrs attaching it to my sleeve. I threw it off, afraid it would come alive again. It disintegrated as soon as it hit the floor, more magic than plant.

"Elijah?" I called again. Had she sent him with me, or had she left him to his fate with the vines and whoever that was outside the car?

I closed my eyes, reaching out in my mind. *Toby?* I whispered. *Please... I need you.*

Nothing but the sound of static responded. Elijah's sleep

spell must still have Toby in its grip. A shuddering breath broke through my lips, and I cried, indulgent self-pitying tears. How could I have been so stupid as to try to shut him out? The melody of the song I'd been singing echoed in my head as if to mock me.

I lay back down, giving in to the exhaustion. Something niggled at my mind, a little sensation at first, like an itch in my brain. The static came in waves, almost like words trying to break through, then the itch became a pull, making me dizzy each time I didn't follow it.

"Toby?" I sat up. The static surged as I did. I stood, letting the pull make my body sway forward. I took a few hesitant steps then broke into a run.

The corridor ended at a glass firestop door. Beyond it, stairs led into shadow. I tried the handle. The locked metal tooth jolted against the frame keeping me firmly out.

"Toby?" I knocked, then banged on the wooden frame with the flat of my hand. "Toby, please!"

I peered down the stairs, but darkness covered everything. He had to be down there. He was the only person whose magic drew me in like that, but why wasn't he answering? A sick feeling clogged my throat. What if he was hurt? I'd left him – left all of them – with those sunflowers growing outside. I thought the danger was in all of us being together, but what if I'd left them to a worse fate? If the sunflowers attacked like the vines, there would have been no way for them to get out of the house.

I leaned my head against the door, reaching out with my mind. Nothing but static replied. Did that mean he was unconscious?

I swallowed and tore myself away. I was no use to Toby just standing there.

I turned the corner, into the next corridor. I didn't recognise the hallway or the rooms flowing off it, though that didn't surprise me. Most of the areas of the school we'd spent time in had been destroyed by Toby's plant.

I stopped, suddenly. Darkness shaded my vision, but I could just make out the shape of someone lying on the floor in front of me.

"Toby?" I whispered.

The figure groaned, raising a hand to rub his face. Light glinted off a silver bracelet, circling his wrist.

"Elijah!" I raced towards him, but the familiar pulsing hum and wave of nausea hit me. I forced my way through it, grabbing his shoulder.

"Wake up! Please just wake up."

He groaned again and opened his eyes. Immediately his magic hit us both like a slap. I scooted back, clutching my head and feeling my stomach turn.

Elijah rolled over, looking like he was going to be sick. "Jesus, Callie. I know I'm irresistible, but..."

I broke into a sudden, high-pitched laugh. He sat up, and I shuffled back further. The nausea subsided as I did.

"Are you okay?" I asked. "Are you hurt?"

He shook his head. "Nah, I'm all right."

He didn't ask if I was okay, but that wasn't exactly unexpected. We'd never been friends, even before we became magnetically opposed.

He eased himself into a sitting position. "Where are we?" He touched one of the bracelets on his wrist, frowning at it.

"The school." I stood, walking away from him. "I think Toby's back here. I can feel his magic, but the door's locked."

The pull still called me. I moved towards it, and waves of static washed over me.

Toby? I called again. Silence greeted me. *Was* it him? No one else's magic had ever drawn me in like this. But that static... it felt like a warning.

Elijah stood, leaning against the wall for support. "I don't recognise this." He moved to look in one of the rooms, leading off the corridor.

"No..." I made my way back towards the stairs, the pull of magic drawing me along. "We destroyed so much of the school. We must be in staff quarters or... it doesn't matter, can you just help me?" I reached the glass door and rattled the doorknob again. "Between the two of us, we can probably get him out."

"Cal..."

I turned, looking back at Elijah. He stared at me, a frown creasing his forehead.

"That's not..." He hesitated, seeming to read something in the air. "I don't know what you're feeling, but your boyfriend's not here."

"But..." I reached out again in my mind. Toby's voice didn't greet me, only that pull.

Elijah watched me, his expression hard to read. I had a feeling he was waiting to see if I'd rise to his "boyfriend" comment, but this wasn't the time for games. I rattled the door handle one more time, as if something might have changed in the last few seconds.

Elijah took a step away. "My magic's stronger than yours," he said quietly, "and I'm telling you, none of the others are here. It's just us."

"Then what is that?"

Elijah stared through the glass. I could tell he felt it too. His body swayed, as if he wanted to give in and walk towards it, then he shook his head.

"I don't know," he said finally. "But if it's trying that hard to get us to walk towards it..."

He turned, walking the other way. I was torn. The pull of magic crept around me, seductively. Maybe Elijah was wrong.

Maybe Toby lay on the other side of that door, waiting for me to find him.

I shook myself. Or maybe it was another siren plant. I took one last look through the door, then ran to catch up with Elijah.

I stayed a few paces back, keeping enough distance so our magic didn't interact. He tried the door handles as he passed them. Most were locked, and the only one that opened led to a cupboard.

I matched his slow pace, still keeping my distance. "How did you end up in the car with Miss Trager?" I asked.

Elijah blinked, as if he'd forgotten that even happened. "Same as you, pretty much. I was walking, trying to figure out where to go, then this guy appeared and started throwing plants at me."

"A guy? Did he have a dog?" I asked, thinking of the man outside Zo's house.

Elijah frowned. "What? No."

"But was it the same man who covered the car in vines?"

"Maybe? I don't know, I couldn't see through the leaves."

It was all so confusing. Who were those people, and why had they attacked? Even more puzzling was the fact that Miss Trager had been the one to save us. But why had she sent us back here alone?

Some instinct made me look down. I froze. "Elijah, stop!"

To his credit, he listened. He halted, midway through a step, and turned back towards me slowly.

"There's a rune line."

"So?" He shook his head. He'd never seen what had happened to me when I crossed the runes while trying to escape the school last time.

I held up my wrist, gesturing to the bracelet. "You can't cross the lines with these on. They'll bind you in place." In the past, they'd also alerted the headmaster to the fact that I was trying to escape. I had no idea if they would do that now – I had no idea if Mr Grandace was even here.

Elijah sighed. Magic trapped us – rune lines in one direction, and some type of siren in the other. He shrugged, then turned around. We made the same slow progress back down the corridor, trying the doors on the other side.

"Why do you think they're coming after us?" I asked. "That man was outside Zo's house – the night before this all started."

Was that yesterday? I was losing track of the days. So much had happened in such a short space of time. I'd gotten used to the peaceful nothingness of living at Zo's. Sure, I'd been missing Toby and the others, but at least life had been calm.

"I don't know." Elijah didn't seem that interested. He focused on rattling the door handles, trying to get one to open. It was silly at this point, and the noise got on my nerves.

I glanced around at the unfamiliar walls. "We're on the other side of the lines," I said. Was that the rune line I'd crossed to distract Miss Trager from finding Toby? The dim light made it hard to tell.

At the time, I'd thought the runes were about keeping me from escaping, but maybe there was more to it. Maybe they also hid something on this side of them.

Elijah tried another door, and it creaked open. He grinned at me, then flicked on the light switch inside. The room lit up, a warm glow spilling out into the hallway. Elijah's eyes scanned the room, until his gaze caught on something. "Woah," he said.

"What's in there?" I asked.

He didn't answer, instead moving into the room, creating enough space that I could join him.

The room was a bedroom, but not like the one we'd slept in when we lived here. Ours had never lost the sense of temporariness that came with our boarder status. This room had been lived in – had grown up with its occupant. It reminded me of Zo's bedroom, with the mix of childhood and teenage decorations, but these were all dusty, abandoned.

"That's the guy who came after me, I think."

I turned around as Elijah spoke. He peered at one of the photos on the wall. He moved back so I could get close enough to look. Three teenagers filled the frame, leaning against each other to pose.

"He was older, but it's him."

"Is that Miss Trager?"

The youngest of the three looked like a gangly, thirteen-year-old version of her. My eyes moved to the girl beside her. She didn't look much like Miss Trager here, but I wondered if she was similar enough for me to have mistaken them. Was she the one who had chased me tonight? She had similar pretty features, but they'd landed in a smug, self-assured expression. Adult Miss Trager only ever looked serious and imposing, never smug. In this photo, she just looked awkward and insecure.

My eye moved to the boy in the photo. "So, he must be her brother."

"No shit, Sherlock."

I rolled my eyes, then turned back to the photo. I studied his face, frowning. Even accounting for changes with age, I didn't recognise the boy. "That's not the man I saw."

Which meant *three* people were coming after us, two of them related to Miss Trager. A niggle of doubt scratched at my mind. Were they against her? Perhaps the four of them had been working together to get us back here.

Elijah stared at something else across the room. He pulled

another photo from the wall, bringing it over. "Is that Mr Grandace?"

Pulsing thrummed in my ears as he gave it to me. There were six teenagers in the photo this time, three of them Miss Trager and her siblings, then a girl and two other guys – one of them clearly a young, beardless Mr Grandace.

"Yeah, that's definitely him."

Elijah didn't back off this time, instead leaning in to look at the other pictures. The air turned solid between us, making it feel like he was pressing against me. From the way his hand rested in the air above my shoulder, he was doing it on purpose. I focused on the images, ignoring him.

There was something so strange about seeing them like this, standing on the front steps of the school, all of them probably stuck there like we had been. Mr Grandace and Miss Trager were even younger than us, though her siblings looked older. I hadn't been able to picture the teachers as teenagers earlier but seeing it didn't help.

"You reckon this is the original six he told you about?" Elijah asked.

I didn't answer. The man I'd seen outside Zo's house stood next to Mr Grandace in the photo, but that wasn't what gave me pause. The other girl, the one standing in the back behind Miss Trager, was my mother.

Chapter Eight

"That's my mum." I felt sick. The other implications of that swirled in my head.

"No shit, are you sure?"

"Yes, I'm sure. She looks just like me." Was she even pregnant with me in this photo? Miss Trager mostly hid my mum's stomach, but the way Mum leaned back made me think she could be supporting a rounded belly.

I turned the photo over, reading the names scrawled on the back. *Arthur, Ursula, Chloe, Benjamin, Joseph, and Samantha.* Samantha... Sammy, as my grandmother always called her.

I'd seen photos of her before, of course. Gran had displayed them all over the house. Somehow, seeing her like this was different. I knew she was young when she had me, but it hadn't occurred to me that she was still in school... this school.

Something in my stomach dropped.

Was this why she'd died? Had the school killed her? Mr Grandace said he and Miss Trager were the only survivors — that the others were destroyed by the magic. It was clearly a lie.

Miss Trager's siblings were still breathing and so was the man with the dog. Only my mum was gone.

Elijah took the photo from me, holding it up next to my face. "Is Mr Grandace..." A frown creased his brow, and his eyes flicked between me and the image.

"What?" My mouth felt like sandpaper around the word.

"You don't think Mr Grandace is your dad, do you?"

"What? No." I snatched the photo back from him. Mr Grandace's arm draped around my mum. Both of them grinned, her head tipped onto his shoulder. "He can't be... he would have told me, right?"

Elijah shrugged. It was a stupid question. Mr Grandace had lied and kept secrets from the beginning – why would this be any different?

"Could be one of the others," he said. "Miss Trager's brother, maybe. That would make Miss Trager your aunt."

That wasn't any better. Gran hadn't told me much about my father, and it had been long enough that the bits she *had* told me floated just out of reach in my memory. Having so many gaps in my past had always been confusing. Now those gaps felt dangerous, like deep pits that would swallow me if I got too close.

I put the photo down and pressed my hands to my temples. "This is insane."

Elijah stared at me, chewing on his lip. "Don't freak out on me, okay?" He reached out, as if to pat me on the arm, but his hand hovered in the air, not quite touching me.

If our magic hadn't been so determined to force us apart, I would have buried my face in his shoulder and cried, no matter what I thought of him. Right then, I wanted him to hold me – to stroke my hair and say soft soothing things.

I wished Toby were here. He wouldn't get it. He'd grown up in a normal family; no way he'd be able to understand the complexities of what I was feeling. But *he* would have been able to hug me. He would have told me it was going to be all right.

I glanced at Elijah, glad he couldn't read any of that in my thoughts. He'd gone still, staring into the empty air in front of him.

"What's-?"

He yanked me back from the doorway, one arm wrapping around me, the other clapping over my mouth. "Someone's here!" he hissed.

The heat of his skin against mine and the pulsing magic made my head feel like it was going to explode. A scream built inside me, and Elijah tightened his grip reflexively. Somehow the intensity of it helped. I clutched his arm, his muscles tight under my touch, and for a moment the magic seemed to pull me towards him rather than pushing me away.

He let go, inching his hand back, ready to clap it over my lips again if I lost it. I turned towards him, and he held my eye, his gaze intense, but I couldn't tell whether he'd felt the same thing I had.

The floor creaked outside the door, and our heads snapped towards it simultaneously.

"Is it Miss Trager?" I whispered. I never thought I'd see her as the best-case scenario, but her siblings terrified me, and I wasn't quite ready to have the "are you my dad?" conversation with Mr Grandace.

Elijah shook his head. "No, I think it's..." He cut himself off and raced out into the corridor.

I followed. Elijah ran to the right, but the pull took me to the left. I found myself moving towards it automatically, almost as if a hand had wrapped around my wrist, coaxing me along. Static swelled in my head, and I couldn't focus on anything except that pull.

"Cal!" Elijah called.

I shook my head, surprised to find my fingers brushing the glass of the door to the stairs. I turned back. "Sorry, I–" Electricity crackled in the air, and something thudded to the floor in front of Elijah.

"Zo!" he yelled.

I gasped, breaking away from the pull. I quickened my pace, reaching Zo. She shivered, her head rolling to the side. Her skin had paled to a waxy grey, the dark of her spiked hair standing out against it. Elijah tapped her cheek, then her collar bone, but she gave no response.

I crouched down beside her. "Zo... Wake up, Zo." I shook her shoulder. "Can you open your eyes?" She didn't stir, but her chest rose and fell in short breaths.

A second thud sounded, sickeningly loud. I spun around. Julianna lay crumpled at the end of the corridor, her wrist bent at an unnatural angle. Elijah got up, running towards her.

I rolled Zo onto her side, first aid instincts kicking in. "Come on, please wake up." Her arm flopped across her body, lifeless, but the silver of a bracelet glinted at me from her wrist.

The bracelets.

My head shot up. "Elijah, wait!"

He crossed the rune line, and his bracelets snapped together, slamming him into the wall. He fell forward, narrowly missing landing on Julianna's slumped form.

"Elijah!" I ran towards him, screeching to a halt at the rune line. He rolled over onto his back, trying and failing to sit up.

"Are you okay?"

He glared at me. "What do you think?"

"Is Julianna?"

He looked over at her and fell quiet. I couldn't see much

from where I stood, but a streak of red slashed across her forehead. A groan sounded from behind me.

"Zo?"

Her breathing turned to gasps, and then to a shriek. I raced back to her. She flailed, not fully conscious yet, only enough to scream. Bruises lined her arms, and a lump formed in my throat. What had I left them to face back at the house?

I put my arm around her, easing her up into a sitting position. Her eyes snapped open, panic filling them. She shoved me off, scrambling back against the wall. Thunder rumbled above us. I moved away, raising my palms, as lightning flashed, and silver sparks rained down on us.

"Hey, hey, Zo. It's me. It's Callie."

She blinked, her eyelids fluttering as her pupils slowly dilated. "Callie. Oh my god, you're here." She crawled towards me, wrapping me in a hug.

"It's okay. It's okay." I rubbed her back. She was trembling, her skin cold to the touch. The storm magistation petered out as she squeezed me tighter, crushing the air out of me. "You were gone."

"I know." Waves of guilt rolled over me again. "I'm sorry. I shouldn't have left."

She let out a sob, and something in my words seemed to register with her. She went still in my arms, then pulled back to look at me. "What do you mean 'left'?" She stared at me, confusion making her eyes wide and childlike.

I couldn't hold her gaze. "I'm sorry. I thought I was doing the right thing."

She shook her head slowly. "We thought they took you. We thought..." She pulled away from me, her voice rising. "You left?! Jules and I were..." Her face paled suddenly. "Where is Jules?"

"Down there. Elijah's with her, but—"

She heaved herself up before I could finish. I lurched after her. "Wait, you can't cross the rune lines." I grabbed her wrist, but she jerked away from me. I grabbed again, locking my arm around her waist.

"Get off me!" She tore at my wrist with her nails, biting into the flesh.

"Woah, listen to her!" Elijah yelled. "I've got Jules, okay?" The bracelets held him in place, but he'd manoeuvred Julianna's head into his lap, his hand clamped against the wound on her forehead.

Zo slowed, her eyes locked on the crimson creeping up between his fingers. "Let me go, she needs me."

Elijah shook his head. "She needs Asher."

Zo flinched, and I tightened my grip. "She needs both of you," I said.

Elijah grimaced. "Yeah, the connection – from both sides."

Zo let out a strangled sound, and her hands flew to her temples. She doubled over, crouching down.

I moved with her, keeping my hand on her back. "Where is he? Was he with you?"

She shook her head, her breath making short, sharp sounds instead of words. She was freezing, and an icy wave of air rushed over me. White flakes of snow danced around her, chilling us both. I never thought I'd miss the sparks of her happy magistations, but we'd all end up with frostbite if she kept this up.

I took her chin in my hand, making her look at me. "What happened?"

She swayed, the blood rushing from her cheeks again. "I don't know... I..." She shivered, her eyes closing. "Sunflowers."

A matching shiver worked its way through me, and not

from the cold. "I'm sorry." I could almost see it, the sunflowers growing, lurching their way across the yard and into the house like the vines had; their stalks wrapping around the inhabitants and strangling them.

"Cal..." Elijah met my eye then nodded down at Julianna. A grey tinge marked her skin and the blood from her head dripped down Elijah's wrist.

I put my arms around Zo again, pulling her to her feet. I clasped her face in my hands, forcing her to focus on me. "Where are Toby and Asher?"

She blinked at me, her eyes drifting back to Julianna. I shook her. "Zo! Concentrate! Were they with you? Who sent you here?"

"We... we woke up and you... were gone..." Her voice crackled, and she took a breath after every second word. Her eyes slid back to mine, finally focusing on me. "Toby and Asher went after you."

I closed my eyes. Of course they had. I'd been stupid to think I could run away without them trying to follow.

"Who sent you here?" I asked Zo. "Was it Miss Trager, or...?"

"Mr Grandace." Zo swallowed, and it was as if her body became solid again. She stopped shaking and words came easier. "There were these people outside. They made the sunflowers grow."

That sounded about right. After their attack on Miss Trager's car failed, they must have gone after the others.

"Do you know if he sent Asher back too?" Elijah asked.

Zo shook her head. "I don't know." She stepped towards Julianna again. "Please let me help her..."

"No."

Something forceful swelled in Elijah's voice making her freeze. Her shoulders rocked towards him, as if the momentum of her body would fling her forward with or without her feet following.

"You won't be able to on your own," he said, "and you'll be useless to Julianna if you get stuck like me."

Zo raised her hands in frustration. "We can't just leave her to bleed!"

"Where are Toby and Asher?" I asked again. "You're connected to them – find them."

Elijah blinked as if trying to contact Asher had never occurred to him. Zo swayed on the spot, perhaps too exhausted to even try. I reached out in my own mind, trying to find Toby, but all I found was static.

Elijah let out a breath. "Asher's in the school."

Zo made a sound, but I couldn't tell whether it was laughter or a sob. I wasn't sure which I wanted to do either.

"I can't feel them," she whispered.

I shook my head. "Neither."

"I'm telling you, they're here!" Elijah's voice shot up.

"I believe you," I said. "I just can't..." I barely had the energy to stand, let alone mentally connect with anyone.

"Where?" Zo asked. Her eyes fixed on Julianna, and her voice had lost the crackle, becoming deep and strong.

"Downstairs."

A pang of something painful flashed through me. The pull I'd felt earlier drawing me to that room... what if that's all Elijah was feeling? What if it was still trying to lure us in?

Zo closed her eyes. For a moment, I thought she was going to collapse, then her eyelids snapped open. She turned abruptly, marching down the corridor away from us.

"Zo, wait!" I stumbled into a run.

"Oh yeah, I'm fine," Elijah called after me. "Just leave me here to rot."

I ignored him, and chased after Zo. "Wait, there was

something here before. It—"

"I don't care!"

I stepped back, Zo's words hitting me like a physical force. Thunder rumbled around us, bouncing against the walls.

"It's your fault Julianna's hurt. If you'd waited until morning like you'd promised, they wouldn't have gone after you, and we wouldn't have been alone."

I opened my mouth, but it felt like it was full of dust. We stared at each other, and the anger in her eyes didn't burn out. She turned away from me.

"The door's locked," I whispered.

She slammed her hand against it. The glass panel shattered, magic scattering the shards into a perfect circle on the ground. It glinted, catching the light as if it would perform its own set of spells, with or without our help.

Zo reached through the gap, unlocking the door from the other side. She walked through it without looking back. My feet felt heavy, but I pulled them into steps, trailing after her. She thumped down the stairs, but I hesitated on the first one. The pull returned, drawing me down. Maybe it was Toby, calling out to me. He would know what to do. His arms would circle me, the magic weaving us closer together until we were cocooned and safe. He would make everything okay again.

I forced myself down the steps. Below me, Zo walked along an identical corridor to the one we had been on above. She stopped in front of a door, reaching for the handle.

I stumbled as my foot hit the floor, expecting another step. She glanced back but her expression was hard. I righted myself as she turned the handle. A vine crept out from underneath the door.

"Zo!" I bolted down the corridor, but my steps seemed too slow. Vines poured out of the door, smothering her.

"Oh my god, no!" I raced towards her, diving into the

tangle of leaves. I grasped her hand, and she clutched mine. "I've got you!" I yelled. "Don't let go!"

But the hand dragged me into the vines with it. "No, stop!" I tried to pull free, but another hand circled my wrist – a male hand, not Zo's.

"Calliope…"

The voice sounded just beside my ear. I whipped around. A face disappeared into the vines – the man from outside Zo's house. His features distorted, gasping for breath. His lips moved, forming words I couldn't make out.

Threads of magic stretched out, pulling me closer, filling my head with static. Vines squeezed my chest, and the air rushed out of me. I went limp, the fight rushing out of me.

He disappeared into the tangle of vines, his hold on me dropping away as we were both swallowed by the plant. He wasn't controlling this. The vines were like Toby's plant, taking over. I had to help him – I had to save both of them.

A spark flashed in front of me, and one of the leaves sizzled, almost catching fire.

"Zo!" I yelled.

More sparks lit up, burning a path through the leaves.

"Hold on Zo. I'm coming." I lunged into the vines. The strands holding me melted, my magic taking over. My hand connected with something, and I felt the brush of Zo's spiky hair, the soft flesh of her cheek. "I'm here! I've got you."

I dived down, finding her shoulder and looping my arm under it. I reached out again, and my fingertips brushed something else. I grabbed it, my hand closing on the man's limp arm.

"Help me, Zo!"

Her magic swelled around mine, and together we pushed backwards, ripping through the vines and out of the room.

Toby! I yelled in my mind. I hoped he could hear me.

I landed on my back, Zo crashing down on top of me, and the man flopped unconscious beside us. Sparks rained down, burning my skin. The vines swarmed above us like a wave. I closed my eyes, not wanting to see when it crashed. Zo turned, clinging to me in a desperate embrace.

"Enough!"

The voice was familiar, but it crackled with power, distorting it. Wind rushed at my face, whipping roughly against my skin. Music came with it, a haunting and disturbing sound.

And then, silence.

I felt the vines retreat, slithering away like cowed children, but I didn't dare look. Footsteps sounded – two sets, maybe more, coming towards us. I creaked my eyes open. A figure crouched down beside me, a grin spreading across his face.

"Can't leave you alone for a second, can I, Reactive Girl?"

"Toby," I whispered.

Chapter Nine

Toby guided me back up the stairs, his hand crushing mine as if he thought I would disappear as soon as he loosened his grip. We passed Elijah in the corridor. We'd been freed from the shackles, but he still sat on the floor, leaning back against the wall, his palms pressed to his forehead. I reached out, grabbing his hand as we passed. It made the air around us distort, the pulse bouncing and echoing around us, but he squeezed my hand, clinging to me anyway.

The rest of the school had come alive. Julianna screamed from somewhere down the corridor, and Zo and Asher's voices piled over each other – both trying to comfort her, both doing all they could to heal her wounds.

I stumbled towards the sound. "We have to help her," I said, but Toby held me back.

"There's nothing we can do. Zo and Asher are taking care of her; we'll just be in the way."

I nodded, though it made me feel useless. I hated knowing she was in pain – knowing that it was my fault.

Toby led me into an old living room and planted me on a sofa. A dust sheet covered it, and the end billowed up ghost-like as I sat. The whole room was shielded in similar covers, as if someone hoped it would be forgotten.

A flash of blonde hair raced past the door, followed by the swirl of a black cape. I wanted to run after Miss Trager and Mr Grandace and beg them to explain what was happening, but both teachers looked wild with energy, focused on their own agendas, no time for questions.

I turned back to Toby instead. "I'm sorry," I said.

He just shook his head. "Are you hurt?" he asked.

"I'm fine, are you?"

"Nah, I'm okay."

He wasn't though. A graze ran along the length of his arm. A rip in my jeans revealed a similar one on my knee. I hadn't felt the skin break, but it stung now. Regardless, we were both doing better than Julianna.

"What happened?" My voice came out croaky, my fear of the answer shutting down my voice.

"I don't know about back at the house." He glanced towards the door, Julianna's screams continuing from down the corridor.

"Zo said you and Asher left?"

Zo had told me she and Julianna were alone. What happened to Josh and her parents? Was it too much to hope that the sunflowers had only attacked my friends and left Zo's family unharmed? God, I hoped they were all right.

"We went looking for you and..." Toby swallowed, his face paling just like Zo's had earlier.

I squeezed his hand. "Show me?"

He hesitated, just for a second, but it was long enough for my stomach to drop. Maybe he didn't trust me anymore – I wouldn't blame him if he didn't, after everything that had happened tonight. But then he squeezed my hand back, his mind seeming to open to me, his memories running through it.

It was like watching my own night play out. I saw him running from vines, Miss Trager's brother in the middle of them. How had her siblings been in so many places at once? The obvious answer was magic. Perhaps the people we'd seen attacking us were no more real than the plants.

Would we have been safer if I'd stayed at the house, or would the six of us have become an easier target, taken out in one swoop? We had all been ambushed tonight, that much was obvious, and Miss Trager had saved us. But what exactly had we been saved from? That part seemed to be getting less and less clear as the night went on.

"Mr Grandace pulled me and Asher out of there. Seems like we arrived back just in time." An image of the wave of vines about to crash over me and Zo ran through his head, the memory raw.

I shivered. "The man who made those vines... they swallowed him too," I said. "He made them, but he wasn't in control." His face gasping for air flashed through my mind.

Toby grimaced. "I know. Mr Grandace is dealing with that."

"What...?" The question wouldn't form, exhaustion stealing my words.

Toby moved to kneel in front of me, cupping my face in his hands. I stared at him, focusing only on his eyes.

Are you okay? he said inside his head.

No, I said back.

He nodded, as if that was the only answer he could have expected. *We need to get out of here.*

We can't. I couldn't form the words, not even in my thoughts. Every time I closed my eyes, I saw that wave of vines collapsing over me. I felt the creep of them tightening around me, compressing the air out of my lungs, but more than that I saw the man's face, the way his magic had drawn me in. When he'd spoken to me, I hadn't been able to make out the words, but I was sure he'd been pleading for help.

Why not?

I reached for Toby's hands, clasping them in mine. I tried to transfer it all to him, every memory from the moment I'd left. Toby's eyes widened, and I could see it all playing again in his thoughts.

"My mum," I said aloud. "She was one of them." I needed to know the truth of what happened here. I needed to stop it from happening again.

Toby studied my face. Too many questions raced in his mind. I saw echoes of what had happened to him tonight. His memory of the moment he'd woken and found me gone flashed through his thoughts. I closed my eyes, as if that could stop me feeling everything he had. Instead, his emotions were washed out by my own guilt.

He and Asher had come after me, and they'd gotten caught up in this because of it. Of course, as much as I blamed myself, the real cause was the school. We would never be free of it until we unravelled everything that had happened here.

Finally, Toby nodded. "Then we'll stay." He crawled up onto the couch, wrapping his arms around me.

I laid my head on his chest. The strain on the magical thread between us eased as I listened to his heartbeat. It bounced and fluttered against his ribcage, and I watched flashes of his thoughts. I never should have left him.

Toby lifted his head to look at me. "Why couldn't I hear your thoughts tonight? What was that sound?"

"The static, you mean? You heard it too?"

"Yeah, what was that?" Toby brushed the hair back from my face. "Why couldn't I reach you?"

"I don't know." I dropped my gaze. "Elijah did something – a spell, but I think it was just supposed to make you sleep longer."

"So, it wasn't on purpose?" No judgement filled his voice. His eyes traced over me, no hint of anger in them, but the touch of his fingertips against my temple was hesitant.

"No. I tried reaching for you when everything happened, but you were just gone."

I *had* tried to hide from him, but only with his trick of repeating song lyrics in my head. I had no idea what caused the static. Was it Elijah's magic working against mine? It sounded different to the hum, but perhaps the effect was growing stronger. Or maybe it was the people who had been chasing us – some magical interference, wrapping around me like the vines.

Toby didn't say anything, and eventually I forced myself to look up at him. His Adam's apple bobbed, and I had an urge to run the tip of my finger over it.

"Why did you leave?" His voice was low.

I didn't answer, but I held his eye, letting him read it all in my thoughts. He had to know I hadn't wanted to go. If anything, it had physically hurt to drag myself away. It was more than the magical pull of being bound to him though. He was the person I felt safest with in the whole world and leaving had been like ripping off a limb.

"I shouldn't have," I said aloud.

He swallowed, pulling me back into a hug. His heart rate finally slowed, and I felt mine do the same.

"Stay this time, okay?" he whispered.

I nodded. I wasn't planning on going anywhere.

* * * *

WE TRIED TO SLEEP, curled up on the couch together. Julianna stopped screaming, but the wailing sound that filled its place was almost worse. Below it, Zo's gentle voice came in shushing waves, soothing all of us. Around us, the school slowly fell quiet, Julianna's tears finally petering out.

I'd never been able to sense anyone except Toby, but my mind kept stretching out, straining to know where each person was. The pull that had drawn me downstairs earlier tickled at the back of my brain, as did a hint of static.

At one point, Elijah made his way down the corridor, and the push of his magic repelling mine pressed against me. He stopped in the doorway, hovering. Somehow it felt too complicated to talk to him. Instead, I pretended to be asleep, and after a few minutes, Elijah walked away. Toby's arms tightened around me as he did.

Eventually, a bar of weak sunlight crept in between the curtains, falling across our faces.

"You awake?" I whispered. I knew he was, but it still felt polite to check.

Toby nodded. "Yeah, couldn't sleep."

"What about the others?"

Toby tilted his head as if listening. "Zo's still with Julianna... actually, I think they all are."

I felt the echoes of all of them in his thoughts. A hint of Julianna's pain filtered through, and he reeled back, distancing himself from Zo's mind to get away from it.

He shifted. "I can still hear it in your head."

"Huh?"

"The static."

The noise had dulled to the point I barely noticed it, but when I listened, it crackled in the background, under the surface of everything.

"It gets louder when you think about those people." Toby

rubbed my arm gently, and I focused on the touch.

I hadn't been conscious of thinking about our attackers, but of course they were running through my mind. How could they not be, with everything that had happened?

"Do you think they're causing it? Like the way Elijah and I repel each other?"

"I think Elijah repels everyone." Toby's mouth twisted into a half-smile.

I frowned. A day ago, I would have said the same. But Elijah had saved me several times in the last 24 hours, even with the magic forcing us apart. The memory of him pulling me back from the doorway filled my head. I thought of the heat from his arms wrapping around me, and that moment when the magic had switched. For once it had been drawing me toward Elijah instead of pushing me away… I hadn't imagined it, had I?

Suddenly, Toby flinched. His hand moved to his stomach.

I sat up. "What is it?"

He shook his head. "Nothing – a ping. The magic wants something."

"The magic, or Mr Grandace?"

"Hard to tell. Both I think." He pulled himself into a seated position but didn't get up from the couch.

A trail of fireflies lit up, guiding me out into the corridor – my version of the ping Toby felt when the magic tried to tell him something. We could ignore it. I wasn't sure I was ready to hear anything Mr Grandace had to say, and I certainly didn't trust the magic anymore.

I looked back at Toby. He met my eye, and his hand moved to take mine, clinging to me or comforting me, I wasn't sure.

You jump, I jump, he said inside his head,

He still wanted to run. It didn't matter how much the magic pulled on him, he wanted to fight against it, and honestly, if he'd told me he was leaving, I would have gone with him, no question. But he'd given the decision to me.

"We should follow it." A flood of anxiety rushed through me, but I squashed it down.

He stared at me a moment longer, his breaths slow, almost sighing, then he nodded. "Then we'll follow it."

* * * *

THE FIREFLIES LED US to a room further down the hallway. Julianna lay scrunched up in a ball on the bed, a faded patchwork quilt spread over her. Asher half-lay beside her, his arms cradling her. Zo sat on the end of the bed. Her hand stretched out, reaching towards Julianna, but she didn't touch her. She looked lost, unsure of her role here. It seemed to hurt her that she couldn't help. She met my eye, briefly, and sparks sizzled around her too quick for me to see the colour.

Miss Trager sat in a corner, her eyes closed. How could she be so calm? How was she unharmed, after everything that had happened last night?

"What is this place?" Toby whispered. "Are we still in the school?"

He stared at the walls. Similar pictures to the ones Elijah and I had found last night lined them, though this time they were peppered with old band posters and pages from magazines. I understood his confusion. The school nestled in the remnants of an old home – Miss Trager's childhood home. No wonder they had kept us so confined when we were students – or should I say prisoners – here. So many questions needed answers, but I doubted we would get satisfactory ones.

Toby and I both jumped at a creaking door, out in the corridor. Footsteps sounded, and Toby stepped in front of me, his hands raised. A pulse started behind my eyes.

"It's just Elijah," I said.

Toby didn't relax his stance, but he lowered his hands.

The hum intensified, as Elijah came through the doorway. He smirked, almost letting it turn into a genuine smile when he met my eye. Then his gaze flicked to Toby, and his eyes narrowed. He took a step towards Asher instead, but then stopped himself. Asher didn't look up, his attention fully absorbed in Julianna. Elijah hovered for a moment, and then he sat down on the end of the bed next to Zo.

She gave him a half-smile and looked back at Julianna and Asher. Elijah and I might be the ones on the ends, but the two of them were the ones being shoved aside.

"I'm glad you're okay," I told him.

His lips flicked back into a smirk. "Course I'm okay. I always am."

That was probably true. Silence fell over us again. A sense of expectation filled the room. It couldn't be a coincidence Elijah had turned up here now. He must have been called by the magic too. Each breath we took seemed to hang, all of us waiting.

Mr Grandace strode into the room, breaking the tension. There were no warning door creaks or footsteps this time; perhaps his magic gave him the advantage of a silent approach. He didn't spare us even the briefest of glances, going straight to Miss Trager. He reached out, stopping short of touching her. She looked up, and her lips parted, but she didn't speak. They were both frozen, locked in eye contact and in each other.

I wondered if they could talk to each other inside their heads in the same way Toby and I did. It seemed like they were playing out a similar conversation to the one Toby and I had just had.

Mr Grandace finally drew his eyes away from her, and

scanned the room, looking at each of us in turn. His eyes fell on me and lingered there. I couldn't read his expression. Regret? Relief? Guilt? Honestly, I didn't care what he was feeling. All I could think of was that picture of his arm wrapped around my mother.

I found my mouth opening. "You lied to me." I didn't plan to say it, the words burst out of me.

Mr Grandace blinked, confusion washing all of the other conflicting expressions away. "I promise you I haven't, Calliope."

"You told me the rest of your circle were dead. You said you and Miss Trager were the only survivors."

Miss Trager flinched. She didn't make a sound, but she bit her lip so hard it turned white. Mr Grandace touched her arm, gently, and the rest of what I wanted to say died on my tongue.

She didn't have any makeup on, and her hair fell in messy, frizzy coils over her face. I'd never seen her like that. For once, she seemed almost human. She swallowed, about to cry, which scared me more than anything else.

"I never said they died," Mr Grandace said, quietly. "We're the only ones who survived unscathed."

Toby caught my eye. He shook his head, his jaw clenched tightly. *Unscathed.* That was a fancy way of skirting around the obvious damage that had been caused to the others. Why couldn't he tell us the truth? What could be so bad that he had to dance around it like this?

"One of our circle died," Miss Trager said, almost as if she were reminding him. "The rest were... lost to the magic."

Elijah scoffed. "So that's why your crazy brother and sister are running around trying to kill us?"

Asher looked up, finally drawing his gaze away from Julianna. Zo shifted and murmured something under her breath.

Of course – the others didn't know about the photos Elijah and I had found.

"They're not crazy," Miss Trager said quietly.

I could almost have felt sorry for her. But she was still lying to me. They were both still lying.

"By one of your circle, you mean my mother." The words tasted like chalk in my mouth.

Mr Grandace's eyes flicked up to meet mine, and Miss Trager took in a sharp breath. I stared back at them, willing them to try and lie again.

"Your mother…" Zo trailed off, and the rest of my classmates shifted, their eyes locked on me.

Toby's hand slipped into mine. I squeezed it tight. Questions circled me, filtering through Toby's thoughts. I ignored them, focusing only on my former teachers.

Mr Grandace cleared his throat. "There's a lot you don't understand, Callie." His voice was low… haunted. He looked to Miss Trager, and she shook her head.

"She was a part of our circle," she said. "She was my friend." Her voice cracked on that final word.

I swallowed. Elijah's question from earlier burned in my throat – was he my father? Was she my aunt? The words stuck in my chest, refusing to come out. I couldn't hold Mr Grandace's eye any longer.

"Samantha – your mother – was important to us, Calliope. She was our friend, and her magic was incredibly powerful. We didn't even know *how* powerful at the time." Mr Grandace hesitated again. He moved forward, his steps jerky and unnatural. "She… she wrote the prophecy."

I reeled back. Toby's grip tightened on my hand, the only thing anchoring me.

"Callie's mother wrote…" Zo trailed off. The others were all talking at once, and the noise seemed to slam against me.

My mother wrote the prophecy. She was the reason Mr Grandace brought me to the school, and the reason Miss Trager had tried to kill Toby.

Suddenly, one more thing became clear. My mother had died because of this – because of the magic. Quite possibly, one of the other people in her circle had killed her. And if we weren't careful, the same thing would happen to us.

Chapter Ten

The others asked questions, but it was too much – too many aspects that needed to be explained. Mr Grandace's jaw clenched, and he kept shaking his head before answering. I wanted to know about my mother, of course I did. But a much more pressing question circled in my mind.

"What is it you want us to do?"

Somehow, my voice broke through the noise. The others fell quiet and Mr Grandace's face relaxed, almost but not quite smiling. I met Toby's eye. The idea of running consumed his thoughts again. I drew my gaze away, not letting myself consider it.

"I want to link the two circles together," Mr Grandace said.

The feeling of the strands of magic wrapping around me engulfed me. My connection with Toby pulled tight, and the frayed ends of my broken tie to Elijah tingled as if they would regrow.

"No way." Toby's voice was firm, cold almost. He slipped his arm around my waist, but it did nothing to ease the tension on the threads of magic.

"But we're already linked," Zo said. I could almost see her connections to Toby and Julianna lighting up.

Mr Grandace nodded. "I know, but the prophecy suggests—"

"The prophecy suggested killing Toby." Asher pulled Julianna closer, wrapping his arm around her. We were all moving in again, closing ranks against our former headmaster. "It's clearly all bull."

My mother wrote the prophecy... It wasn't possible.

"The prophecy never told me to kill Toby." Miss Trager didn't look up. "I was trying to stop what she'd predicted from happening."

Suddenly, she seemed so small, no different to the teenager in the photo. She'd always been so imposing, terrifying even. Now she just seemed afraid.

"The magic is unbalanced," Mr Grandace continued. "Both circles are missing links – between you and Elijah," he gestured to me, "and where your mother would have been in our circle. The prophecy talks about intersecting circles – *none will be complete until all interlink.*"

He said that last part as if quoting. I looked to Elijah, but he didn't return my gaze. He stared at Mr Grandace.

"If we'd known to link ourselves back then," Mr Grandace said, "maybe we could have controlled the magic better, but..."

But my mother's prophecy hadn't told them to. Or maybe it had, and they hadn't listened.

"If we join both circles together, we think it will stabilise all of us. But we need you to be in agreement. The others in our circle..." Mr Grandace hesitated, and Miss Trager grimaced. "The power has corrupted them. They won't be willing to give it up easily," he said finally.

If tonight was anything to go by, that was an understatement. They were clearly willing to fight or even kill us to keep the status quo.

They killed my mother...

How had it happened? Was it an accident or had they meant to hurt her? I thought of the photo of the six of them, all so young and fragile. One day, would I look back at a photo of the six of us and think the same? Would I even get the chance?

"I know you all have so many questions," Mr Grandace said as if he had heard my thoughts. "I promise you, I will answer all that I can, but joining the circles is urgent. Ursula and I can't keep the others contained for much longer."

The wave of vines flashed through my head again, and the face of the man swallowed by them. By keeping them contained, he didn't just mean locking them up. The magic was overwhelming them, and they were all drowning in it.

Mr Grandace cleared his throat. "We'll leave you alone to decide." His eyes were on me, but I didn't look up.

He put his arm around Miss Trager, guiding her out of the room. She leaned on him heavily, limping. So much for my belief that she was unharmed, though the biggest damage was to our view of her. All I could see now was that tiny teenage girl from the photo.

Toby stood as soon as they were gone. "There's no way we're doing this."

"Why not?" Elijah's voice was level but filled with a bitterness. "At least we're getting a choice this time."

I blinked at Elijah's words. I hadn't expected him to be on the teachers' side. But perhaps he wasn't on *their* side, just against Toby's.

Toby shook his head. "I had to link us; you know that. We all would have died if I hadn't."

"So you say." Elijah's gaze fixed on Toby, but I felt him pull at the frayed edges of our severed connection, almost as if he were trying to speak to me through it. Funny how I could still feel it, even after it broke. Would the connection between us regrow, or would I be joined to Mr Grandace or one of the others? Nausea flooded me at the thought.

"I think I want to do it." Julianna raised her head, too weak to sit up properly. It was the first time she'd spoken, and we all turned to stare at her. "I want this to be over."

Zo and Asher didn't say anything, but it was like I could see the connections light up again. They both loved Julianna enough to follow her, no matter what they actually wanted to do.

"We can't trust them!" Toby's voice strained. His eyes flicked to mine, pleading. "He said we have to all be in agreement."

Zo scoffed. "Like that's ever going to happen."

"Well, it's going to have to." Asher's raised voice silenced everyone.

"What do you want to do, Cal?" Elijah's voice was steady, none of his usual snark. All eyes turned to me, both Elijah and Toby expecting me to side with them. Whichever way I went, Toby would follow me, same as Asher and Zo followed Julianna. I could turn this into a consensus, or I could hold out and maybe save us.

I swayed on the spot, exhaustion catching up with me. Toby stepped towards me, but I held out my hand, stopping him. "I want to read the prophecy."

* * * *

I HEADED DOWN THE corridor to the bathroom while Toby went to find Miss Trager. I didn't really need to go; it was an excuse to take a breath. Everything Mr Grandace had told us was just... it was a lot of information to get in a short space of time.

The picture of my mother with Miss Trager and Mr Grandace haunted me. They had been friends. I'd had no idea my mother had magic, though that wasn't surprising. I'd had no idea *I* had magic before a few months ago.

I needed time, but I wasn't going to get it. What if I made the wrong choice? I felt like I'd been spinning for so long making wrong decision after wrong decision. Toby binding us together had made things better – it had saved us at the school, but it hadn't been the right thing for us since then. I didn't know if binding us to more people would be either.

I splashed some water on my face and stared at myself in the mirror. Julianna was right. This needed to be over.

I opened the door to the corridor. Miss Trager stood right outside, and I stumbled back a pace. She'd tidied herself up a bit, smoothing back the frizzy hair at least, but the paleness of her skin betrayed how worn out she was.

"Toby said you wanted to see the prophecy," she said.

I nodded. Toby hovered further down the corridor, Elijah behind him. Toby would see the pages in my mind, and he could pass them on to the others, but they were giving me the space to do this on my own. I wasn't sure what I was looking for, but somehow, I felt it would help if I could see it in her words.

Miss Trager gave a mouth shrug, then put her hand on my shoulder, gently guiding me back towards the room where we'd found the photos. I'd never seen her as anything remotely maternal, but knowing she knew my mother – that she could be my aunt – the touch felt more affectionate. I shrugged away, not willing to feel that from her.

I hovered in the doorway while she sat down on the bed, opening a drawer in the base of it. She ruffled through the contents, pulling out an old makeup palette and a couple of grubby soft toys. She placed them gently on the bed beside her, as if they still meant something to her.

I looked away, picking up the photo of the six of them again and studying my mother's face. This was Miss Trager's room – her childhood room, which meant she lived here even before it became a school. There was something so strange about seeing evidence of her being human, especially seeing them all together in the picture. I glanced over at her. She'd shrunk before my eyes. I couldn't see her as an adult anymore – just a fragile teenage girl, as helpless as me.

She pulled out a stack of battered exercise books and flicked through them. "Here." She selected one of the books from the pile, but she didn't hand it to me, clutching it in both her hands on her lap instead.

I hesitated, then walked over, sitting down on the bed beside her.

She took a heavy breath, trying not to cry. "You're so like her, Callie. I..."

She didn't finish that, but I was sure she'd been going to say she missed her. I didn't know what to say in response. I couldn't tell her that I understood. I'd never known my mum. I missed the *idea* of her, but that was all I had.

"I'm not trying to keep things from you, but you may not be able to read it."

"Why not?"

Miss Trager's fingers tightened on the edges of the book, biting into them. "The way your mother wrote... she said you could only read her words when you needed them the most."

That sounded like some new-age hippie bunk. Was that what my mother was like? Swanning around writing enigmatic prophecies no one could read?

Miss Trager placed the book on my lap. "Here," she said again. "I don't know if you'll find what you're looking for, but there it is."

She stood quickly and moved out of the room, her hands flying to her face as if she was ashamed to let her tears fall.

Doodles and scribbled words crisscrossed the cover of the book. I made out the names of her classmates, and that strange "S" everyone draws. But mostly she'd drawn circles. Layers and layers of them, overlapping. Apart from that, it looked like a normal exercise book, like one of mine from my old school. So strange that a prophecy that had nearly gotten us killed would be written in something so ordinary.

I flipped the book open, trying to read a page at random. The writing scrawled over the page in a stream-of-consciousness rant. Again, this wasn't what I'd expected. Strings of letters dripped and weaved over the lines, some of them barely legible. Certain words and phrases had been underlined, and notes made in the margins.

I understood what Miss Trager meant about not being able to read it. Though I could see it was written in English, the words seemed to move, impossible to focus on. A few lines jumped out at me.

Siren plant...

...all six survive or none of them do...

...catastrophic power...

I ran my hand over the page. There was something so perverse about this. Our whole lives had been upended because of this – the handwritten ramblings of a girl not much older than me.

The girl will know only that her mother died, and her grandmother raised her.

The next line blurred, disappearing just as I tried to read it.

She will live sixteen summers, and on her seventeenth birthday, the sky will burst into fire, and it will begin.

Why was the book only showing me things that had already happened? They weren't exactly prophecies anymore.

Perhaps it would have been nice to know I was going to set Zo's ceiling on fire before things got out of control, though I'm not sure I could have stopped it.

...only the sacrifice can save them...

...She will be tuned to the family, and she will choose them...

The family? She was my only family, and she was gone. I flicked through the pages, but nothing else became clear, the words remaining disjointed scrawls. I couldn't find the bit about circles Mr Grandace had quoted, though I kept scanning the pages for it.

Maybe this was a lost cause. I'm not sure seeing it would make the words more meaningful anyway. I had to make this decision for myself – I wasn't going to get any guidance from these pages, and definitely not from my long-dead mother.

My eye fell on the annotations in the margins. They'd been written by someone else in a different colour pen. It wasn't the words themselves that caught my attention; it was the hand-writing. The same handwriting from the birthday cards I'd gotten every year from my father.

"What do you mean, you let her look at it?"

I looked up at the sound of Mr Grandace's voice in the corridor. Miss Trager said something in response, but I couldn't hear it over the thumping of my own pulse. Or maybe that was his footsteps, pounding down the corridor towards me.

I stood, clutching the book to my chest.

I thought of trying to run again, but I couldn't do that to Toby or to Zo, or to any of them. Even Elijah had grown on me and become part of the weird family we'd created.

I forced my feet into steps. Mr Grandace appeared in the doorway, meeting me halfway.

"Calliope." He strode towards me, his arms reaching out as if to pull me into a hug, or maybe to rip the book from my hands.

"She wanted to see for herself." Miss Trager stopped outside the room. She looked from Mr Grandace to me. Shivers worked their way up my body, and I clung tighter to the book – to my mother.

"I'm sorry. She shouldn't have let you try and read that. It's too much." He placed a hand on my arm, his touch gentle, like Miss Trager's had been. It made me shiver more.

I stared at him, trying to find something familiar in his face. "Are you...?" I couldn't get the words out.

His eyes dropped to the notebook. He reached for it, but I held it back.

"The cards," I said. "Are you...?" But I still couldn't say it.

He reached for the prophecy again, but I didn't let him touch me. I could feel the fizzing of energy coming from his skin. It may have been meant to be soothing, to manipulate me into being calm, like the clouds of coloured energy Toby said he used to send out at the school. All it did was make me angry.

"My father sent me birthday cards," I forced out. "The handwriting..."

Understanding finally dawned on his face. Miss Trager made a noise in her throat. She came closer and I let her. I wasn't sure when she had become the more trustworthy of the two, but I found myself moving towards her, wanting the comfort of someone who had loved my mother.

"I'm not your father, Calliope," he said.

I wasn't sure whether to believe him. He and Miss Trager had lied and omitted and stretched the truth so many times. He reached for the notebook again, and this time I let him take it, along with the photo.

His expression fell, and he ran his thumb over the faces of the six of them. He opened the book, tracing the lines of writing as if he understood far more of it than I ever could.

He looked up at me. "But I did write those cards. I'm sorry."

I shook my head. "Why?"

Miss Trager cleared her throat. She moved closer to me again, and I let her. She pointed to the third boy in the photo. "Joseph... he's your father. He was a part of the original circle. He and your mother came to the school together."

Not Miss Trager's brother, but the man with the dog. The one who had been watching me and started those sunflowers growing, triggering all of this. The one who had nearly drowned us both in the wave of vines.

"He's one of the bad ones," I said. The words choked me.

"No... no." Mr Grandace took hold of my shoulders. "Your father is not a bad person," he said firmly. "None of them are. The magic, it..."

It had taken him over, just as it would take all of us over if we let it. I thought of the way he'd reached for me – saying my name as if asking for help. Maybe he had been asking for help all along.

"Ursula and I, we promised your mother we would look after you. She loved you very much."

Miss Trager nodded, her eyes filling with tears, and I found I believed them.

"Your father... he knew the magic was going to take him over. He wanted us to make sure you knew he was alive – that he still loved you. We didn't know how else..." Mr Grandace's voice petered out, perhaps realising it was a pathetic explanation. "We couldn't do much else. We didn't want him to find you."

I heard the unspoken end of that. My father had loved me and wanted me to know that once upon a time, but now the magic had taken him over he was just a danger to me. The one good memory I had of him was those birthday cards, and he hadn't even written them.

"This is why we need to link the two circles," Miss Trager

said. "We can bring them back to us – my brother and sister, and your father. We can fix what the magic broke, like Samantha wanted."

Mr Grandace raised the notebook in his hand, as if to invoke her. He made it sound so simple, but was it? Did he really believe he could bring my father back after all these years?

Toby appeared in the doorway. He looked between me and the teachers. *Are you okay?* he asked me inside his head.

I didn't answer, because honestly, I didn't know. "Can I talk to him?" I asked.

Miss Trager winced. She opened her mouth to answer, but Mr Grandace spoke over her. "It's not a good idea. You saw what happened last time."

Toby's memory of finding me covered in vines flashed through his head. I understood why he was afraid, but surely there were ways we could make it safe? If Zo hadn't opened that door, we wouldn't have been overwhelmed.

I wondered if she had forgiven me, now Julianna was healed. Somehow, I didn't think it was really about that. I'd been beginning to think of her as family, but she'd kept her feelings for Julianna a secret from me, and then practically cast me out when Julianna got hurt. Perhaps we had never been that close after all.

"He's asleep right now. We used a spell on all of them," Miss Trager added. She stared at me, and I got the feeling there was something else she wanted to say. Would she have answered differently, had Mr Grandace given her the chance?

"It's time," Mr Grandace told me. "We need to link the two circles."

He didn't ask if I'd made my decision – didn't ask if any of us had. Somehow, he seemed to know it had all come down to me, and he was sure he had me onside.

Chapter Eleven

My classmates made slow, limping progress down the corridor. Julianna could barely stand. Dried blood coated her clothes in blotches, like a brown floral pattern, and flecks of red speckled her face. She clung to Asher and Zo, and they bore her weight on each step.

The glass from where Zo had broken the door had scattered across the floor, her perfect circle destroyed by running feet. Toby and I swept it into a pile in the corner, then stood in front of it, like we were protecting a glittering hoard. In reality, we just hoped to save our classmates' bare feet from being shredded.

Downstairs, my father was a prisoner, just like I had been at the school. Magic had been forced on me. Was I really about to do the same to him? I didn't know if this was the right thing. Would he be free once we joined the circles? How could he be after he and Miss Trager's siblings had been responsible for my mother's death?

Mr Grandace and Miss Trager crouched on the floor of the corridor below, laying rune lines. Supposedly they would keep us safe as we bound the circles. The teachers had asked us to give them twenty minutes to lay the magic, and then to follow them down there. It had taken nearly that long to get Julianna this far.

She reached the broken door and let out a little high-pitched groan at the sight of the stairs. Her legs gave way, and she slumped against Asher.

"Jules!" Zo dived forward to grab her, but Asher scooped Julianna up, pushing Zo away as he did.

"I've got her."

Julianna made another noise, as if in pain, but her head fell against Asher's shoulder, relieved at not having to walk any further.

"It's okay," Asher told her. "This will be over soon." He glanced at me and Toby, and the look in his eyes was a challenge.

He carried Julianna down the stairs, disappearing into darkness at the bottom.

Zo hesitated. Her arms dangled at her sides, as if she wasn't sure what to do with them, now she wasn't supporting Julianna.

"Zo, I–"

She half turned towards me then cut the movement short. Her head froze at an odd angle, as if she was trying to pretend she hadn't heard me. She kept it there as she drifted down the stairs, more willing to risk tripping than accidentally making eye contact with me.

Toby squeezed my arm. "She'll be okay. She just needs time."

He was wrong. Zo was cutting me out, the same way so many families had done before. Even if he had been right, time wasn't something I could give when we were all linked to each other. In a few minutes, we would be linked to even more people – to my father. Would I feel more of a familial connection to him once the magic joined us? The idea of being able to read his thoughts terrified me.

Toby pulled me into a hug. I leaned into him, resting my head on his chest. In all honesty, I was scared of losing this. Even though it was hard sometimes, being linked just to Toby felt special. I had lost so much already. Would we still have this closeness if I was attached to someone else on the other side?

He pulled back to look at me. *You could never lose me, Reactive Girl.* He brushed the hair back from my face, his touch gentle.

I kissed him. I felt his surprise, then he was kissing me back. The feel of his lips mixed with the sensation of mine meeting his, each of us experiencing it from both sides. I pulled him closer, until I couldn't separate where my skin ended and his began.

The sound of a throat clearing startled me. I sprung back, spinning around. Elijah stared at us from the stairs, an expression I couldn't read crossing his face.

"If you're quite done, they're almost ready," he said.

I nodded, my face flushing. Neither Toby nor I made any move to go downstairs, though.

Elijah hesitated. His gaze flicked between me and Toby, finally landing on me. Heat rose in my cheeks, and I found I couldn't hold his eye. The severed end of the thread between us tingled, as if trying to regrow. Toby's arm slid around my waist, the pressure of his touch comforting.

Elijah cleared his throat again. "We need to do this, Cal. It's the only way."

I hadn't realised my hesitation was so obvious. Elijah turned, making his way back down the stairs.

Toby turned to me, stepping in close again. I rested my forehead against his. *Are you sure?* he said in his mind.

I shook my head. *No, but what other choice do we have?*

Since when did I trust Elijah over Toby? My gut told me we shouldn't be doing this, but my father... this might be my only chance to bring him back.

Toby dropped his gaze. He didn't try to hide his reservations, and I read it all in his thoughts. Finally, he looked up at me. "I trust you."

I could tell it was true. He didn't want to do this – didn't believe for a second that our former teachers had our best interests at heart – but he trusted me enough to follow me. He pressed his lips lightly against mine again. *You jump, I jump, right?*

I found his hand, and we walked down the stairs together.

* * * *

MISS TRAGER CROUCHED in front of the door where my father was being held, adjusting the chalk rune lines. Identical lines ran in front of the doors on either side, presumably trapping her siblings inside.

She stood as we came downstairs, giving me a half-smile. "Good timing."

I nodded. My voice didn't seem to be working.

"Here." Mr Grandace took Julianna's arm and helped her to lean against the wall, opposite the door. He arranged the others on either side of her into a semi-circle. He gestured for me and Toby to take our places. Zo, Julianna, and Asher linked up, holding hands following the lines of magic.

I looked over at Elijah. He stood between Asher and Miss Trager with both hands in his pockets. I met his eye, and he nodded once. He took hold of Miss Trager and Asher's hands, completing his arc of the circle.

I turned to Toby. "It'll be okay. We'll be okay." My voice

was not convincing, a tremor running through it.

His shoulders slumped, deflating, but he linked up with Zo anyway. I'd known he would follow me, whichever way I chose. It didn't make me feel any better about it, though.

"Thank you, all of you," Mr Grandace said.

I thought I sensed a little of that calming magic Toby had talked about floating out from him. "We're not doing it for you." I held out my hand, but he didn't take it.

"You won't be linked to me," he said. "You'll be linked to your father."

My stomach lurched. I thought of his hand, pulling me into the wave of vines, and I could almost feel them regrowing, slithering over my body.

"We're going to have to wake them," Miss Trager said. "So once we start, do not let go under any circumstances. We'll need to work the magic as quickly as possible."

A flash of fear passed around the room. Mr Grandace and Miss Trager looked at each other. Years of stress, tiredness, and connection seemed to pass through their eyes. Then there was a click as the spell dropped away.

Even though I wasn't connected to him yet, I felt my father wake. I could hear all three of them moving around on the other side of those doors. I gripped Toby's hand so tightly, it hurt us both, but I didn't want him to let go. He squeezed back just as intensely. Fear rolled inside him, anxious thoughts bouncing through all of us.

Mr Grandace's magic sent out a call. Julianna and Zo's magic resisted at first, then it intertwined with his. He moved on to Asher and Toby. Elijah and I would be next. I took a breath, trying to let my mind relax, to let my magic flow ready to answer Mr Grandace's call.

It wasn't the same as when Toby had done it. Then, it had almost been automatic, the reactive magic taking over. This felt forced, unnatural. But Elijah was right – what other choice did we have? We couldn't spend our lives running from Miss Trager's siblings and my father, nor could we leave their magic to continue destroying them and anyone else they came into contact with.

Perhaps this would be good. Perhaps the two of us would finally feel connected, instead of the horrible push we always had against each other. I tried to imagine how it would be. Each of us balanced, no longer being dragged towards Toby and repelled away from Elijah.

I squeezed Toby's hand, and he opened his eyes, meeting mine. Mr Grandace's magic reached out for me, and Toby gave me a nod. This would be okay. It had to be.

Something invisible slammed into me. I opened my mouth to scream, but nothing came out, my body winded by the force. A second slam threw me backwards, and my hand ripped out of Toby's. Elijah flew backwards too, the magical force repelling him as well.

Static shrieked around me. I clutched my ears, trying to block it out.

Toby ran towards me. "Callie!" his lips said, but there was no sound.

I reached for him, and he was flung backwards, hit by the wall of magic. I felt the wave of it slamming into me again.

Toby! I screamed.

Calliope, I heard in amongst the noise, but it wasn't Toby.

I tried to scramble up, but the static exploded in my head, even louder than before, bringing me to my knees. I reached for the thread tying me to Toby. It flung me back again. I stared at the others; all of them sprawled on the floor, their faces peering at me in identical shock.

For once, I could see all of the magic around us. Tattered strings of it hung in the air. New threads reached out. They wrapped around me, drawing me in. I felt a familiar pull, but it wasn't bringing me closer to Toby.

Come here, Calliope, fuzzy words formed in the static, voices becoming clearer, like a radio tuning in on a station. I felt my magic responding to it. I tried to fight, but I couldn't move. My magic reached out, independent of me. The threads bound me, wrapping tighter and tighter until I couldn't move or speak.

And then, suddenly, the static was gone.

Hello, my daughter. The voice was clear. I felt myself turning, my head moving without my permission.

"The circle is complete," Elijah said, but it didn't sound like his voice. He turned, walking to the locked door and opening it. His movements were jerky, robotic. He unlocked the next door, then the third.

No one else moved. Everything seemed to be in slow motion, all of us suspended in a strange, liminal space. Miss Trager's sister walked out of one of the rooms. She stared at me, with the smug, self-satisfied grin I'd seen in the photo of her.

And then my father appeared. I found myself standing, greeting him with a hug. I fought against it, but I wasn't in control of my own limbs.

"Callie!" Toby stared up at me, from where he'd fallen.

No resonance filled his words, the sound dull and hollow. A sickening realisation grew inside me. I heard only his external voice. I couldn't hear his thoughts anymore. I tried to reach for him, but I couldn't move.

Heaviness filled my mind. Toby's image blurred in front of me. Some part of my brain told me I should be worried about him, that I was still tied to him and wanted to be near him, but more than that I wanted to be near these people – near my father. Their magic wrapped around me like a hug.

"I have to go," I heard myself saying.

Elijah took one of my hands, and my father took the other.

"Callie!"

I heard Toby's voice, but there was no Callie now. We walked away, leaving the old circle behind us.

VOLATILE

REACTIVE MAGIC BOOK 3

Helen Vivienne Fletcher

Chapter One

Ursula Trager - Age 14

The beating of hammers sent rumbles through the floor beneath my feet. Thumps vibrated in my chest, a rhythmic beat that shook me. It made it hard to think, unsettling me as energy tingled in little pulses.

I stood at the window, watching. The students wouldn't arrive for another few hours, but anticipation charged the air, mingling with the sounds of the building work below me. If I were more comfortable wielding magic, I would be able to use this, to turn it into something spectacular. I closed my eyes, imagining that the vibrations came from the earth itself. I inhaled, pretending I could feel the movement of the very planet.

"Grow," I whispered.

Immediately, dread built in my stomach. I opened my eyes a crack, terrified I would see darkness – vines covering the windows, or trees having sprouted up to block out the light. Instead, I was greeted with the exact same view I had seen all my life.

Soon, I told myself. Soon, things would change.

The thumping from downstairs had increased as my parents sought to get the school finished before the students got here. The chances of that happening were low, given they were arriving today, but still my parents persisted.

Footsteps clattered on the stairs down the corridor, and a moment later Chloe burst into my room, blonde braid carving an arc in the air around her shoulders like a weapon. "What are you doing?" she asked. She moved to stand beside me, her gaze flicking to the window.

I stepped back from it. "Nothing," I said, not willing to admit I had spent the whole morning staring out. A slow, sly smile spread across her face.

"They're not coming here for *you*," she said.

I felt my cheeks flush. "I know that." I did know that, but it didn't stop me hoping.

Chloe let out a little giggle. "Whatever you say." She turned, flouncing towards the door. "Mum and Dad want to see us downstairs. But do something with your hair first, you look a mess." She didn't wait for me, her feet clattering down the next set of stairs before I'd even crossed the room.

My fair hair was a mirror image of Chloe's, though somehow it never looked as nice, hanging limply around my shoulders. I pulled it into a ponytail – practical and less deadly than Chloe's braid – and smoothed out my crumpled T-shirt. Chloe didn't seem to care whether or not I followed, but I trailed after her anyway. The heat in my cheeks didn't cool as I circled down the flights of stairs. I hated that she was right. I *was* hoping that the students arriving would be at least a tiny bit interested in me. But they wouldn't be. No one ever was.

I came out into the entryway of our house. That still looked the same at least – high ceilings and skylights looking down over Mum's ever-increasing collection of houseplants. If she kept this up, soon it would be more greenhouse than foyer.

Muddy footprints crossed the black and white tiles, one of the builders leaving their mark. All around us, workers were transforming home into school. They might as well have been carving off pieces of my flesh. I dreaded seeing the cosy spaces of my childhood turned into sterile classrooms. At least our bedrooms were staying the same. Our floor would be left untouched, a safe place in all this chaos.

Dad stood in the middle of the foyer, Chloe and Ben facing each other in front of him. My stomach gave a flip, and I contemplated turning tail and running back up to my room.

"Ursula, get down here," Dad's voice rang out before I could. "Your sister might be about to beat Ben for once."

Chloe grimaced, and I reluctantly made my way down the last few steps. Ben gave me a wink, which was more than Chloe would ever do, but it was brief, his focus turning away almost immediately. My brother and sister both raised their palms, a glow forming between them.

"Over here, love." Mum reached out, drawing me to the side. I took her hand, gratefully. Magic crackled in the room, not helped by the continued pulsing of hammers.

"Unless you want to help Chloe?" Dad asked. "Perhaps the two of you would be a match for your brother."

I shrank behind Mum, and I felt her stiffen. Dad's voice held a laugh, but I didn't trust him not to actually force me into it. I hated when he made them fight, and my mother's cries of "Ursula's too young for this" wouldn't protect me for much longer.

Chloe's hands trembled, the colour emanating from them shuddering. She kept up a good fight, but she wouldn't beat him. She was too focused on trying to use force. My brother just made himself immovable, drawing magic from everything around him until Chloe tired herself out.

My father made a noise in his throat. "Come on, Chloe!

Don't be so weak."

Sweat beaded on her forehead, and Dad's lip quirked, delighting in Ben's victory already. Mum's hand tightened on mine, but she didn't say anything. *She's not weak,* I wanted to yell. *Ben's just stronger.* But Chloe wouldn't appreciate me speaking up any more than Dad would.

"Steel yourself!" Dad yelled. "Don't let him force you back."

Chloe's legs shook, her physical strength waning along with her magic. Mum's plants drooped as Ben pulled energy from them, and Chloe stumbled backwards, her magical glow disappearing.

"Yes!" Dad's arms flew into the air. "Unbeaten!"

None of that delight lit Ben's face. He watched Chloe, concern creasing his forehead. "You okay, kiddo?"

"Shut up!" Chloe shoved him, no magic, just fury in her hands this time. "I'm not a kid."

Ben dodged backwards out of her way, a half laugh escaping him. "Okay, okay! Clearly, you're a mature adult."

"Don't be a sore loser, Chloe. You just have to accept your brother is better than you." Dad patted Ben on the back, congratulating him, and Ben's jaw tightened in response. I could see in Dad's eyes that he wanted to make them try again, despite the fact that Chloe was still shaking. For once, I was glad to be almost invisible. I couldn't do that a single time, let alone as often as my father wanted.

"We had some things to discuss," Mum said quietly. She picked up one of her plants, grimacing as she inspected its withered state.

"Hm? Oh yes, come, come." Dad moved to stand next to Mum, drawing us to him. I had an urge to line up next to my brother and sister in height order, like we were the von Trapp children. I couldn't see Chloe ever singing songs on the mountain though, and she definitely wouldn't wear dresses made from curtains.

"The new students will be arriving here this afternoon," Dad announced. He said that like we were students ourselves. We were his children, but perhaps he'd forgotten that in his excitement over the strength of Ben and Chloe's powers. "This will be a new era in our family's magic, and I want you all to make the most of it."

Chloe rolled her eyes and gave a snort. It annoyed me that she was acting like she was above all this. She was half the reason our parents had decided we needed magic training in the first place. If she and Ben had just kept things simple, Mum and Dad might not have made such a big deal out of everything.

Dad gave Chloe a hard look. "I'm expecting you to welcome the new students. You need to learn from them – become as strong as you can be."

"They've had just as hard a time of it as you have with developing powers," Mum added quietly. "Harder maybe, since they didn't have the benefit of parents who know about magic."

Ben made a noise in his throat which could have been agreement or irritation. "We'll do everything we can to make them feel comfortable."

Mum smiled at him, ignoring the hint of sarcasm in his voice. "I know you will, darling." She gave me a warm smile too and squeezed my shoulder. I relaxed a little at her touch. We were still a family. Becoming a school didn't have to change that.

"Excellent." Dad clapped his hands together as if dismissing us. He started to walk away, heading off to yell at some of the workers no doubt, but then called back over his shoulder. "You should be excited about the lessons, Chloe. You might actually learn to beat your brother."

Chloe scowled, and I felt my face form a similar expression. I hated the way he goaded her. Chloe turned to Mum as soon as he was gone. "Why couldn't you just get us private lessons?" she whined. "Why did you have to build a whole school?"

"It's not just about the three of you, love." Weariness filled Mum's voice. This wasn't the first time she'd had this argument with my sister. "Your magic is twinned with theirs; geminus magic has the potential to be very dangerous if not handled correctly."

Chloe rolled her eyes. "I just don't get why it's our responsibility."

Literally for the reason Mum just said, I thought, but I kept my mouth firmly shut.

"Of course you don't." My brother took up the eye rolling. "You don't think anything is your responsibility."

Chloe flushed a little, but she held Ben's gaze, refusing to back down. He didn't take the bait, turning to Mum. "Was that all you dragged us down here for?"

Mum blinked, perhaps deciding whether or not to chide Ben. He'd grown taller than her, surpassing Dad too, and he seemed to be forgetting all of us as he reached heights we couldn't.

"We thought you'd like to see the new classrooms," Mum said finally.

Chloe let out a long breath. "We're going to be stuck in them all week, aren't we? We don't need to start early."

Ben clearly agreed with the sentiment, but he and Mum stared at each other, a silent conversation passing between them. Then he looked at me, his face softening. "Do you want to see them, Ursula?"

I hesitated. Choosing to go with Ben would piss Chloe off,

but honestly, everything I did pissed her off. I looked to Mum instead. She gave a little smile. "It might make you feel better to see the changes now, love."

Ben squeezed my shoulder. "Come on, I'll race you." He bolted up the stairs, giving himself a head start, not that he needed it. I chased after him, Mum's laughter and Chloe's snort of derision following after us.

*   *   *   *

THE NEW ROOMS WERE not that interesting. My parents had turned the floor below ours into a dormitory of sorts, where the new students would sleep, then the bottom two floors were now a series of classrooms. The house had always been far too big for us, and the changes made it feel not only vast but sterile.

We didn't stay long in the classrooms. The huge shelves of textbooks and rows of desks made me feel odd. There were only three students coming, but so many desks – a visible sign of my parents' unspoken plans.

"Make sure you stay out of Dad's way this week," Ben said, as we passed a couple of builders in the corridor.

"I *always* try to stay out of Dad's way," I told him.

Ben frowned. He opened his mouth, but then closed it again without speaking. "Good idea," he said finally. "Keep doing that."

I followed him upstairs into the dormitory. "If we're supposed to stay close to the new students to help their magic, why are they sleeping on a different floor?"

Ben snorted. "Can you imagine asking Chloe to share a room?"

I laughed at the thought. "She doesn't even like sharing a wall with me."

Ben grinned. "Eh, you're not so bad. Just like having a little mouse live next door." He reached out, ruffling my hair.

I squirmed away. My gaze fell on the door at the end of the hallway. Jagged black marks spread out across the walls around it, and streaks of ash surrounded the doorhandle. "What happened to the library?"

Ben didn't look up. "Don't worry about it. Mum and Dad moved the important books downstairs."

"But the door..." I took a few steps forward. I couldn't explain it, but there was something wrong with the air at the end of the corridor. I couldn't see anything exactly, but it *felt* different. There was a dull sort of... *nothing* to it, as if it wasn't real. It seemed to suck inwards, like a black hole or a vacuum. I took another step towards it.

"Don't!" Ben's hand slammed down on my shoulder.

I gasped, cringing away from him. His face fell, and he crouched down, pulling me into a hug. "I'm sorry, Urse. I didn't mean to scare you."

"Why...?" The question died on my lips.

Ben sighed. He shifted so he could look me in the eye. "You heard about the fire?"

I nodded. My siblings' experiments with magic had gone very wrong. I hadn't been there when it happened, but as far as I could gather, they'd tried to create indoor fireworks and nearly burnt the place to the ground. Not that their outdoor fireworks had been much better.

Ben nodded towards the library. "There was a lot of damage. Chloe and I fixed some of it with magic. That's probably what you can feel."

"Why can't I go down there if you fixed it?"

Ben gave a short laugh. "I said we fixed *some* of it. Neither of us are that good yet."

If the dull sucking feeling was anything to go by, they'd

had no idea what they were doing. It didn't feel like they'd fixed anything, only charged it with a strange energy. I supposed Mum and Dad would be able to reverse it, and the builders could repair the physical damage once they were done with all the other work. "You didn't burn any of the books, did you?'

Ben grinned. "Only the evil ones." He gave my hair another ruffle and then sighed. "Do you want to see the rest of the dormitories?"

I could tell he had no interest in seeing them, and suddenly neither did I. "No. It feels weird to go into someone else's bedroom."

"True." Ben glanced at his watch. "Hey, I've got some stuff to finish before they arrive. Shall we head back up to our floor now?"

I nodded and followed Ben to the stairs. I paused in the doorway, looking back towards the library. That dull, empty feeling followed me down the corridor. I didn't like the idea of the new students sleeping with that right beside them. Then again, our magic was supposed to get stronger once we met our geminus pair – the person our magic was twinned to. Perhaps together, we'd be able to fix what Ben and Chloe had broken.

My stomach tensed. I'd been waiting days for my geminus pair to arrive, but what if they didn't like me? What if they were just like Chloe?

Ben glanced back at me. He followed my gaze down the hallway, and his face tightened. "Come on, little mouse," he said, forcing a smile. "Ready for another race? See if you can beat me this time." He took off, leaving me to chase after him. I pounded up the stairs, watching him get further and further away from me, with about a mouse's chance of catching up.

Chapter Two

Mum called us downstairs again that afternoon. My stomach flipped, knowing that this time it would be because the students were here. I trailed down the steps, passing workers carrying a large whiteboard up to the second-floor classrooms.

"Hi... yes, thanks," I said, as they stood back to let me pass.

Silence greeted my words, and I scurried past, getting out of their way. Their eyes all held a vague, glazed look, and they moved with a heavy lethargy as if the boredom of the work drained them of energy with every passing minute.

I made my way down the rest of the stairs and found Mum in the foyer. She ushered me out to join my siblings on the doorstep.

"Where's Dad?" I asked.

"He's talking to the builders. Don't worry about him." Her face switched back and forth between over-excited beam and nervous lip chewing.

Chloe rolled her eyes when she saw me. "You still look a mess, squirt."

I blushed, trying once again to smooth my clothes. Ben clucked his tongue. "Leave her alone, Chloe."

She made a face at him, then her expression returned to a practised, disinterested glare. Ben popped his lips, boredom etched across his whole body. They still both snuck eager looks every time an engine roared from the street, though.

Finally, a car pulled into the drive, and we all stood up straighter.

"Remember – be welcoming." Mum beamed at us. Ben and Chloe both rolled their eyes this time.

The car stopped at the base of the steps, but the doors didn't open. Through the tinted windows, I could just make out three figures – one in the front, two in the back. Chloe craned her neck to peer in, her attempt at nonchalance forgotten. The driver hugged the other two, and the back doors finally opened, a boy and a girl getting out.

"I didn't know they knew each other," Ben murmured.

"Hello! We're so glad you arrived safely." Mum moved forward to help them with their bags, but my siblings and I stayed frozen on the steps.

The girl turned towards us, dark wavy hair swishing across her shoulders in a way that was both messy and beautiful. She smiled at me, and I liked her instantly.

Chloe gasped. "Is she pregnant?"

Ben smacked Chloe's arm. "Be nice," he said, looking at both of us. I hadn't said anything; why was I getting told off?

The girl's face flushed, and the boy reached for her hand, pulling her close. I could see what Chloe meant. The girl's peasant dress rose abruptly at her waist as if covering a huge baby bump.

"Welcome." Mum took the girl's hand, drawing her towards the house. "These are my children, who will be joining you in the new school."

The girl glanced towards the boy as if seeking reassurance. He didn't notice, his dark eyes focused up at the house instead. He reminded me of Ben – tanned, athletic and projecting confidence... but in his own world, like he was above the rest of us.

Chloe stepped forward, surprising me. "Nice to meet you. I'm Chloe," she said. After a moment she seemed to remember us. "And this is my brother and sister, Ursula and Benjamin."

The girl looked to the boy again and this time he grinned. He dropped her hand to reach for Chloe's. "I'm Joe. This is Sammy."

Chloe looked Sammy up and down, her expression not altogether friendly. "So, are you pregnant?"

"Chloe!" Mum and Ben said at the same time.

Sammy seemed to shrink under our gaze. I wanted to say something – to reassure her – but I felt myself shrinking just as much as she was.

"Yes, we'll be having a baby in about a month," Joe said. He put his arm around Sammy, and she relaxed a little.

"How old are you?" I asked.

"Ursula!" Mum frowned at me. "That's not nice either."

"I didn't mean it like that. I just want to know..." I trailed off as Mum glared at me. All I wanted to find out was whether they were young enough to be my friends, or whether they would instantly dismiss me as "just a kid" like Ben and Chloe.

"Don't mind my sisters." Ben shook his head. "They don't get out much."

"It's okay," Sammy said. "We're both seventeen. We know we're young to be parents." She fiddled with a collection of silver bangles around her wrist, then looked to Joe as if she wanted him to add something, but he was back to staring up at the house.

Seventeen – older than Chloe, and just younger than my brother's eighteen years. Sammy seemed nice, but if it came down to it, she'd be far more eager to hang out with my brother and sister than with me.

"How old are you?" Sammy asked me.

"Fourteen," I mumbled. Chloe often reminded me I looked more like twelve.

"Come on in. We'll show you to your rooms." Chloe aimed this towards Joe, ignoring the rest of us.

"There's one more student to arrive," Mum said.

Chloe gave another eye roll and shifted her weight into a posture that screamed irritation. Honestly, I was starting to feel the same way.

"So you both have magic, huh?" Ben asked.

Mum shot Ben a frown as he asked this, but she didn't interrupt. Joe and Sammy looked at each other, a whole conversation seeming to happen behind their eyes.

"A little," Joe said, finally.

Obviously, that wasn't true. I didn't need to be an expert in body language to notice the lies, but even without that, they must have had more than a little magic to get noticed by my parents.

Ben raised his eyebrows. "Oh yeah? What can you do?"

Joe and Sammy glanced at each other again. At first, I thought they were going to refuse, but then Joe closed his eyes. Little daisies peeked up through the grass around us. He didn't stop there. Tiny plants crept out through the gaps in the concrete path as well, stretching up to greet us.

He let out a breath, opening his eyes. "I'm good with plants," he said. He lent down, picking one of the flowers and handing it to Sammy. She smiled, getting even prettier as she blushed.

Chloe wrinkled her nose, but I could tell she was impressed. Ben regarded Joe, his assessment of him clearly rising at least a few points too.

He turned to Sammy. "What about you?" he asked.

Sammy opened her mouth, but Joe squeezed her hand, stopping her. "Can't give away all our secrets now, can we?" He raised his eyebrows and grinned.

If anything, this seemed to impress my brother even more. Chloe just stared at Sammy, her eyes narrowing slightly.

Another car turned in to the driveway – an older, beaten-up wreck that made a chugging noise like it was barely running. It pulled up in the same spot as the first car, barely stopping before a back door flew open, no pauses for goodbye hugs. A boy leapt out, dragging an oversized duffel bag with him.

I stepped back, the chaos of his energy confusing me. His dark curly hair bounced around him for a moment after he came to a stop, and his long, black eyelashes flickered as he stared up at the house. "Jeepers." His jaw dropped open. "They didn't tell me I was coming to a mansion!"

A laugh burst out of me, and Ben pressed his lips together, trying not to follow suit. I could see the others were holding back sniggers at the word "jeepers" too. The kid's eyes finally travelled down from the house to meet ours. The laughter died in my throat as his gaze met mine. His eyes were beautiful, but full of that same chaotic energy, making my heart pound.

He blinked and his face brightened. He bounced forward to greet us – like actually bounced, there was no other way to describe it.

"I'm Arthur. Pleased to meet you. Arthur Grandace." He held out his hand to my mum.

"Welcome," she said. "I'm Candace Trager. I spoke with your parents."

My brother grinned, clearly taking a liking to the kid. He held out his hand. "Benjamin."

"Arthur," Arthur said again. He moved down the line, shaking hands, which elicited further giggles from the others as they mumbled their names. I found myself shrinking back, dreading him reaching for my hand.

Thankfully, Ben picked up Arthur's bag before he got to me. "Come on." Ben nodded towards the house. "I'll introduce you to the rest of this lot properly inside."

"Wait, wait," Mum called. "I want to get a picture of you all. We have to commemorate your first day at magic school!"

The others all either groaned or laughed, but let Mum gather them together for a photo on the steps. "Everyone say cheese!"

I forced my lips to stretch into something resembling a smile, but inside my stomach tightened. *Our first day of magic school.* This was supposed to be a happy thing, and it mostly was. I just couldn't help thinking it might also be my last day of family.

* * * *

MUM ASKED US TO GIVE the new students a tour. Arthur kept up a steady chatter as we walked up the stairs. Ben joked and laughed with him, while Chloe rolled her eyes behind his back.

Sammy and Joe kept to themselves. She seemed to be having some trouble with the stairs, and he hung back to walk with her, the two of them speaking quietly in a way that didn't involve the rest of us. I walked between the two groups, already unsure of where I fit.

"This is where you'll sleep," Ben told them. "You can pick your own rooms."

"Cool." Arthur took off through one of the doorways. A moment later, there was a thump as he jumped on the bed.

Sammy and Joe looked at each other, then at the remaining two doorways. I felt awkward, as I realised they were deciding whether or not to share a room. Seventeen was only three years older than me, but Joe and Sammy's world felt an entire lifetime away from mine.

"What's down there?" Sammy asked. She stared down the corridor towards the blackened door.

I'd almost forgotten about the library, but as soon as Sammy mentioned it, that strange, empty feeling tugged at me again.

"Nothing," Chloe said quickly.

Joe and Sammy both looked up at that, and Arthur's head poked around the doorway of his room. Way to make it seem more interesting, Chloe.

"Ignore her," Ben said. "We just screwed up some magic and she's embarrassed."

"Been there." Joe grinned, but Sammy's eyes drifted back to the door, tension clouding her face. I wondered if she could feel the same thing I could. The others didn't seem bothered by it.

"What are these marks on the floor?" Arthur asked. "Are they runes? I've been learning all about ancient languages. What do they say?"

Ben waited for the stream of questions to stop. "Yes, it's a rune line. My parents lay them around the house. Don't cross that one. In fact, don't go down that end of the corridor. The magic's still a bit volatile."

Chloe gave a snort. "It's not that bad!"

Ben raised an eyebrow. "She never thinks her failures are 'that bad'," he told the others.

The rune line hadn't been there this morning. The group began swapping magic-fail stories, laughing as they tried to top each other. I didn't have any of those, scared to try any of the showier spells Ben and Chloe seemed to favour. I slipped away from them, inching towards the rune line. I stopped when I reached it, but stretched out my foot, touching a toe to the symbols etched on the floor. Buzzing zapped through me.

"That's powerful," a quiet voice said beside me.

I started, turning to see Sammy. I hadn't realised she'd followed me. She glanced back at the group. Joe hadn't come with her. He stood with Ben, coaxing a vine he'd created to grow up the wall.

"It's just a rune line," I told Sammy.

She shook her head. "I mean what's behind that door. I don't like the idea of sleeping next to it."

I nodded. It's what I'd thought this morning. "I'm sure Mum and Dad will fix it soon."

"Yeah." Sammy's voice didn't hold that much conviction. She looked like she wanted to say something else, but she drifted back towards the group instead. She folded her arms over her bump, holding herself tightly as if trying to ward off the magic.

I waited until she was absorbed, talking to Joe, then I crouched down, examining the symbols on the floor. They were well formed, but not as strong as I would have liked. I closed my eyes and ran my hand over the line.

Relax, I said to myself, releasing the mental stranglehold I used to keep my power hidden and contained. My magic began to flow, and I poured protection into each symbol, doubling what my parents had started.

I opened my eyes. The vacuum feeling from the library eased – still there, but now only as background noise. I smiled, the anxious rush in my head quietening now the magic was contained. I turned to go back to the group.

They were still deep in conversation, swapping stories and showing off little spells. All except Chloe.

My sister's eyes flicked between me and the rune line, a scowl on her face. She didn't speak, letting the silence hang heavy between us, but I could tell she'd seen what I'd done. She knew exactly how powerful my magic really was.

Chapter Three

I woke early the next day, but skipped breakfast, too nervous to eat. Today, we would be entering the classroom as students for the first time. I brushed my hair in front of the window, watching my reflection in the glass. A single ivy vine had crept up over the window frame overnight, clinging to the flaking paint. For a moment, I feared my magic had coaxed it to grow, my ill-conceived, impulsive spell from the previous morning finally taking effect, but it was more likely down to Joe or Sammy.

I wound my hair into two tight braids, even though it played into Chloe's comments about me looking young. Today I wanted my sister to see me as little – vulnerable.

My throat went dry as I thought of the moment with the rune line. Would Chloe tell Dad what she'd seen? I couldn't bear to think what he'd do if he knew I'd been hiding how powerful my magic really was.

I ran my hands down my T-shirt and shorts, smoothing them out, then made my way out into the corridor and down the first set of stairs, trying to calm myself with the thudding rhythm of my steps. Perhaps it would have worked, but a shout from downstairs had my heart pounding again – Dad, yelling at some of the workers. Power boomed in his voice, and his fierce magic expanded through the building.

I froze, considering turning tail, but it was too late. A group of builders trudged up the stairs towards me, Dad leading the way. He caught sight of me but gave me only a cursory glance. The workers didn't acknowledge me at all, filing past with uniform, dragging steps. They looked like zombies, shambling after Dad.

I stumbled on the next stair, something sticking in my throat. *Were* they zombies? Was my dad controlling them with his magic, forcing them to work to exhaustion in the pursuit of finishing his perfect school?

I stared up at the trail of people, disappearing onto the floor above me. No... surely, he wouldn't do that. I swallowed, hard, but the tight feeling in my throat didn't clear. My father was a man who made his own children fight. Could I really put anything past him?

The dormitory-floor door burst open next to me, sending me skittering back a pace. I blinked, all thoughts of zombies shambling away on their own.

"Ursula." Sammy's voice was high and tight, and her cheeks held a bright flush. "Why are you standing in the stairwell?" She shook her head, not waiting for an answer. "You haven't seen a notebook, have you?"

"I don't think so."

Sammy let out a puff of air. "I'm sure I brought it. I *know* I brought it. It must have fallen out of my bags."

"Maybe Mum has it? If she does, she'll bring it to the classroom." Hopefully it would just be Mum visiting us today. I'd rather Dad stayed as far away as possible.

Sammy nodded, but she chewed on her lip. She fell into

pace beside me, circling down the next flight of stairs to the classrooms. Her silver bangles clattered together, creating a tinkling soundtrack to her steps.

"Is it your diary?" I asked. "The notebook, I mean."

Sammy shook her head. "Not exactly."

I waited, but she didn't offer any further explanation. We made our way down the stairs in silence, our feet hitting the floor in unison and her jangling jewellery the only interruption to it.

I took a breath before stepping into the classroom, steeling myself. The room had changed even since yesterday, becoming more sterile. A large whiteboard had been installed, dominating the front wall of the room, and an imposing teacher's desk planted in front of it. I pictured a terrifying figure standing behind it, school master from my nightmares.

"Morning!" Arthur called. He stood staring up at the wall of textbooks, eagerness lighting his face.

"Morning," I mumbled back, but he didn't seem to hear. His eyes traced over the spines, widening occasionally as a title caught his attention. Chloe sat on one of the desks, an exercise book in her hand.

Sammy stopped dead in the doorway, her face turning pale. I glanced between her and Chloe. "Is that...?"

Chloe looked up, her eyes landing on me. "Is this yours, little mouse?" she asked, raising the notebook. "What's so secret you're writing in code?"

"Give that back!" I grabbed for the book, but Chloe held it out of my reach.

"Calm down, it's not like I was reading it. What even is this?"

"It's not yours, that's what it is." I reached for the book again, and Chloe dodged out of my way.

"Touchy-touchy!" She flipped through the pages, pretending to read them. The spine bent back, threatening to rip.

"I said, give it back!"

Chloe held the book above her head, and danced backwards, waving it side to side like a little kid. "How ever are you going to get your book back?" she said with mock concern. "If only your magic was stronger."

I froze. Chloe smirked, and I cursed myself for giving her the reaction she wanted. She wouldn't tell Dad about my magic, would she? Not over something like this?

"It's not Ursula's book; it's mine," Sammy said quietly.

Chloe's eyes widened. "I..." For a moment, it seemed like she would apologise, then something else crossed her face. She smiled – a twisted, mean smirk. "Well, that still doesn't explain why *you're* writing things in code, Samantha."

Joe and Ben chose that moment to walk into the room. Joe grinned as he saw Sammy, then his expression fell, taking in the tension in the room. "Hey, is something wrong?"

I ignored him, still focused on my sister. She made a show of flicking through the notebook pages. "Maybe my parents should know about..." Chloe trailed off, something in the pages catching her eye. "Their magic will flare out of control," she said softly to herself, reading. "And she will realise..." she cut herself off abruptly, her eyes widening.

"What's going on?" Ben asked.

"Chloe stole Sammy's notebook," Arthur said, before anyone else could speak. I looked up. He still stood by the bookshelf, silent the entire time we'd been arguing. So strange that he had so much energy, such eagerness and frenetic movement, yet managed to disappear into stillness when it suited him.

Chloe blinked, dragging her eyes away from the page. "Don't be so dramatic. I didn't steal it; I found it."

Ben grabbed the book from her hand. "Cut it out, Chloe. You're not seven." He glanced down, and his gaze caught in the same way Chloe's had. His eyes flicked across the page, reading, then his expression hardened into something I couldn't interpret. He looked up at Sammy. She'd gone pale again, fear sparking in her eyes. She reached out for the book. Ben hesitated, then handed it over.

Joe touched Sammy's shoulder. "Are you okay?"

Sammy nodded, clutching the book to her chest. His arm slid around her shoulder, pulling her into a hug. Something shifted in the room, everything becoming charged. A look passed between Chloe and Ben, then her eyes flicked towards Sammy. Whatever they'd read, it seemed to have unsettled both of them.

But the book was back in Sammy's hands, where it should be. I sank down into one of the desks, all of the fight going out of me. Funny how things worked like that. I could barely hold a conversation, shyness sticking the words in my throat, but when someone was threatened, I could argue for them, *fight* for them.

Arthur slid into the chair next to me. "Are you okay?" he asked. I frowned, anticipating some kind of punchline, but he stared back at me, his dark eyes open and curious.

"Yeah, I'm fine," I said. "My sister can just be..." I let that hang, the end of the sentiment clear enough without me having to say it.

I stared down at the desktop. My parents had bought the desks from a local high school, and they were covered in scribbles, layers of pen scraped into the surface. Was this something we were supposed to do too? Carve our mark into the furniture to prove we'd been here?

Suddenly, it felt important to do just that. I took out a pen, pressing hard and carving my initials on top of all the others.

Arthur watched me, probably puzzling at my strange actions. I dropped the pen as soon as I was done. It landed with a clatter, bouncing off the table. Arthur picked it up. He leaned over, adding his own initials below mine.

"You're nervous," he said. It wasn't a question.

I swallowed. "Is this what schools are normally like?"

His eyebrows rose a little in surprise, and I blushed. I shouldn't have said that – shouldn't have admitted I had no understanding of such a normal thing. Mum and Dad always said we'd learn more in home school. Now I knew about the geminus magic, I wondered if the choice to keep us out of regular school had been made simply to avoid us accidentally killing other kids.

"Mostly," Arthur said finally. "It's never going to be completely normal with magic, though, right?"

We would never be completely normal with magic.

"All right, children." A firm voice rang out from the hallway, and a young woman stepped through the doorway, high heels clicking against the floor. "Come take a seat. My name is Miss Caraway, and I will be your instructor in magic."

Joe and Sammy extracted themselves from each other's arms, and everyone settled into seats. I snuck looks at Miss Caraway. She wore a thin, floral dress – not the sort of thing I would have expected with that loud voice – and soft, curly hair bounced around her shoulders. She looked sweet, but that wasn't exactly a good thing when it came to teaching my sister. I had a feeling Chloe would have her in tears by the end of the first week.

"In the coming months, other instructors will arrive to teach you in the traditional subjects, but for now we are focused on gaining control of your powers."

I turned to Arthur. "Do you think she's a—"

"No talking, please." Miss Caraway's voice snapped with

a force that had to have magic behind it. I shrank automatically, and Chloe let out a giggle, earning herself a stern look.

I took a breath, letting it out slowly. This would be okay – it had to be. Whatever Miss Caraway's style of teaching, it couldn't be worse than Dad's.

Miss Caraway looked at each of us, in turn, her gaze serious. "As you know, the six of you hold magic."

"Hell yeah, we do," Joe said. He raised his chair, levitating it an inch off the floor. His magic wasn't strong enough to hold him, and he came clattering back down.

Miss Caraway raised her eyebrows. "Yes, quite."

I suppressed a smile. I'd underestimated her. It would take at least *two* weeks for Chloe to have her in tears.

"Joseph, is it?" Miss Caraway asked.

Joe nodded, feet firmly on the ground now. "Joe."

"All right, Joe. You will probably have already noticed that your magic is somewhat unreliable?"

Chloe looked at me when Miss Caraway said that, but I didn't return her gaze.

"Yeah, I guess," Joe mumbled.

"This is an unfortunate side effect of geminus magic," Miss Caraway continued. "You've heard this term, yes?"

Only about a hundred times. The way Dad went on, it was like he thought we'd won the magic lottery. Mum seemed more concerned one of us was going to blow up.

"Our magic is twinned with another person's," Sammy said.

"Indeed," Miss Caraway said. "Your magic will be stronger and more stable when paired with another person's. Alone, you will struggle to control it – for some geminus magic wielders, their magic will fade completely if they don't find their pair, but that is best case scenario. In other cases, it becomes dangerous. Explosive even."

Perhaps that explained why my siblings had been so drawn to making fireworks.

"So how do we stop that?" Arthur asked.

Miss Caraway smiled, evidently appreciating the sensible question. "Before we do anything else, I think it would be a good idea if you all get to know your pair a little better."

My heart did a leap then started to hammer. I snuck a look at Arthur, but he didn't look back at me.

"Joseph, you'll be with Chloe," Miss Caraway said.

Chloe blinked, and Joe raised his head, surprise taking over his usual self-assured expression. "I thought I'd be with Sammy."

Miss Caraway shook her head. "No. The magic is strongly indicating you are twinned with Chloe."

Sammy looked towards Chloe and frowned. Her eyes flicked back to Joe. "Then who am I paired with?"

"Your magic seems to be gravitating towards Ursula's."

Sammy looked around at me as if she had forgotten I was even there. She caught herself and schooled her face into a smile. "I'm sure we'll work really well together."

"Have fun babysitting." Chloe smirked at Sammy then turned her gaze on me. I glared back at her for a moment before I wavered and dropped my gaze.

"I guess that leaves me and Arthur." Ben got up, moving over to sit next to Arthur.

"Neato," Arthur said. My brother suddenly became very focused on wiping something from his eye. I couldn't tell how he felt about it, other than being amused by Arthur's excited exclamation. Then again, I'm not sure any of us knew how we felt about these matches yet.

"Hey." Sammy made her way over to my desk. "I'm glad we're working together. Hopefully it will mean great things for both of our magic."

Shyness overcame me, and I found I couldn't do anything except smile. Even that may have come out as more of a mouth shrug. I felt Ben's eyes on me, then he leaned over across the aisle from his desk to say something to Sammy. I didn't hear what it was, but she smiled at him and then nodded. My cheeks flushed, knowing he was probably warning her I was socially inept.

She turned back to me. "Thanks for helping me before – with my book."

I nodded, though I hadn't actually got it back for her. She tilted her head to the side, clearly waiting for me to say something.

"You're welcome," I choked out eventually.

She smiled. "Ursula's a pretty name."

"No, it's not," I said automatically.

Sammy looked horrified, and I started to laugh. She joined me, a grin spreading across her face.

"If we're twinned, does that mean I'm connected to your baby's magic as well?" I blurted out. I glanced at her stomach, and then pressed my lips together, shushing myself. Maybe I still wasn't supposed to mention it.

Sammy just looked thoughtful. "I don't know. I don't even know if she'll have magic yet."

I nodded, running out of questions. Her focus had turned to the notebook she'd taken back from Chloe. She thumbed through it, reading, then drew a star in the margin. I glanced down at the page, but I couldn't make out her handwriting.

I snuck a look at what the others were doing. Chloe and Joe had their palms pressed together in front of them, in the same way as when Dad made her and Ben fight. Chloe's had her eyelids lightly closed, but Joe kept blinking, as if unsure of what he was supposed to be doing. I felt the magic building between their hands from where I sat.

I looked back at Sammy. Should magic be growing between us too? But of course, it wouldn't unless I released mine. I took a breath, easing my grip on my power. Suddenly, I felt a tug at my stomach. A glowing rope of energy lit up between me and Sammy, like an umbilical cord joining us. I glanced around at the others, spotting similar cords growing between Chloe and Joe, and Ben and Arthur.

"The geminus connections," I whispered.

"Huh?" Sammy drew her eyes away from my brother. He and Arthur tossed a balled-up piece of paper back and forth between them. They'd levitated it and used their power to fling it from side to side, both of them laughing.

"We should set it on fire!" Arthur said, way too loudly. I shuddered at the thought.

"Can you do that sort of thing?" Sammy asked me.

I shrugged. "Maybe. I've never tried." I'd kept my magic use to a minimum around Dad. Besides, "fireball" didn't sound like much fun to me.

"I can't," Sammy told me. "My magic doesn't work like that."

Strangely, I could tell she had a lot of power, though it was a different sort to my brother and sister's. They seemed to gather energy to them, pulling it from everything around them when they wanted to do something. Sammy's just hummed quietly on her skin, coming from inside. I liked it. It was calming to be around.

Miss Caraway gasped. "What are you doing? Stop!"

I spun around. Chloe's hands glowed, colour flaring around them too bright to look at, but Joe's had turned black. Dark, ashy colour crept up his arms, his limbs withering under its touch. Chloe's eyes glazed over, reflecting the light.

"Joe!" Sammy shot out of her chair, but I stepped in front of her, shielding her as sparks shot out from Chloe's hands.

"Oh god," Sammy whispered. "She's draining his energy!"

"I said stop!" Miss Caraway grabbed Chloe's shoulders, yanking her away. The light around Chloe flared, and Miss Caraway jerked, a shudder running through her. She fell backwards almost in slow motion. A choked sound rasped through her lips.

"Miss Caraway!" I ran towards her but stopped just short of touching her. Dark veins crept up from her fingertips, her skin blackening.

"No, don't touch him!" Ben yelled.

I spun around, just as Arthur grabbed Joe's shrivelled wrist. Colour flared out from Chloe's hands, engulfing Arthur's. I shielded my eyes, the glow too bright. A rune lit up on the inside of my eyelids.

Arthur shuddered. He turned towards me, and it seemed to take forever. Behind him, another surge of bright colour flared in Chloe's hands.

"Arthur!" I darted forward.

Sammy scrambled after me. "Ursula, don't!"

I caught hold of Arthur as the flare of colour faded, and yanked him back before another could surge. He swayed under my pull, dead weight resisting my rescue. Sammy caught his head before it smashed into the floor.

"Did it get you?" Ben grabbed my wrists, examining my hands. "Are you okay?"

I stared down at my palms. My skin remained pale, no signs of the dark ash. "I'm fine," I said. "I'm okay." I looked back at the others – at their blackened, withered flesh. Why hadn't it affected me? I felt magic tingling in my fingers, scratching against my skin.

Chloe blinked as if waking, and the light died down to a weak glow around her hands. She took in the slumped forms of our classmates and teacher, her eyes going wide. "What happened?"

"What do you think, Chloe?" Ben spat the words at her.

Blood trickled from Miss Caraway's nose, but her eyes were open, blinking. Arthur's fingers stretched out, as if still trying to catch the paper ball, his skin black and crumbly, desiccating in front of us.

I grabbed his hand on impulse. It felt warm to the touch, but something cold rushed through his veins. A tunnel of icy air opened up inside him, and I felt myself falling into it.

"No," I whispered. I pulled back, scrambling to escape, but Arthur kept falling.

Sammy grasped my other hand. She closed her eyes, pouring all of her magic into me, and I squeezed my eyes shut too. Something warm built inside me – warm, then hot, and then boiling. It rushed in my veins, pushing against the chill in Arthur's blood.

"My hands!" Joe gasped.

I opened my eyes. Colour rushed back into Joe's skin – into Arthur's and Miss Caraway's too. Arthur blinked at me, his healed hand tightening around mine.

Ben's mouth dropped open. "How are you doing that?"

I shook my head. "I... I don't know." I didn't loosen my grip on Arthur. In my mind, I saw his fingers crumbling, turning to ash between mine.

Ben stared at me for a moment longer, frowning, then he rounded on Chloe. "What were you thinking? You could have killed them."

Chloe shook her head, her face pale. "I don't know. I didn't mean to do anything."

"We just wanted to see if we could connect our magic." Joe balled his hands against his chest, as if protecting them. Sweat beaded on his forehead, and I was sure he was about to vomit.

Suddenly, Miss Caraway groaned. She sat bolt upright, her whole body shivering.

"You're okay." Sammy knelt beside her, gently rubbing her arm. "It's all going to be okay." But Miss Caraway made a keening noise, that didn't sound okay at all.

Ben shook his head. "Mum and Dad are coming," he told Chloe. I could feel them moving towards us, drawn by the unusual magic.

Chloe went a shade paler, a shiver of her own working its way through her body. "I'm sorry," she whispered, and for once, I think she actually meant it.

Chapter Four

I stayed in bed late the next morning. My palms still itched with magic – the same magic that had protected me and saved my classmates. I stretched my fingers out, searching for its source. Nothing. I had no idea how I'd done it.

Then again, I hadn't done it alone.

Their magic will flare out of control... Chloe's words, read from Sammy's notebook, echoed in my mind. Sammy had been so sure of herself, grabbing my hand and joining her magic to mine. Had she known this was going to happen? If so, why hadn't she tried to stop it?

My parents had cancelled classes for the rest of the week, so Arthur, Joe and Miss Caraway could recover. Joe and Arthur didn't need it. Within hours of waking, Arthur had had a stream of questions about what happened, his magical curiosity far outweighing any ill effects he'd felt. As for Miss Caraway, I wasn't sure. My parents had whisked her away, and I wondered if my prediction about Chloe driving her to tears might have been a little too on the nose.

I got dressed, then stepped out into the corridor. Immediately, all the resolve flew out of me. I could go downstairs and demand to see Sammy's notebook, or I could march into my sister's room, and ask what exactly she thought she was doing draining Joe's energy like that. Instead, I stood, wavering as I tried to decide which option felt less impossible.

"What are you doing, brat?" Chloe's voice rang out from behind her bedroom door. It sat ajar, but knowing Chloe, that didn't constitute an invitation.

I pushed it open, not quite crossing the threshold. It had been a while since she'd let me in her room. Photos lined her walls, and I was surprised to see my own face peering out from some of them. In between the pictures, she'd hung band posters and images from magazines, creating an onslaught of colour.

She cleared her throat, and I snapped my gaze back to her. "Are you okay?" I asked her.

Chloe blinked, surprise chasing away her irritation. Had anyone else asked her that? We'd all been so concerned about the others, she'd been forgotten – or rather blamed – but yesterday had to have affected her too.

She shook her head, her expression returning to her regular disinterested glare. "I'm fine. You all overreacted. I would have got things under control if you'd given me another minute."

I frowned. "Really? It seemed like…" I trailed off as Chloe made another irritated noise in her throat.

Dark circles lined her eyes, and her cheeks were drawn. I doubted she'd got much sleep last night – I certainly hadn't. "What did you and Ben read in Sammy's notebook?" I asked.

She frowned. "Sammy's notebook…" she repeated. Her eyelids flickered, as if she was trying to dredge the memory from the depths of her mind, then she shook her head and shrugged. "I don't know. I don't remember. It was just some stream of consciousness nonsense, I think."

That didn't make sense. She and Ben had looked so worried by what they'd read, then part of it had come true. How could Chloe have just forgotten?

Suddenly, I noticed the way she was sitting, her hands cupped protectively over something, shielding it from my view. "What are you doing?"

Chloe wrinkled her nose like she was going to tell me to piss off, then her face softened. She beckoned me over. "Come here, I'll show you." She moved her hands, revealing a pair of white mice on the bedspread beside her.

I gasped. "Where did you get those? Mum will kill you if she sees rodents in the house."

Chloe rolled her eyes. "Well, you're not going to tell her, are you?"

I hesitated. I *probably* wasn't going to tell Mum. "Depends. What are you doing with them?"

Chloe grinned and shifted over in the bed so I could sit down. She held up her hand, a sparkling swirl of magic forming in her palm. It stretched out into a thin cord which wrapped itself around the mice. I tensed, my fingers digging into the bedspread.

A rune sparked in the air, disappearing again just as quickly. Chloe pulled on the end of the cord, leading the mice on a path across the bed. One of them followed willingly, seeming happy enough to go with the magical pull. The other's head twitched as if it was straining against her.

"How did you learn to do that?"

Chloe hesitated. "Joe showed me how to do it," she said finally. "My magic is getting stronger – must be the geminus connection. I think I might be able to lead a person eventually."

I recoiled, disgusted by the idea. Chloe didn't notice, her focus fixed on the mice and her Pied-Piper-like magic. She drew one of the mice closer to the side of the bed. In a second, it would topple over, walking straight over the edge into nothing.

"Stop it. You're hurting him!"

Chloe glanced up at me, her eyes widening. "No I'm not." The defensive note in her voice told me she had no idea whether this magic hurt the mice or not. She released them, and I gathered them up in my hands, stroking them gently. They cowered into me. "Where did you get them?"

Chloe's eyes flicked away from mine, and she shrugged. "Joe bought them at a pet shop in town."

"They're so little. You have to be careful." That wasn't what I wanted to say. I wanted her to stop completely – to let them go free.

She looked down at the little creatures in my hands. She reached out a finger, stroking their heads ever so gently. There was something in her expression I couldn't quite read – a heaviness that almost seemed like sadness. One of the mice sniffed her fingertip, and the hint of a smile crossed her lips.

"Maybe you're right," she said finally.

She got up and pulled a small cage from her bedside drawer, holding it out to me. "Here."

I hesitated. I didn't want to surrender the animals to her, but what would I do with them otherwise? I studied her face. Her gaze was soft, repentant, and her shoulders slumped. "I promise I won't hurt them, okay? I was just trying to figure out the spell."

"Okay." I stretched out my hand and let the mice climb off it into their home. They scurried into their bed, happier once they were inside, though of course they didn't know who was holding the box. Chloe closed the lid and set it down on the top of her dresser. She placed her hand gently on the side of the cage as if offering an apology.

"So are Arthur and Joe okay?" she asked without turning around.

"I don't know. I was going to go down to the dorm and see how they're all doing."

"That's a good idea."

"Do you want to come with me?" I stepped out into the corridor.

Chloe took half a pace towards me, then stopped herself. Something shifted in her posture, and her lips quirked into a smirk. "Pass," she said.

I frowned. "Really? You don't want to—"

Chloe rolled her eyes. "I said *pass*. Leave me alone, brat." She closed the door, shutting me out. The sound of the latch clicking into place told me she wouldn't be opening it again anytime soon.

"What the...?" I stood for a moment, blinking at the closed door. What *was* that? The change in Chloe had been so sudden, like she'd flicked a switch and just didn't care anymore. I opened my mouth to yell at her, then shut it again without speaking. If she wasn't worried enough to check on our classmates after she hurt them, I couldn't make her. Besides, her trick with the mice made me nervous.

I turned away. Light flared from behind her door as I did. I glanced back, but the glow had faded, leaving behind only the tiniest streak of ash around the doorknob.

"Chloe?" I called. She didn't answer.

*　*　*　*

BY THE END OF THE WEEK, we were all climbing the walls. Chloe seemed to have given up on spells involving the mice, instead meeting Joe in the garden early each morning to practice growing plants. I was glad there was no further errant magic, but the utter tedium of long days with no classes was almost worse. Sammy said her power didn't manifest in a way we could practice, and I was too scared to unleash mine beyond what I had to.

Our parents set up a common room for us, next to Chloe's and my bedrooms, but the space was dull. We lounged on old couches that smelt of dust and sadness, the blank white walls looming as if they would topple down on us like dominoes. I'd taken to reading one of the magical textbooks to stave off boredom – an encyclopaedia of spells. I was already up to F.

"What are we supposed to do now?" Joe asked, flopping down onto the couch beside Sammy. "You don't even have a TV."

"Who cares? At least we're not stuck in the classroom with that flighty old bat." Apparently, Chloe's repentant phase had lasted for less time than it took Arthur to recover.

Ben clicked his tongue. "Show some respect, Chloe. You could have killed her."

Chloe rolled her eyes. "Give off, she'll be fine. Look at Arthur and Joe. She was being dramatic."

I frowned. Dramatic didn't seem like Miss Caraway's style. I had a feeling her image was carefully curated – that floaty dress against the booming power of her voice. It was designed to surprise, to draw attention. There was no way she would give up that powerful image for the sake of feigning sickness.

"Forget about what happened. Joe's right – we should do something fun." Arthur practically jiggled as he spoke. "We have the whole night to ourselves."

Mum and Dad had gone to a function, dragging themselves away from their lurking watch over us after eliciting promises we wouldn't try any magic while they were away.

They may as well have written a sign saying: "we're going out – start the explosions after 8 PM!"

It was all very well for Arthur to say we had the evening to ourselves, but there was nothing exciting for us to do. I almost suggested a board game, but that would have had Chloe rolling her eyes so far back she'd do herself damage.

"So, what do you do for fun around here?" Sammy asked.

Joe raised his eyebrows. "I think you're looking at it."

Chloe's cheeks turned pink at that. "We can head into town," she said. "We could see a movie or…" She frowned, as she scrambled for anything remotely interesting. Her eyes flicked towards Joe. "We could… Actually…" Chloe's face brightened. "I've got a friend who could probably get us some beer."

Ben frowned. "Oh, really? Who's this friend?"

"No one you know." Chloe tossed her hair, a smirk on her lips, and Ben's frown deepened.

Joe watched Chloe, his eyes narrowing, but the hint of a smile played at the corners of his mouth. "That doesn't sound too bad. I'm in – we're in, right Sammy?"

Sammy hesitated. She looked from Joe to Chloe, but Arthur cut in before she could say anything. "I'm in," he said. He got up and moved towards the door almost as if he would lead the way.

Drinking did not appeal to me – I'd probably just make a fool of myself – but I didn't want to be the only one left behind. "Yeah, I'm in too," I said.

"No." Ben shook his head. "No way, Urse."

Chloe scoffed. "Who said you were invited, squirt?"

"If you're all going, then I'm going." I hated how petulant that made me sound. Chloe glared at me, like I'd threatened to tell Mum and Dad if they left me. I wouldn't have done that, but it was tempting to say it if it would make Chloe include me.

"Sure," Arthur said, as if he had any authority in the situation. "Of course Ursula can come." He grabbed my hand, pulling me up beside him. I stumbled with the sudden movement, and his fingers tightened on mine, steadying me.

"No, she can't." Chloe crossed her arms.

I stared at Ben, giving him my best pleading look. He stared back, and for a moment, it seemed like he might relent. But then he shook his head.

"No, little mouse. I think you should sit this one out."

Behind him, Joe sniggered. I could have killed Ben for using that nickname. It wasn't fair. I was only a year younger than Arthur, but they were treating me like a baby.

"All right, it's settled. The rest of you..." Chloe's gaze fell on Arthur. She opened her mouth as if to protest him going too, but my brother slung his arm around Arthur's shoulder.

"Perhaps this will be a good geminus-bonding exercise," he said.

Arthur glanced at me. "If Ursula's not going..."

"It's fine," I said. "I don't like beer, anyway."

Chloe scoffed, knowing full well I'd never tried it.

"See you later, little mouse," Joe said, winking at me.

My cheeks flamed. Ben ruffled my hair, probably in a lame attempt at an apology, but all it did was annoy me more.

Joe stopped in the doorway. "You coming?"

I glanced up, ready to glare at him for making fun of me, but his eyes were on Sammy, who hadn't moved from her spot on the couch. She hesitated, looking at me. I shook my head. She couldn't hang back out of pity; that was humiliating.

"I'm going to stay with Ursula," she said finally. "If it's a geminus bonding thing, I should probably..."

"Seriously?" Joe frowned. Behind it, there was something else though... a hitch in his voice that almost sounded like he was hurt.

She swallowed and looked down. "It's not like I can drink anyway."

It got weirdly quiet in the room. We all had this stupid fascination with Sammy's pregnancy, but in a lot of ways, it wasn't real to the rest of us – just something to gossip and speculate on. Suddenly, it was almost as if the baby was already here, judging us for wanting to feed it beer.

"You could still come," Joe said. "You don't have to—"

"I'll see you all later." There was something final in Sammy's tone. Joe just stood there, staring at her. I felt like I'd watched an entire argument play out with only half the words spoken aloud.

"Fine. Suit yourself." Joe looked away, his expression dark.

Chloe slipped her arm through his and pulled him towards the door. "Don't worry. I'm sure we'll still have fun without them."

I shook my head at my sister's callousness. She smirked in response.

"Come on," Sammy said to me, once the others had gone. "We don't need them. We should do something fun ourselves."

It was sweet of her, but the idea felt forced. "You don't have to do that. You don't have to stay either. If you want to go with them—"

"I don't," she said firmly. "Even if you weren't staying back, I wouldn't have gone." She shook her head, then flicked her hands as if she was brushing off the others and their night out. "I mean it; let's do something fun. Let's... I don't know... Let's have a picnic. You can show me around the grounds."

I frowned. I could just imagine Chloe laughing at us if I told her we'd had a picnic, but it couldn't be worse than sitting on these lumpy couches, listening to the never-ending hammer beats. "Okay," I said begrudgingly, then I softened. "Actually, there is somewhere cool I could take you. It's not far – still on the grounds – but no one else knows about it."

Sammy's smile widened, lighting her face. "That sounds perfect." She took my hand, though I had a feeling it was mostly because she needed help getting off the couch. "Don't tell anyone, but I have a secret stash of chocolate," she said. "Not even Joe knows where I keep it."

I smiled at being let in on the secret. I didn't have the heart to tell her I wasn't that big a chocolate fan. "We could make chocolate strawberries," I said instead.

*   *   *   *

WE MELTED A COUPLE of Sammy's chocolate bars on the kitchen stove, tempering them ready to coat the berries. I would take Sammy up onto the roof of the old disused barn. It didn't sound that impressive, but the view from up there spread out across the hills and the sky. When I was little, I'd wanted my parents to build me a treehouse. They never did, but I'd figured out how to get up onto the roof of the barn, and that was almost as good. The best part was neither Ben nor Chloe knew about it.

Sammy pilfered a few other treats from the pantry, packing them all up in a Tupperware container. It wasn't a picnic basket, but it would do. We let the strawberries set, then headed out into the garden.

"Doesn't it give you the creeps, having all these people wandering around your house all the time?"

"Huh?" I glanced up.

Sammy nodded to a group of workers milling around the grounds, finally having laid down their hammers for the night.

I shrugged. "I guess I'm used to it. They've been here for a while."

"They're so strange though. They almost don't seem human."

Zombies, I thought again. Now that they were off duty, it was even worse. Without my dad giving orders, they just drifted across the lawn, eyes glazed.

"I think my dad is using magic on them." As soon as the words were out of my mouth, I wanted to pluck them back out of the air.

Sammy shivered. "He wouldn't do that to us, would he?"

I swallowed, unable to give the answer I knew I should. Sammy studied my face for a moment, her own expression unreadable. I couldn't hold her eye. Memories of Dad forcing Chloe and Ben to fight flashed through my mind. He'd never really hurt them, though, would he? It was just about making their magic better.

Sammy squeezed my hand, drawing my attention back to her. "Where's the spot you wanted to show me?"

I forced a smile, grateful for the distraction. "This way."

I pulled Sammy over to the tree beside the barn. The wide branches stretched up over the roof, solid... stable. I rested a hand on the bark, and the tree seemed to press back against me in welcome.

On the far side of the lawn, the workers had given up on milling around and now sat in the grass, like they were joining us in their own foodless picnic.

Sammy looked from me to the tree, frowning.

"You're not expecting me to climb that, are you?" Her hands tightened over her belly.

I laughed. "No, of course not. It's just where I hide the key." I crouched down, retrieving the key from the roots of the tree. I unlocked the side door of the barn, and led Sammy to the narrow staircase leading up to the roof. Sammy looked almost as dubious about climbing the steps as she had about the tree.

"I won't let you fall," I told her. "I promise."

She took a long breath, letting it out slowly through her lips. "I trust you," she said finally. "You better catch me and bub if I slip, though." She laughed as she said it, but I nodded, making the promise seriously.

I walked up first with the food, opening the trapdoor to the roof, then came back to help Sammy. She gripped my arm tighter than I was expecting, fear turning her fingers into wiry claws. I guess it was a bit daunting with no handrail and one side of the stairs open to the barn. But still... she trusted me enough to do this. I wasn't going to take that lightly.

"I've got you," I told her.

She took a breath and then nodded. We took the steps one at a time. I gripped her tightly, pulling her up partly with magic and partly with sheer strength. Perhaps it had been insensitive of me to suggest this. I hadn't thought how hard it would be for her, with the baby weighing heavily on her. By the time we reached the roof, her breath came in sharp, ragged gasps. She lay back on the corrugated iron, laughing, letting the heavy rise and fall of her chest slow, and I flopped back too.

"Oof. That's my exercise for the week," she said.

From up here, we could see all of the stars, far enough away from the lights of the house for the sky to really show its magic. The bright dots danced against the inky darkness as if performing just for us.

"Wow," she said softly, not letting her voice disturb the night. "This is beautiful."

If I'd brought Chloe up here, she would have scoffed, even if she thought it was pretty. I settled back next to Sammy, letting the soft night sounds wash over us.

"You're good at protective magic, aren't you?" Sammy asked.

I shrugged. "I guess."

"You are. You helped Arthur the other day when the rest of us couldn't even touch him."

"*We* helped Arthur the other day." I couldn't have done it if Sammy hadn't taken my hand. I still wasn't entirely sure *what* we had done, but I knew it hadn't been me alone.

Sammy fell quiet, her earlier laughter completely disappearing. "I guess that's this geminus thing they keep talking about." Her voice was low, making it hard to judge how she felt about it. I wasn't sure either. Sammy's magic had made me feel stronger, but I wasn't sure I wanted to have to hold someone's hand every time I used my power.

"You knew it was going to happen, didn't you?"

Sammy looked up at me, her gaze sharp. I swallowed, not wanting to back down now I'd said it. "That bit Chloe read out from your notebook – you'd written about what was going to happen."

Sammy nodded slowly. "Sometimes, I write things, but—"

"Then why didn't you try to stop it? How could you let them get hurt?"

Sammy hesitated, then slipped her hand inside her jacket. She pulled her notebook from inside the lining. "Here."

I took the notebook from her, but I didn't open it. Suddenly, I wasn't sure if I wanted answers to any of my questions. Sammy bit her lip, and nodded, gesturing towards the book. "Read it."

I opened the book. Pages of scrawling words greeted me. I flicked through them. Names jumped out at me – my own, Chloe's and Ben's – but each time I tried to focus on the words around them, they moved, letters shifting and changing under my gaze.

She took the book back. "I don't remember writing it. I can only read bits when it's important," Sammy said quietly. "Until then, it's gibberish."

So that's what Chloe meant about Sammy writing in code. "But Chloe and Ben both read it."

Sammy nodded. "I think the magic was trying to stop Chloe from hurting the others. That must be why she found my book in the first place."

I shivered, cold suddenly. I knew magic could influence things – nudge people in a different direction or sway outcomes, but this was a different kind of power than any I'd witnessed before. "You've written a lot about us," I said.

Sammy's eyelashes flickered. "Yes."

Something curdled in my stomach. She'd read some of it, I was sure of it. I drew breath, ready to ask her if there was something she knew, ready to beg her to let me read what she had written, but a scrabbling sound cut me off.

Sammy grabbed my hand, her nails biting into my skin. We both looked towards the trapdoor where we'd just climbed up.

"There you are." Arthur's head appeared. He grinned at us.

Sammy let out a nervous laugh. "Oh, it's you."

I couldn't tell from her tone whether she was happy to see him or just relieved he wasn't someone worse. She moved back across the roof so he could climb out. I frowned. There was so much more I wanted to know about her prophecies. How could she be sure she was just predicting things and not causing them to happen?

"How did you find us?" Sammy asked.

Arthur shrugged. "Magic, of course. Ooo, strawberries." He dove into the Tupperware container, grabbing two of the chocolate berries, and then settled himself beside me.

"Why did you come back?"

Arthur shifted uncomfortably. His knee brushed mine as he did, but he didn't move away. "They got drunk really quickly. Then they were using magic on people, and..." He trailed off and glanced at me, falling silent.

That told me everything I needed to know. When he said "they" were using magic on people, he really meant Chloe.

"I bet Joe was egging them on." Sammy picked at some lint on her skirt. She didn't look up at either of us.

"Yeah, he was." Arthur didn't seem to register her mood. "The two of them started letting off fireworks, but then that turned into explosions and the whole thing got out of control. Joe seems like kind of a loose cannon. I don't know if I want to be around him, to be honest."

I nudged Arthur in the side, and he glanced up at me. I looked meaningfully at Sammy, especially her stomach. She still worried at the lint on her top. If she kept going any longer, she would pull a hole in the fabric. She chewed on her lip, perhaps trying to tear that too.

"I mean, it was fine," Arthur said quickly, his voice too high to be believable. "They were just having fun, I guess."

"Fun at other people's expense." Sammy flopped back on the roof, staring up at the stars. I leaned back with her, looking up, and after a second, Arthur joined us.

"He's not a bad guy," Sammy said. "He's actually a really *good* guy, I love him a lot. But it's just..."

I think I knew what she meant. People could get influenced by magic really easily, get carried away with it. Ben could be like that. Sometimes I had doubts about my sister's morality, but it wasn't like that with Ben. He just got excited and took his magic too far. I could see the same thing might be happening with Joe.

Sammy closed her eyes, resting her arm across her forehead. We let the silence hang damply over us for a moment.

"What type of magic do you have, Arthur?" I asked, breaking it.

Arthur blinked at the change of subject and looked towards me. I stared back at him, hoping he got the hint that we were done talking about Joe and my sister.

"I can do a little bit of everything," he said finally. He said it shyly, as if he wasn't all that sure in his own abilities. Somehow, that made me certain he was actually very good. Funny how things worked like that.

"That sounds cool," I said.

We both looked at Sammy, but she didn't open her eyes. Part of me resented Arthur for that. I'd been enjoying talking to Sammy alone. It reminded me of when Chloe and I were younger, and we used to stay up talking, long after Mum and Dad thought we had gone to bed.

"You two can obviously do some powerful stuff. I felt when you stopped that magic in the classroom."

I was surprised he'd felt anything, given how much it had been affecting him. An image flashed through my mind, and my thoughts scrambled after it, trying to catch hold.

"Did either of you see a rune?" I asked. With everything else that had happened, I'd forgotten about the brief spark of light I'd seen marking the rune on the inside of my eyelids, but suddenly it felt important.

Arthur frowned. "Like the ones on the floor?"

I shook my head. "No, it flashed in the air when the light flared." Just like the one that had sparked when Chloe led the mice. "You saw it, right?" I turned to Sammy.

She shook her head. "I don't think so."

Arthur looked down at his hands, rubbing them gently together, perhaps remembering the way his skin had turned black and withered. Even in the dark, I could see him shiver.

Sammy reached out, gently squeezing Arthur's hand. "Whatever it was, it's gone now." She smiled, but it didn't light her face the way it normally would.

"Can you see the geminus connections?" I asked.

I reached out as I spoke, grabbing hold of the cord of magic between me and Sammy. It sparked as I made contact, a small wave of power rippling off it. The others reeled back, feeling the energy even if they couldn't see it.

Sammy touched her stomach, where the cord connected to her. "Woah... that was strong."

Arthur prodded the air in front of him, as if feeling for his connection to Ben. He missed it by a good twenty centimetres. That was probably a good thing.

"You must see magic in ways we can't," Sammy told me. Her voice dropped low again, and I couldn't help feeling she saw some significance in that. I lay back, retraining my focus on the night sky. It didn't look quite so beautiful now.

Arthur seemed to register the heavy mood that had fallen over me and Sammy. He pointed out the constellations above us, perhaps as a way to distract us, but I found I couldn't concentrate on his words. Instead of faraway celestial lights, I saw runes flashing in my mind.

The rune in the classroom had been significant, I was sure of it. I'd been thinking of what happened as an accident – another example of Chloe's overenthusiastic magic use, but doubt crept in now. What if she had known exactly what she was doing?

I shook my head, brushing the thought away. My sister wasn't like that. She was self-absorbed sometimes, and a bit mean, but she never set out to actually hurt anyone, did she? Suddenly, I wasn't sure of the answer. The world was tipping underneath me, and if I wasn't careful, my sister might lead me right off the edge.

Chapter Five

Sammy looked about ready to collapse by the time we got back to the dormitory floor. She gave us each a hug, which made me stiffen, not used to physical affection from... well, anyone except my mother.

Arthur walked down the hallway with me. "I'm sorry Ben and Chloe didn't let you come with us tonight."

"I don't care," I said automatically, then I realised I actually meant it. I'd felt left out before, but I'd had a better time here with Sammy and Arthur than I would have had in town.

"I'm glad I came back," Arthur said. "It was fun getting to know you and Sammy."

"I'm glad you did too." I was surprised to find I meant that as well.

Arthur opened the door to the stairs and light poured through. He turned towards me, and I saw him clearly for the first time all night, our conversations having been sheltered in darkness. A dark swirl marked his cheek.

"You've got something on your face," I said. "It looks like..." My stomach dropped. It looked like ash, but that wasn't what made me pause. The mark curved into the shape of a rune.

I shook my head, trying to clear it. It couldn't be. The mark didn't mean anything. It *couldn't* mean anything.

Arthur brushed his cheek. "I think that's from the fireworks... and the fire."

The weight in my stomach grew. "There was another fire?"

"Oh, it was just an accident. They got it under control quickly."

Accident or not, Chloe hadn't learnt anything from the last time. I turned towards the old library, almost against my will. The lines of ash seemed to scream a warning, forcing me back.

"I have to go," I blurted out.

Arthur blinked, his eyelashes fluttering.

"Sleep," I said. "I need to sleep."

Arthur's gaze relaxed, releasing me from its intensity. "Yeah, me too." He smiled and touched my arm gently. "Dream well, Ursula."

I forced myself to keep a slow, steady pace on the first few steps, breaking into a run only once I heard the bottom stairwell door close. The pounding of my heartbeat turned to pulsing in my ears, reminding me of the hammers. Always the hammers; I couldn't escape them.

I closed the top stairwell door behind me, leaning against it. It was irrational, right? My fear had no base. Magical accidents happened; the library didn't need to fill me with all this dread... *my sister* didn't need to fill me with all this dread. Arthur would be fine. He had to be.

I let out a slow breath and opened my eyes.

Ben and Chloe weren't back yet, their rooms sitting empty in darkness. My exhales came a little easier at that. My fear may have been irrational, but I still didn't want to face my sister tonight.

A light came from down the corridor – my parents' room. I hesitated, straining to hear if they were home.

A voice floated towards me. "There's something wrong."

I frowned. That was Miss Caraway. What was she doing in Mum's room? I edged my way along the corridor, listening.

Her pacing figure moved back and forth across Mum's doorway. "None of their powers are as strong as they should be. *My* power isn't as strong as it should be."

Nausea rolled in my stomach. I thought I'd got away with hiding my magic, but it sounded like Miss Caraway had noticed. Except... she wasn't just talking about me.

None of their powers are as strong as they should be... How much magic was she expecting us to have?

An image of those dark veins creeping up her arms flashed through my head. My sister had taken some of her power – some of Joe's and Arthur's too – but that wasn't permanent, right? They had regained it once Chloe stopped, surely.

I swallowed. Unless Chloe had done irrevocable damage to them. I shuffled forward, hoping to get a glimpse of Miss Caraway's arms now.

"I know, but..." Mum stopped suddenly, and so did Miss Caraway. Everything went quiet – too quiet – that hollow, stretching sort of silence when someone is listening. I froze with them, willing myself to turn to stone.

"Ursula?" Mum called.

Damn. I hadn't made a sound, had I? But somehow they still knew I was there. I hesitated, then padded my way down the corridor.

The room was lit just from Mum's bedside lamp. It cast a warm glow, creating a cosy atmosphere. Miss Caraway and Mum both smiled as I appeared in the doorway. There was no sign of the worry I'd heard in their voices just before, except for the fact that Miss Caraway's smile didn't reach her eyes.

"Hello, dear," she said.

"Hi..." I said. "You look better."

Miss Caraway raised her eyebrows, and I blushed, but then she nodded. "Thank you. I feel better."

"Where's Dad?" I asked.

Mum frowned. "He had some things to finish up downstairs."

I thought of the zombie-like workers drifting over the lawn, waiting for him to return, and my stomach curdled once more. Would he gather them up again, forcing them to pick up tools and trudge after him until the early hours of the morning?

Miss Caraway studied my face, as if she saw some trace of what I was thinking. "I was just about to head off," she said. "Why don't you walk with me, Ursula?"

I glanced at Mum. They'd been mid-argument just moments before; it hadn't sounded like she'd been about to leave.

Mum chewed on her lip, her eyes flicking between me and Miss Caraway. "Yes, go on, love," she said finally. Then she looked back at Miss Caraway. "We'll finish this tomorrow."

There was an urgency in Mum's voice that made me want to run to her, but Miss Caraway's hand clamped down on my shoulder before I could object. I stared back at Mum, as Miss Caraway guided me away. Mum looked so small, suddenly. Had she always been that thin, or had creating a school carved pieces of her away along with parts of the building?

"How are you finding learning magic, Ursula?" Miss Caraway asked.

I turned back to face her, blinking as I tried to refocus. How was I supposed to answer that? We'd had only half a magic lesson before everything had gone wrong.

"It's okay," I said finally. *It's scary*, was the real answer. Scary and confusing.

The cosy feeling of Mum's room dropped away the further we got down the dark corridor. Shadows seemed to move around us, closing in. They were just like the ash outside the library, creeping closer and closer. Even worse, that hollow, empty feeling was coming with them.

Miss Caraway stopped and turned towards me. "Trust your magic, Ursula. It's stronger than you realise."

I didn't know what to say to that either. I made myself nod, and she frowned slightly. She studied my face for a moment longer, then touched my shoulder gently. "Goodnight, dear."

I forced myself not to shrink from her. "Goodnight, Miss Caraway."

I watched her walk to the stairs. The shadows shifted away from her, almost as if she could bend the light to her will. Or, more likely, they weren't just shadows, and they knew to run from her power.

Could she feel it too? That sense of something bad coming? Sammy had said I saw magic in ways the others didn't, but Miss Caraway had seen something too, I was sure of it.

*   *   *   *

I WOKE TO THE SOUND of voices, then a sharp knock on my door. I dragged myself up, groggily, and opened it. Miss Caraway stood in the corridor, Sammy beside her.

"Good, you're awake. Can Samantha share your room for a while?" Miss Caraway didn't wait for me to answer. She pushed Sammy forward, closing the door behind her. We heard the click of it locking... except I didn't have a lock on my door.

I tried the handle, but it was stuck fast, magic sealing us in here.

Sammy turned to me. Her face blanched pale, and she pulled her robe tightly over her stomach as if she could protect the baby with her grip alone. Lines of blue ink marked her hands; she'd been writing again.

"What's going on? What time is it even?"

"It's just after 4 AM." Sammy swallowed, a shiver working its way up her body. I took her hand, pulling her towards the bed. We sat down cross-legged, facing each other. "There's something wrong with Arthur," she said.

My hand flew to my mouth automatically. Though I'd tried to convince myself I was imagining it, I'd felt something was wrong last night – a growing dread that something was going to happen. I'd seen the rune drawn in ash on Arthur's cheek, but I hadn't done anything. I hadn't even wiped it off for him; I just left him to sort it alone.

"We have to help him."

Sammy shook her head. "We can't. They've closed off the whole floor. Joe's in Ben's room. There are workers stationed at the doors, not to mention the runes your mum laid."

"What happened? What's wrong with Arthur?"

"They say he's sick, but he's not. It's like all of his power is being sucked out of him. He stumbled into my room, and he was so hot – burning – but so, so pale."

My own forehead burned, a restless feverishness coming over me.

"It's the magic," Sammy told me firmly. "It's doing something strange, like it's being drawn out of everything, not just him. I don't know, can't you feel it? The wrongness of it?"

Out of the corners of my eyes, I saw black shadows stretching across the room; fingers of ashy darkness reaching for me. They disappeared when I looked directly at them.

"We need to tell someone," Sammy said. "Your parents?"

I swallowed, nausea building in my throat. I loved my mum, but she had looked so frail last night. Would she help us if we asked? *Could* she even help? And my dad...

"I don't know if we can trust them." My voice cracked on the words. They felt like a betrayal to my family.

Sammy's eyes went wide. "What do you mean?"

Where did I start? Sammy was right, there was something wrong with the magic, but how did I explain that I thought it might be my sister causing it? How could I tell her that Chloe might have hurt Joe – tried to drain his magic for her own use – on purpose?

Sammy squeezed my hand. "Please, Ursula... I need to know."

I closed my eyes. She was my geminus pair. If anyone could help, it would be her. "That rune I saw, when Chloe hurt Joe – I saw it again."

"When?"

"Chloe did a spell with some mice. She was controlling them."

Sammy's hand flew to her mouth. "And you think that's what she was trying to do to Joe?"

"Maybe... I don't know. I think it's what my dad is doing to the workers." I shook my head. My family had always pulled energy from plants and other objects to fuel their magic, but never to this scale. I'd never seen them take power from people before.

Sammy closed her eyes. She shook her head slowly back and forth. She didn't ask for more details, but it was like she was plucking them from the air around us, filling in the blanks of all the things I couldn't bear to say aloud. I knew my dad misused magic, gaining money and status because of it. But this was something even darker.

"I don't think Chloe's doing this on purpose," I said quietly. "I think the magic is influencing her – taking control."

"That's almost worse."

Was my sister really all that bad? If Dad hadn't pushed her to fight Ben, she never would have cared how strong her power was.

Suddenly Sammy opened her eyes and pulled her notebook from inside her robe. She whipped through the pages, nearly tearing them as she flung them back.

"What is it? Did you write something?"

She shook her head. "I don't know, it just sounds familiar." Something caught her eye, and she stilled, reading. I peered over her shoulder, but the words remained gibberish to me. She murmured to herself, then pressed her lips together, thinking. She closed the book, her focus landing back on me.

"If we can't trust your parents, then who can we talk to?" she asked.

I studied her face. Her cheeks were drawn, worry changing her features in the short time she had been here. Miss Caraway had said that none of our powers were as strong as they should be. I hoped that didn't mean Chloe was draining Sammy too.

An even more uncomfortable thought occurred to me then – was Chloe draining *my* power? Would I be able to tell if my sister was leaching off me, taking away my magic?

"Miss Caraway," I said finally. "She'll help us."

"You're sure?"

I nodded. "She knows something is wrong; she can feel it too, I'm sure of it."

"Okay, that's a start. Anyone else?"

"Ben," I said, though my voice didn't come out with as much conviction. Would he listen to me, or would he dismiss me with a pat on the head, calling me "little mouse"?

Sammy didn't answer, perhaps having the same doubts I was.

"What about Joe?" I asked. I didn't know if I trusted Sammy's boyfriend, but he was Chloe's geminus pair. Maybe he could help her. We had to at least try.

Sammy nodded slowly. "I'll talk to him. Your magic is the strongest, so you should go help Arthur."

"But the door's locked."

"Don't worry about that. We can break it."

She said that so certainly, but I glanced at the door, dubious. Breaking through a normal lock was one thing, but I had no idea where to start with Miss Caraway's magical one.

Even if we weren't trapped in here, I had another issue with Sammy's plan – one that I didn't want to voice. I was scared of going downstairs alone.

Sammy studied my face, seeming to read some of what I was thinking. "Can you put your magic into objects?" she asked. "Protection, I mean, like when you kept me from falling down the barn stairs?"

"I don't know. What type of objects?"

She slipped one of the bracelets from her wrist. "This?"

I took the silver band. If I could add the magic to it, it would double my natural protective magic... but that was a very big if. Sammy had already told me she couldn't do this kind of magic – that hers was confined to writing. If we tried to work this spell, it would all be on me.

I glanced at Sammy's notebook. Her magic manifested as writing, but maybe she had written *this*. She mentioned the bracelet like she'd just thought of it, but the steadiness of her gaze told me different. She'd read something important in her notebook just now, I was sure of it. Maybe she wasn't coming up with the idea here, in the moment, but following a plan her unconscious self had left for her.

I reached for her hands, and she gripped mine. "We can try," I said.

Sammy nodded, then closed her eyes. I felt her magic reach out. It twisted around mine, glimpses of it flickering at the edges of my vision. My power was strong, but unpractised. A heavy tiredness pressed me down towards the mattress, and my hands shook with the effort, but I kept going. I had to. I could feel the danger around us building – the "wrongness" as Sammy called it.

I forced magic into the metal, driving power right down into its core.

"That's it," Sammy whispered. "Keep going." She slipped the other bracelets from her wrist, laying them out on the bedspread. I pushed magic into all of them until they hummed with it, shimmering with supernatural strength.

This was stronger than anything I could have done alone. I looked up at Sammy, and she nodded, pleased with what we'd created. Together, we might just protect the others, and if we were lucky, we might even be able to protect Chloe from herself.

Chapter Six

The stack of bracelets clicked against each other as I walked down the stairs. I clasped a hand over the top to silence them. Sammy had only taken one, giving me the rest. They didn't make me feel any safer about going downstairs, but Sammy was right; I had to be the one to help Arthur.

The halls were quiet, and dimly lit, as the sun outside the window inched up above the hills. A worker stood in the stairwell in front of the dormitory door, his face in shadow. I remembered Sammy's words about the whole floor being closed off, guards posted at the doors. I hesitated, then walked towards him.

"I want to see Arthur," I said, making my voice as firm as I could muster.

He blinked, his eyelids fluttering to show he'd heard, but he didn't answer. I almost turned back right then, but Miss Caraway's voice echoed in my mind. *Your magic is stronger than you realise.*

"I'm going to go see him," I told him, almost as firmly. Then: "Okay?" Not at all firm now – weak and pleading – but

I had said the words. That was something.

The man still didn't respond. His eyes shone with a glassy glaze, and he swayed ever so slightly. What was I doing, trying to reason with zombies? I pushed past him, half expecting him to reach out an arm to stop me, but no barrier came down, and no clutching hand held me back. He blinked as I touched him, though, his eyes clearing just a little.

Good. Perhaps he would snap out of it and stop letting my dad siphon power off him. I let the door close behind me and padded down the corridor to Arthur's room. My feet tingled as I crossed the rune line – my own protective magic seeming to scan me and assess whether it would let me pass.

"It's me," I whispered, half to Arthur, half to the line of power defending the entrance. The tingling swelled to humming, vibrating up my legs. I turned Arthur's doorhandle, quietly pleased that the magic recognised me.

Arthur's room was warm – too warm. A wave of heat hit me as soon as I crossed the threshold, coming from Arthur himself.

"Arthur?" I whispered.

He didn't stir. Bright spots of red bloomed in his cheeks, but the rest of his face was unnaturally pale. I could feel a rush of energy flowing away from him, just like it had in the classroom when he touched Joe.

I pulled the strongest bracelet from my wrist, slipping it over his hand. "This will protect you," I said.

Power thrummed from it. I felt it swelling out from the jewellery, wrapping Arthur in a thin layer of protective magic. But he didn't wake. His hand flopped back onto the bedspread as soon as I let go of it, the bracelet dangling.

Energy leached out of him. If I followed the thread of it, I was sure I'd find my selfish sister at the other end, or worse, my father, who was well old enough to know better.

"You have to fight back, Arthur," I told him.

No runes marked his flushed cheeks now, but I rubbed them with the heel of my palm anyway, as if I could ward off the invisible symbol. "Come on, Arthur! Wake up."

Something tingled against my skin, and I gasped, jerking my hand away. Black streaks of ash lined my palm, coming from his cheek. I scrubbed at his face. "Wake up!" I told him fiercely. "You have to wake up!"

The bracelet was useless. All the magic we had poured into it, yet it did nothing. Anger built inside me, and with it heat. Why had Sammy's stupid book told her to waste that magic when it didn't even work? I hated this!

I reached for his hand, squeezing it. I wanted to say something reassuring, promise him I would figure out how to stop the magic draining from him, but there was only one way to make this stop for good, and that was at the source.

"I'm going to fix this," I told him. "I promise."

He didn't open his eyes, and if anything, he just got paler. I gave his hand one last fierce squeeze, then turned and ran from the room.

The worker outside the door glared at me as I passed him, finally showing some independent thought. I didn't wait for him to yell at me – to ask what I was doing on the closed floor. I just kept running, praying he wouldn't leave his post to chase me.

I found Joe and Chloe down at the bottom of the garden, where they practised each morning. Joe had covered every inch of one of the walls in vines. It was impressive really, though the strength of his magic scared me. He reminded me of Chloe, in a way. Unpredictable – nice one minute, playing with dangerous spells the next.

"I need to talk to you," I told Chloe.

She glanced my way, then back at Joe's ivy wall. "We're

busy, squirt. Why don't you go bug Sammy?"

I wavered, half ready to turn away. A part of me wanted to give up – to find Ben or Miss Caraway and tell them how dangerous Chloe's magic had become. But I couldn't do that to her. She was my sister; I had to at least give her a chance to get it back under control first.

"Please, Chloe. It's important!"

She let out an exaggerated breath. Her hair was loose, falling in messy waves around her shoulders. It made her look younger; it made her look more like me.

She stared at me for a moment, then glanced up at the vine wall. "How fast can you make them grow?" she asked Joe.

Joe grinned. "Fast as you want, baby." He waggled his eyebrows.

"Chloe, please!" I stomped my foot like a little kid. "This is serious! Arthur's really sick."

"Okay, okay!" Chloe grabbed my shoulders, pushing me towards the wall. "Stand here, and we can talk."

I shook my head. "Your magic is out of control. I know you've been—"

"Hold your hands out to the sides." Chloe raised my arms, moving me like a mannequin. She stepped back, beckoning to Joe. He looked from her to me, a puzzled grin on his face.

"What are you doing?" Panic rose in my chest. I dropped my arms, moving to step away from the wall, but she held up a hand for me to stay.

"I want to try something."

"But—"

"You say my magic is out of control, well this is how I learn to manage it." She fixed me with a stare. Her lips curled into a smile, but there was a challenge in her expression.

Was this an ultimatum? Would she leave Arthur alone if I helped her with this spell? Reluctantly, I stepped back against the wall, lifting my hands to the sides. Joe grinned. Apparently, he didn't even need to know what Chloe's idea was to think it was a good one.

"Can you make them grow?" she asked him.

My heart hammered. "Wait, what are you going to do?"

A slithering sound came from behind me. Chloe moved towards me, raising her hand. Vines shot out from the wall, wrapping around my arms. I screamed, jerking away, but they held me fast. "Chloe!"

The vines circled my limbs, tighter and tighter. Suddenly, they lurched up, taking me with them. I let out a shriek.

"It's working!" Chloe burst into giggles.

Joe's mouth fell open. "Woah," he said. "I never thought of doing that!"

I drew breath, ready to shriek again, but the vines didn't drop me. They held me securely in the air.

"See?" Chloe called. "I can control my magic when I want to. Do you want to go higher?"

The little gleam in her eye told me she was going to send me higher anyway. Joe closed his eyes, pushing the vines to grow faster. Chloe whispered something, directing them up, and I shot further into the air. I shrieked again.

"Chloe!" Ben's voice rang out from across the garden. I turned my head to see him and Sammy racing towards us.

"What are you doing!?" Ben grabbed Chloe's arm and the vines loosened. I gasped, throwing out a lasso of magic to anchor myself.

Chloe shook him off. "Relax. Ursula's having fun."

Fun was an exaggeration, but I was okay, and the more energy Chloe focused on me, the less she would have available to drain Arthur. Ben peered up at me, and I raised my hand, giving him a thumbs up.

"You sure you're okay, Urse?" His narrowed eyes traced

the lines of the vines supporting me. I nodded, though the movement made the vines shake.

"Sammy, you'll love this," Joe said. "You should try it after you have the baby."

She frowned. "I don't know. Are you sure Ursula's safe?" She stared up at me, chewing on her lip.

I found I couldn't quite meet her gaze. I should have updated her after I left Arthur's room. This wasn't what Sammy and I had agreed, but I still wanted a chance to talk to Chloe, to persuade her to reign her magic in. Ben stared at Chloe, his gaze hard. Had Sammy already told him everything? Something about the way he was looking at Chloe made me feel cold.

My sister's face darkened at Sammy's criticism. "Of course it's safe." She twisted her hand slightly, and the vines tightened around my raised thumb.

I gasped. "Don't, that hurts." Suddenly, the vines were growing faster, wrapping around me.

"Hey, stop that!" Ben shoved Joe's shoulder, but Joe shook his head. "I'm not doing anything. They shouldn't be growing anymore."

I looked back at Chloe, and her hand twisted again. "I can make them grow too," she said. Her breath came out in a puff. She curled her fingers, excitement lighting her face.

"Please, Chloe!" I gasped.

Something flashed in the air in front of her – a spark of light. Then the vines covered my face. One of them found its way into my mouth. I spat it out, a strange taste crossing my tongue. I tried to pull away, but foliage bound my hands. I squirmed, breaking the stalks, and I lost hold of my own magic. Suddenly, the only thing supporting me was the thin strings of leaves. Fleshy pops sounded as they snapped, straining under my weight. I opened my mouth to scream but vines poured into it.

"Oh my god, stop!" Ben scrambled up the wall towards me. The vines wrapped around him too. He grabbed my ankle and immediately vines bound around us like handcuffs. "God dammit, make it stop!"

"I don't know how!" Joe yelled. He joined Ben at the wall, ripping vines free. But they were growing faster and faster. I could barely breathe through the leaves wrapping around my face.

That strange taste filled my mouth again. Ash – that's what it was. The vines were withering, energy leaching out of them even as they grew.

Suddenly, Chloe shrieked, then there was a thud. The vines dropped away, and I fell. Joe and Ben tumbled backwards too, all of us landing in a heap.

Chloe lay on the ground, her face indignant. Sammy stood over her, her hands splayed out, as if she'd just shoved Chloe. It took me a moment to realise that's exactly what had happened.

Ben pulled me upright. "Are you okay, Ursula?"

The others crowded around me, and Sammy's hand slipped into mine, squeezing it.

"Yeah..." I started to say, but my voice sounded very far away. The vines – Joe and Chloe's spells – had dissolved, as had the magic I had been using to keep myself safe. Sammy's bracelets had fallen from my wrist, scattering in the grass. I reached for one, but my limbs felt heavy, almost as if I wasn't in control of them.

"You didn't have to push me!" Chloe got up, dusting herself off. "I would have figured out how to stop it." She glared at Sammy.

Sammy shook her head. "Oh yeah? When exactly? Ursula could have been hurt! And after what you did to Arthur—"

"What do you care? She's my sister, not yours."

Sparks appeared on the surface of my skin. They drifted out, floating away from me. I reached for one, but the magic slipped out of my grasp, no longer mine. I felt weak, suddenly. Dizzy. More sparks floated away, coming from my arms. They left black spots in their place. Black, ashy spots like my skin was burning.

"Are you okay, Ursula?" Sammy reached out to touch my arm.

I jerked away. "Don't!"

Her hand connected with one of the black spots. She gasped, flinching back. Then she shuddered, going rigid.

"Sammy!" Joe caught her as she fell. Her eyes went wide, her skin paling instantly.

"The ash!" I hissed. "She touched the ash!" But no one was listening to me. Chloe screamed something at Ben, her words incomprehensible.

"Help her, Ursula!" Joe yelled.

I scrambled to grab the bracelets, pushing as many as I could find onto her wrist. They felt like cheap, useless trinkets in my hands, the magic not strong enough to help anyone. Sammy's eyes rolled, trying to find mine. I felt Joe start something, some spell growing around her, and I added my power to his. Sammy's fingers inched out, reaching for my hand. I gripped hers, pouring all of my protective magic into her palm.

Sammy gasped and so did Joe. I shuddered, as I felt an icy rush of air inside her, just like I had with Arthur and Miss Caraway. But it was different this time – grittier and bitter tasting. Filled with ash.

And something else was different. This time it wasn't trying to pull me in.

"No," I whispered.

Sparks flowed from my skin, my magic drifting away. But the icy rush came from inside me. *I* was draining Sammy's magic, siphoning it through the geminus connection.

I clasped my free hand to my stomach, as if I could dam up the flow. Sparks appeared around my fist. I pulled my shirt up, revealing an ashy burn mark around my belly button. "No, no, no!"

The others stared at me, unable to see the magic the way I could; unable to see the damage I was causing. "Help!" I screamed, putting every ounce of magic I had left into the call. "Make it stop!"

The words echoed out, drawing every magical member of staff to us. They came running, bursting out of the doors of the house. Mum and Dad ran towards us. My mother took in the scene, shaking her head slowly. "What have you done?" she whispered.

Chloe opened her mouth to speak, but Mum didn't wait for an answer, turning to Sammy instead. She hovered over her as if afraid to touch her.

"It wasn't—" I started to say, but my father pushed me away.

"That's enough, Ursula!" he said. "Let go of her."

"It's coming from me!" I said, but no one was listening. My father gathered Sammy up in his arms, pushing both me and Joe away. In a blink, they were gone again, all of the adults disappearing, taking Sammy with them.

Chapter Seven

Sammy wasn't in her room. Joe grabbed her pillow, as if he thought he might find her hiding under it, then he hurled it across the room. "Where did they take her?" he screamed at me.

I shrank back, and Ben automatically stepped in front of me, hands raised protectively. Chloe put her arm around me, but I cringed at the touch.

"I don't know," I whispered. "They shouldn't have taken her away." They should have let me help her.

"There's a medical bay – there *will be* a medical bay," Ben said. "It's not finished but they might have taken her there."

"They'll be worried about the baby," Chloe added.

"Where is it?" Joe lurched towards the door, but Ben pressed a hand to his chest, stopping him.

"I'll go. They'll tell me more than they will you. I'll let you know anything I find out, okay?"

"But I need..." Joe wavered for a moment, the end of the sentence disappearing with his resolve. He sank down on the bed, clutching his head in his hands. "Please, just find out if she's okay? They both have to be okay."

Ben tilted his head towards the door, gesturing for me and Chloe to join him. Chloe's arm fell from my shoulders as we walked into the corridor. Ben shut the door, and he and Chloe rounded on each other.

"What the hell were you thinking?" he yelled at her. His eyes blazed, and he flung out a hand emphatically.

"Me? I wouldn't have had to if you hadn't—"

"What's going on?" Arthur appeared in his doorway.

I gasped. "You're awake!" I grabbed him, pulling him into a hug. He squeezed me back for a moment, then I pulled away to look at him. Dark hollows marked his cheeks, but he was up and standing unaided, so that had to be a good sign. "What happened?" I asked. "How are you better?"

He shook his head. "I don't know. I just woke up a few minutes ago."

A few minutes ago, as in at the same time Sammy collapsed? That couldn't be a coincidence.

"What's going on?" Arthur asked. "Why are you yelling?" He looked to Ben and Chloe. They just stared at each other, fury clouding their faces.

"Sammy's hurt," I said. "Like you and Miss Caraway."

Arthur's eyes flicked towards Chloe, but I shook my head. "It was my fault. Sammy touched my arm, and..." I gulped, tears shutting the words down.

Ben turned away from Chloe, blinking. "What? This wasn't your doing, little mouse."

I just shook my head. The sensation of the icy air rushing through me still chilled my core. I had drained Sammy's magic... Maybe it had been me all along.

"Ben's right," Chloe said, her voice strained. "It wasn't your fault, Urse." A silent conversation seemed to pass between my brother and sister, none of it accessible to me. Arthur looked between us, his brow creasing.

"I told Joe I'd find out what's happening," Ben said finally.

Chloe gave a sharp nod. "I'll go with you. We need to talk." She looked back at me, and her face softened. "It will be okay. I promise."

The fact that Chloe was trying to reassure me unnerved me more than anything else. Ben took hold of Chloe's arm, not altogether gently, and they set off down the corridor.

Arthur turned to me once they were gone. "What on earth is going on?"

I shook my head and took his hand, pulling him down the corridor away from Joe's door. I stopped at the rune line. "It's a long story."

He gave a short laugh. "I've got nothing but time."

Something was different from this morning. He seemed stronger somehow, more life in him. Whatever had been draining his magic was well and truly gone now. The observation almost pleased me, until I remembered the exact opposite was true for Sammy.

"It's my fault," I whispered. "I didn't mean to, but I hurt her."

Arthur's face went serious. He touched my arm, gently. I flinched, but nothing happened. Whatever had infected my skin earlier didn't seem to affect him.

"Tell me what happened," he said.

"Joe and Chloe were playing this game – they made these vines grow and they lifted me up in the air." My stomach lurched at the memory of the sensation. It had been almost fun at the time, but now it made me want to throw up. "Then Chloe got pissed off, and... I don't know. The vines started strangling me."

"She tried to hurt you?"

I shook my head. "No, I don't think so... I don't know."

"But she hurt Sammy?"

"No." That part I was sure of. "*I* hurt Sammy. After the vines dropped away, my magic started floating away from me. It left these dark patches on my skin, and Sammy touched one of them." I risked a glance at my arm. The ashy spots were still there, singed into my limbs. I shuddered and looked away.

Arthur shook his head. "That doesn't... Your magic can't just float away, can it?"

I shrugged. That wasn't the important part. "I don't know. But it was the same as with you and Miss Caraway. I could feel this icy rush of air, but this time it was coming from inside me. I couldn't stop it."

Arthur stared at me. He clearly didn't understand anything I was saying, but then a flash of recognition crossed his face. "I remember that feeling," he said quietly. He touched his stomach. "But it wasn't air."

"It was filled with ash," I said. "I could taste it on the vines, and—"

"No, Ursula, it wasn't air. It was magic. I remember now. It was draining my magic."

"What was?" I desperately hoped he wouldn't say Chloe, but deep down, I knew it had to be her. I'd seen the flash of light just before everything went wrong. It must have been a rune. She'd been trying to control me, trying to steal my magic, and Sammy had got caught in the middle of it.

"I..." Arthur hesitated; his eyes flicked back and forth as if the memory was just out of reach. "I don't know how to explain it," he said finally. "But it was someone else's magic draining mine. I could feel it."

"They should have let me help Sammy. I think I'm the only one who can." I'd never said anything so arrogant in my whole life, but suddenly, I was absolutely sure it was true. If my parents didn't let me try to stop the magic draining Sammy, then there was no chance anyone else could.

Arthur studied my face. "You really think you can help her?"

"I'm sure of it. But there's no way they'll let me. I'd have to get to her before anyone notices, but there's no way I can reach the sick bay before Ben and Chloe do."

"I think I can help with that."

"Yeah?"

He nodded. "Do you trust me?"

"I…"

He grabbed my hand, not waiting for an answer.

"What are you—?" I didn't get a chance to finish the question. Arthur closed his eyes, and it was like the lights had gone out with it. Darkness slammed down on us, knocking the air from my chest. I tried to breathe in, but my chest shuddered instead. It wasn't darkness; it was nothingness. We were in a vacuum, and I was going to suffocate.

The lights came back on, slamming into me just like the darkness had. I gasped, an awful wheezing sound coming out of my chest. Arthur wrapped his arms around me before I collapsed.

"I know," he said. "It's awful the first time. It gets better."

I nodded, though I couldn't imagine ever letting him do that again. He lowered me to the floor, and I sat, sucking air back into my lungs.

Voices came from the next room – my mother's and Miss Caraway's, and maybe the entire staff who weren't zombies. I couldn't make out the words, but their voices rose and fell in sharp peaks, anger and worry tumbling out as they argued about how to help Sammy. I pressed a finger to my lips, shushing Arthur, though I was the one making all the noise.

We were in a bedroom – or at least a space for students to convalesce. I could see my mother's touch in here. The bedspread was green, a print of cool, tropical leaves covering it, matching the soothing pale green walls. There were real plants in here, too, but like all of my mother's attempts, they were wilting, soon to succumb to plant death.

Arthur's hand found mine, and he pulled me up. "Come on. We can get to Sammy and heal her before they even decide who they're mad at."

I nodded, though my heart thumped in my ears. With every beat it seemed to say: *"My fault. My fault."*

We crept down the corridor, and Arthur pushed open a door at the far end. "She's in there," he whispered. He stepped back as if to let me go in alone, but I tightened my grip on his hand.

"Come with me," I whispered.

He hesitated, but I could feel it. He *had* to come with me. He had to help me.

"Okay," he said, glancing back down the corridor. "But quickly."

We slipped into the room. Sammy lay on a bed, covered with an identical green-leaf bedspread. More ailing plants surrounded her, along with quickly sketched symbols on the walls, floor and headboard. They created a rough rune line around her, but it wouldn't be enough – she needed much stronger protection magic.

I felt it as I got closer, the rush of icy air running through Sammy.

"I don't understand." I touched my stomach, but the magic no longer ran through me. It veered around, as if afraid to touch me. I tasted ash in my mouth, though, and felt the sandpapery burn of grit and dirt flying past me.

"You say it's all magic?" I asked.

Arthur nodded. "Her magic, being stripped away, just like mine was."

And mine, floating away in sparks. "It really wasn't me," I said, half to myself.

"Of course not." Arthur shook his head. "I don't know what you saw, but you didn't cause this."

"Except, I did. Or, not me, but..." Someone had used me. *Chloe* had used me, controlling me with that sparking rune.

She hadn't taken much of *my* magic, but she'd sent that rush of air running through me, those sparks flying out from me, in order to steal Sammy's. Did it latch on to her just because she had touched me? Or had my magic targeted her because she was my geminus pair?

Sammy groaned, and we both turned back towards the bed. She didn't stop, the sound turning into a long moan. Arthur shook his head. "That didn't... that's not from the magic."

"No?"

Sammy's whole body seemed to contract, curling her forward. My heart plummeted. "She's going to have the baby... but it's too early, isn't it?"

"Can you still help her?" Arthur asked.

I nodded. "Yes," I said, my voice coming out more confident than I really felt. I could make sure her baby survived; I would have to. Sammy had said she wasn't sure if her baby would have magic, but suddenly I could feel her – the tiny child and her power surging around her.

"We have to wrap her in protection," I told Arthur. "Both of them – her and the baby."

He nodded, though I could tell he didn't understand what I meant. Sammy moaned again, her unconscious state not deep enough to protect her from the pain. I took hold of one of her hands, clutching tight to Arthur's with the other. He did the same, taking Sammy's free hand and closing the link between the three of us. I took a thread of magic, visualising it as bright red in my mind, and drew a line from the top of Sammy's head. I traced all the way around her shoulders, down her arm and over the outline of each of her fingers. Arthur followed me, winding his magic over mine, until the two threads merged together into a hard, protective barrier.

Sammy's eyes opened, a scream escaping her lips. I gripped her hand as tight as I could. "Keep going," I hissed at Arthur.

Sammy's body contorted, pulling away from us, but I couldn't break the thread. We traced down her side, around one leg and then the other, and then back up to her other arm.

Sweat beaded on my forehead, and my palms felt slick against Sammy's and Arthur's. Sammy's scream petered out, and a third strand of magic appeared – Sammy's, stretching out to join ours. She didn't speak, the strains on her body and mind too great, but her eyes met mine, and there was life in them again.

A small part of my mind was conscious that the raised voices from the other room had dropped to a normal volume, that they had finished arguing, and were instead working together to come up with a plan. Soon, they would walk down the corridor to implement whatever they had come up with. A bigger part of my mind was focused on the heaviness creeping up my body like a black sticky tar.

"You can do this, Ursula," Arthur dug his nails into my palm, and the pain woke me a little. "I know you're tired but keep going!"

Sammy's hand tightened on mine too. I nodded, my head lolling with the movement. Keep going... I could do that. Sammy was about to give birth, and yet they were encouraging *me*.

It struck me as unfair that Arthur was still so alert, even after being so sick. Why could he manage to do magic without it exhausting him the way it did me? Perhaps he had had more practice, or perhaps he was like Ben and Chloe, pulling energy from everything around them. No wonder Mum's plants always died. No wonder the workers all looked like zombies.

My eyes snapped open. "They look like zombies," I repeated aloud.

Chloe had never been able to beat Ben, but suddenly her magic was so much stronger. It wasn't the geminus connection increasing her power, and my dad wasn't controlling the workers. It was all her.

And that's how we could stop her – cut her power off at the source. We had to get everyone out.

I turned to Arthur to tell him, but the heavy tar creeping up my body had reached my head. "They have to go," was all I managed, and then I felt Arthur catch me, as the tar took me over.

Chapter Eight

Time blurred. I felt myself moving, but it was as if I was being carried. Then I was lying in a bed, everything hazy. I woke at one point and my sister was holding my hand.

"Fight back, little mouse," she whispered.

Magic pulled at me, or rather, something pulled my magic away. It stretched out from me like shining cobwebs, sparking every so often as pieces broke off.

I gathered them back to me, reaching out with both my mind and my arms to clutch at handfuls. I caught hold of them, but something felt wrong. The magic wasn't all mine.

My sister squeezed my hand, and energy seeped off her. Threads of her magic wrapped around me, burrowing their way into my skin. I tried to pull away, but she squeezed tighter, tugging at me. I looked up, and her eyes were wide, but blank, glowing almost. I didn't recognise anything behind them.

* * * *

VOLATILE

I JOLTED AWAKE. THE sick bay room was light, the curtains half closed, and a bright column of evening sunlight streamed through the gap. I was alone, the chair where my sister had sat now empty.

I scrambled out of the bed. I had to stop her.

My muscles ached as if I had been running, and the hair at the back of my neck stuck to my skin in damp, sweaty mats. The green, leafy bedspread lay bunched at my feet, like I'd spent the night thrashing, fighting against whatever Chloe had tried to do to me.

No more. I forced my feet into steps, into a run.

I raced down the hallway, trailing along the twists and turns of corridors. An eerie quiet greeted me at every step. Runes ran across the floor, line after line of them. That's where the silence came from. The symbols had thrown the building into a stasis. They kept everything in place, stopped the magic from moving between rooms. Even I could barely cross them, my whole body buzzing every time I stepped over one.

Finally, I found some of the workers. None of them spoke to me – none even made eye contact. They all sat or stood in a stretch of corridor, staring hauntingly into nothing. They weren't just zombies. Bones jutted out under their skin, muscles withering away along with their energy, and burnt patches marked their limbs. They'd been drained of everything but the reflex to inhale and exhale.

I approached one of them. He sat in a chair, and our faces were almost level, yet his eyes still didn't meet mine. "Run," I said. "Get out of here."

He didn't even sway.

"Go!" I yelled. "All of you, leave. Now!"

Still nothing. I grabbed his arm, pouring power into the gesture.

The man finally stood, not running, but slowly shambling forward. He stopped as soon as he got to a rune line, his whole body seeming to shut down.

I shoved him, forcing him over the line. "Keep going," I told him. "All of you, keep going."

But he only took a few more steps. Anger coiled in my stomach. "Go!" I screamed. "Go, you useless zombies!" I shoved him again, harder and harder. "Go!"

Power erupted from me.

He stumbled forward, gasping. "What the...?" He turned towards me, his eyes clearing but horror building in them. Magic flared on my skin, propelling the worker away.

He was right to be horrified. All the magic I'd ever kept hidden was rising to the surface. Around us, the other workers woke from their daze.

"Run," I said, my voice low and resonant. "Go now!"

They scrambled over each other in their escape, nothing uniform in their movements now. I let myself breathe as they did, but my power didn't retreat back inside me. It stayed humming on my skin. My whole body changed with it, my spine straightening and chest opening out. I felt elated... I felt powerful... But behind that was something darker I couldn't quite identify. I had cut off Chloe's source of energy by freeing the workers, yet a sense of impending danger still ran through the walls of the school. I felt the magic bubbling up, ready to swallow all of us.

I turned, running in the opposite direction to the workers, towards my sister. All around the school, I felt other workers leaving, the very building seeming to shift with their exit. A pungent smell of rotting plants came from the main foyer, but so did light. I ran towards it, eager for any signs of life.

"It's out of control!"

I slowed as I heard my father's voice. He sounded agitated,

and I remembered the rise and fall of words as my parents had argued about how to help Sammy.

Sammy. Where was she? *How* was she?

Heavy footsteps strode across the foyer towards me, and I shrank back against the wall, slipping behind a wilted Ficus plant.

"We're going to have to strip her of her powers," my father said.

My stomach clenched. I stepped back automatically, clutching my newly unlocked magic to me. It spilled out around me, no forcing it back inside now.

Stripping away my magic would be like carving away pieces of my skin. How could they do that to Chloe? It didn't matter what she'd done, that was too cruel a punishment. Something niggled at the back of my mind, and I shook my head, trying to force the memories to solidify.

"Fight back, little mouse."

Why had Chloe said that if she was the one causing all of this?

"Surely that has to be a last resort," my mother said. "What about the boy?"

The boy... did she mean Joe? Would the geminus bond mean his powers would be stripped too?

"I'm afraid we're already at the last resort stage."

I peeked out from behind the Ficus. Miss Caraway stood with my parents, still in that ridiculous floral dress. She wore a coat over it, and a duffle bag lay at her feet. Was she leaving? I wasn't sure if that made me feel relieved or more frightened.

"The boy is an unfortunate casualty," she said, "but we don't have a choice."

"She's right, Candace. And if it doesn't work, then..." Dad trailed off.

I swallowed. Whatever he was going to say, it couldn't be

worse than what I was imagining. My mother looked from Dad to Miss Caraway.

Mum looked even smaller than she had a few days ago. She made a sound that was almost a sob. "This could kill them both."

I gasped, slapping a hand over my mouth. Mum looked up, alarm firing in her eyes, and Dad turned slowly towards me. "Chloe?" he called. His voice boomed with a power that didn't quite reach me. I turned and fled.

"Ursula..."

I heard Mum race after me, but I didn't look back.

"Ursula, wait!" she called again, but her footsteps came to a halt, like always. She had never fought for us. She had always just given up.

My own feet thudded against the stairs, making a dull, echoing sound in the silence. I didn't stop running until I reached our floor, even though no one was chasing me. What did it mean that they hadn't – why wouldn't they follow? Were they that afraid of Chloe? Had her power become so strong that even my parents cowered away, hiding behind rune lines?

I passed my sister's room, glancing in. She wasn't in there, her empty bed unmade. The mouse cage sat in the middle of it, open and abandoned, no sign of the rodents she had been trying to control.

I reached Ben's room and threw open the door. "Ben..." I couldn't get anything else out. I leaned forward, out of breath.

He looked up at me, startled. "Little mouse... you're awake." His voice didn't hold the same laughter it usually did when he used my nickname. His eyebrows drew together in a frown. He stood, moving towards me, and placing his hand gently on my shoulder.

I panted, still trying to get my breath back. "It's Chloe," I choked out.

Ben sat down on the bed, drawing me to sit next to him. "What's she done now?"

"They're going to strip her powers." I shivered, all the heat from running rushing out of me. "She's the one behind it. She's been stealing energy."

Ben's frown deepened. "What do you mean?"

I shook my head. "Can't you feel it? She's draining the whole building. It's like you do with the plants, but bigger. The workers look dead on their feet. But it's okay, I sent them away. She won't be able to steal their power anymore."

"You did what?" His voice had an edge to it, and his hand suddenly felt heavy on my shoulder.

"I sent the workers away – cut her off at the source. But you're missing the point. I heard Mum and Dad talking about stripping Chloe's magic. They said they have no other options."

Ben's grip on me tightened. "They can't do that!" His fingers bit into my skin and I squirmed away. He released me but didn't apologise. He stood, moving away from the bed.

"I know," I said. "It could kill her, and Joe too! I know she's done some bad things, but—"

"It doesn't matter what she's done!" Ben spun around as if he would strike me.

I shrank back against the bed. "That's what I'm saying," I said quietly. He didn't seem to hear me.

"I have to find her." His hand massaged his bottom lip, hard enough to tear it

Something in my stomach unclenched when he said that. I wanted to help my sister... or maybe I didn't, maybe I just wanted to stop her. Either way, I didn't know what to do. I wanted Ben to do it. I wanted him to take over.

A noise outside the room caught my attention. Ben's head whipped up, staring out into the corridor. "Chloe...?"

Footsteps thudded against the floorboards, just as mine had done only moments before. Ben hesitated for only a second, and then he was off down the corridor, chasing after her.

I stood, taking a few steps after them. "Wait," I yelled. But they were both gone.

Chapter Nine

I sat on the bed for a long time, waiting for them to come back. The unnatural silence of the building settled over me, and I shivered. Eventually, I couldn't stand it any longer, and I made my way back to my own room.

Warm cosiness greeted me. I reached out, and echoes of my own magic reached back, welcoming me home. A humming came from the floor. No, not from the floor – from Arthur's room below mine. He was in there, his magic stretching out to meet mine.

I'm coming, I whispered back to it.

My mother had placed some kind of ward on the door to the dormitory floor. I felt it trying to push against me, to turn me away. If my magic had been weaker – if I hadn't unlocked all of it just an hour earlier – it would have worked.

More rune lines crossed the floor inside – layers and layers of them, drawn over multiple times. Voices came from Arthur's room, but I didn't immediately turn that way. Fingers of ash spread out from the library, almost as if they were reaching for the runes. The lines bent around them, the symbols

261

curving to fit. Had they been drawn that way or had the runes moved to avoid the ash? I stepped towards them, reaching out to feel the hum of both sets of magic competing against each other.

"We have to get out of here," Joe hissed.

I froze. I stepped backwards and the floorboards creaked under my foot. Silence stretched, then feet pounded towards Arthur's door.

"Get the hell away from us!" Joe flew through the doorway, his hand raised in front of him, fingers splayed as if he would hurl magic at me.

I took another step back, raising my own hands in defence. Arthur appeared beside Joe, grabbing his arm. "It's Ursula. It's just Ursula."

Joe dropped his hands, relief and horror crossing his face. Arthur stepped towards me, pulling me into a hug. "You're awake."

I sank into the embrace, relief filling me. He pulled back to look at me. "And your magic is different."

I dropped my gaze, ashamed to admit how much I had been hiding until now. "Is Sammy okay?" I asked.

Arthur squeezed my arms gently, then released me. "Yeah, she's in here."

Joe stood back to let us into the room, and Arthur drew me inside, shutting the door behind us. Sammy sat propped up in the bed, the tiniest baby I'd ever seen on her chest. A weight lifted inside me at seeing them both healthy.

Joe's face softened as he looked at them. "Ursula, meet Calliope – Callie."

Sammy held out her hand, beckoning me over. "She's here because of you. You saved us."

I moved forward but didn't dare touch the child. "She's beautiful."

Magic swirled around her – Sammy's, Joe's, Arthur's, mine and her own. The protection around her was strong; Chloe wouldn't be able to touch her. But still, she was so tiny. This wasn't a safe place for her.

I looked around at my classmates. Dark shadows marked their eyes, and heavy weariness shrouded all of them. "You're trying to leave," I said.

Sammy hesitated and her eyes darted away from mine as if she was afraid of my reaction.

I frowned. "I think it's a good idea."

Sammy and Joe looked at each other, then he moved closer to the bed and put his arm around her. There was a greyish tinge to his skin that wasn't there before. "We want out," he told me. "We all do. The magic is getting to us."

Something didn't seem right about Joe's words. The way he said *we*. If they were all in agreement, why didn't they just go? And why had they been afraid to tell me? Suddenly, it dawned on me. The ward on the door... the rune lines... My parents had trapped them in here.

I had got those workers across the lines, but it would be different with my classmates. I could already feel there was strong magic around them, keeping them here. Magic I wasn't sure I knew how to break.

I didn't know if I could help them – I didn't know if I could get them out – but I owed them the truth. It was the least I could do after the destruction my family had caused.

"I got the builders out," I told them, "but I don't know if I can do the same for you. I promise I will try."

I saw it register on Joe and Sammy's faces then – they could see the change in my magic, just as Arthur had. Joe shifted, perhaps uncomfortable with my strength.

"I can't come with you," I said, ignoring his unease. "My parents want to strip Chloe's magic, but it might hurt Joe too.

It could even kill both of you."

My words seemed to hit Sammy like a physical blow. "No..." she whispered. She shook her head, fiercely. "That can't... they can't do that!"

Joe's arm tightened around her shoulder. "Shouldn't I have been able to tell if Chloe's causing this?" he asked. "Our magic is supposed to be twinned."

And she's my sister, I nearly said. Instead, I shook my head. "I think she's got really good at hiding things."

Should *I* have known? Should I have been able to tell what she was up to? But I'd never known what Chloe was doing, even before the geminus magic.

Maybe that was the problem.

Joe and Sammy looked at each other, then down at Calliope, another silent conversation happening between them. Joe squeezed Sammy's hand, and she nodded.

"We're staying," she said. "We can't let them strip Chloe's power. Not if it could hurt her and Joe."

Joe nodded. "Use your magic to fix this; don't waste it on getting us out."

Arthur moved closer to me, offering me his strength too. They all stared at me, determination and belief in their eyes. I felt their trust in me – their faith in my newly unlocked magic. There was just one problem with that. I had no clue how to fix this.

When had it all gone so wrong? Had Chloe always been dangerous, and I just hadn't seen it? Had the geminus magic damaged her in some way, warping her powers? No. It had started before that, I was sure of it. It had started...

Suddenly, it hit me. I opened the door and strode back out into the corridor.

Arthur followed after me. "Where are you going? This is the only safe place."

"Nowhere is safe until we fix this."

A flash of Chloe sitting beside the bed holding my hand came into my mind. *Fight back, little mouse.* There was more to this, I was sure of it.

I walked towards the library door. Joe and Arthur followed me, and then a moment later Sammy did too, clutching Callie to her chest with one hand and leaning heavily against the wall with the other.

I sent a wave of healing magic out to her, trying to ease some of her pain. I felt Joe do the same, and Sammy stood up straighter, her body responding and gaining strength.

"You should stay in bed," I told her. She shook her head, though she tightened her grip on Callie.

I traced the lines of ash with my eyes. This was where it had started, where Chloe and Ben first lost control of their magic, where Mum and Dad first realised we were all part of geminus pairs. Would I have eventually lost control if Sammy and I hadn't found each other? But then why hadn't Chloe and Joe's magic stabilised now they were together?

I turned to Joe. "What did you mean when you said the magic started to get to you?

His hand went to his wrist, one of Sammy's silver bracelets circling it. "I don't know. It's like Miss Caraway said about the geminus magic – that it can become dangerous. I could feel it exploding inside me, making me change. I couldn't control it."

"But the geminus pair is supposed to stop that."

Joe shook his head. "I think maybe Miss Caraway got it wrong. My magic only gets calmer when I'm around you three. It's way worse around Chloe and Ben."

That seemed to fit with what I was thinking. Chloe wasn't in control of her magic anymore, so how could she possibly help calm someone else's?

There was only one thing for it. I took another step towards the library.

"Where are you going?" Sammy called after me.

I didn't answer. Numb emptiness hit me as I crossed the rune line, the magical vacuum pulling me forward. Sammy gasped, and Joe swore. They felt it too, even without crossing the line.

"What is that?" Arthur asked.

"Ursula, come back. Don't go down there!" Sammy's voice held a note of panic, but I kept walking.

"This is where it started. Where Chloe first lost control of her magic." I opened the door.

Books lay strewn across the floor, and a dull, muffled blanket of dust, ash and silence fell over me. Suddenly, I understood why it felt like a vacuum. Chloe had sucked every ounce of energy out of the books – out of the room itself. No wonder she had started a fire. She had overloaded herself.

Arthur and Joe crept into the room after me, peering around at the destruction. Sammy stayed in the doorway; her hands clasped protectively over Callie.

"Who's been in here?" I turned back to the others.

Arthur shook his head. "None of us. I didn't know there was anything down here."

I looked to Sammy and Joe, and they shook their heads too.

"No, the closest I got was when I asked you about the rune line," Sammy said. "Honestly, I forgot about it after that."

So had I – almost. That must have been part of my mother's spell. I picked up a book that was lying open, face down. The pages were coated in grime. I brushed them off, revealing a spell on removing excess magic. Arthur took it from me, examining the page.

I picked up another book, and this time it fell open on a page about severing magical connections. The spells in these pages reminded me of something, but it wouldn't quite come clear. I'd read something in the encyclopaedia of spells, and it floated just at the edge of my memory, almost as if it was trying to signal its own importance.

Joe picked up a third book from the floor. "Symptoms and side effects of stolen magic," he read.

"She's trying to fix it," I said. "She knows she's losing control."

"She already *has* lost control!" Arthur took the book from me, skimming through the pages.

The others all looked alarmed by the discovery, but I felt a lightness inside my chest for the first time in days. Chloe was trying to fix it. My sister was still in there, trying to regain control of the magic.

Fight back, little mouse.

My eyes fell on Sammy. She still stood by the door, rocking slightly as she soothed Callie. Her eyes traced around the room, almost as if she were looking for something in particular.

"You wrote something about this, didn't you?" I said.

Her gaze shot to mine, eyes almost guilty. She hesitated, then nodded. "I've written a lot, but most of it's still jumbled. I can only read a few pages."

I touched the bracelets on my wrist. "But it told you we needed to enchant these?"

"Yeah, my writings told me we would do it. I don't know why; they don't seem to help."

I ran a finger over the silver bands, letting them clink together. "I do," I said. The plan was only just starting to form in my mind, but I said it with as much confidence as I could muster. I needed them to follow me. I needed them to trust me, and I needed to trust myself.

"I read something in one of the textbooks about using

objects to control magic." I slipped one of the bracelets from my wrist, squeezing it tightly, letting the metal cut into my palm. I'd never got further than F in the encyclopaedia, but that didn't matter. B for bracelet – B for binding spell.

"We're going to use these to bind Chloe."

Chapter Ten

I found Ben downstairs, no sign of Chloe. When I saw him, I almost backed away. He sat on the bottom step, his head in his hands, and everything about him screamed broken.

I could tell from the way he stiffened that he'd heard me approach, but he didn't turn around. I sat down next to him, bumping my shoulder against his.

"Did you find Chloe?" I asked. It was a silly question – he wouldn't be sitting there if he had.

Ben shook his head. "No."

He rubbed at his face. His skin had turned red, where he'd been worrying at his temple. Obviously, my parents hadn't found Chloe either. She and Joe were safe for a little longer at least.

"We went into the library," I told him.

His head shot up. "I told you not to."

"I know, but she's been in there. We found these books, and…" I didn't know how to explain everything we'd found. "It's worse than we thought. I think Chloe's in over her head."

That was the best way to describe it, I decided. I didn't believe that Chloe had done any of this on purpose, and the fact that she was looking up side effects of siphoning magic made me sure she knew what she'd done was bad. I remembered the way her eyes had glowed when she sat by my bedside – so blank and unfamiliar – the way she'd told me to fight it. She was saying it to herself too.

"I think that Mum and Dad were right about her power."

Ben pulled away from me. "You can't be serious! Mum and Dad can't take her magic away."

I wasn't even sure they would be able to. The way the magic was behaving – that icy rush of air I'd felt when it was running through me – there was no way to stop once it started. As much as I had tried to dam it up, I couldn't. Geminus magic was even more powerful than they had warned us. If Chloe was stuck in the middle of that, she'd have no way to stop it.

"I know, I know," I said, trying to soothe Ben's ire. "That's not what I meant." I chewed on my lip. I should have got Joe or Sammy to come with me. Ben still saw me as a baby – his little mouse of a sister. But I wasn't so small anymore. I could fix this, if only he would listen to me.

"I want to bind her instead," I told him. "I read about it in one of those textbooks from the classroom."

Ben's forehead creased with a frown. "Bind her?"

I nodded. "It won't take her magic away permanently; it will just stop her using it. It will still all be inside her."

Ben started to shake his head, then hesitated. He rubbed his fingers together as if reassuring himself his own power was all still there. "Her magic will all be intact? You're sure?"

"As sure as I can be." The textbooks hadn't gone into specifics about what happened after the binding, but it couldn't be worse than her and Joe dying, could it?

Ben nodded slowly. "That sounds... well, it doesn't sound awful," he said, finally.

"Not awful" was probably about as good as we could hope for right now. I just prayed my parents would see it that way.

Ben stood and reached out a hand. I let him pull me up. "We have to find Chloe first," I told him.

He made a noise in his throat. "No, let's go back to the library. I think I can draw her there."

My stomach flipped a little at the idea of going back to that burnt-out room. Honestly, it creeped me out. Mum had been right to block it off with runes. "Why there?"

Ben grimaced. "It's where this all started," he said, his voice heavy. I could hear the regret in his tone. It wasn't just Chloe who had lost control of the magic that day. "It should be where we end it." He turned, walking away before I had a chance to ask anything else.

*　*　*　*

SAMMY STAYED IN THE doorway, not coming all the way into the library. She'd put Callie down for a nap in Arthur's room, and she hovered between the two rooms. We'd wrapped the room in protective magic, but her eyes still darted back towards the crib at every hint of noise.

"You can stay with her, if you want," I told her. "You don't have to be a part of this."

She smiled, but there was something sad in her eyes. "I think I do."

I frowned. She'd read something. She might not know exactly what was going to happen, but it was obvious she had an idea of how things were going to play out.

Sammy shook herself off, smiling lightly. "Besides, Callie's safe in there," she said. "I trust your magic."

I touched the bracelets. "*Our* magic. Let's hope this works."

She nodded, then hesitated. She drew her notebook out of her pocket. "I think you should have this. I finished the last page last night."

I frowned. "But I can't read it."

"You will be able to, when the time's right."

That sounded like the kind of thing my mum said when I got frustrated about home schooling and all the other things we weren't allowed to do. I clutched the book to my chest, then slipped it under my shirt to keep it safe. "Thank you."

"All right." Ben clapped his hands, drawing our attention to him. "I want you to gather piles of ash. Bring them all into the centre of the room."

I glanced down at the debris beneath our feet. Images of those long, dark, shadowy fingers reaching for me played in my mind, and I shuddered. The ash was magically charged, I could feel that even from here, and I didn't want to touch it.

"It will help," Ben said. "I'm going to draw Chloe here, and I need to use material from a spell she cast. Bring all of it in – right from the corners of the room."

Ben headed towards one corner of the room, and Joe to another, so I took the third. Arthur followed me, dropping into a crouch beside me as I swept ash into my hands.

"Are you sure about this?" he whispered.

I looked up at him, frowning. "I thought you were on board with binding Chloe."

"I am. It's just..." Arthur hesitated, and his eyes flicked towards Ben. Ben's back was to us, and Arthur took my hand, pulling me out into the corridor. "I didn't realise you were going to involve your brother," he said.

"Why wouldn't I?"

Arthur chewed on his lip, staring back into the room. "The way he uses magic worries me sometimes."

Sammy was back in Arthur's room, singing to Callie. The

lullaby made a strangely ominous soundtrack to Arthur's words. I'd never seen Ben use magic in bad ways – that had always been Chloe's department.

"What do you mean?"

Arthur made a noise in his throat. "That night in town when we went out and he started throwing fireworks at people..."

"Wait, *Ben* was throwing fireworks?"

Arthur had told me and Sammy about the fireworks when we were up on the barn roof, but I'd thought he meant Chloe. Had he actually ever said that, or had I just jumped to conclusions, blaming my sister as I always did? To be fair, if there was a chaotic spell happening, she was usually the one behind it.

"Yeah..." Arthur shook his head, as if brushing off images. "He just seems really different when he uses magic. It's like it takes him over."

I frowned trying to fit that image of my brother to the one I knew and loved. The only times I'd really seen him work strong magic were when he fought Chloe. But that was different – Dad made him do that.

"I don't know..." I said finally. "Maybe he was just drunk that night. Alcohol makes people do strange things, right?"

"Sometimes, I guess." Arthur didn't sound sure.

"Ursula, what are you doing?" Ben called. "Come help us."

I glanced at Arthur. He shrugged, but didn't turn away. "Up to you," he said. "If you're sure it's okay."

I hesitated. Ben was my safe sibling – he always had been. This had to be okay. "I'm sure," I told Arthur.

Ben had arranged piles of ash in the middle of the room. He beckoned for us to come closer. "All of you, stand near this one. It represents us."

Joe, Arthur and I dutifully moved to stand beside the pile

of ash as directed. Sammy stayed out in the corridor, looking in from the doorway. I knew there was no such thing as good and black magic, only the intentions of the person using it. Even so, involving the remains of a fire like this felt dark. Arthur's hand slipped into mine, and I squeezed his.

Ben drew out a long thread of magic, then started to draw runes around the second pile of ash.

"What is he doing?" Joe asked.

I watched the magic, transfixed. "It looks like that leading spell," I said.

"What leading spell?"

I dragged my eyes away from Ben, turning to face Joe. "The one you taught Chloe – the one she was practising on the mice."

He frowned. "What mice?"

"The ones you bought at the pet store. You know... she used the same spell on the vines too, to make them grow upwards."

Joe shook his head slowly. "I didn't teach her that. I'd never seen it before."

I frowned. Why would Chloe have lied about that? "Then where did she learn it?"

He shrugged. "Looks like your brother's the expert."

I turned back towards Ben. The pile of ash representing Chloe was shifting, slowly inching towards the one at our feet, drawn along by the thread.

What was it Chloe had said to Ben after the vines? *I wouldn't have had to if you hadn't...* She never finished the sentence.

I watched Ben now, his loop of magic drawing the pile of ash closer. My stomach dropped. Surely, this could only work if he had already looped a thread of magic around her, giving him control.

"Oh no." I let go of Arthur's hand, jerking forward. Sammy's notebook fell from under my shirt as I did. "Ben stop, please!"

He raised a hand, holding me off, and like the silly little mouse I was, I froze.

Joe picked up the notebook. "This is Sammy's. Why do you have it? Did she give it to you?" He opened the book, and a note fell out, written in Sammy's spidery writing.

I stared at the page it had marked, horror setting in as a string of words became clear.

Their magic will flare out of control, and she will realise she is under her brother's power...

That's what Chloe had read that day in the classroom. If Ben made those fireworks that night in town, then he was the one who had got the ash on Arthur's cheek. He was the one who had marked him with the magic that made him sick. And everything that Chloe had done had been because Ben was influencing her.

Joe picked up the note that had dropped from the book. "What the hell?" He looked up at me, his eyes wide. He held the page out to me.

Take my daughter to my mother, it read. *Keep Calliope safe.*

I spun around, searching for Sammy's figure outside the doorway. Sammy thought something was going to happen to her. She *knew* something was going to happen to her. Joe met my eye, the same realisation clear in his expression. He turned to run, but the ash swirled up in front of us, pushing him back. It drew itself into lines, forming runes in the air.

"Ursula, what is this?" Arthur clutched my arm.

I slashed a hand through the air, scattering the runes. "Ben, stop!"

But it was too late. Chloe walked into the room, drawn by Ben's magic.

Chapter Eleven

I'd been so stupid. *Ben* was the one who drew magic from the plants, killing them each time. Ben was the one desperate to increase his powers. Why had I been so quick to blame my sister? I knew the answer, though I didn't want to admit it. Because Chloe was Chloe – complicated and prickly.

But Ben was the one who had always been stronger, and he was the one who always won.

Chloe strained against the magic now, fighting with every step. "Don't do this, Ben, please!" she whispered. "You have to stop."

Fight back, little mouse... She'd been saying it to herself as much as me.

I turned to Joe and Arthur. "We've made a mistake." My voice came out as a whisper too. "It's Ben – he's the one controlling this."

Joe's eyes were wild. "I have to help Sammy!"

"Go!" I told him. Did Sammy really believe she wouldn't survive this? That couldn't be true. We *all* had to get through this, somehow.

Joe hesitated. He looked between me and Arthur. "If anything bad happens to me and Sammy, you look after Callie, yeah? You make sure she's safe and that she knows I love her."

"Of course. We'll protect her," Arthur said, at the same time as I said, "Nothing bad is going to happen." I didn't know if either answer was true.

Joe gave a firm, single nod. He turned to run for the door, but then froze. His limbs seemed to short out, stopping abruptly in a way that would have been comical in any other circumstance. Only his eyes still moved. They roved now, panic lighting behind them.

Sammy gasped from the doorway. "Joe!" She jerked forward as if to step into the room.

"Don't! Don't come in here." Chloe let out a hiccupping sob. "It's the geminus magic."

I saw it then – the cord of shimmering, silvery energy stretching from Chloe to Joe, like the one between me and Sammy. Anything Ben did to Chloe, he would also do to Joe. That was why Joe had felt worse – like the magic was taking him over – when he was around my sister. *Ben's* magic had been taking over Chloe and rippling out to Joe.

I met Chloe's eyes and opened my mouth, but all words froze on my lips. *I wouldn't have had to if you hadn't...* She'd been trying to stop Ben. I'd seen the rune flash in the air just before the vines, and blamed her, but it was Ben all along. Chloe hadn't been trying to hurt me, she'd seen Ben start to drain my magic and was trying to disrupt him.

Sammy looked between Joe and the room where Callie slept, her face stricken. *Stay there*, I said inside my head. We all had to get out of this room, out of this house. As if he'd heard me, Arthur's arm tightened on mine. He took a step towards the door, pulling me with him.

Ben turned towards us, almost like he'd only just remembered we were there. He studied our faces, reading the fear and horror that must have oozed from every inch of us. "Ursula, come here," he said calmly. "Give me the bracelets."

I shook my head. Arthur's grip turned to a stranglehold, his fingers biting into my arm. He took another step towards the door, and I stumbled after him.

Ben frowned. "Don't be silly, little mouse, come here." His voice was so steady – so normal. "I know it's hard, but Chloe's magic is out of control. You know we have to bind her."

I swallowed. "Why are you doing this?"

"Doing what? This was your plan, Urse." Even now, he was still holding on to the lie. He gave me a small, encouraging smile and held out his hand. When I didn't move, his face hardened. "Get over here, Ursula. Mum and Dad will strip her powers otherwise."

"Let them!" Chloe screamed. "It's better than you having them."

"Chloe, no..." I could barely get the words out. "It could kill you and Joe."

She'd tried to make me see what was happening to her by showing me the spell with the mice, and I hadn't understood it. I stared at her, trying to communicate silently how sorry I was, but she wasn't looking at me. Her eyes met Joe's, searching them. He stared back, and then slowly, deliberately, he blinked once.

Chloe nodded back. Just as slowly, just as deliberately. And then she threw back her head. "Mum!" she screamed. "Dad!" She poured power into the word, amplifying it and calling them to us.

"Stop it!" Ben lunged forward, aiming for Chloe. I got in his way, and Arthur ran to protect Joe.

"Mum!" I yelled, pouring all my magic into it too.

"Shut up, Ursula! I'm doing this for you." Ben grabbed my

arm, yanking two of the silver bracelets off it. "It won't hurt Chloe, so just calm down. I wouldn't even have to do this if you hadn't sent the workers away."

My stomach dropped. I'd meant to weaken Chloe by getting rid of them, but all I'd done was make him double down on draining Chloe's power. "No! I won't let you." I scratched at his face, trying to grab the bracelets back. Arthur hurled himself forward, knocking Ben to the ground. Chloe gasped, and Joe stumbled forward.

"Run!" I yelled. "Arthur's room. Go!"

Joe grabbed Chloe's hand, and together they bolted for the door. Arthur gave a strangled cry and fell back. Joe and Chloe's steps slowed.

"No, keep going!" I yelled. But their movement dragged, magical threads wrapping tighter around them, slowing them to a crawl.

Ben held Arthur down, marking the lines of a rune on his cheek. Ben stood, brushing ash off his hands. He picked up the silver bracelets he'd taken from me and walked towards Chloe, his steps unhurried. She strained to look back at him, her own steps a painful crawl now. When I suggested binding Chloe, Ben didn't ask if it would hurt her; he'd just asked if her magic would still all be intact. He wanted to keep using it, and I'd made it easier for him.

More threads stretched out from him now, wrapping around Joe and Chloe. "All of you need to calm down," he said. "I'm not going to take more power than you can handle."

Chloe let out a strangled sound that was almost a laugh. "What about Joe and Arthur?" Chloe said. "You took more than *they* could handle."

Ben's jaw clenched. "That was an accident. The geminus connections made me stronger than I realised. I have it under control now."

He didn't, but he couldn't see it. Ben stepped towards Chloe, taking hold of her arm almost gently. "I mean it, Clo. I'm doing this for us. You think Dad will stop at you and me? You really think he won't force Ursula and the others to fight next?"

They both turned to look at me, and the threads of magic turned too, slithering towards me and Arthur.

"I can protect myself," I told him.

Ben shook his head, his focus going back to Chloe. "Not against Dad, little mouse," he said. "I had to get strong enough to stop him."

Maybe that had been true once. Maybe he had started stealing energy to protect us from Dad, but he was the one hurting us now. His eyes went wide, shining like Chloe's had.

I brushed the ash off Arthur's cheek, blurring the rune. He'd turned pale, sweat beading on his forehead. "What do we do?" I said under my breath. Arthur just shook his head. He looked like he was going to pass out.

"Ursula?" My mother appeared in the corridor beside Sammy. "Ben, what's going on?" She moved to come in the room, but Ben held up a hand, stopping her. My father stepped through the doorway beside her, but he too stopped at Ben's raised palm.

"Everything's fine. I have it all under control."

"No, he doesn't!" I yelled. "It's him! He's the one—"

Ben turned towards me, and a wave of magic slammed into me. I fell back, dazed. It tasted sweet, and it hummed against my skin in a way that felt familiar. I stretched out my hands, letting the magic settle against me. It was Sammy's, not his – the magic he'd stolen from her.

"Ben, that is enough!" Dad strode towards my brother. "How dare you hit your sister like—"

Another wave slammed into Dad, sending him flying back

into Mum. She fell backwards, and both their heads hit the floor with sickening cracks.

"Mum!" Chloe yelled. I tried to yell too, but all that came out was a rush of air.

Ben dropped his hands. "Oh my god, Mum." He took a shaky step towards her. "I didn't mean to..." He crouched beside her, but Mum and Dad didn't move.

I tried to stand, stumbling under the weight of the magic in the room. I caught sight of Sammy, out in the corridor. She stood still, no longer looking between this room and the other. She mouthed something to me.

"What?" I mouthed back.

She mouthed again, and this time I made out the words. "The book." Her prophecy. I reached under my shirt, but it was gone. I scanned the floor, looking for it. Ash coated everything. I dropped to my hands and knees, scraping it aside. Arthur heaved himself up, joining my search, though he could barely move, and I don't think he knew what he was looking for.

Ben took Mum's face in his hands. "I can fix her," he said. He lurched back towards Chloe, grabbing her right wrist, shoving one of the bracelets on it.

"No!" She let out a sob. Threads of his magic tightened around her, keeping her in place.

"Shh... No, it's all right, Clo, I'm not going to hurt you. Just calm down." Ben's tone was gentle – so calm and rational – so like *him*. He was our brother. How could he be doing this? He put the other bracelet on her left wrist. "I just have to get enough power to help Mum."

"Ben..." I stared at the bracelets, holding my breath. This is what we'd planned – *my* plan. I waited for the bracelets to snap together, binding Chloe in place, protecting us by trapping her magic.

Nothing happened. Chloe looked down at her wrists, still

free. It hadn't worked. Ben grabbed Chloe's hands, mashing them together. "Why isn't it binding her?"

"Got it!" Arthur pulled Sammy's notebook from under the ash. I grabbed it, opening it to the end, but the pages moved by themselves, flicking to one in the centre.

"What does it say?" Arthur whispered.

I shook my head. "I don't know." I still couldn't read the words. But then, it was like they unfurled in front of me. The letters climbed up my arms and buried themselves into my skin.

"Oh, I get it. Very clever." Ben let out something that was close to a laugh. "I didn't make the bracelets, so I can't control them. Ursula, get over here."

I shrank back, and Arthur moved in front of me, hands raised. He was too weak to work magic, especially with Ben stealing his, but there he was, still trying to protect me. Ben took a step towards us.

"She didn't make them alone." Sammy's voice rang out from the corridor. Ben spun around, and she stared him down, a hardness in her eyes I had never seen.

Ben drew in a long breath. "Fine." He took a step towards Sammy.

She turned and fled.

"Wait!" He ran after her. Joe and Chloe stumbled along behind him, dragged along by the threads of magic.

I leapt up too, scrambling over my unconscious parents. I heard Arthur stumble after me. Sammy's words from the book pounded with each step, like flashes of light in my head. Suddenly, I understood.

I heard a scream. I surged towards it, bursting into the foyer. Ben held Sammy as she struggled against him. Joe and Chloe just stood there, their eyes blank but bright, completely under his power now.

"Bind Chloe now!" he screamed at Sammy.

"I can't!" she gasped. "I told you; I can't do it alone."

Ben rounded on me, his eyes just as blank as Joe and Chloe's. "Come here, Ursula,' he growled.

Arthur moved to step in front of me, but I reached for his arm, stopping him. His skin was cold, clammy, and when he turned to look at me, his face was so, so pale.

"Do you have your bracelet on?" I asked.

He nodded, but it was like the movement was too much for him. The last shred of colour drained from his face, and he crumpled, collapsing at my feet. I let go of him, though it felt like a betrayal to do it. "I'm sorry," I whispered. I walked towards my brother, slipping a bracelet from my wrist as I did.

Ben smiled, but there was nothing comforting in it. "Good, little mouse." He said he was trying to help Mum, trying to protect us from Dad, but only hunger for power lit his eyes. He turned towards Chloe. "Bind her," he told me.

Chloe was practically bound already, so tightly wrapped in his magical control. But he wanted more. He always wanted more. I met Sammy's eye, and she gave just the briefest of half nods.

"Okay," I said.

Sammy stomped on his foot, and brought her head back, smashing it into his nose. He let go of her, clutching his face. She ran up the stairs. I grabbed Ben's wrists, shoving the bracelets onto them.

Ben actually had the gall to laugh. "You can't do it alone, little—"

The bracelets snapped together, binding him in place. He looked down at the handcuffs in surprise. "How...?"

"You threw Sammy's magic at me. I had both."

He smiled slowly. "Very clever, little mouse, but do you really believe this will hold me?"

"No." I looked up at Sammy. She grabbed the air in front of her, and the geminus connection sparked. I felt a tug deep inside me, then the wave of energy rippling out. I grabbed Ben and Arthur's connection.

"Now," Sammy screamed.

We both yanked back, snapping the invisible cords of the geminus bonds. Ben and Arthur both howled, a horrifying, animalistic sound. I doubled over, pain setting me on fire. Emptiness rushed in, my connection to Sammy severing.

Alone, you will struggle to control your magic. Miss Caraway's words about geminus magic wielders came back to me suddenly. *In other cases, it becomes dangerous. Explosive even.*

Something was building, rushing up inside me. "Get down!" I yelled.

The wave of power threw us back. It hit the walls, crashing against them. And then everything burst into flames.

Epilogue

My eyes were open. I blinked to check, but somehow it still felt like I was in a dream. Someone was singing, a quiet lullaby, and cosy warmth surrounded me.

I sat up.

"You're awake." Arthur smiled at me from across the room, then glanced down at the baby in his arms. Callie.

"Oh my god, Callie!" I half rose from the bed, but Arthur raised a hand, gesturing for me to stay.

"It's okay. She's okay. The magic protected her. Miss Caraway and I have been taking turns looking after her."

I sank my head into my hands, relieved. "I didn't know..." I whispered. I hadn't been able to read Sammy's prophecy. I'd only known in the moment what it was asking me to do. I hadn't known that the power would be so strong, or that it would cause an explosion.

Sammy. I felt an ache deep inside me where my connection to her was missing.

"It's okay," Arthur said. "You did what you had to. None of us could have known."

His words didn't make me feel any better. He resumed the lullaby, rocking Callie gently. I watched them, unease building inside me. He'd said he and Miss Caraway had been taking care of Callie.

"Arthur, where's Sammy?" Panic tightened my stomach. "Where's Ben?"

Arthur's eyes slid away from mine. "Everyone who wore a bracelet was protected from the blast."

"But... Oh god, my parents?"

Arthur shook his head slowly. "I'm so sorry."

I pressed a hand to my mouth, not sure if I wanted to throw up or scream. Arthur hesitated, perhaps unsure if he should continue. I couldn't speak, but I gave him a nod. I needed to know.

"The blast severed Ben's connection with the energy in the house – the energy he was draining from the house I mean – but he still had hold of Chloe and Joe. He got free of your binding, and they fled. Miss Caraway had only just got to town. She came back when she sensed the force of the magic."

My siblings were alive. My siblings were alive, but corrupted by selfish, dangerous power. "It was all for nothing," I whispered.

"No!" Arthur shook his head fiercely, waking Callie. She let out a cry, and he rocked her, lowering his voice. "No... not for nothing. Ben would have enslaved or killed us all if you hadn't stopped him. He's considerably less powerful now – considerably less dangerous."

Was that worth my parents' lives? Callie continued to fuss, and he stood, jiggling her gently. He started singing again, his voice strangely haunting.

I watched them, dread growing in my stomach once again. "Arthur, where's Sammy?"

He didn't look up at me, finishing the lullaby. I started to cry, all of it becoming real in one go. "She was at the centre of the blast," he said finally, his voice soft, conscious of the baby in his arms. "I couldn't find..." He swallowed, then moved a hand from around Callie, pulling something from his pocket. A bracelet.

Everyone who wore a bracelet was protected from the blast.

"No..."

"I don't know if it fell off or she took it off, but... I'm so sorry."

The hollow in my stomach where the geminus connection used to be seemed to grow, engulfing me. "She knew it was going to happen." She'd given me the prophecy and that note because she knew she was going to die in trying to stop them. But we didn't stop them. It had all been for nothing.

"She wanted us to take Callie to her mother," I said.

Arthur looked up. "We promised Joe that we'd look after her – that she'd know he loved her."

That was for if he died, but he wasn't dead. What was he now, taken over by magic like my brother and sister? All three of them were trapped in it.

"You can't. You can't tell her anything about him. We have to protect her from them."

"But we promised."

I shook my head. It felt too impossible. The child had to be protected – from her father, from my siblings. Maybe even from us. "So we'll send her letters, or cards or... I don't know. Something."

Arthur swallowed. "There's one more thing."

I closed my eyes. I couldn't take one more thing.

"Sammy's prophecy," he said. "You need to read it."

"I can't. Even before the blast, I couldn't read it. It was like it burrowed into me, telling me what to do."

Arthur was quiet for a moment. "I think you'll be able to read it now."

I opened my eyes and he nodded towards the bedside table, where the battered notebook lay. I opened it, and it flicked automatically to a page. I stared at it, and slowly the gibberish formed into words.

The girl will know only that her mother died, and her grandmother raised her. The magic will be in her, and when the time is right, she will defeat him. She will live sixteen summers before magic finds her, and on her seventeenth birthday, the sky will burst into fire, and it will begin.

I looked at Arthur, not knowing what to say. But he wasn't looking at me. He was staring at Callie. I read the rest of the page, my horror growing with each word.

"It's all going to happen again," I said. "Another three sets of geminus pairs. When Callie is sixteen."

Arthur nodded, still staring down at her. "Yes, and Callie's going to be at the centre of it."

I pressed my hand to my mouth again. "We promised we'd protect her."

"And we will."

"We can't!" The words wrenched themselves out of me, the awfulness of all of it seeming to pour out with them. "I just exploded the school. I destroyed everything!"

Arthur finally looked up at me. "So, we rebuild," he said, simply. "And in sixteen years' time, we'll be ready."

EXPLOSIVE

REACTIVE MAGIC BOOK 4

Helen Vivienne Fletcher

Chapter One

Toby

Mr Grandace's magic sent out a call. Julianna and Zo's power resisted at first, then it intertwined with his.

I stood in the school corridor, my classmates and former teachers joining me to make a half circle. In front of us were three doors, behind which Callie's dad and Miss Trager's siblings were being held prisoner.

Mr Grandace moved on to me and Asher, his magic reaching out for us like it would swallow us whole. I didn't want this. I didn't want to be joined to these people.

It wasn't the same as last time. Then, my magic had reached out, and my classmates' had reached back as if it had been something we were all subconsciously waiting for. This felt forced, unnatural.

Callie squeezed my hand, and I opened my eyes. Mr Grandace's magic reached out for her, ready to bind her to her father and Miss Trager's siblings.

I gave her a nod, trying to tell her it would be okay. But would it?

Callie jolted backwards, as if something invisible had

slammed into her. She opened her mouth, but nothing came out.

"Callie!" I screamed. A second slam threw her across the room, ripping her hand from mine.

Toby! she screamed inside her head. And then all I could hear was static.

I ran towards her, but power threw me back. Then everyone was on the ground.

Tattered strings of magic hung in the air. I reached for my connection to Callie and found only shreds. The newly formed connections to Miss Trager and Mr Grandace were gone too. Our circle had been cut in half.

"Callie!" I called again. I tried to get up, but it was like moving through toffee.

A stab of pain shot through me, doubling me over. Not my pain – Julianna's pain echoing through Zo's mind. Zo's thoughts distorted, like a radio not quite tuned to a station. The thread between us was still there, but weakened, only just holding together.

"The circle is complete," Elijah said. It didn't sound like his voice. He turned, walking to the locked door and opening it. His movements were jerky, robotic. He unlocked the next door, then the third.

No one else moved. Everything seemed to be in slow motion, all of us suspended in a strange, liminal space. Miss Trager's sister walked out of one of the rooms, and then Callie's father appeared.

Callie stood, her movements just as jerky as Elijah's had been. She greeted her father with a hug. Her eyes darted around the room, panic filling them.

"I have to go," she said. The words seemed to terrify her.

Elijah took one of her hands, and her father took the other. They started to walk away.

"No!" Miss Trager yelled. "Ben, please don't do this!"

Mr Grandace threw out a spell. It fizzled in the air, disappearing.

EXPLOSIVE

I couldn't move. All I could do was watch as Miss Trager's siblings and Callie's father walked out of the school, taking Callie and Elijah with them.

* * * *

"TOBY!" ZO HISSED.

I blinked, clearing my head of images from the night Ben had taken Callie and Elijah. No matter where I was, every moment of quiet had my mind slipping back there.

"I'm okay," I told Zo, though I was about ready to burst with anxiety.

We were crouched in the bushes at the edge of a parking lot. In front of us was a tower block office building. If Mr Grandace was right, then Callie and Elijah were inside.

The chill of the night turned my breath to steam. I covered my mouth with my collar, breathing into my sweatshirt. It was midnight-dark, likely no one would notice the tiny puff of crystalised air escaping from my lips, but I couldn't take the chance.

It had been three months since Ben had taken Callie and Elijah. Three months of him dragging them from place to place, never staying anywhere for more than a few nights. Three months of us trying to find them, knowing he was stealing their magic and forcing them to create destruction and chaos to further fuel his powers. We saw the aftermath of it all the time – burnt out buildings, withered wildlife, people injured or stripped of energy to the point of collapse. This was the first time Mr Grandace had managed to predict where they might strike – the first time we might actually have a shot at stopping it.

"Hey," Zo whispered. "Surveillance only, remember?"

I nodded, but if I got the chance to grab Callie, I would be taking it.

I froze as a low hum rose at the base of my skull, tickling the back of my mind.

"Callie?" I whispered. No answer came, but the humming continued. What was that sound? I'd heard it vibrating through my bones every time we got close for the last few months, but I still had no idea where it came from.

I peered into the darkness. Everything was still, too still. Then, more vibrations started, discordant notes competing against each other. I clapped my hands over my ears. Between the notes, I heard something else. The slithering of vines crawling towards me.

"Dammit!"

My classmates burst from their hiding places. Zo shrieked as a vine reached her. No... no! I just needed a moment longer. I'd heard Callie, I was sure of it!

"What are you doing, Toby? Get out of there!" Asher ran past me, Julianna just a step after him. Explosions boomed behind us, the flash of light blinding me for a moment. But still, I didn't move. I strained, listening for that first humming note, for Callie.

"Toby!" Zo grabbed my arm, yanking me up. She dragged me along behind her, half physically, half with magic. The bush where I'd been crouching exploded a second later. I turned back, but Zo's magical hold pulled me forward. Suddenly, I understood how Callie and Elijah must have felt, being on the ends of our magical human chain.

"Seriously, get it together!" Zo shook my arm. "We're losing them."

That got my attention. So much for surveillance. I turned, racing to keep up with her. We'd been close so many times, but we'd never quite managed to catch Callie or any of the others.

She was here tonight, though, I was sure of it.

Ahead of us, Asher and Julianna ran towards the building entrance. I couldn't see Miss Trager or Mr Grandace but they would be here, somewhere. This watch and wait was their plan after all. They had traced Ben to this building, traced the signs of his destructive magic and chaos. We had to stop him – we had to get Callie and Elijah free of him.

A ball of fire flew from the front entrance, knocking Asher and Julianna to the ground. I grabbed Zo, flinging her down and covering her with my body as the flames rushed over us.

The fire turned green above us, morphing into a twisted tangle of vines and leaves. Julianna and Asher didn't move. I scrambled to my hands and knees, crawling over to them, keeping low.

Julianna groaned, eyes closed, but Asher raised his head. "Go! We're fine. They're getting away!"

Figures darted through the smoke and footsteps hit the pavement around us. I dragged myself up, stumbling after them. Zo scrambled to her feet too, giving chase.

We couldn't let them get away; it might be months before we got another chance. We'd seen their patterns, hiding for weeks, then reappearing to cause chaos as they drained whole city blocks of energy, taking it from everyone and everything to fuel their magic.

The smoke obscured my vision, but I kept running, desperate not to let them get away this time. Suddenly, I felt someone move. I reached out, clasping hold of their arm. My palm jolted, familiar bolts of electricity shooting off their skin. They spun around, hitting me, nails scraping across my face as they tried to free themself.

"Callie," I breathed.

She gasped. "Toby." Her voice cracked. She swayed like she was trying to take a step towards me, then a shuddering sound broke through her lips. "I'm sorry," she whispered.

"Please just come—" a blast of magic threw me back, wrenching her from my grip. She stumbled, falling to her knees. Lank hair fell over her face, haunted eyes staring out from behind it. The blast knocked the air out of me, but I tried to pull myself towards her.

She shrank back, like a wounded animal. She was all angles, sharp collarbones sticking out from the neck of her shirt.

"Please, Callie," I whispered. "Let me help you."

Something seemed to break inside her. She reached out a hand, but before I could grab it, her father was beside her. His arm snaked around her waist, and he pulled her to her feet. The discordant humming melody intensified, blocking out everything else inside my head. Callie met my eyes once more, and tears pooled in hers.

Joe dragged her away, and they were gone.

Footsteps pounded behind me. "Are you okay?" Zo asked. She grabbed my chin, turning my face to hers.

I jerked away. "I'm fine," I said, my voice rough. "But they're gone. I couldn't stop her."

Zo ran a few paces, as if she could catch up with them anyway, but she quickly gave up, returning to my side.

I leaned forward, hands on my knees as I tried to catch my breath. "I saw her, Zo. We were this close."

She nodded, and her lips pressed together into a thin line. I peered into the smoke and the remains of the disintegrating vines, desperate to catch one last glimpse of Callie. Was it too much to hope that she'd dropped some kind of clue? I prayed for a glass slipper or trail of breadcrumbs left in her wake.

Instead, another of Ben's victims stood in the wreckage. I stumbled forward. "Hey! You there, wait!"

The man turned towards me, and a violent vibrated note

reverberated in my head. I took a few steps towards him, but then flames exploded around him.

"No! Oh god, no!" I lurched forward, but Zo grabbed me.

"Toby, you can't!"

"We can't leave him!"

"I know." She closed her eyes. Her magic swelled up around us. I poured my own into her, letting her use it. The flames let off swirls of energy. They flew up into the air, then began to coil, joining together into one long rope of power.

I grimaced. Ben was calling the energy back to him.

Is that man okay? Zo said inside her head. The flames died down, her power counteracting them. The man lay on the ground, shivering. No burn wounds marked his skin, but only because Zo had stopped the fire. I could feel from here that Ben had stolen a dangerous amount of energy from him. How many times had Ben made Callie or Elijah hurt someone like this? How many more people had Ben killed when we weren't here to stop him?

I turned away. "He's fine. Let's go find the others."

Zo stared at the man for a moment longer, biting her lip, then she linked her arm through mine. She leaned heavily against me, though she tried to disguise it. I couldn't say I was doing much better. I heard thoughts chasing themselves through her head, too fast to catch.

"I know it doesn't feel like it, but this is a good thing," she said aloud. "We found them. It means Mr Grandace's methods are working."

I frowned, not even dignifying that with an answer. Letting them get away wasn't "working". For that matter, I wasn't convinced Mr Grandace really had "methods". All he seemed to do was pore over the gibberish in Callie's mother's prophecy, and study news reports for signs of destruction that could be linked to Ben.

If I hadn't faffed about in that bush, maybe I would have been able to help Callie. I swallowed, ignoring the fact that she'd just blasted me with her magic. Was she like this all the time now? Did she have no control over her life or her actions? The thought made something compress around my chest as if I was the one trapped.

Zo stopped. Her arm slipped from mine as I kept walking.

I looked up, then my steps ground to a halt. "Oh my god!"

Asher lay face down in the dirt in front of us. Zo broke into a run, the soles of her shoes hitting the concrete hard. I stumbled after her, my feet clumsy underneath me.

Ben stood over Asher. Dark red magic swirled around Ben, stolen from Asher.

"Hey!" I yelled. "Get away from him." I raised my hands, willing my reactive magic to sprout into action. Zo did the same, racing towards him.

Ben flicked a wrist and Zo flew backwards, landing with a crash. He stepped towards her, and I launched myself forward, trying to get between them. He flung me back too. Murky red-black energy slipped from my skin, flowing out towards Ben. I clawed at it, trying to catch hold. It slipped through my fingers.

Ben shuddered as it reached him, his outline blurring almost as if the extra magic reshaped him. My head swum and the world closed in at the sides.

"No!" Julianna screamed.

Suddenly, she was beside Ben, launching herself at him. She shoved him, not with magic, just with sheer force. He stumbled back, startled. She raised her hands, landing a punch before he could right himself. She hit him again and again.

I blinked hard, trying to stay conscious. He was getting up. He was walking towards her.

"Jules!" I yelled. I tried to stand but my limbs felt leaden.

Ben raised his hands, and Julianna cowered. Asher's eyes

opened. He scrambled up, throwing a magical blast at Ben.

Zo followed suit, a weaker attack exploding from her hands. I got to my feet, but my magic was spent. Instead, I grabbed Zo's arm, using our connection to give her the little energy I had left. Ben was strong, but surely he wasn't stronger than the four of us... except he was. He stood tall in the face of our attack, it barely seeming to register.

Julianna hit him again. She stomped on his foot, then kicked his shin. He backed away from her blows, breaking into a run.

None of us had the energy to chase. We watched him disappear into the smoke, almost as if he was turning into it.

"What the hell were you thinking?" Zo yelled at Julianna. "Did you really just *punch* him?"

Julianna had been funny about using magic since we got back to the school, but launching herself at Ben with nothing but high school self-defence skills was reckless beyond words. Yet somehow it had worked.

Julianna shook her head, then her legs gave way. Asher caught her, moving to do it almost before she started to fall. She buried her face in his chest, and her whole body shook, all the strength she'd displayed just moments before gone. Asher met my eye over the top of her head.

"How the hell did she just do that?" I asked.

Asher shook his head. "I have absolutely no idea."

Chapter Two

Toby

We walked back to the meeting point in silence. The streets were empty – unnaturally so. We were in an industrial area on the outskirts of a suburb. The people living nearby would have no understanding of what happened tonight. They might have heard the explosions, they might have seen the flames, or even the plants growing out of control, but they would never put the cause down to magic. They would hunker down for the night in their nice safe homes, and in the morning, they would do everything they could to forget about it. I just wished we could do the same.

Asher supported Julianna, practically carrying her to keep her moving. I couldn't tell whether she'd been hurt again or if old wounds had opened up – physically and metaphorically. Either way, Asher's worry circled her, shutting me and Zo out.

Miss Trager and Mr Grandace hadn't joined us at the office building. They'd left us to keep watch but were supposed to return later in the night. I couldn't help feeling there was a reason they hadn't. What hadn't they told us about tonight?

Somehow, they always managed to leave out the most important details.

Of course, there was another possibility – that they hadn't joined us because they'd been hurt or worse. I shook my head. I couldn't let myself think about that.

Zo bumped my shoulder, falling into step beside me. *What happened tonight?* she said inside her head.

"Huh?" I responded out loud, not willing to have her delve too far into my thoughts. Gravel and broken glass crunched under my feet, and I kept my eyes on it, kicking stray pieces along in front of me.

Zo clicked her tongue. "You were all over the place. I know you lose it every time you see Callie, but—"

"I didn't lose it." I thought of that bush exploding just after I got clear of it, and my confidence in my own words wavered. "I knew she was there. I could hear her."

Zo frowned. She didn't argue with me, but I heard it all in her thoughts. She didn't believe me about the humming. I wasn't connected to Callie anymore; Ben had severed my link to her and Asher's to Elijah, leaving only me, Zo, Julianna and Asher connected in our magical chain. I shouldn't have been able to hear anything from Callie, but somehow... somehow, there was that vibration every time I got close. Somehow, there was still electricity when I'd touched her skin.

Zo's eyes flicked away from mine, and my cheeks heated. "Sorry," I muttered. Thinking about Callie sometimes took us into uncomfortable territory. I schooled my mind back to safer topics.

Zo's steps slowed. I looked up, taking in the empty bus shelter ahead. Mr Grandace and Miss Trager had told us to meet them here if we got separated, but there was no sign of either of them.

"They're not here," Zo said, rather redundantly.

Asher cursed under his breath, and my stomach lurched. I glanced back the way we'd come, ready to turn back and start searching, but Zo strode ahead, picking something up off the bench.

"Looks like they left us a ride home." She held up a handful of silver bracelets.

Julianna let out a noise that was somewhere between a gasp and a groan. Honestly, I felt like doing the same. I'd never been a fan of our teacher's magical handcuff bracelets, but after learning they'd belonged to Callie's dead mother, they straight out creeped me out.

"At least it means they're alive," Zo said, responding to my unspoken thoughts.

Asher's jaw tightened. "That's a weak-ass silver lining."

Irritation flooded Zo's thoughts, but she turned away from Asher, a slight eyeroll the only visible sign of her mood. "Over here," she said. She pointed to a roughly drawn rune line on the ground beside the shelter.

As much as the woman frustrated me, I couldn't help but admire Miss Trager's quick thinking in setting this up. The rune line was shakily drawn, the symbols scratched out in pink chalk. A broken stick of it lay abandoned on the ground beside the last rune. I pocketed it just in case I ever needed to repeat the trick.

Zo doled out the bracelets. I slipped one on each wrist, but Julianna backed away.

"No... I can't. I can't do it."

Asher wrapped his arm around her. "It's okay. We can find another way home."

Zo scoffed. "Like what? Are you going to piggyback her ten kilometres?"

Asher frowned at Zo's flippancy, and he opened his mouth

to snap back, but Zo turned to Julianna, placing her hands on her shoulders.

"I know you hate using magic, but it will be two seconds and then we'll be back safe at the school, okay?" Zo stared straight into Julianna's eyes, and I could almost believe she was using mind control.

"You don't have to," Asher said again. "If you want—"

"It's fine." Julianna took a long deep breath. "I just want to get out of here." She took two of the silver bands from Zo. Her hands shook, and it took her a moment to fit them to her wrists, but then she stood up straight, raising her head high.

Asher studied her face for a moment. I heard echoes of their silent conversation passed on through Zo's mind, and Zo and I both looked away. That part was harder for Zo than me.

Finally, Asher nodded. He put on his own bracelets, then wrapped his arm around Julianna's shoulders. Zo gave her a firm nod, which Julianna returned.

It amazed me how they did that – figured out what Julianna needed between them. Whether Asher and Zo liked it or not, the three of them were a team. I just wished seeing it didn't give me a lonely ache in my chest.

I slipped my hand into Zo's, squeezing it tightly. *Okay?* I said inside my head.

She nodded and squeezed my hand back. It didn't completely remove the lonely ache – only Callie would be able to do that – but it eased it just a little.

As one, we stepped over the rune line. Darkness crushed in on me from all sides, knocking the air from my lungs. I forced myself not to inhale, not to panic in the vacuum. Just a moment longer and... light and sounds slammed back into me. I let go of Zo's hand, falling forward onto my knees.

"I will never get used to that," Zo said, as she landed with a thump on her butt.

Asher and Julianna arrived a bit further down the corridor. Asher pulled himself up immediately, moving to crouch in front of Julianna. He held her shoulders as she shook.

I couldn't imagine what it was like for her, reliving the moment she'd almost died every time we made one of these leaps. Even so, I wished we could teleport everywhere. It would make searching for Callie so much simpler, but the bracelets only worked to bring us back to the school, their magic tied to it. Occasionally, Callie's reactive magic had given her the ability to jump elsewhere, but that was the problem with reactive magic – you couldn't control it. It reacted to the moment, doing what it thought was right, whether or not you agreed.

Zo watched Asher and Julianna for a moment, then tore her eyes away. I did the same, giving Julianna the only small measure of privacy we could offer.

Zo pushed herself up and brushed imaginary dust off her shirt. "What are the chances they'll let us head to bed and sleep for a couple of hours?"

"Approximately zero to zero, give or take a margin of error." Even if they did let us sleep, I knew I wouldn't be able to. What the hell had happened that they just left us tonight?

As if in response to that thought, I felt a ping in my stomach. Zo rolled her eyes, something that was not quite a grin crossing her face. "Not even time for a bathroom break? Rude." She made her way down the corridor to the toilets anyway.

I considered refusing to go downstairs, making them come up to us. I wanted to see for myself that Miss Trager and Mr Grandace were safe, but I did not want to rehash the night. It wasn't like our teachers' "debriefing" meetings ever amounted to much. Ninety percent of the time, we wasted hours rereading cryptic paragraphs in Callie's mother's prophecy, trying to match them up to things that had already happened. I couldn't help with that. While the others all had moments where Sammy's writing revealed itself to them, I'd never been able to read so much as a word. It all looked like gibberish to me.

The magical ping pulled at my stomach again, more insistent this time. I sighed and ducked into my room, grabbing a hoodie. I pulled it on and wandered back into the hallway.

Asher emerged from Julianna's room, closing the door softly behind him. He stayed holding the doorhandle for a moment, his eyes closed, swaying ever so slightly. Then he looked up, meeting my eye. His jaw tightened.

"She okay?" I asked. *Stupid question, Toby. Of course she isn't.*

"She's just tired."

Somehow, I didn't think it was the type of exhaustion sleep would fix.

Asher made his way downstairs, but I hung back, waiting for Zo. She reappeared and linked her arm through mine.

"This place could really use a lift, huh?" She gave me a tired smile.

I shrugged. "I don't know. I kind of like the rhythm of the steps." I thumped down them as if to prove my point, letting gravity do half the work.

"Each to their own, I guess... weirdo." Zo bumped my shoulder. She let go of my arm and jumped the last two steps, landing on the other side of the rune line at the bottom. I felt the buzz as she crossed it, and she let off a couple of sparks. They died out too quickly to see the colour.

I frowned. When had I last seen red and gold sparks from Zo? In fact, when had I seen any magistations? Surely there'd been something tonight – some flash of fear or frustration? I couldn't remember. Perhaps we were all too numb to feel anything.

I stepped over the rune line myself, shuddering a little at the buzz.

We made our way down to the "planning room" on the second floor. Mr Grandace insisted on calling it that, but in reality, it was just one of the old classrooms. I think he was trying to show us he saw us as equals – that we were no longer his students, but something closer to colleagues in the fight against out-of-control magic. A better way to show us that would have been to stop ordering us around and actually tell us what was going on.

Zo hesitated outside the door, glancing back at me. Asher stood just inside the doorway, not fully entering the room either.

"What is it?" I asked.

Zo tilted her head towards the room, and I stared in. Mr Grandace strode across the floor, yanking several books off one of the shelves as he went. He flipped through them, scanning the covers, before grabbing another handful. Miss Caraway rummaged in a desk drawer, pulling out pens.

"I'm telling you; I left it on the table. It's gone," Miss Trager snapped as she scrawled something across the whiteboard, her pen squeaking in protest at how hard she was pressing. "They tripped the wards. One of them was in here."

Ben or one of the others was here? No wonder Miss Caraway and Mr Grandace had left us to fend for ourselves at the office building.

"They can't have taken it," Mr Grandace said.

"Well, it's gone! Stop tearing things apart and help me record what we can."

Mr Grandace hesitated, pinching the bridge of his nose with one hand. "Blast it. Okay." He dropped the books he was holding and whipped around to the whiteboard. Miss Caraway placed a whiteboard marker in his hand, and he joined Miss

Trager in scribbling across the surface of the board.

Zo and I shuffled into the room. "What's going on?" I asked.

"The prophecy's gone," Miss Trager said, without looking up. "I'm sorry we had to leave you tonight, but the magic flung Arthur back here when someone broke in and tripped the wards. I only just had time to draw the runes before following."

Her words tumbled over each other, as if she was still rushing against the pull of the magic. This was too much information to take in all at once.

"The prophecy's gone?" I repeated, focusing on the only bit I understood. "Gone where?"

"Taken." Miss Caraway chucked a couple of pens in our direction. Asher caught one of them; the other landed at Zo's feet. "Write down everything you remember – everything you ever read." She clicked her fingers and pointed at the other white board.

Zo and Asher glanced at each other, then Zo picked up the fallen pen. They each took half of the whiteboard, beginning to write. I hovered, unsure what to do with myself. I had a vague memory of Callie reading something aloud when she'd first seen the book, but that wasn't going to be much use now.

"Was it him?" I asked.

Miss Trager didn't turn around. "Who else would want it?"

I shivered. Ben's looming figure was burned into my mind like the boogieman of childhood nightmares. I didn't know why the idea of him having the prophecy made that image so much more frightening. It wasn't like it had done us any good – most of the time the writing in it stayed stubbornly gibberish, and when it did unscramble itself into words, they were so cryptic we could only understand them after the fact.

"This is bad, right?" Zo asked. "Can he use the magic from it?"

None of the adults answered, but the lines around Miss Trager's mouth tightened. Mr Grandace just kept writing.

I hadn't thought about that part. Whatever magic Sammy had poured into the book must be incredibly strong. The idea of Ben gaining that, on top of the power he was siphoning from Callie, Elijah and everything else... well, it didn't bear thinking about. There was a reason Sammy and Miss Trager had fought so hard to keep their magic from him.

Asher gave up writing. "That's it. That's everything I remember."

Zo scrawled another couple of lines, then stopped too, her list of prophecy fragments running out. It wasn't surprising. Our former teachers had been protective of the book, only allowing us glimpses.

I scanned the lines Mr Grandace had written. He'd moved onto paper now, the board full. Unfamiliar strings of letters and words filled it, his writing devolving into nonsense.

"What are you...?" I trailed off. He was recording the gibberish. He'd run out of revealed prophecy and was now wasting time scrawling down the lines of unrelated letters Sammy had filled the pages with in her magical fugue state.

A part of me was impressed he could remember it... but a bigger part of me was suddenly really angry.

"This is bullshit!" The words exploded out of me.

Zo jumped, letting off a shower of sparks, and thunder crackled above us. So much for her being too numb to feel anything.

"Why are we wasting time on this?" I yelled. "Ben's escalating things, right? We need to get Callie out of there now!"

A small voice in the back of my mind told me I should be saying "Callie and Elijah," but a bigger voice knew that if it came down to it, I would leave him behind to save Callie, no question. I didn't want to think about what type of person that made me.

"Nothing has changed, Toby," Miss Caraway said. "It's still safer to leave Callie and Elijah where they are until—"

"What do you mean nothing's changed? He's getting more powerful and we're just watching him!"

Ben drew energy from everything around him, and magic where he could get it. The more chaotic the energy the better. Those explosions today would be enough to fuel his magic for months, let alone adding Sammy's notebook into the mix.

"I know it's hard," Miss Trager's voice was flat, exhausted. "But I genuinely don't think Ben plans to hurt Calliope."

"What would you know? You didn't even notice he'd enslaved your own sister!"

"That's enough!" Mr Grandace stepped between me and Miss Trager. A coloured cloud of magic seeped out around him, forcing me to calm down. I didn't need it. Miss Trager's face had frozen at my words, and I instantly regretted them.

"I'm sorry," I said and meant it. "It's just... you didn't see Callie tonight. She looked..." I couldn't even bring myself to say it. She looked scared and in pain. She looked like she was dying.

Zo touched my arm, squeezing it, but I didn't get much comfort from the gesture.

Miss Trager blinked, seeming to properly take us in for the first time tonight. "You saw her?" Her face paled and she sank back against one of the chairs. "Oh god, it was just supposed to be surveillance! I never would have left you if I'd—"

"We're fine," I said sharply, cutting her off. I didn't know if that was true in Julianna's case, but it had to be. "We'll be okay. But Callie won't."

Miss Trager swallowed. "We will get them out of there as soon as we can, I promise."

Her voice came out tight. She meant that, I'm sure, but given she hadn't managed to free her sister or Callie's father in the sixteen years they'd been Ben's prisoners, I didn't have high hopes of "as soon as we can" being any time soon.

"It's been a long day," Miss Caraway said. "How about you all get some rest and you take us through everything in the morning?"

I wanted to argue, but Asher was already moving to the door, ready to head back upstairs to check on Julianna.

Zo took my arm, squeezing it tight. "Come on," she said. "Let's go get something to eat."

I opened my mouth to protest, but my stomach rumbled at the thought of food. I closed my eyes for a moment, trying to will the sensation away, but I wasn't stronger than my own biological needs. "Jules nearly defeated him tonight, you know?" I said.

"Toby…" Asher's voice was a warning, but I ignored it.

"What do you mean?" Miss Trager asked. I didn't think it was possible, but she turned a shade paler at the thought.

"She hit him. The magic did next to nothing, but she punched him and it nearly knocked him out."

The teachers looked at each other, a silent conversation passing between them. Then Miss Caraway stepped towards me. "Come on. You can tell me everything while we eat."

Asher and Zo both glared at me, on the same page for once. Was I doing the wrong thing by revealing what Julianna had done? She was so fragile these days. It might actually break her if our teachers interrogated her over what happened. Honestly though, I didn't care. I'd let them break all of us if it meant getting Callie back.

Chapter Three

Callie

Heavy sobs wracked their way through me. The sound echoed in the tiny room, the concrete walls and floor closing in on me. I pressed my face into my pillow, trying to stifle my tears. I'd seen him. I'd been close enough to touch Toby, and instead, I'd shoved him away. Not just shoved him, I'd sent a blast of magic throwing him backwards. Was he hurt? Did I even have the right to ask that?

A soft knock sounded against my door. I froze, pressing a hand to my lips to muffle my ragged breath.

Be silent.

Be still.

I wouldn't survive this if I couldn't make myself small.

"It's me," Elijah whispered. He opened the door just a crack, then slipped through closing it behind him. "You have to stop crying."

I nodded but even as I did, a muffled hicuppy sound came out of my mouth and my chest shook. Elijah clicked his tongue, irritated, then padded the two steps across the dark room to reach the edge of my mattress. I shifted over so he could join me.

He lay down next to me, then slipped his arms around me, pulling me against his chest. My skin tingled as he touched me, and suddenly I realised how cold I was. His warmth felt charged, and I moved closer.

He made a noise in his throat, shaking his head. "Of all the people I could have got stuck with, I had to end up with the one that cries all the time."

I let out a laugh, and he shushed me. I swallowed, the humour dying in my throat. We both froze, listening.

I had survived years in foster care by making myself small enough not to be noticed. Why was I finding it so hard to do it again now?

Elijah traced soft circles on my back, gently soothing me despite his purported annoyance with my tears. "You saw him tonight, didn't you?" He didn't say Toby's name, but it was obvious who he meant.

I frowned. "Yeah. Didn't you?"

"I can't see anything when Ben's controlling us."

I wasn't sure whether that was a good or a bad thing. We'd caused so much destruction over the past few months. I wished I could forget some of the things I'd seen, but a part of me wanted to bear witness to it. A part of me wanted to know exactly what awful things I was doing, even if I couldn't stop them.

"Toby grabbed me," I told Elijah. "I... I hit him."

I couldn't get Toby's face out of my head. The shock in his eyes when I threw him backwards, then the way they'd shifted as he stared at me. What did I look like to him? I knew my body had changed in the last few months – I knew I had changed, my brittle shell thickening, petrifying the few parts inside of me I'd managed to keep soft. How much of that showed on the outside?

Elijah pulled back a little to look at me. His eyes flicked back and forth between mine. "Toby will be okay," he said. "He's a weedy little loser, but he's tough as anything."

I raised my eyebrows. "You, giving Toby a compliment? My crying must really be annoying you."

Elijah shrugged. "You already know you're annoying, Cal. Don't make me say it."

I let out a silent half-laugh, and a smile tweaked the corners of Elijah's lips. I could feel his breath on my neck and suddenly this all felt way too intimate. I pulled back, angling my face away so I didn't have to meet his eye. Even so, I could feel him watching me. He didn't remove his arms from around me.

Even after all this time, it still felt strange to be this close to him. There was no magnetic charge forcing me away, no magic trying to tear us apart. His warm arms circling around me were one of the only safe places I had... but still, it felt wrong.

He seemed to sense some of what I was thinking, and his face closed off. He shifted away a little, not meeting my eye. I had to fight the urge to draw him back – to pull him closer.

"Now you're done leaking everywhere, can we give this a go before the others wake up?"

I let out a slow breath. Of course. He hadn't come in here to comfort me – he wanted to keep trying with his pointless attempts to fix our magic. I was annoyed to find a part of me was disappointed. I squashed that down and pulled myself up into a sitting position.

"Yeah, okay." My voice came out hollow – my lack of enthusiasm flattening it out.

He sat up and raised his palms in front of him, ignoring

my lacklustre attitude. I half-heartedly raised mine, mirroring him.

He frowned, and grabbed my left hand, stretching my fingers out. "Can you concentrate, please?"

"Sorry." I tensed my fingers, putting more effort into keeping them flat. It was so strange how we had reversed roles. Elijah had always been the one the rest of us had had to reign in.

He closed his eyes, and I did the same, doing my best to "connect" to my magic. I felt it heavy and alien inside me, uncomfortable even after all this time using it. Honestly, I still found it hard to believe I had magic at all.

Elijah's energy reached out, finding the ends of the frayed connection between us. The loop of Ben's magic around me tightened as he did, almost as if Ben sensed our rebellion from the depths of his sleep. Elijah and I both froze, waiting. After a minute the constriction eased.

Elijah let out a breath. "It's okay. He doesn't know what we're doing."

Neither do we, I nearly said, but I kept the thought to myself. A few months ago, I couldn't have done that. Toby being able to read my thoughts had made me feel trapped at the time, but I'd had no idea how free I had really been. The bonds Ben held us with didn't join us in the same way that the connections to my classmates had. The rope of magic was only there for Ben's purposes – to contain us, to drain our energy, and when he deemed necessary, to puppet us like the slaves he believed we were.

Suddenly, magic flared in front of me. Tiny lines of fireflies lit up in the air, marking out the ends of my broken connection to Elijah. I gasped, pulling away, but they reached for me, stretching out to touch my fingertip.

"You can see it?" Elijah asked.

"Yeah."

"Take hold of the magic," he told me. "You can do it. It's yours."

It didn't feel like mine. I pinched the air next to one of the fireflies, gently tugging it towards me. It followed with little resistance.

Elijah let out a breath that was almost a laugh. "I *felt* that," he said.

"So, what do I do now?"

Elijah shrugged. "Let it tell you what to do. The magic should want to heal itself."

I frowned, but a second string of fireflies appeared, stretching out from my fingertips... almost as if they were reaching for Elijah, wanting to heal the bond between us just as he said.

The magic tickled against my fingertips, like insects crawling over my skin. They seemed to claw at me, just as disquieted by this as I was. My heart raced, and the fireflies jostled with each beat.

"Tie the ends together if you have to." A hint of impatience crept into Elijah's voice. "Just try something."

The pounding in my chest shot up a notch, and the fireflies blurred, their lines becoming less defined. I took a breath. New sparks lit up between me and Elijah, the fireflies guiding me like they always had.

I took hold of two tiny threads, one from Elijah, one from me. But as I did, other lines of lights lit up in the air, different colours fighting for my attention. I blinked, trying to focus on the remains of our connection. My eyes blurred, the pounding of my heart and the colours all too much.

Something slammed into me, throwing me back. I crumpled against the wall. Tiny flames burst into life on my skin, pain erupting with them. I drew breath to scream.

Suddenly, Elijah was beside me again, clapping his hand over my mouth. "Don't! Ben will hear you," he whispered.

The flames lapped at his palm, but he didn't let go. His fingers tightened against my cheek, flexing in pain.

God, it hurt. Nausea rolled through me, but the flames slowly shimmered then burnt out. *What was that?* I wanted to ask... but I already knew the answer.

Elijah removed his hand carefully. There was no sign of burn wounds. "I guess I still repel you," he said. His voice was tight, and it seemed to hold a question he didn't ask.

"I guess so." Something heavy settled in my chest.

We both fell silent. It wasn't like before. I wasn't being forced away from him – I could stay beside him without it hurting – but still... something in the magic didn't want the connection between us to be rebuilt.

His breaths were heavy, and I found myself matching my inhales to his.

"E?" I whispered.

He raised his head, but still didn't quite look at me. I slid my hand across the mattress, reaching for his.

The door opened. Elijah shot out of the bed. I froze, my throat tightening. A dark figure appeared, silhouetted in the doorway.

"Joe," Elijah said.

I let out a slow breath, mirroring Elijah's. Not Ben – just Joe.

Joe looked from me to Elijah, and my cheeks heated up. "I was crying," I blurted out. "Elijah—"

"Came to comfort you?" A scoff burst through Joe's lips, and there was no mistaking the sarcasm in his voice.

The heat in my cheeks turned to flames. "It wasn't like that," I mumbled.

I couldn't blame Joe for his scepticism. Elijah had never

been known for his empathetic abilities, and I knew what this must look like.

Elijah shrugged. "She was keeping me awake." He started towards the doorway, but Joe grabbed his arm.

"You need to watch yourself." Joe turned to me. "You both do."

I forced myself to look up – to hold Joe's eye. "Are you going to tell?" In another lifetime, we might have had this argument if I been caught sneaking out or hiding a boyfriend in my room, but there was no fatherly warmth or concern in Joe's face. All that flickered through his features was fear.

"I can't protect you if he catches you," he said.

"Well, it's a good thing he didn't." Elijah's voice dropped low, a hint of a threat in it.

Joe stared at him for a long moment and then he stepped aside, allowing Elijah space to leave the room.

Instead, Elijah glanced back at me. "We'll talk later, yeah?"

I made myself nod. I desperately wanted to flick my gaze to Joe, to see what he thought of this exchange. I didn't let myself. He was my father, yes, but I had no idea if he was on my side.

"Get to bed," Joe said. "Both of you."

I reluctantly settled back down on the mattress, though sleep was out of the question. Elijah gave a single nod of his head then turned away, leaving me with Joe.

Joe stared at me for a moment. He shook his head slowly, and I didn't know how to interpret the gesture.

"You need to be careful of him," he said finally.

"You got Mum pregnant at 17. You don't get to warn me about boys."

Joe blinked, and his mouth fell open, but no words came out.

I shouldn't have said that. It was petty and cruel, but something about being around Joe turned me into a child.

"You don't need to worry," I said, my voice barely more than a mumble. "It's not like that with Elijah. He really was just trying to comfort me."

Comfort me and connect to my magic so we could escape, but Joe didn't need to know about that part.

"That's not what I'm worried about."

I glanced up, frowning. Joe looked like he wanted to say something more but instead he moved to the door.

"Just be careful, okay? I meant what I said – I can't protect either of you from Ben."

"You dragged me away from Toby tonight," I said. "Your lack of ability to protect me is pretty obvious. Don't try to act like a dad now."

Joe frowned, and I grimaced. I shouldn't have said that either. I wasn't supposed to be aware of anything that was happening while I was under Ben's control.

I studied Joe's face. Had he figured out what Elijah and I had been doing? Did he know that I wasn't under Ben's control in quite the same way he, Chloe and Elijah were? He didn't give anything away, just stared at me, his frown deepening until it seemed his face would crack.

"I'll be careful," I said, breaking the silence. "I promise."

His expression remained blank, no sign of whether that answer satisfied him or not, but he nodded and turned away. He closed the door behind him, blocking out the dim light from the corridor.

I lay back against the mattress. Even if Joe did know what we'd been planning, did it matter? For months, Elijah and I had been trying to regain the connection between us. I never thought we would manage to do it, but now I was realising it might not matter even if we did. We still repelled each other –

polar opposites in the dangerous magnetic energy field we'd created.

I stretched my fingers out, feeling an echo of Elijah's magic pushing me back. I plucked at the thin threads of my own power, slowly coaxing the fireflies out. Why was this so different to my connection to Toby?

My heart squeezed at the thought of him. Toby had been right in front of me tonight. He had been within arm's reach, and I'd pushed him away. I let my eyes close, silently begging the universe for something else to fill my head.

Footsteps pacing the corridor answered. My eyes shot open. I clenched my fists, the fabric of the mattress gripped tightly in my hands as if that could somehow protect me. The footsteps got closer, until Ben was right outside my door.

Leave me alone, Ben, I whispered inside my head. *Please just leave me alone.*

He took a slow steady stream of energy from me at all times, but if he was coming closer, it meant he was going to take more. He kept the four of us prisoner, so he could get close enough to tear power from us, leaving us with next to nothing.

The loop of magic tying me to him tightened. It crushed my chest, forcing the air out of my lungs. But I could hear him breathing, right outside the doorway. Then I felt it, the slow drain speeding up, pulling more energy from me, taking away what little magic I had left.

Chapter Four

Callie

In the morning, I lay on my mattress for a long time, hoping to fall back asleep. When I didn't, I tried teasing out the threads of magic again. The lines of fireflies swayed towards my fingertips every time I moved as if they were trying to help, but they still felt alien to me, like pressing against a limb numb with pins and needles.

Joe, Elijah and Chloe's voices floated through from the other room. I couldn't hear the words, but from the cadence, they were chatting about nothing. Sometimes these were the worst parts – when things were calm, almost normal. Almost normal, but also so far from it it hurt.

My door was ajar, and Mosby padded his way in.

"Hey, buddy." I reached out a hand, but Mosby went straight for my face, wet nose snuffling against mine.

"I don't have any food, bud."

Mosby licked my face to check anyway, then padded back out of the room. From down the corridor, I heard Joe greet him in a high-pitched, excited tone, then the answering thump of Mosby's tail.

Chloe had told me Joe found him stray a few years ago. A part of me wondered if Joe had been trying to replace me by keeping him, but I didn't like thinking about that too much. Whatever Joe's reasons, having a friendly Labrador around did make things less bleak. Perhaps that's why Ben had let them keep him.

I pulled myself upright, and my head swam. My skin burned, every touch of my clothes stinging. I stretched out my fingers, watching them shake. Ben must have siphoned even more energy than usual.

I dragged myself down the corridor to the bathroom. We'd stayed here a few times before – one of several places Ben had set up for us to squat. He shifted us every time his paranoia got to him, so I had no idea how long we'd be here before he felt the need to uproot us once again. I didn't understand how Chloe and Joe had survived like this for seventeen years.

This was an old factory. The bathrooms were rows of stalls and sinks, with only one cold and mouldy shower, but at least the toilets still flushed. We'd stayed in much worse places over the last few months.

I stared down at the plug hole. A tiny vine had crept up through the pipes overnight, spreading into the basin. Was it my magic or Joe's that had coaxed it to grow? I stared at the leaves, willing them to grow faster. An out-of-control plant like Toby's would surely disrupt Ben's magic enough to free us. Instead, the vine withered, curling up and retreating back down the pipes. I turned on the tap, flushing it away.

I washed quickly with cold water, standing over the sink, too nervous to fully undress. Sometimes Elijah and I stood guard for each other, but I still didn't trust Ben not to drag us away from here half-naked.

My hair clumped together in greasy strings, but there wasn't much I could do about that. Hopefully the next place he towed us off to would have hot water, or at the very least shampoo.

I made my way down to the old employee staffroom. It had cooking facilities, and the smell of something savoury made my stomach rumble. The power was off, of course, but Ben allowed Chloe and Joe enough use of their magic to deal with practicalities like that. If I asked nicely, she might even heat enough water for me to fashion a bath.

Joe and Elijah fell quiet as I came into the room. That bugged me – that Elijah was forming a relationship with my... Joe. It didn't feel right to call him my dad. I wasn't sure what he was to me, but it wasn't that.

Chloe handed me a plate of eggs. They were overcooked, and heavily peppered by the smell, but I took them gratefully. Chloe served up a plate for herself and sat down next to me.

When I'd first seen her, however many weeks ago it was, I'd thought she was Miss Trager. Now, I wasn't sure how I'd made that mistake. Sure, she had the same fair hair, but Chloe's face was harder, her manner flintier. Miss Trager had seemed broken the last time I'd seen her.

I shook my head, trying to clear the image, and shovelled a couple of forkfuls of eggs into my mouth. Almost immediately, my stomach objected. I forced myself to swallow but pushed the plate away.

"Too burnt?" Chloe asked.

I shook my head. "No, they're fine. My stomach just hurts."

Joe frowned. "You need to eat."

I looked up, meeting his eye, then shook my head. I was sure I'd vomit if I opened my mouth again. Chloe and Joe glanced at each other, then Chloe reached a hand across the table. Magic seeped off her, and I jerked away.

"Let me help you." Chloe's voice was low. "Joe's right, you have to eat."

I glanced between the two of them. Their expressions told me nothing. What had prompted this show of paternal concern?

Elijah gave a mocking shake of his head. "Only you could need magical help to eat a plate of eggs, Cal." His tone was light, but the muscles in his neck were tight, and I could feel his leg jiggling under the table.

Chloe gave me something which almost passed for a concerned smile. I must have looked worse than I thought if they were all this worried. Or perhaps they just wanted me to get stronger, so Ben didn't decide I was too weak and start farming more energy from them instead.

I picked up my fork, scooping another mouthful of egg on to it. Waves of magic flowed out from Chloe, competing with the waves of nausea. I resisted the urge to pull away this time. Despite myself, I relaxed into her power. My stomach eased, and I managed to eat another few bites before the sick feeling returned.

Chloe let the magic fall away. "Good. It's annoying when you let my cooking go to waste." She picked up my half-finished plate and took it out to the kitchen. Joe gave me a nod, then followed after her.

"What was that about?" I asked Elijah, once they were out of earshot.

"Huh?"

"The three of you staging a breakfast-intervention?"

Elijah rolled his eyes. "If you would just eat like a normal person—"

I touched his arm, making him stop. "E, what's going on?"

Elijah glanced towards the kitchenette, where Joe and Chloe stood together, speaking in low voices. Elijah let out a heavy breath, then nodded towards the door. "Outside."

I followed him down the corridor towards the dirt yard outside the factory. If you could call it a yard. The narrow strip of bare earth was a bleak parody, but I'd take any outdoor time over being trapped inside twenty-four seven. We stepped through the door, and immediately, the ropes of magic around me tightened, straining at the slight distance from the building. I stopped, breathing lightly as they constricted around my chest. *It's okay*, I whispered inside my head. *We're not trying to run.*

Slowly, the tension eased, allowing me the tiniest bit more freedom. We walked to the fence, leaning back against it.

"Would you believe it's just Joe trying to be a good dad and look out for you?"

I frowned. "No. And don't be an ass."

Elijah smirked. "Fine, no playing on your daddy issues."

"E..." A little pang of guilt hit under my ribs. Him bringing up my relationship with Joe was manipulative, but so was me using that nickname. I could tell he liked that I had a special name for him. I could tell he thought it meant more than it did.

He fiddled with a loose loop of wire on the fence. "Last night – it was a distraction. He was trying to draw Mr Grandace and the others out."

Draw them out for what? Something caught in my throat. "He didn't hurt them, did he?"

Elijah shook his head. "No, but he sent Chloe to the school."

"Why?" Was it bad that I hadn't noticed Chloe wasn't with us last night? In all the chaos, it had been hard to keep track of the others.

"He got her to take the prophecy."

I blinked. "You mean..."

"Your mum's prophecy, yeah. The one Miss Trager used to start all this bullshit."

There was a lot to unpack there. I'd held Mum's notebook for approximately two minutes before everything went to shit. Even thinking about it gave me *Feelings* with a capital F, but what did Ben want with it? He wouldn't be able to read it. Even if he could, all it ever seemed to have done was lead Miss Trager and Mr Grandace down dangerous and confusing paths, creating more and more chaos as they went.

"What does that have to do with me eating Chloe's gross eggs?" That was not the most important question by far, but it was the only one that felt safe to ask.

Elijah yanked the piece of wire, ripping it free from the fence. He stared at it, as if surprised by his own strength, and then tossed it across the yard, letting it land in the dirt. "He drained energy from you again last night, didn't he?" he asked. "After I left?"

I swallowed, fighting the urge to shudder. The hollow sound of Ben's footsteps walking towards my room echoed in my mind, as did the tight feeling of his magic constricting around my chest.

Elijah touched my arm, squeezing it gently. I couldn't help but notice that his hand closed nearly all the way around my bicep. Perhaps Joe and Chloe were right when they said I needed to eat.

"This could get worse," he said. "We need you to be strong. *I* need you to be strong."

I understood that, but a plate of burnt eggs wasn't going to steel me enough to break us out.

"Tonight, we'll try again, yeah?" he said. "With the magic?"

Dread built in my stomach at the thought of trying to persuade my magic to behave the way we wanted it to. "You really think that will work?"

Elijah studied my face for a moment, then slowly let go of

me. His palm brushed softly down the length of my arm. There was no charge forcing me away this time. My skin tingled under his touch, and I had to resist the urge to shiver, but the contact didn't repel me, quite the opposite.

He said something under his breath. I wasn't sure I'd heard correctly, but it sounded like: "It might if you let it."

I automatically took half a step away but forced myself to stop there. Maybe he was right. Maybe last night was a fluke, and our magic wouldn't magnetically force us from each other if we tried again. Maybe...

"One more shot," I told him. "But after that, we stop. I can't keep getting my hopes up."

He nodded, relaxing a little now he'd got me to agree.

None of this really mattered anyway. Whether or not we managed to reconnect our magic, there was something much more important at stake now – the prophecy. We had to figure out a way to stop Ben using it. Nothing good ever came from that book, and I had a feeling we were all going to be sorry that Ben had got his hands on it.

Chapter Five

Toby

I didn't sleep that night. Every time I closed my eyes, it was either Callie's face staring at me from behind my eyelids, or an echo of that humming. What was that sound?

When the sky outside my window turned light enough that I could plausibly call it morning, I got up, too frustrated to try to sleep any longer.

The dormitory floor was quiet, all of the rooms dark except for Julianna's where a thin line of yellow snuck under the doorway. I hesitated outside it. Jules and I had never been close, and these days she seemed so broken it was hard for anyone to connect with her at all. In that moment, I wanted to talk to her anyway – to question how exactly she had managed to fight Ben – but it was obvious she didn't know either. Forcing her to talk about it would be cruel.

I stared at Zo's door instead, willing her to wake and join me. It just hadn't been the same since Ben's magic weakened our links to each other. Being so deeply connected that we constantly dragged each other in and out of sleep had been annoying, but I'd give anything to be able to see parts of Callie and Zo's dreams right now. Hell, I even missed the six of us sleeping in the same room – the closeness of it. I never thought I'd hear myself say that about those damn bunkbeds.

I turned away from the girls' rooms, leaving them to their peace, and made my way downstairs to the planning room. I got half a step through the doorway before I stopped, staring.

Miss Trager sat on a chair in the middle of the room, wrapped in a blanket and sipping a coffee. A battered and dirty book lay open on her lap, and loose pages of writing surrounded her, all of it scrawled in red ink. When I say they surrounded her, I mean *surrounded* her. Sheets of Mr Grandace's handwriting covered every inch of the floor, table, and walls. He sat on the carpet in the corner, still scribbling.

"Morning, Toby," Miss Trager said.

"Morning..." I said, not taking my eyes off Mr Grandace. "What the... What is this?"

Miss Trager nodded to herself slowly, as if she'd asked herself that same question several times today already. She closed the book on her lap, carefully folding a bookmark between the pages.

"It's the prophecy," she said finally. "All of it." She waved a hand at one section of floor. "Black ink is stuff that's already become clear. Red is still indecipherable."

I glanced over, noting the pages she'd indicated. There was a hell of a lot more red than black. "How did he remember all this?" I scanned the pages on the walls, taking in the strings of unconnected letters.

It didn't seem to matter that I was talking in front of Mr Grandace. His focus had 100 percent narrowed to the page in front of him.

"He read it so many times over the years. He spent years poring over it to find the six of you. He thought it could stop it

– all of this." She flapped her hand in a vague gesture encompassing "everything".

I noted that she said "he" not "we". Something told me she'd given up hours ago, staying only to stop Mr Grandace going completely over the edge. Her tone was either serene or numb, I couldn't quite tell which.

"Woah…" Zo's voice sounded behind me.

I turned to see her in the doorway, staring just like I had. She stepped towards me, and linked her arm through mine, as if she needed an anchor to avoid being swamped by the words. Fragments of her thoughts rushed through my head, our connection sparking back into life now she was awake. Her internal narrative amounted to much the same as what I was thinking – this was amazing and terrifying, and perhaps we should be concerned for Mr Grandace's mental health.

He raised his head, as if I'd said that aloud. "Can you read any of it?" he asked.

Miss Trager glanced around but made no effort to get up and properly look at the pages. To be fair, she'd probably been staring at them all night.

Zo and I looked at each other, then she let go of my arm to wander towards one of the walls of red text. I did the same, taking the other side of the room. Given I'd never been able to read any of the prophecy, even when it was written in Sammy's original script, the likelihood of me deciphering any of this was low. Honestly, I wasn't sure this would work for any of us. I stared at the lines of text anyway, willing them to turn into proper words.

"The girl will know only that her mother died, and her grandmother raised her…"

I whipped around. Zo stood at the wall, her finger tracing along lines of Mr Grandace's scrawl. Miss Trager's head shot up too, and we both converged on Zo.

"You can read it?"

Zo nodded. A flush of excitement rose up inside me.

"The magic will be in her," Zo continued. "And when the time is right, she will..." she trailed off, squinting. "I can't read the next bit."

"And when the time is right, she will defeat him," Miss Trager murmured. She closed her eyes, remembering. "She will live sixteen summers before magic finds her, and on her seventeenth birthday, the sky will burst into fire, and it will begin."

The excitement I'd felt a moment earlier crashed down, hard. We'd already read that, and it had happened months ago. Well, most of it at least. The fire at Callie's birthday had been the start of everything going wrong.

"Why does it have to do that?" I slammed my hand against the page on the wall. "Why does it keep showing us the same things, when they don't help?"

Mr Grandace shook his head. "No, this is a good thing, Toby. Don't you see?" He got up, gesturing around at the pages. "We can still read it. I was scared it wouldn't work without the actual book, but we can still decipher Sammy's words—"

"No, we can't!" I grabbed one of the sheets of paper, pulling it from the wall. "We just get the same things over and over. It doesn't mean anything!"

I raised the page, ready to tear it in two. Zo and Miss Trager grabbed my wrists. Waves of colourful magic spewed out from Miss Trager as she tried to force me to calm down.

"Don't do this, Tobes," Zo said. There were no colours from her, only sparks which burned my skin, but I didn't let go. "You know you'll regret it."

I did, but it would feel so good to be destructive right now. She squeezed my arm, and the fight rushed out of me.

"I'm sorry," I told her.

"I know. It's okay." Miss Trager pulled gently on the page. I didn't release it. I wasn't sure why, but I couldn't quite let go yet. Almost as if in answer to that unspoken question, something shifted on the page.

"Woah..."

The letters rearranged themselves, blurring and reshaping into something different.

Miss Trager's hand slipped from my wrist to my arm. "What is it? What can you see?"

The words appeared one at a time. "They must... break the connections, and it... must... end in... flames."

Mr Grandace grabbed a black pen. "See? It's working. We've never read that bit before."

I took a breath, bubbles of hope rising inside me. But then I caught sight of Miss Trager's face.

"Except that's already happened, hasn't it?" I asked. "You and Sammy broke the connections, and..."

Miss Trager winced. I trailed off, not wanting to make her feel worse.

"It's okay, Toby," she said, her voice tight. "It's still useful. That's a bit we hadn't read before." She pulled another sheet from the wall. "Try again. See if you can read anything else."

I took the sheet from her, but the bubbles of hope had well and truly popped. The strings of letters on this sheet remained gibberish. I shook my head. Zo handed me a third piece of paper. Immediately the red text swirled.

"Everything... good... comes in... cardboard."

I looked up at the others, but silence greeted my words. That was... not helpful.

"Excellent!" Mr Grandace grabbed another sheet of paper, writing that down in black ink. "Now we're getting somewhere."

Zo and Miss Trager exchanged a look but didn't stop him. Fuck, I was useless. The only time I'd ever been able to read anything from the prophecy, and it was something so utterly pointless, I couldn't even be sure I'd got it right.

"Keep looking!" Mr Grandace said. "There's sure to be more."

Zo and Miss Trager glanced at each other again, then slowly turned back to the walls. They did as they were told, eyes scanning the pages for anything that jumped out, but I could tell their hearts weren't in it. Neither was mine.

"I can't," I said. "This is fucked. We should be out there looking for her, and you all know it."

Zo sighed. "Toby..."

I didn't wait for her to finish. I turned and left the room, heading back to the dorm. At least there, I didn't have to pretend my failures were helping anyone.

* * * *

ZO KNOCKED ON MY bedroom door later that afternoon. I felt the warmth of her magic and the edges of her thoughts through the wall.

I'd spent the day in my room, moping, pacing, and trying to plan some great rescue where I could race in and drag Callie out of Ben's clutches. So far, I'd been thwarted by one pretty big problem – I had no idea where she was.

The humming I heard when she was close helped, but it only worked in a certain proximity. Much as I wanted to, I couldn't wander the entire city listening for it. If she was even still in the city, of course.

I didn't answer Zo's knock, and eventually she popped her head around the doorway. "You sulking?"

I rolled my eyes. "I'm not sulking."

She made a face that made it clear she didn't believe me. "I brought you some food," she said. "Guessing your pride didn't let you come out for snacks."

My stomach rumbled as if in response, the traitor. Zo grinned and held out a plate. In the centre was a sandwich, with a necklace of alternating red and green grapes around the edge. I popped two of them in my mouth, my mood instantly lifting at the promise of a blood sugar hit.

"Thanks. You're a good friend."

She shrugged. "Miss Caraway made it, I just volunteered to bring it up. No one else wanted to deal with Hangry Tobes." She grabbed one of the grapes and bit into it.

She sat down on the end of my bed, and I pulled myself upright to join her, folding myself into cross-legged position.

"For what it's worth, I agree with you," she said. "We can't sit around trying to read that nonsense. We need to get out there looking for them."

"So, why didn't you say anything?"

"Because *they're* not going to agree with you. There's no point arguing."

"We can't just leave her there, Zo."

"I know, I know."

Callie's image kept appearing in my mind. She'd been so thin, so desperate looking.

Zo studied my face and chewed on her lip. I couldn't quite catch the thoughts that ran through her mind. She had a song in her head – perhaps as a cover to hide her thoughts, or maybe just an earworm. I had this stupid feeling that I *missed* her. She was right there in front of me, not lost like Callie, but the closeness we'd once felt was absent.

It wasn't like I wished things could go back to the way they were, because they had never been good. We'd been prisoners at the school, even though we hadn't known it, and then everything had gone so badly wrong once we left. I wanted life to be the way it felt like it should have been. Magic *should* have been easy; *our connection* should have been easy. And most of all, Callie should have been here.

"Thing is..." Zo said quietly. "I think I might know where they are..."

I jerked, sending the grapes rolling off the plate and onto the floor. "What?"

"That thing you read – the bit about the cardboard – I think I know what it means."

"What?!" Everything good comes in cardboard? How could that mean *anything*, let alone be the answer to finding Callie?

Zo hesitated. She picked up one of the escaped grapes and squished it between her fingers.

I grabbed it off her, dumping it back on the plate. "Zo, you can't just say something like that and then not tell me. Where is she?"

Zo shook her head. "Eat something first. I'm not dealing with you when you're all low-blood-sugar grumpy."

"Zo!" The edge to my voice probably didn't help my case.

She stared at me, her eyebrows raised. I wanted to throw the food at her more than I wanted to eat it, but I picked up half of the sandwich, shoving the whole thing in my mouth in one go.

Zo made a face. "Classy."

"Just tell me," I said around the stodge of bread.

"Can I trust you not to do something stupid?"

I groaned. "Zo, seriously?" I swallowed the last of the sandwich, fighting back the urge to cough.

She shook her head slowly, a decision flickering behind her eyes. "I'm not going to tell you where she is."

I opened my mouth to protest, but she held up a hand, indicating she wasn't finished. "But I will go with you."

My automatic response was to refuse. It was one thing for me to put myself in danger, but it was quite another to drag Zo into it with me. She shrugged, almost like she didn't care either way.

"Take it or leave it, Tobes. Either we go together, or I tell Miss Trager and Mr Grandace what I know, and they sit on it for months like everything else."

Zo leaned back on her elbows and picked up another grape. She chewed on it, her expression thoughtful, but as far as I could tell there was nothing but that song in her head.

I knew her. If she said she wasn't going to tell me, she wouldn't; there was no getting around it. I didn't want to think about our only lead going to Miss Trager and Mr Grandace, who would indeed do absolutely nothing.

I nodded, slowly. "Okay," I said. "But if anything happens, you let me take the fall, yeah?"

Zo gave a snort. "Naturally." She got up from my bed and started towards the door.

"Um... excuse me? Aren't you forgetting something?"

Zo looked back, raising her eyebrows. "I already said I'm not telling you. You think I trust you not to run off during the night? We know how that played out last time."

"I'm not Callie."

"Yeah, but you're just as stupid when it comes to rescuing her." Zo gave a stretch, calm and casual as always. "We'll leave in the morning. Try not to think too much about it. We don't want the others getting wind of it."

The song she'd been singing rose up again in her thoughts, blocking out everything else. I suspected I'd be hearing it from her all night.

"In the morning," I echoed.

Zo reached out and squeezed my hand. I squeezed back,

pact made. She shut the door quietly behind her. I turned back to the food she'd left me and bit into the other half of the sandwich, stopping to chew it this time.

The last time Zo and Callie had seen each other, Zo was mad at Callie. For a while, I'd thought that might make Zo less motivated to help find Callie, but honestly, I think it was part of what fuelled her. We all had amends to make – we all wanted to fix the things that had been broken. And for the first time in months, I had a spark of hope that we might be able to do it.

Chapter Six

Callie

Ben's lurking figure reappeared that afternoon. We all felt him before we saw him. A tightness rushed through the room that made us all sit up straighter. Mosby raised his head from my lap to growl, and the hairs on my arms stood on end, all senses tingling, ready for an attack.

We were back sitting in the staffroom again, but the atmosphere was easier than this morning. Joe and I had even exchanged a few words. Nothing of consequence of course, but it was better than the awkward attempts at avoiding each other's eyes we usually did.

Ben's entrance plunged us back into silence. He limped into the room, moving stiffly. "Did you leave me any food, Clo?" he asked.

God, he was an arrogant asshole, expecting her to cook for him after everything he'd done.

Chloe just shrugged. "On the bench."

I'm pretty sure the only thing on the bench was my half-eaten plate of eggs, and the thought of Chloe feeding him my gross leftovers gave me more pleasure than I cared to admit. I saw a flicker of recognition on Elijah's face too. I avoided looking at him in case I laughed.

Ben picked up the plate and ate a forkful of the eggs. He grimaced at the taste but ate another bite anyway. He came over, sitting on the arm of Chloe's chair.

I always had a hard time reconciling his physical presence with the looming figure in my mind. His power felt huge – overwhelming – but the man in front of us was old beyond his years. His eyes were sunken, and his shoulders hunched. He'd been tall once, that much was obvious, but his body had withered down, shrinking him as his spine compacted.

"Can either of you cook?" he asked, looking at me and Elijah.

Elijah's jaw tensed, and I reached over Mosby to grab Elijah's arm before he did something stupid like try to hit Ben.

Be silent.

Be still.

Mosby licked Elijah's hands as if he understood the risk and wanted to soothe it too.

"Fuck, you're an asshole." Chloe shoved Ben off her chair. "We're not your slav—" she cut herself off, probably remembering we *were* in fact his slaves.

Ben's brow creased, but he didn't yell at her. If Joe or Elijah had said anything like that, they probably would have landed themselves a magical blow to the chest. I'd seen Elijah laid out enough times in our first few weeks under Ben's control to know how bad it could be. Personally, I'd never been brave enough – or stupid enough – to try to defy him.

But Chloe? Chloe was his sister, and she could get away with things we couldn't.

"Whatever," she said quietly. "Cook your own food if you don't like mine."

She got up and moved over to the couch beside Joe. Ben

took her chair. He sat down properly and ate the rest of the eggs in silence.

I gave Elijah's arm a squeeze before releasing it. It was always hard to assess what to do at times like this. I wanted to run away – go and hide in my room or Elijah's until Ben decided he'd had enough of "company" and pissed off to wherever it was he went when he wasn't around us.

But sometimes he got mad when we did that. Sometimes he got suspicious and wanted to know what we were hiding, lashing out at us or stealing more energy just to be punitive.

Ben put his empty plate down on the floor. Mosby abandoned me to go and lick it, even allowing Ben to stroke him. I loved the mutt, but his stomach definitely took priority over loyalty.

"Are you feeling okay?" Ben asked.

I looked up. He still held the fork and twisted it between his fingers. He stared at me, the question clearly directed my way. This was new. He didn't normally care how we were coping – or perhaps he just didn't want to know the answer.

Elijah spoke before I could. "How do you think she's feeling?" he said, his voice hard. "Steal more energy from her last night, did you? Why is it always Callie? You got some fetish for teenage girls?"

I kicked Elijah's leg hard. Fortunately, Ben ignored him. He studied my face for a moment, and then his jaw unclenched enough to speak.

"I need something from you," he said, evidently giving up on the pretence of checking up on me.

Elijah made a noise in his throat, and I could already hear the snark about to spill out of his mouth.

"E, don't," I said under my breath. I didn't look at him, but I could practically feel his teeth clamp hard on his own tongue, shutting down whatever antagonistic thing he'd been about to say.

I turned my focus back to Ben. "What do you need?"

A muscle in my face twitched at the measured tone coming out of my mouth. Playing nice was to keep me and Elijah safe, I reminded myself. I could still judge Ben for his awful life choices in private.

Ben hesitated, then he reached inside his jacket, pulling out a notebook. My breath caught. Even though Elijah had told me Ben had the prophecy, it was different seeing my mother's book in his hands.

Ben held it out. "Can you read it?"

I shrugged. Honestly, I didn't know. A few phrases had become clear to me, in the two minutes I'd been allowed to hold the book, but I hadn't exactly had the chance to peruse it, what with him enslaving me less than an hour later.

I did know, however, that even if I could read every word, I wasn't going to tell Ben a single goddamned thing.

Ben stood. He moved towards me, opening the book and splaying the pages in front of me. "Try," he said.

Mosby wandered over, reaching up to sniff the book, and Elijah leaned in, peering over my shoulder. I couldn't blame him. Our whole lives had been upended because of the prophecy. Had Elijah even seen it before? I suspected he was about to be sorely disappointed. My last encounter with my mum's book had been a monumental anti-climax.

I scanned the page. Scrambled strings of letters scrawled across it. They shifted as I tried to read them, but none of them rearranged themselves into words.

I looked up at Ben, shaking my head. He grimaced, then turned the page. "Try again."

I sighed. This could stretch out for hours, if not days – Ben making me stare at the book until something became clear.

Perhaps that would be a good thing, though. At least it would keep him distracted from creating more explosions.

I shook my head. Nothing on the second page became readable either. Ben turned to another. Immediately the letters swirled, forming something coherent. My eyes widened, scanning the lines before I could stop myself.

She will see the threads, and she will follow them. They will all find the way out when they untangle the web.

Ben's hand closed tight on my arm. "What is it? What did you read?"

"I…" Damn my lack of poker face. I scrambled for something I could say instead, but my mind went blank.

Threads – just like Elijah and I had been trying to regrow between us. But Ben couldn't know about that.

Ben yanked me to my feet, displacing Mosby. And suddenly everyone was moving. Chloe grabbed Ben and tried to pull him off me, but Ben shoved her back with a blast of power. Mosby started growling, then barking at Ben. Joe stepped in front of Elijah, pre-empting his attack.

Ben twisted my arm, making it burn, and the magic rope tightened around my chest, locking me in place. "Read it, goddamn it. Read it aloud!" He thrust the book into my face.

"Read it yourself!" I shoved him, and to my surprise, he stumbled backwards. He righted himself and a rush of cold ran through me.

He stepped towards me, and I dropped my gaze to the ground, making myself small.

Be silent.

Be still.

He came right up close, his eyes burning into me. My heart hammered but he made no move to hit me. Instead, he turned towards Elijah.

I gasped. "Wait…"

Ben pushed Joe aside, then took hold of Elijah's hand. Elijah's eyes went wide then blank.

"What are you doing? Leave him alone."

"I'm not doing anything," Ben said, his tone light. He stepped back.

My stomach dropped. Ben had placed his fork in Elijah's hand. Elijah lifted his arm, slowly, muscles straining against Ben's control. I looked desperately to Joe. He grimaced but made no move to help either of us.

Elijah raised the fork, pointing the tines towards his own eye. They moved closer... closer... and then suddenly jerked back.

"Okay, okay! Stop," I gasped.

Elijah froze, fork still in the air. Chloe's breath came out in a rush.

"I'll read it," I said. "Just let me..." I reached for the book. "I didn't see it properly."

Apparently, this was the right bluff. The constriction around my chest relaxed, letting me breathe. Elijah remained frozen, the threat still in place. I felt Chloe's eyes on me. I could almost hear her willing me to lie.

I scanned the page again. *She will see the threads, and she will follow them...*

I couldn't tell him that. Another section of the page swirled, letters rearranging themselves, as I scrambled for a plausible lie. Woah. This one was different. This one was...

"Callie will read of her mother's love in the prophecy," I read aloud. "And she will tell her father he is forgiven."

My voice cracked. The prophecy was a lot of things, but an "I love you" message from beyond the grave wasn't one I'd been expecting.

"Oh my god," Joe whispered.

I looked up at him. He met my eye and his whole face

crumpled. For a moment, I had forgotten he was the father in question. Not that he had acted like it just now.

"Bullshit!" Ben yanked the book from my hands, hurling it at the floor. "That can't be all you read."

Elijah and Chloe both came to life, Ben's outburst breaking his hold on them. Elijah pulled me back, putting me behind him. He threw out some magic, but Ben walked straight through it, almost seeming to get stronger as it touched him.

"It is," I said. "I'm sorry." I wouldn't tell him about the threads. No matter what, I wouldn't tell him.

"You're lying. There has to be more."

The loop around me tightened, and my knees buckled. He pulled energy from me, tearing it free like strings of sinew ripped from my limbs. I groaned, the sound turning to a shiver. Spots danced in front of my eyes, and everything dissolved into blobs of colour.

Chloe grabbed me and wrapped an arm around me, as if she could protect me that way. "Stop it, Ben! She's too weak, you'll kill her."

"Maybe that will make her read the prophecy faster."

Elijah punched him, hard. "Touch her again, and I'll kill you."

Ben crumpled under the blow. He blinked, dazed, and blood spurted from his nose. Elijah raised his fist again. Ben threw out a magical blow, sending Elijah flying back. Elijah hit the floor with a crack.

"Ben, don't!" Chloe's hand flew to her mouth.

Ben stalked after Elijah.

"Please," I whispered, but it barely made a sound.

Fear flickered in Elijah's eyes. He let out a cry and folded over. His skin went pale, the colour rushing out of him as Ben took his energy. A second later, Joe doubled over too.

"Stop it, you're taking too much!" Chloe yelled.

I tried to get up, but I couldn't. Colours still danced in front of my eyes. I could see the outlines of Chloe and Elijah, but their features were gone. Ben's outline shifted, patches fading in and out. He was barely person-shaped, just a swarming mass of other people's power. I cringed away from it, horrified.

"Fireflies," I whispered.

If Chloe heard me, she didn't react. Suddenly, all I could see was magic. The ends of my severed connection with Elijah lit up, but there were more lines than that – new ones I'd never seen before. A string joined Elijah to Ben. I watched as energy slipped along it, pulled from under Elijah's skin.

Threads tied Ben to me, Joe, and Chloe, and energy leached along those too. The chord between Joe and Chloe pulsed. Magic travelled along it in huge sucking gulps. It flowed onto Ben, through Chloe's connection to him.

"Oh my god." I blinked, hoping fresh eyes would change what I was seeing. "No... it can't be her. She can't be..." Was Chloe intentionally helping Ben steal energy?

The lines disappeared, reality settling back into place. Ben stalked towards us, slow and deliberate. Elijah forced himself upright, refusing to fold. He stood in Ben's path, ready to attack. In a fair fight, Elijah might have won. But this wasn't a fair fight. This was an ambush from a grown man pumped up on other people's magic.

I strained my eyes, trying to make the magic light up again. Panic made my vision blur. I would do as my mum had said – I would follow the threads and unravel the web if only she gave me the chance. But there was nothing – only the sound of Ben's ragged breathing as he moved towards Elijah.

Elijah's fingers tightened around the fork still in his hand. The muscles in his arm twitched, as Ben regained control.

"Don't. Please!" I yelled.

Ben's eyes flicked to me, and I tried desperately to hold them there.

"Are you ready to read the prophecy, Calliope?" he asked.

"I'll keep trying, but Chloe's right; I'm weak." It killed me to say that, because I had spent my whole life trying to be anything but. "I can't use magic when you keep draining me," I told him. "Just... just..." Just don't hurt Elijah over my lies was what I really wanted to say.

"Just let her recover," Chloe supplied. "She can try reading it again tomorrow."

Ben looked between us. Joe lay in a heap on the floor. Elijah squared off, ready to fight to the death, and Chloe and I cowered as Ben drained the life out of us.

"Tomorrow," he said. "Tomorrow, you tell me everything it says."

"Yes. I promise."

He nodded at my acquiescence then turned away. I held my breath, listening to his footsteps retreating down the corridor. I almost broke down at the sound.

Chloe grabbed my arm as soon as he was gone. "Come on." She dragged me out into the corridor.

Her touch felt like it was burning me. What had she done? What had Ben promised her to make her help him steal energy like that?

She yanked me along, not letting me stop until we reached my room.

"What about Joe?" My voice came out as a croak.

She closed the door behind us. "He'll be fine. He's always fine," she said, her mouth set into a grim line.

That wasn't comforting at all. I eyed the door. "And Elijah?"

Chloe shrugged. He would never be her priority as much as he was mine. I'd always thought Chloe seemed to care about me a little but ultimately, she was just trying to survive. If it came down to it, she'd probably let Ben skin me and Elijah alive if it meant she got out of this. Skin us alive… or drain us to death.

I glanced towards the door again. I wished she hadn't shut it.

Chloe hovered, her gaze tracing over the concrete walls. I eyed her, warily. Did she know what I'd seen? All this time, I'd thought she was a prisoner just like us, but if she was feeding energy to Ben, then…

"I saw something in the magic." My voice was hard, the words a threat.

Chloe's eyes narrowed. "What do you mean?"

I swallowed, my throat painfully dry suddenly. "I—"

Elijah opened the door. I let out a breath, all my resolve disappearing with the puff of air. What had I been thinking? You don't confront the beast alone.

Elijah crossed the room in a single stride and sank down onto my mattress, laying his head in his hands. He was pale, shaking, and sweat beaded on his forehead.

"Are you okay?" I sat down beside him and touched his shoulder gently. He flinched. How much energy had Ben taken from him?

He pulled his palms down his face, a low hiss escaping through his lips. "Are *you*?" he asked.

I didn't know how to answer that. A heaviness had settled over my chest, perhaps from where Ben had stolen energy from me, perhaps just from the knowledge that he had the prophecy and planned to use it.

"I will be," I said finally.

An image of the tines of the fork inching towards Elijah's face flashed through my head.

Did Elijah know what had happened? Did he know how

close he'd just come to losing an eye because of me, or had Ben's control shielded him from that?

"And Joe?" Chloe asked.

I made a noise in my throat. "Like you care."

Chloe frowned. "What's that supposed to mean?"

I stared her down for a moment, and then dropped my gaze.

Be silent.

Be still.

Why was this so much harder than it used to be?

"Cal?" Elijah squeezed my knee.

"It's nothing." I made myself flick my gaze up, briefly meeting Chloe's eye. "I didn't mean anything." This room was too small for three people.

"What did you read in the prophecy?" Chloe asked.

I shook my head. "I told you. *Callie will read of her mother's love —*"

"Not that bit. What else?"

I shook my head again. "Nothing. That was it."

Chloe narrowed her eyes. "Are you sure?"

I nodded, not trusting myself to lie convincingly. She studied my face, and something flickered in her expression. She didn't believe me.

"Fine, be like that. You're so like Ursula sometimes."

I was like Miss Trager? As far as I was concerned, I was about as different from my former teacher as you could get.

Chloe paused, as if she was expecting me to argue with her about that, then she shook her head. "I'll talk to you later then."

I was surprised to hear a hint of hurt in her voice. She was a damn good liar. If I hadn't seen her sucking energy from Joe with my own eyes, I never would have believed it. She left the room, slamming the door behind her. I slumped forward as she did, all the tension rushing out of me. I lay down, dizzy and exhausted suddenly.

Elijah was quiet for a moment, then he lay back next to me, staring up at the ceiling. "You did read something else, didn't you?" he asked.

I nodded. "And saw something. We can't trust Chloe."

A slight frown puckered between Elijah's eyebrows but otherwise his face remained blank. "Good thing I didn't trust her to start with."

I gave a half-laugh. "Never trust a Trager, eh?"

He rolled onto his side, propping his head up to look at me. "So what happened?"

Where did I start? "When Ben was stealing energy from us, I could see it." I shivered. The way the magic had taken over made me feel strange. It was like someone had changed the channel in my brain. "Only, it wasn't just him. I saw Chloe take energy from Joe. She fed it on to Ben."

Elijah frowned. "You mean she's—"

A sound in the corridor cut him off. We both froze. Elijah pressed a finger to his lips, but he didn't need to tell me to shut up. He got up slowly and walked over to the door. He inched it open a crack and peered out. "All clear," he said. "If Chloe was listening in, she's gone now."

But was it too late? Thank god I hadn't said anything about what I'd read in the prophecy.

Elijah closed the door again, pressing on it firmly until it clicked. I beckoned him over, and he sat down close to me, leaning in so I could whisper. Once again, I wished we had managed to regain our connection. Well, if I was wishing for things, I wished our connection had never broken.

I told him the whole story in whispers, pausing every time I heard even a hint of noise in the corridor.

"So we can't trust her," I said finally. "Not until we figure out why she was helping Ben."

"Agreed."

It was the first time Elijah had spoken since I started the story – not one snarky comment or interjection. I don't think I'd ever heard him so quiet.

He chewed on the inside of his lip, thinking. "Question is, do we tell Joe?" he said finally.

I hesitated. If it were me, I would want to know that Chloe was stealing energy from me, but at the same time, Joe had just stood there as Ben hurt Elijah. He hadn't even tried to stop him.

I shook my head. "No. No one else, just us."

Elijah nodded, accepting that without hesitation. Mum might have forgiven Joe, but I sure as hell couldn't. If we were going to survive this, we couldn't trust anyone.

Chapter Seven

Toby

Zo kept to her word and adamantly refused to tell me where we were going. Even so, I probably could have picked up the trail after a while. Evidence of explosions became clearer and clearer. Broken asphalt lined the empty streets, as if something had been repeatedly hurled at them. The surrounding trees were all weathered, barely alive with the energy drained out of them, but vines of ivy flourished, strangling everything. The few people we saw stared blankly at us, zombies under Ben's control.

"God, what is he doing here?" Zo asked.

Probably the same thing he'd been doing everywhere – gaining energy by dragging it out of everything else. The thought made my skin crawl. If he'd done this to the trees, what was he doing to Callie and Elijah? Maybe I should be thankful for the explosions. Sucking up all the energy from big releases like that was probably the only thing stopping him from killing everything in his vicinity.

Suddenly Zo tapped my arm. "There – look!"

She pointed to an old mouldy sign out the front of an

abandoned factory. *Everything good comes in cardboard.*

I shook my head, slowly. "How did you...?"

"Cardboard factory – I remembered reading it in a list of stupid slogans. I looked it up and the company went out of business two years ago. Seemed like the prophecy might be trying to lead us here."

I let out a half-laugh. "You're a genius, Zo."

"Or I spend too much time online reading stupid listicles."

I turned back to the factory. "So, how do we get in?"

Zo shrugged again. "I don't know."

"What do you mean you don't know?"

"I told you I could get you here. I didn't promise anything beyond that."

It didn't matter. This was the closest I'd gotten to Callie, other than last night. If there was even a chance I could get her out, then I had to take it. I took a step forward.

Zo grabbed my arm. "We've got to be smart about this, Tobes."

The urge to push her away and run towards the old building was strong. "What do you suggest?"

Zo studied the building for a moment, her eyes narrowing. Then she pointed to the right-hand side. "From the pictures online, there's a kind of yard around the other side. It's surrounded by a big fence, so we won't be able to get in, but..."

But we might be able to talk to Callie and Elijah. "Okay, let's go."

"You have to stay hidden, okay?"

I nodded, though everything in me wanted to barge in there, metaphorical guns – or at least magic – blazing. Instead, I let Zo take the lead. She took us around the side of the building at an agonisingly slow pace. She stopped every few steps, crouching low in the bushes, her head cocked like a rabbit's, listening.

Finally, we reached the yard, though yard was definitely an exaggeration. It was a bare stretch of dirt, maybe a couple of metres wide down the side of the building, opening out into a patch maybe four metres by two. Only the odd tuft of grass managed to survive, the rest was just bare dirt surrounded by a high chain link fence.

I dropped my head. This was pointless. There was no way we'd be able to scale the fence without being seen, not to mention the barbed wire on the top.

"Look," Zo whispered.

I raised my gaze as a figure came out of the building. He paced the length of the building, kicking the dirt in front of him.

"It's Elijah," I said.

"No shit, Sherlock."

I cracked a smile. That's just what he would have said.

We watched for a moment as Elijah continued pacing, looking more like a caged animal than anything else. He was thinner than when he'd been at the school, his cheeks drawn like Callie's. Dark hollows shadowed his eyes, and his skin was a sickly pale colour.

"Do you think I can get closer?" It took everything in me not to just run straight towards Elijah, begging him for news of Callie or a way to help them both escape.

Zo studied Elijah for a moment longer, then nodded. "I'll keep watch. But only for a minute, okay?"

I crept towards the fence. Elijah turned before I got there, walking away from me. Damn my bad timing. I waited, crouched just at the edge of the bushes.

Finally, he turned back. I felt, rather than saw, the moment he spotted me. A slight shudder went through his body almost as if he was holding in a shout. Then within a breath, he was back to pacing slowly. It took him a full minute to walk the few metres towards me. He stopped at the fence and turned, leaning back against it and closing his eyes.

"You can't be here," he said under his breath.

"I know, but..." Suddenly everything I wanted to say flew out of my head.

"You're putting her in danger," he said.

Funny how he phrased it like that – putting her in danger. Surely, I was putting him in danger too, but it seemed we both cared about Callie more than ourselves.

"I just want to help. Can I see her?"

Elijah tipped his head forward, rubbing his temple. He turned ever so slightly towards me. "Half an hour," he said so quietly I almost missed it. "Once it gets darker." He pushed himself off the fence and walked back into the building.

What did he say?

I started at the sound of Zo's voice inside my head. *He wants us to wait half an hour.*

Zo crept forward. "We need to get back," she whispered. "Miss Trager will notice we're gone."

"I'm not going unless I see her. Go back if you have to, but I'm not leaving."

Zo let out a frustrated sigh. She ran her hands down her face, tension tightening her shoulders. Her shoulder blades stuck out, the flesh withering from her frame just as much as Callie's. I should have noticed that before. How had I not seen how drawn she was becoming?

"We wait half an hour," she said finally. "But no more. And we move away from the fence until then, okay?"

I shuffled back from the wire mesh. It felt like wrenching a part of myself off to move away from the fence – from Callie – but Zo was right. We couldn't get caught before we had a chance to talk to her.

Zo rested her head against my shoulder, closing her eyes.

She wasn't just thinner, she was exhausted. If I could honestly look at myself, I'm sure I'd see exactly the same things on my own face.

It didn't matter. We had to keep going until the others were safe.

Despite how wired I was, I dozed a little, leaning my cheek against the top of Zo's head, the feel of her spiky hair comforting and familiar.

After what felt like only minutes, she shook me awake. "She's there."

My head shot up, all stealth forgotten in my urgency to see Callie. Zo grabbed my arm, her nails digging into my bicep. I slowed at her warning, my instincts returning.

I waited as Elijah and Callie moved out of the building and away from the door. They walked in opposite directions, Elijah towards the far side, and Callie towards the fence where I'd talked to him earlier. Finally, Zo squeezed my arm, gently this time.

"Go," she whispered. "I'll keep watch."

Chapter Eight

Callie

My eyes snapped open when I heard the humming.

I raised my head. It was still early, but I was already lying on my mattress, trying to sleep. Of course, there was little chance of that actually happening. Every time I started to drop off, imaginary lines of magic lit up in my head. I'd sit up to follow them, and they'd blink out, leaving me in darkness.

But the humming was something new. I scrambled to my feet, rushing out into the corridor. The discordant sounds seemed to come from everywhere, impossible to follow.

I closed my eyes, alistening to the notes. They sounded familiar, some vibration my body knew but couldn't name. I let myself respond to them, humming too under my breath. I turned, almost without realising I was doing it.

A line of fireflies lit up. I waited, but they didn't blink out. One end of the thread disappeared into my stomach, anchoring somewhere deep inside me. The other led down the corridor towards the door to outside.

The humming swelled up around me, drawing me forward. I took a hesitant step. The sound tingled against my skin, almost like it was wrapping around my limbs, tiny fingers of magic latching onto me and drawing me outside.

A figure appeared at the end of the corridor.

"Toby?" His name barely made a sound, my throat refusing to believe. "Is that—"

"Cal?" Elijah called.

The humming disappeared as did the fireflies. I let out a breath, and suddenly I was desperate for air. I gasped, trying to refill my lungs.

Elijah was beside me in seconds, his hands on my shoulders. "What is it? What's wrong?"

I looked to the end of the corridor. "Did you hear that?" I asked. "The humming?"

He frowned, then slowly shook his head. I studied his face, looking for... I wasn't sure what. Signs of deception? Signs that he was the one causing the sound? I used to hear vibrations when I was around him – a pulse in the air that forced me away.

He stepped closer, but still the humming didn't reappear. He brushed the hair back from my face, staring straight into my eyes. "Are you okay?" he asked.

I shook my head. "I don't know." Was I losing my mind? Was I seeing magical threads because the prophecy had put them in my thoughts, or was there really something here trying to help us? My mother? I couldn't let myself think about that. It was too much, too confusing.

Elijah held my eye for a moment longer and then dropped his gaze. Strangely, I felt a loss at the movement. I wanted him to look back up at me.

I reached out, touching his arm. "Were you trying to find me? What's going on?"

He still didn't look up. Instead, he closed his eyes, shaking his head ever so slightly. His hands dropped from my shoulders, and he turned away, gesturing for me to come with him.

I didn't follow immediately. My skin tingled, feeling the absence of where he'd touched me. My whole body ached, and exhaustion made everything swim. The last few days, I'd felt weaker, not seeming to be able to regain my power after Ben took it. It was more than that, though. I felt like a part of me was giving up, giving in to the depression. I was so tempted to run back to my room and bury myself on the mattress. But another part of me wanted to follow the path of that magical thread.

Elijah stopped a few paces ahead of me and looked back. There was something about his manner, some urgency to it. I couldn't tell if it was a good or a bad thing.

"Okay, I'm coming."

Elijah's shoulders sagged, and his eyes flicked away from mine. I frowned. What was I supposed to make of his behaviour right now?

He turned away from me, and I padded after him, shivering a little now the adrenaline of mysterious magic had worn off.

Elijah gestured down the hallway. "Outside," he said.

The last thing I felt like doing was going and standing out in the cold. At least indoors, I could pretend I had the option to leave. Once out in that barren stretch of dirt, looking up at the fence, there was no mistaking the fact that we were prisoners. I'd almost go back to the silver bracelets locking me in place over staring at that towering wire barrier.

It was all stupid. The coil of magic wrapped around my chest linking me to Ben should have been enough to tell me I was trapped here. I didn't know why seeing the criss-crossed mesh of the fence made it so much worse.

Elijah started down the corridor, and I stumbled into a jog to catch up with him.

"Go to the right-hand side," he said under his breath. "Right to the fence by the bushes."

I turned to look at him, but he kept his eyes on the door ahead of us. My heart started to hammer, and something tugged at my stomach as if that string of fireflies was pulling at me. We saw our classmates yesterday. We saw Toby. Could he have…?

I didn't even let myself finish the thought. It was too much to hope for. Toby wouldn't risk coming here, would he?

Elijah pushed open the door, and a wave of cool air hit me. I didn't let myself look around, walking straight over to the edge of the yard as Elijah had instructed. He didn't follow me. He wandered over to the other side, then leaned back against the fence. He folded his arms, watching me.

I strained my ears, listening with my whole body. I leaned my arms against the fence, propping my head against them, and closed my eyes. There was a strange emptiness to the night here – only man-made sounds. The absence of wildlife was deafening. Ben had dragged the energy out of all the life around here for miles. I guess I should have been grateful. It was probably the only thing stopping him from killing me.

"Callie?" Toby whispered.

I froze at his voice. I opened my eyes, slowly. At first all I saw were the droopy outlines of the bushes, but then he shifted, and like an optical illusion his figure became clear.

"Toby," I breathed, barely letting it make a sound.

I felt it – the tingling at the edges of our broken magical connection. It took everything in me to turn around, away from him. I leaned my back against the fence, pressing my palm to the wire, reaching out to him as much as I dared.

"What are you doing here?" I whispered.

"We came to get you out."

A desperate laugh slipped through my lips. "You can't."

He knew as well as I did that I was stuck here. I wouldn't have been doing the things I'd done over the last few months – causing that level of destruction – if I wasn't trapped. But still, Toby was here... He was still trying to save me despite the awful things I'd been forced to do.

"Are you okay?" he asked,

I heard him shift and I could almost imagine him reaching out to touch my palm on the other side of the fence. How could I answer that? Of course I wasn't okay. My energy was being drained by a power-hungry dictator. I'd been forced to destroy things, to hurt people, and I didn't even know why. I didn't understand what Ben wanted other than to take magic from me and Elijah. I was trapped here with my father and Chloe, and I didn't trust either of them.

"We're okay," I said finally. "Elijah is looking after me."

Toby went silent at that. I opened my eyes, staring at Elijah across the courtyard. His gaze locked on mine, but he stayed leaning back against the fence on the other side, watching, giving me space.

Suddenly Zo's voice hissed, "Toby, what are you doing?"

I couldn't help myself; I jerked around to look. Toby stood, coming forward from his hiding place in the bushes. I pressed my hand to the fence. He mirrored the movement, our hands connecting without either of us having to think about it.

I heard Elijah take a few steps forward, and I spun back, shaking my head to hold him off. "Please," I mouthed at him.

He stopped, looking to the entrance of the building. A flash of fear crossed his face. Something dropped in my stomach, and my eyes darted to the building too.

I spun back to Toby and pressed my fingers through the fence. He gripped my hand through the wire, his face just inches from mine. Threads of his magic stretched out, reaching as if they would wrap all the way around me.

"Let us get you out of here, please."

I could feel his breath on my cheek. In another lifetime, I could have kissed him.

"Toby!" Zo hissed. I could just see her crouched in the bushes behind him. She stared at me, her eyes darting between me and Toby, her fear evident.

Suddenly, Elijah was right behind me. He gripped my shoulder. "We have to go, Cal. If they catch us…"

I started to shake. Ben's magic – the rope wrapped around my chest – tightened. "Give me one minute, please."

Elijah's fingers bit into my shoulder, but I grabbed his hand. I poured every ounce of desperation I could into my grip, and I knew he felt it.

"One minute," he said. "Just one minute." He backed away a few paces, keeping himself between me and the door. I doubted it would make much difference. If Ben or one of the others came out here right now, we were done. I turned to Toby.

"I have to go," I whispered.

He shook his head. "I can't leave you here."

"You have to." I swallowed. The words felt like they were ripping a hole in my chest. I leaned towards the fence letting the edges of Ben's magic come into contact with Toby's hand. "You feel that?"

Toby drew in a sharp breath, his eyes flicking from his hand to my face.

"That's why I can't leave. And it's why you can't get caught."

He hesitated then nodded. "I love you."

I swallowed. I couldn't say it back, not when it meant he

would risk himself to get me out. "And that's why you have to leave me here."

His face fell. Zo shifted forward, reaching for Toby's hand. "Come on Toby. Please?"

Toby didn't look at her, keeping his eyes locked on mine. "Are you surc you're safe here?"

A lump stuck in my throat. I looked back at Elijah.

He took a step forward. "I can protect us," he said. "But only if you leave."

I wanted to cry, but I couldn't. The only way for Toby to stay safe was for him to believe that I already was.

"I hear humming," Toby said. "When we get close. Every time, I know when you're near."

I froze. Elijah pulled me away, but I grabbed the fence hard. "Humming? You're sure?"

Toby nodded. "It's you, isn't it? Inside your head." He started to hum, the same low tone I'd been hearing for days.

"That can't be a coincidence." I looked from Toby to Elijah, but neither of them knew what I was talking about. We were still connected. Somehow, the magic still had us joined, even if we couldn't feel it. Was that why I'd seen that thread? Was that what the prophecy was trying to tell me about?

Zo tugged on his sleeve. "Please Toby. We have to go."

She pulled him back a pace. He kept his hand pressed to the fence. Elijah's arm slid around me, pulling me away too. I pressed my hand to Toby's.

"We'll figure it out, I promise," he said. The ends of his magic stretched out as he spoke, no coaxing needed. They wrapped around mine, and I shivered at the sensation. Suddenly my magic didn't feel so alien to me.

Toby's eyes went wide. "Did that just...?"

I didn't dare breathe. For months Elijah and I had tried, and nothing. But maybe... just maybe it would work with Toby.

Fireflies appeared, swarming over our linked hands. They didn't burn, the sensation warm like sunshine.

Callie? he said inside his head.

Yes. I hear you.

He grinned, and sobs rose in my throat. I closed my eyes, forcing myself to remember everything. The threads... Chloe stealing Joe's magic... every piece of destruction we'd caused over the last few months. He had to know all of it.

"Elijah... Callie!" Joe shouted from inside.

My head snapped towards the door. Footsteps thundered down the corridor, coming towards us.

Toby sucked in a sharp breath. "Did you just show me—"

Another shout from inside cut him off.

"Go!" I hissed at the same moment Elijah yanked me away from the fence. Zo broke into a run, dragging Toby with her. I moved with Elijah, going back inside, not daring to look back.

I love you, I said inside my head. I wasn't sure if I wanted him to hear it or not.

Chapter Nine

Toby

Zo didn't let go of me until we were back inside the school. I shrugged her off once we were through the doors, in the main foyer.

"You didn't have to do that," I snapped at her.

"Oh, yeah? Would you have left if I hadn't made you?"

I started up the stairs to our rooms without looking back at her.

She followed after me. "That's what I thought."

My head pounded, trying to make sense of all the new information Callie had shared. The images she'd passed to me felt like memories, but they made me nauseous to watch. What had she gone through the last few months? What had I left her to go through now?

I turned at the landing, starting on the second flight of stairs. Zo followed at my heels, and I increased my pace, trying to get away from her. She would have seen it all in my thoughts, of course, but it wasn't the same for her. She didn't care about Callie like I did.

Honestly? If Zo hadn't dragged me back here, I would

probably still be outside the fence. Or, more likely, I'd be inside facing Ben and the others.

"Toby..."

I shook my head. I just needed a moment alone. My hand tingled, almost itching. The memory of Callie's magic reaching out to mine was fresh, and the sound of her voice echoed in my mind. Would it hold? Were we connected like we used to be? I almost couldn't bear to hope. I needed to test it – to see if I could reach her.

"Toby, you can't ignore me forever."

I let out a frustrated noise. "Just five minutes, Zo. Can't you just give me five minutes' space?"

Asher looked up as we stepped off the stairs onto the dormitory floor. "What's going on?" He sat on the carpet outside Julianna's room, keeping guard like her personal lapdog... or perhaps warden. I couldn't help feeling Jules was just as trapped as Callie was.

I looked at Zo. She stared back, and I could feel the thoughts flicking through her head. I couldn't quite read them, but I knew she could read mine.

Don't, I said inside my head. Did Callie hear it too? The possibility made my pulse speed up.

Zo turned away from me, focusing on Asher. "We found their base," she said. "Toby talked to Callie."

Shut up, Zo! I said inside my head.

Asher's eyebrows shot up. "You went to their...? Where is it? Does Mr Grandace know? You have to—"

The sound of a throat clearing cut Asher off. Mr Grandace stepped out of the stairwell, followed by Miss Trager.

"He does now," Mr Grandace said dryly.

I grimaced, frustration building inside me. I refused to believe he had just happened to be walking past as Asher said that. They were listening in on us, I was sure of it.

Miss Trager's eyes were bloodshot, and the dark circles underneath them extended almost to her chin. Mr Grandace wasn't faring much better. His beard had gone from straggly to sticking out in all directions, giving him a bedraggled wizard look. Somehow, the dishevelment only increased how intimidating the pair looked.

Miss Trager shook her head. "Do you have any idea how dangerous that was, especially for you, Toby? Ben got to Callie and Elijah, because of the break in their connection. That's exactly the same position you and Asher are in now!"

I glanced at Asher. It hadn't occurred to me that I was putting him in danger.

"Planning room, now." Miss Trager's tone left no room for argument. Zo, Asher and I all looked at each other.

"What about Jules?" I asked, less because I was worried about her being included, more because I was stalling.

Miss Trager glanced towards Julianna's closed door. "Leave her. She's not feeling well."

Asher and Zo both looked towards Julianna's room too. She wasn't sick, she was hiding from the magic. It frustrated me how everyone let her. We all had to fight if we were going to beat Ben.

Miss Trager's face softened as she looked at Asher. "I'm guessing you weren't a part of this?" she asked. Somehow, she'd singled me and Zo out as the naughty kids. I'd be annoyed, if she wasn't right.

Asher shook his head, eyes still glued to Julianna's door. "Nah, I've been here all afternoon."

Miss Trager nodded, then her gaze hardened again as she turned to me and Zo. "Just you two then. Both of you, downstairs now."

Zo sighed and linked her arm through mine. I flinched away, still mad.

We trailed down the stairs and into the planning room. Miss Trager and Mr Grandace had made a little progress – re-arranging the screeds of scrawling writing into some semblance of order. It still looked like the raving-lined den of a serial killer.

Miss Caraway stood by the far wall, pinning up the re-maining loose sheets with thumb tacks. She looked from me and Zo to Miss Trager and Mr Grandace.

"I'll finish this later," she said, quickly removing herself from the room.

Dammit. I'd half been hoping we could claim we were interrupting her work, and delay this telling off for a little longer. Instead, I slumped in one of the chairs in the middle of the room. Zo moved the book Miss Trager had been reading from the seat beside me and placed it carefully down on the floor. I glanced at the title, but the whole thing was covered in ash, making it hard to read.

"Why didn't you tell us you knew where they were?" Miss Trager asked. "What on earth possessed you to go off on your own?"

"It was my fault," I said. "I made Zo come with me."

Miss Trager made a soft sound that was almost a scoff. "I very much doubt you could make Zo do anything against her will."

"Why? He made her sleepwalk." I gestured to Mr Grandace.

Everyone went quiet, and Zo shook her head slightly. "Dude…"

I slumped back in my chair. That was petty, and I knew it, but right now I felt petty. I was sick of being told what to do. They weren't my teachers anymore, and they were the ones who'd got us into this mess. I was sick of them acting like they knew what was going on when everything they did just made things worse.

Zo cleared her throat. "That cardboard thing Toby read – it was a slogan for an old factory. We went to check it out. No, we didn't tell you, but we didn't know if it was going to pan out."

Miss Trager and Mr Grandace exchanged a look. Even though they weren't connected in the same way Zo and I were, they still seemed to be able to talk inside their heads. I closed my fingers over my palm, feeling the tingle of Callie's magic.

"Did you learn anything?" Mr Grandace asked finally.

Zo and I glanced at each other. Part of me wanted to keep everything Callie had shown me to myself. Miss Trager and Mr Grandace would just sit on it, analysing it, but ultimately refusing to act on it like everything else.

Then again, Callie had shown me a lot of stuff I didn't really understand. If there was even a slight chance they could figure it out...

"She'll see the threads, and she'll follow them. They will all find the way out when they untangle the web," Zo said before I got a chance to. "Something like that at least – Callie read it in the prophecy."

I glared at her. Why was she being like this? Why couldn't she trust me to make the right choice?

Mr Grandace grabbed a pen, scrawling that out on yet another sheet of paper. He stuck it to the wall, layering it over another page. "Anything else?"

Zo shrugged. "She showed Toby a bunch of other stuff, but it was too quick for me to follow. She looked really sick. I don't know if she was in her right mind."

That wasn't fair. Callie wasn't crazy. Then again, maybe it would spur our former teachers into action if they thought she was.

"We have to get her out of there," I said. "There's no other option."

Miss Trager waved her hand as if I were a phone screen she could clear. "Go back," she said to Zo. "What do you mean she showed Toby?"

Zo looked at me, and I grimaced.

"We regained our connection. At least, I think we did." I raised my hand, uncurling my fingers, as if she would be able to see the end of the connection etched on my palm.

Mr Grandace grabbed it and ran his hand across mine. "Yes, I can feel it," he said. "But it's not quite as strong as last time."

That, I'd already figured out.

Miss Trager touched my hand too, more gently. "It should still offer her some protection and stabilise her magic. If she and Elijah can find a way to rebuild their connection, they may even be able to shut Ben out."

My heart hammered inside me. Had I actually done something right for once?

"And she was able to show you something?" Miss Trager asked.

I nodded. "A lot of things. I don't know if I understood them all. A lot of stuff about the threads, a lot of fireflies. That was always how she saw magic." I closed my eyes, trying to tease out the memories. "There was something about Chloe... Callie thought she was stealing magic from Joe, passing it on to Ben."

Miss Trager's head whipped up. "What?"

I shook my head. "I don't know. It was like she could see all these strings light up and energy rolling along them. She thought it was Chloe stealing magic, not just Ben."

Miss Trager got up, striding across the room. She pulled one of the pages from the wall, scanning it.

Mr Grandace followed her reading over her shoulder. "What is it. Did you read something?"

"Maybe... I don't know." She set the page of writing down and grabbed another one.

That bloody prophecy.

"Here..." Miss Trager brought the paper over to us. She pointed at a string of red letters. The words swam under my gaze, refusing to settle into anything coherent. She looked up at me expectantly.

I shook my head. "I can't read it."

She sagged visibly.

Mr Grandace patted my shoulder gently. "Don't worry about it, Toby. This is still more than we knew this morning."

"Can you read it?" Zo asked Miss Trager. "What does it say?"

"Pretty much the same thing Callie showed you, except this bit here..." she trailed off, not elaborating on what the extra bit was.

How could we even call it a prophecy when all it seemed to predict were things we already knew?

Suddenly, she strode back across the room and picked up the book Zo had placed on the floor. "Side effects of stolen magic..."

She brought the book over to the wall and picked up the piece of prophecy. She placed the page back on the wall, smoothing it out carefully, then held the book up next to it as if comparing the two texts. She mumbled to herself, too fast and quiet for the rest of us to understand. We were done getting anything coherent out of her for the day, that much was obvious.

"Anything else we should know?" Mr Grandace asked.

Zo shook her head and looked to me. I clenched my hand into a fist, balling my other hand over it.

Callie? I whispered inside my head. I held my breath, waiting for an answer. The silence stretched out in response.

"No, nothing," I said aloud.

Chapter Ten

Toby

I spent the rest of that night talking to Callie in my head. I replayed memories; my favourite ones of her, and also things we had learned since she left. I gave her every single piece of information that might be able to help her. I had no idea whether she could hear any of it, but I had to try.

Zo would be able to hear it, of course. I was probably massively pissing her off, but I didn't care.

At some point, I fell asleep and dreamed about Callie, Elijah and the others. The dreams felt almost as real as the memories she'd shown me. I woke several times in a cold sweat, blinking to clear the images of buildings exploding, their zombie-like owners stuck inside as Ben's control froze them in place.

Before it was even light out, Miss Caraway woke us, telling us Mr Grandace wanted us up and ready for "training". I dragged myself out of bed to shower and eat breakfast.

"You still pissy with me?" Zo asked as we sat down in the dining room.

I shrugged. "Are you?"

She shook her head. "Nah, but if you could have less involved dreams tonight, that would be great."

"You saw that?"

Zo nodded, stifling a yawn. "You think it's coming from Callie?"

"I don't know... I hadn't thought of that."

"You spent all last night trying to show her stuff. You think she's not obsessing about you enough for you to end up with her dreams? Even without the *actual* connection, you two are connected."

That made a lot of sense, but I wanted to vomit at the thought. What she'd shown me voluntarily had been bad enough. If she'd lived through everything I'd seen last night, I had no idea how she was still standing.

"Alright," Mr Grandace called. "Five minutes, then I want all of you in the foyer ready for training."

Zo rolled her eyes, but we both got up to put our dishes in the kitchen. Every time Mr Grandace started down this track, a little niggle of irritation tweaked my stomach. Training. What were we training for? To fight Miss Trager's siblings and the others, obviously, but training implied he had a plan on how to achieve it. Why did he keep refusing to tell us what it was?

It didn't matter. I had a plan of my own now. I just had to keep Zo out of my head long enough to put it into place.

Mr Grandace had us run up and down the stairs in the foyer for a while. Usually Miss Trager joined in, helping with the drills, but she'd left the dining room after breakfast, heading towards the old burnt-out library. It was always a sign of a bad day when she ended up in there.

When we first did training sessions, I thought the running part was pointless – I wanted to get into growing our magic. Now, I was starting to see the value. I'd done more running chasing after Callie in the last couple of months than I had in the last few years. Ben and the others weren't going to just stand there and let us try to overthrow them.

Today especially, the running would come in handy.

"Okay, let's try practicing some magic skills," Mr Grandace said.

Julianna whimpered and turned away. I rolled my eyes. My patience for her magic-aversion was wearing thin.

I expected Asher to rush over and start coddling her like he usually did, but instead he walked over to me. "How about we pair up today?" he asked.

I blinked. I glanced over to the side of the foyer, where Julianna now sat, staring at the tiled floor. Her hair was loose, and it hung greasily over her face. Zo followed my eyeline, and her eyebrows pinched together.

"Yeah, I'll work with Jules today," she said.

Asher nodded. "Yeah... okay. That's a good idea."

I got the feeling they'd planned this, given Asher very rarely thought anything Zo did was a good idea. Whatever. It worked in my favour. If I paired with Zo, she'd be stuck to me like a limpet, but with Asher as my partner, I might actually get a chance to sneak off.

I turned back to him. "What did you have in mind?"

He gave me the briefest of smiles. "I thought we could go outside. Maybe try something bigger?"

I grinned. That was perfect. Not in the magical sense – "bigger" magic wasn't exactly in my wheelhouse – but the idea of getting out from under Zo and Mr Grandace's watchful gazes appealed.

Out in the garden, Asher sat down on the ground, picking up a couple of rocks. I frowned. When he said he wanted to do bigger magic I wasn't picturing cobbling together stones. He closed his eyes, holding them in his hands. They started to grow and to multiply.

I picked up a pebble of my own. I closed my eyes, pouring my magic into it. Slowly, it warmed and then started to expand.

"Nice one, man!" Asher said.

I smiled faintly at the praise. Mine hadn't doubled in size in the same way as Asher's had, but it had gone from a pebble to... a slightly larger pebble. It was a start at least.

"Will this work with other stuff?" I asked.

He shrugged. "Should do. You want to grab some things and try it out?"

Perfect. Asher could have levitated anything he wanted over to us, but I didn't point that out. "Yeah, man," I said. "I'll be back in a sec." Or not.

I made a show of collecting a few sticks, then wandered around the side of the building. The main gates to the property were closed – of course they were, things could never be that easy – but what was the use of magic if you couldn't scale a few fences with it?

I found a spot hidden from the house by the trees. The fence was old, made up of creaking metal railings that didn't seem like they'd hold my weight, but that was where the magic came in.

An image of Callie and I falling from the tree as we'd tried to escape the school flashed through my head. Maybe we should have kept going. Sure, we'd saved our teachers and classmates that night, but only for a little while. My choice to join our magic together had hurt them just as much as it had helped.

I took a firm hold of the fence, then braced my foot against it, pushing myself up.

A hand slammed down on my shoulder. I gasped and let go of the fence, falling back onto the person behind me. We hit the ground hard.

"Shit!" Asher yelled.

I rolled off him. "Sorry!" I scrambled to my feet. "I thought you were Mr Grandace."

Asher groaned. "Nah, I'd never have a beard like that."

That was actually pretty funny for Asher. He pulled himself up to a seated position and brushed the dirt off his back. "What were you doing?"

I glanced awkwardly at the fence. "Would you believe I was trying to get higher to gather sticks straight off the trees?"

"About as much as I believe you wanted to work with me to improve your magic skills." He sniffed, wrinkling his nose, then looked from me to the fence. "I'm not Mr Grandace," he said slowly. "But I still can't let you go running off by yourself, Tobes."

I huffed out a breath that was almost a laugh. "Yeah, I get it."

If the situation had been reversed, I probably would have been saying the same to any one of my classmates. I wouldn't let them go off to face danger on their own – I'd been furious when Callie had run off all those months ago... but what choice did I have?

"I can't just leave her there."

Asher nodded, slowly. "I know, man. It sucks. I feel like an asshole for leaving Elijah there."

That wasn't the same thing. Honestly, I wasn't even sure if Asher liked Elijah, he just felt guilty.

Asher tilted his head towards the house. "Come on." He got to his feet, walking a few paces before looking back.

I hesitated and glanced at the fence again. If I was fitter, perhaps I could have done some kind of parkour leap and vaulted over the fence to freedom before Asher had a chance to catch up. Instead, I turned away and trailed after him.

He waited for me to reach him, then started walking again, keeping pace with me. "Tell me about what you saw," he said.

"What I saw?"

He kicked a heavy stone along the ground in front of us. It was one of the ones he'd enlarged, its edges unnaturally perfect and smooth. "When you went to their hideout. Describe it to me."

I shrugged. "We didn't see much. There was a big fence around the building, and just this kind of dirt yard. Elijah came out, and he went and got Callie. We talked for a little while."

We rounded the corner to the main gardens. Zo had brought Julianna outside. They walked slowly around the circumference of the lawn, their arms linked. So much for magic practice. It didn't look like they were using any power whatsoever.

Asher turned towards me, stopping suddenly. He stared dead into my eyes. "Jules isn't going to last much longer like this," he said.

Immediately, I felt like an asshole. I was getting annoyed at Julianna for not wanting to use magic, but in all honesty, she was probably just as unwell as Callie was. She was crumpling before our eyes, and Mr Grandace and Miss Trager were just watching it happen.

"Do you remember where to go?" Asher asked.

I frowned. "What do you mean?"

"Zo said she didn't give you the address, but do you remember where to go? To get to the factory?"

I nodded slowly. Asher's gaze dropped to the stone at his feet. He picked it up and tossed it lightly back and forth as if it weighed nothing.

"Let's go," he said suddenly. "Tonight. Let's get Callie and Elijah out of there."

"How? Ben has them wrapped in magical ties."

Asher shrugged. "Magic can be broken. We've proven that already." He tossed the stone into the air. It arced upwards, then slowly started to drop. Asher flicked his hand, and the stone burst in mid-air, showering us both with a cloud of dust.

He turned back to stare at Julianna. "It's my fault that Elijah ran off that night." Asher didn't look at me, his focus entirely on Julianna. "I was connected to him. He was my Geminus pair, but I didn't even try to help him. I can't let this shitshow keep destroying Jules," Asher said, his voice grim. "She needs to be able to go home."

It wasn't Asher's fault. Callie had run off too, and I should have been the one to stop her, but neither of us had been able to do anything.

The Geminus pairs had been a mistake; we were all connected to each other, both with the natural field of magic between us, and the links that I had created to try and stabilise it. If only it had worked – we probably would have been able to keep Ben out – but that broken link between Elijah and Callie had caused so many problems. The irony was, now they were more connected than any of us. I couldn't help but feel a pang of jealousy about that.

I closed my hand over the fragile connection between me and Callie.

"So, tonight?" Asher asked.

I nodded. "Tonight."

One way or another, we would get Callie and Elijah out of there.

*　*　*　*

WE WAITED UNTIL THE others fell asleep, and then crept out. I'd underestimated how dark it would be, but Asher seemed to have some sixth – or perhaps magical – sense for moving around in the limited light.

We made it outside before anyone challenged us, but a voice hissed from behind us, as we were crossing the gardens.

"What are you doing?" Julianna's silhouette appeared in the open doorway.

Asher turned back, his face stricken, and I sighed. There was no way we would be leaving now.

Zo pushed past Julianna and strode across the grass towards us. "What the hell, Toby? Did you really think we wouldn't notice you were gone? We're connected to you, for god's sake!"

"Please, Zo..." I didn't know what to say. She knew how much we needed to do this. I could barely function knowing that Callie was out there under Ben's control.

Zo shook her head and looked to Asher. "Toby I get, but what's your excuse? You're supposed to be the disgustingly level-headed one."

Asher clenched his jaw, then his eyes flicked towards Julianna, still standing in the doorway. She looked so small, almost waiflike. I could practically see through her.

Zo followed his gaze, staring at Jules for a moment. *Stupid boys losing their heads over girls*, she thought. *Thank god I'm a lesbian.*

I caught myself before I pointed out that she had also come pretty close to losing her head over Julianna. Zo raised her face to the sky, breathing deeply as she studied the stars.

"We just want this to be over," Asher said quietly. "We need it to be."

Zo closed her eyes, but she nodded slightly. "When this is all over, I'm moving to Latvia. That ought to be far enough away. I'll meet some nice girl, settle down, and never think about any of you again."

Asher and I looked at each other, then back at her. I inched backwards as if we could sneak off before she noticed. Finally, she opened her eyes and levelled her gaze.

"Come on, then," she said.

"Huh?"

"I know I've got balls-all chance of stopping you, so I guess I'm coming too. Someone's got to look out for you muppets."

Asher huffed out a breath, but I couldn't tell whether it was in irritation or admiration. He glanced back at Julianna.

"I'll stay here," she said quietly. "Cover for you if I can."

I didn't know how much use Julianna would be in covering for us. She shivered in the night air, as if the lightest breeze would knock her over. Asher wavered. He took a step towards her, but she shook her head. She reached out as if she would take his hand, though she was too far away, then dropped it to her side. "Go. End this."

Asher's whole body seemed to steel as if in response to her words, and he nodded once. He turned back to me and Zo. "Let's do this."

Chapter Eleven

Callie

Elijah slipped into my room that night. "You awake?" he whispered.

"Yeah." I'd been asleep earlier in the night, and strange dreams about Toby, Miss Trager and my mother had filled my head. In them, I saw my mother's death over and over. She stood at the top of a staircase, then she and Miss Trager snapped the chord of magic between them, causing an explosion. Again and again the image played, and each time I felt more like I'd actually lived it.

Elijah pressed a finger to his lips. "Ben's roaming like a drunk toddler tonight," he whispered, then tilted his head towards the corridor. "Let's go somewhere he can't hear us."

I pulled myself out of bed and followed after Elijah. A part of me had been hoping he was waking me because Toby was back, but a bigger part of me hoped my former classmates stayed far away. The last thing we needed was for Ben to start stealing their magic too.

Elijah led me down the corridor to the warehouse part of the factory. Mosby lay asleep outside Joe's room. He thumped his tail when he saw us. I pressed my finger to my lips, and he laid his head back down.

We didn't often come down to the warehouse – the space was full of old machinery, not to mention stacks of rotting cardboard. We slipped in behind a pile of it, hoping it would keep us hidden if Ben came looking.

"So?" Elijah asked, once we were settled.

I sniffed. The mould from the piles of cardboard had my sinuses streaming already. Maybe this wasn't worth the cover it provided. "So... what?"

The air around Elijah seemed charged somehow, almost like it used to be. It didn't completely push me away – if I'd wanted to, I could have moved right in close to him – but if I listened hard enough, I could almost hear a hint of that pulsing hum. He didn't speak. Instead, he chewed on his lip, watching me.

"Spit it out, E," I said finally.

"Huh?"

"Whatever it is you're debating saying."

He let out a half-laugh. "You know me too well." He sounded almost bitter when he said that.

He touched his right palm, and tiny threads of power lit up. The hum I'd thought I could hear went from a hint to a rumble. Strings of fireflies rose, reaching for me.

"You managed to connect to Toby's magic, didn't you?" He stared at his hand instead of me, though I could tell he was aware of every movement I made.

"I..." I shook my head. Guilt trickled through me, though I wasn't sure why. "Yeah. I think so, at least. It happened automatically, but it's not as strong as it used to be. I haven't been able to hear him since he left."

I should have tried to strengthen the connection – made sure I could actually use it – when Toby was in front of me. But in that moment at the fence with Toby, all I'd been able to think about was how much I'd missed him.

"Everything was so rushed," I added.

Elijah nodded. He looked up at me, his eyes tracing my face, searching for... something.

"And you and I can keep trying," I said. I didn't know why, but that felt like a lie.

Elijah made a soft noise in his throat. I dropped my gaze, my cheeks heating.

"Perhaps with all of us joined we'll be able to break Ben's hold," Elijah said.

I couldn't help hearing that as a jibe. If I hadn't broken our connection, maybe Ben would never have been able to take hold of us in the first place.

"If we can figure out what my mum meant about the threads, we won't even need the connections."

That was placing a lot of hope in a vague note from my mother's notebook. Then again, what else did we have to place hope in?

The silence hung between us for a long moment. Or not silence as it was. Elijah moved towards me, and the humming rose in a wave like feedback from a microphone.

"Do you know why?" he asked.

"Why what?"

He hesitated, then reached out, touching my palm. "Why you can connect to Toby and not me?"

Something squeezed inside my chest. The way he said that, it was like he thought I'd chosen this, but his and my magic had always repelled each other. I had no control over it. At least... I didn't think I did.

"I don't know," I said finally. "I guess Toby was the first person I trusted at the school."

He had been one of the first people I'd trusted full stop,

but that was beside the point. "Maybe that made the magic stronger."

"You don't trust me?" Elijah's eyes flicked up to mine.

"I didn't say that." I hadn't said it, but did I mean it? I honestly wasn't sure.

"But you don't." Elijah looked away, closing off from me.

"I didn't say that!" I said again. "But I mean, back at the school—"

"I was behaving like an ass, I know. I wasn't worth trusting. But I've changed. You see that, right?" He ran a hand through his hair, the gesture stilted and jerky. He was breathing fast, and his eyes telegraphed enough pain that I couldn't hold his gaze.

"Yes," I said. "I know you've changed."

"But not enough."

"I didn't say that." I was going to be repeating that same mantra all night. I'd trusted him enough to tell him about Chloe. That meant something, didn't it?

We both fell quiet again. Even without being connected to him, I could feel what he was thinking. I could feel his desire to step closer to me, and the humming rose up almost as if in warning. He swayed towards me, and I raised a hand to stop him.

"Those flowers you gave Julianna," I said, almost before the thought had fully formed in my mind. "Back at the school – the poisoned ones. Why did you do that?"

Elijah went still. He half turned away from me and when he spoke, his voice was tight. "I didn't know you knew about that."

I swallowed. "Were you trying to hurt her?"

"No... I don't know."

"Were you jealous?" The way both Zo and Asher flocked around Julianna, it wouldn't surprise me if Elijah was in love with her too. He'd also been weirdly clingy with Asher.

He started to shake his head again, but then stopped himself. "Maybe. You don't know what it was like – before you arrived, I mean. They were all friends, but I was on the outside."

"So... you figured if they were going to reject you anyway, you'd give them a reason to do it?" I'd been there. When being small and quiet didn't work, I'd burned many a bridge trying to keep myself safe.

"Maybe." The corner of Elijah's lip twitched, fighting a grimace. "No one ever likes me, why bother trying to make them?"

"I like you."

Elijah frowned as I said that. He studied my face as if looking for deception. I stared back, trying to make my expression as open as I could. I might not have liked him at the start – might have been afraid of him even – but I cared about him now, that much I was sure of.

He reached out, hesitantly running his hand down my arm. "Would things have ever been different? If you'd met me before Toby?"

I took a breath, then let it out without saying anything. How could I answer that? What would it even matter if I did? His expression darkened at my silence.

A noise from the other room made us jump. Elijah's hand closed around my arm, his fingers biting into my skin. More thumps sounded, like a foot pounding against the wall. I scrambled up.

Elijah leaned in close, his lips brushing my ear. "We have to get back to our rooms."

I nodded. We'd been stupid to stay out this long.

We crept along the wall, aiming for the sliver of light coming from the corridor. Mosby stood outside the door to the warehouse, his tail between his legs. He pressed up against me, his head turned back to peer in the direction of the noise.

"Go," Elijah whispered. "I'll distract Ben."

I shook my head. The noise was coming from the staff-room, and light spilled out from the doorway. There was no way I'd get myself and Mosby down the corridor straight past that open doorway without Ben noticing.

Then I saw it. Strings of fireflies lighting up, leading me towards the room.

"What is it?" Elijah whispered.

"Threads," I said.

Elijah hesitated. He looked between me and the staffroom, and for once, I thought I saw fear in his expression. He turned back to look at me properly. "You're sure the prophecy said to follow them?"

I nodded. "Definitely."

"What the prophecy wants, the prophecy gets, right?"

Was that right? Every time we'd tried to do something it suggested we'd made things worse for ourselves. Perhaps my mother had been unhinged all along. Maybe the prophecy was nothing but rambles, predicting the future only in the same way magazine horoscopes did, with a lot of confirmation bias and liberal interpretation of vague statements.

Elijah slipped his hand into mine. He pulled me forward, and without thinking I was following – him and the thread. My heart hammered, several thumping beats for every step. The fireflies got brighter, and they let off a low sound. The noise swelled until it reverberated inside my head. Was this a warning? Was something trying to force me away, despite the prophecy urging us to follow? For all the power magic was supposed to hold, it really lacked in the communication department.

I squeezed Elijah's hand, reassuring myself, and he tightened his grip in response. Ben's voice came from inside the room. We paused outside the door, looking in. He'd tossed the room, furniture upended and couch cushions hurled across the floor. He rummaged in the base of the couch now, as if looking for spare change.

"Where did it go?" he said. "It's not in the book. It's not here."

He looked up. I froze, but no anger flashed in his face. He waved the prophecy at me. "I thought she put it in here, but there's nothing."

"Is he drunk?" Elijah said under his breath.

I didn't dare nod, but yes, Ben was definitely drunk.

"I just want to stop. But I can't until I get it."

"Get what?" I surprised myself by saying that. Though most people got more dangerous when they were drunk, Ben suddenly felt a lot less threatening. His movements were big but floppy, nothing intimidating about them.

"The magic! I just want it to stay. I thought if I had all of them, I'd be done, but then Sammy went and died."

I felt like he'd hit me. My mother didn't just *go and die*. He killed her. Or at least, he caused her death.

"I thought she'd put it in the book – stored it away for safe keeping, but there's nothing here." He waved the book again. The pages scrunched up under his fingers, and I cringed at the sight. As much frustration as it had caused me, the prophecy was still my one link to my mother.

I hesitated, then reached out my hand. "Can I have it?" I asked.

Ben stared at me, then slowly looked down at the notebook, almost as if he'd forgotten what it was. He held it out, swaying slightly as he did. I took it gingerly, afraid he would snatch it back at the last second, but he let me take it from him. I smoothed the pages out under my hand.

"What are you doing?" Elijah said under his breath.

I didn't reply. The book hummed now it was in my hands, but it wasn't a discordant sound like the ones I'd been hearing. This seemed familiar... welcome.

"I just want the magic to stay inside me," he said. "But it always drains away. I always have to take more."

I frowned, and I felt Elijah glance at me. Chloe had explained how she and Ben had to take energy from objects and other people to fuel their stronger magic, but she'd never said anything about it draining away.

I reached out in my mind, tentatively feeling the edges of his power. The rope around me tightened, warning me off, but I kept going. He always seemed so strong – magically at least – but there was a sort of flux to the energy around him. It flowed towards him, dragged out of me and everything around us, but there was also magic flowing away from him.

"It's leaching out of you," I said. "You really can't hold onto it."

Ben's eyes widened, and he almost smiled. "See? You get it now."

Could it be that he wasn't trying to make himself stronger, but to simply keep his own magic – his own energy – from draining away?

"Side effects of siphoning magic," he said as if quoting something.

A memory flashed through my head. No, not a memory exactly, but something from the dream I'd had. A book – Miss Trager holding it out in a room full of ash. Other memories crowded in around it, all of them too fast for me to understand.

Suddenly, the prophecy felt hot in my hands, no longer welcoming but urgently drawing my attention. I almost dropped it. *Tell me what to do*, I wanted to ask it. *Tell me how to escape this.*

In response, the humming sound swelled.

Ben's head snapped up. "What is that?"

Elijah stiffened. He could hear it too, I was sure of it.

Every last hint of benevolence rushed out of Ben's face. He rubbed at his ears, scratching the skin in front of them. "All night... All night it's been going on. I can't sleep with that noise."

Elijah pulled me back, putting himself between me and Ben, but Ben's eyes were locked on me.

"You know something, don't you? You're keeping it from me – lying, always lying, just like Chloe!" Ben's loop of magic tightened around me, draining me. I gasped, the air disappearing from my lungs.

He reached for the prophecy, but I pulled it tight against my chest. It burned there, too hot to hold, but I couldn't let go. Ben lunged forward. Elijah got to me first. He shoved me back. I stumbled, falling into the corridor. Elijah slammed the staff-room door, shutting me out, and closing himself inside with Ben.

I scrambled to my feet. Humming swelled around me, blocking out everything else. But then Elijah's voice, somehow inside my head, became clear.

Callie, run!

Chapter Twelve

Toby

"So, what's the plan?" Zo asked. "Scale the fence?"

I stared up at the height of the wire fence from our spot hidden in the bushes. I was embarrassed to admit that I hadn't got that far. I'd been so relieved when Asher decided that he would come with me – that he would help me get Callie and Elijah out – that I hadn't thought through what we were going to do once we got here.

Asher shook his head. "I think we can do better than that." He closed his eyes, concentrating. Zo and I looked at each other. I could practically feel her heart rate rise at the thought of doing magic so close to someone who was literally an energy vampire. Would this alert Ben to our presence?

Asher opened his eyes, a satisfied smile spreading across his face. I looked around. Nothing appeared to have happened.

He rose into a stooped crouch and scuttled over to the fence. He pushed against it gently and a piece of it swung forward like a gate.

Zo let out a breath that was almost a laugh. "Nice work, man."

Asher didn't respond to the praise. His eyes traced the building. "Can you talk to Callie?" he asked me.

Callie? I called inside my head. I counted my breaths as I waited for her reply. Nothing, not even that humming.

"It's okay, man," Asher said. "We'll figure it out."

I leaned my head back, looking up at the sky. The last few months, "figuring it out" had meant doing nothing and hoping the problem solved itself. I couldn't do it anymore.

"Fuck it," I said. I got up and ran.

"Toby! What are you doing? Stop!"

I heard Zo calling after me, but I didn't slow my pace. I ran straight inside... and then I abruptly halted. The adrenaline went out of me in a rush. The corridor was dimly lit, about half of the long fluorescent bulbs burnt out. It smelt like mould and dead things, and I was suddenly thankful for the lack of light.

The slap of feet behind me made me turn. Zo and Asher dodged through the door. "Dude, what the hell?" Zo hissed.

I shook my head. I hadn't meant to lead them into danger, but I couldn't stand out there doing nothing. Zo and Asher looked at each other again, and I could tell they were questioning my sanity. A silent conversation seemed to pass between them, then Asher turned back to me.

"I have a plan, if you don't," he said.

I don't think any words have ever brought me more relief than those ones did. He opened his backpack and took out a stack of silver bracelets.

"Here." He handed us each a pair. "Escape route home. I've got some for Callie and Elijah too. Ben won't see it coming."

"But we have to break Ben's bonds first," I said.

Asher shook his head. "Teleporting ought to snap them, right?"

I couldn't even form words; my mouth just gaped open at

him. Ben had ropes of magic tying Callie to him. Yeah, maybe they would snap with the force of the teleportation magic... but what if they didn't? Visions of Callie suffocating as the bonds tightened around her filled my head.

Asher threw his hands in the air, the bracelets flashing as he did. "Well, what's your plan then? I say we jump them out of here while we can, and deal with the consequences later."

"Are you crazy?" Zo practically shouted the words. I pressed a hand to her mouth, and she shook me off. "Toby, are you actually talking about kidnapping your girlfriend?" At least she lowered her voice this time.

"Not just Callie," Asher said. "If we can, we're going to grab Elijah too. Besides, it's not kidnapping if they want out of here."

I hadn't thought about Elijah. Between the three of us, we might be able to get Callie out, even if she was kicking and screaming, freaking out about the rope, but Elijah was bigger and stronger. There was no way we'd be able to manhandle both of them.

"Do you even know what this will do to her?" Zo hissed at me.

Asher shook his head. "It doesn't matter. We have to end this. Julianna's going to lose it if we don't fix this soon, and the rest of us will be next."

"Stop saying stuff like that!" Zo shook her head. "Julianna is fine. Her only problem is you treating her like she's breakable."

I cleared my throat. "I think we're getting off track here."

"She's not fine." Asher didn't seem to register I'd spoken, his glare firmly fixed on Zo. "She can barely eat."

"She's stronger than you give her credit for," Zo said. "She was the one who stood up to Ben while you were unconscious on the ground."

Asher blinked. "She what?"

"See, she didn't even tell you because you're too overprotective."

Zo had a point. Asher was too overprotective of Jules. Wait... what about me? Was I too overprotective of Callie? Was I only avoiding pulling her out of here because of the potential risk when it might be a risk she'd *want* to take?

"I think Asher's right," I said, though I still wasn't a hundred percent on that. "We grab Callie, get her back to the school, and we deal with whatever happens once we're there."

My mouth went dry at the thought. Could this kill her? But then again, Ben would kill her if we didn't get her out.

Zo stared at me, slowly shaking her head.

"We have to," I said finally. I tried to pour everything I was thinking into the connection between me and Zo. Her face flickered through a range of emotions, reading my thoughts.

I didn't wait for her to answer, instead looking to Asher. He gave a single grim nod. "Which way?"

I glanced one way down the corridor then back the other. The building was so bare, both directions looked identical. I'd always thought the hallways of the school were intimidating, but they had nothing on this. A ping sounded in my stomach, pulling me to the right.

"This way." I set off down the corridor. "I can feel it."

"Are you sure?" Asher kept pace with me, and after a second Zo trailed after us.

"Tobes, please just think about this—"

"Elijah!" Callie screamed from somewhere behind us, cutting Zo off. Thuds echoed after the shout, like fists pounding against a wall.

Zo spun around, running towards the sound instinctively. I went to follow, but Asher grabbed my shoulder. "The magic said this way, right?"

"What?" I shook him off. "Yeah, but—"

A dog burst into a series of barks and growls down the corridor. Callie screamed again.

"It's Ben messing with us," Asher said. "Misdirection. We should follow the magic – follow the threads, like you said." He took off in the opposite direction to Zo.

My head flicked between Zo and Asher, watching both of them get further away. Which way? My head said follow Asher – go the way the magic had said. But my heart heard Callie scream, and everything else went out the window.

An image flashed in my head. Fists hitting a door, shouts and crashes coming from inside, a dog pressing against Callie's legs, his hackles raised.

I gasped, coming back to myself. *Callie? Come on, Reactive Girl. Tell me where you are.*

The ping sounded in my stomach again. *Follow the threads.* I had to trust the magic. I took off in the direction it pulled me.

I turned a corner, and the lights went out with an unnatural hiss. I froze. Solid black pressed in on me from all sides. I reached out, finding the wall and navigating along it. "Callie?" I whispered. "Please, Callie, it's me!"

The ping cut out abruptly. I stopped. What did that mean? Go back? I spun around. Footsteps thundered towards me. I raised my hands, spreading my fingers, hoping like hell my reactive magic would kick in.

"Toby?" a familiar voice said from the dark.

"Asher!" I hissed.

He raced over to me. "Did you find her? I feel like I'm going around in circles."

"No, and I lost Zo." Or, more honestly, I'd abandoned Zo.

He grabbed my arm. "Come on, let's go back the way you came."

But just as he said it, the ping hit my stomach again. Asher took a sharp inhale. He could feel something too. This time it was stronger, more urgent, jerking me forward.

Asher's hand tightened on my arm. "In there?" he asked.

"Yeah." We both reached out, feeling the shape of the door in front of us. I strained, trying desperately to sense something through my connection with Callie.

"Open the door," he said. "I'll grab her."

I hesitated, all the earlier doubts rushing back. "What about Zo?"

"You worry about getting Callie home. I'll get me and Zo out."

He shoved me towards the door, and before I even registered what I was doing, I'd opened it. It was pitch black. I heard a gasp, and then footsteps running towards me. I couldn't see anything, but magic swirled around me, taking over. My limbs moved against my will. I grabbed Callie around her waist. She shrieked and her hair flew into my face.

"It's okay!" I called. "It's me! It's Toby."

But then Asher's hand was over her mouth, and any comfort she might have felt from my words was lost. She let out muffled screams and thrashed against me. Then there was more noise, someone else running towards us.

"Here." Asher shoved two of the silver bracelets into my hand, then I felt him grab Callie's arms. "Put them on her."

I wanted to vomit. She screamed, twisting away from him.

"Just do it Toby," Asher yelled. "You have to."

I found her hands and shoved the bracelets over them. She screamed again at the touch of the metal, and I tightened my grip on her. "It's okay," I told her. "We're taking you home."

Asher swore under his breath. "I forgot about the rune line!"

I pulled the piece of chalk from my jeans pocket. "Here."

He took it and crouched down in front of me, scrawling

runes across the corridor floor, I assumed.

"You have to get Zo," I told him. Guilt ate at me that I wasn't going after her myself, but Callie was straining against me, swells of Ben's magic wrapping around both of us. I had to get us out, or Ben would strangle us both.

"I'll look after Zo," Asher said. "Just go. The rune line's right in front of you."

Asher gave me a shove and I half dragged, half carried Callie across the line. Nothingness slammed into us from all sides, compounded by the magical rope tightening around us. Then sounds and light rushed in.

I fell forward, letting go of Callie as I did. She sprawled on the black and white tiles of the foyer floor, unconscious, hair covering her face. I landed on my hands and knees, gasping. I couldn't get air into my lungs. I blinked, trying to make sense of what I was seeing. Instead, confusion and horror filled me.

Blonde hair covered her face. The woman I'd just dragged back here wasn't Callie.

Chapter Thirteen

Callie

I hammered on the door. "Elijah!"

Magic flashed inside the room, light flaring out under the door.

"Ben, please! Let him out!" Wind whipped around me, ruffling the pages of the prophecy. Mosby growled low in his throat then started barking his head off. He circled around me, snapping at the wind.

Suddenly he froze. I turned, terrified of what I would see next. A figure raced past at the end of the corridor too quick to see properly. The sound of humming floated towards me.

"Toby?" I yelled. It couldn't be him, but that humming... The prophecy's pages ruffled again as if answering me.

Mosby shot off, chasing after the figure.

"Mosby, wait!" I ran after him. *Toby, wait!* Could he hear me? Was it even really Toby?

I turned a corner, and the humming swelled to a painful, rumbling volume. The figure appeared in front of me. Sparks burst from it. I gasped and stumbled back. That wasn't Toby. I turned and ran.

"Callie!"

That was Zo's voice. I turned back, but the darkness had swallowed her.

"Zo?" I yelled.

She didn't answer. Instead Toby's voice called from somewhere ahead of me. What was happening? Was any of this real?

Elijah screamed. Mosby bolted back towards the staff-room, but I froze.

Which way? Which way?

I couldn't let either of them get hurt.

Callie...

I gasped at the voice in my head. Toby would save us. Toby would get me and Elijah out.

I'm coming, I called back.

I ran towards him. I couldn't see him in the dark, but I heard his voice. His and someone else's, then the muffled sound of Chloe screaming.

"Chloe?" My steps ground to a halt. If Chloe was with Toby, then...

A flash of light lit up the corridor. Toby stood in the centre of it, Chloe imprisoned in his arms.

"Toby, wait!" I ran towards him. The flash burned out, and the humming stopped. "Toby!" I screamed. But they were already gone.

Another flash lit up from the other end of the corridor – Asher and Zo silhouetted in its glow.

"No, wait! What are you doing?" Then they were gone too. The humming intensified once more, crashing down on me. I crumpled under the weight of it. Suddenly there was a figure beside me. I screamed, pushing it away.

"Callie, stop! It's me. It's Joe."

I shrank back against the wall, and slowly sunk down

against it to the floor. Joe crouched in front of me, holding my shoulders.

"Callie, what's happened?"

I let him hold me, not caring for a moment about our complicated father-daughter relationship. "Toby took Chloe," I whispered.

Joe grimaced. "Why?"

"I don't know."

Toby didn't know what he'd done. Chloe had stolen energy from Joe. She could steal energy from any of them, and they'd brought her right into the school.

I tried to get up, but Joe held me in place. "You saw them take her?" he asked, his voice low.

What the hell *had* I seen? Toby had taken Chloe, but why?

"Where's Elijah?" Joe asked.

My stomach dropped. "Oh god, Elijah! Ben's got him."

I had left Elijah. I'd chosen Toby over him, and just left him to Ben. I started towards the staffroom, but Joe grabbed my arm again.

"Wait." Joe gestured to my chest. "What's that?"

I looked down, only then realising I was still holding the prophecy. Joe reached out, gently prying it from my hands. It took a moment for me to let go, my hands refusing to unclench. Once free, it fell open on a random page. Joe scanned it, then flicked to the next. I couldn't tell whether he was reading words or more random letters. A range of expressions flickered across his face, and he went very still.

"What is it? What did you read?"

"Nothing." He closed the book and handed it back to me. "We need to hide this. Put it under your shirt," he said.

I did, pressing it to my stomach. Joe's hands started to glow, and a thin vine appeared – half plant, half magic. He wrapped it tightly around my waist, holding the book in place. I let my shirt fall over it.

"That should hold but try not to draw attention to it."

That I could do.

Be silent.

Be still.

Don't let anyone notice you.

Joe took my hand. "Come on. Let's go find that idiot friend of yours."

I stumbled after Joe. The vine he'd wrapped around me felt comfortingly warm, almost like an embrace. "I don't trust you," I told him.

He gave a half-laugh. "That's fair. Your mother didn't either."

"Chloe's stealing energy from you." I didn't mean to tell him that, it just popped out. He slowed his pace, turning to look at me.

"I saw it. She fed it to Ben."

Joe's jaw worked as he chewed that fact over. I couldn't imagine what he was feeling. I might be his family by blood, but Chloe was all he'd had for seventeen years. How could she betray all that? Then again, Ben was *her* blood. Maybe those ties could never be broken, no matter how much you wanted to rip free of them.

Joe started to walk again, slowly. He tugged on my hand, pulling me along with him.

"Why would Toby take Chloe?" he asked.

I shook my head. "I have no idea."

The corridor outside the staffroom was quiet, and the door stood propped open. "E?" I called.

No answer. I glanced at Joe then pushed the door wide. Elijah lay on the floor in the middle of the room. Mosby was curled up beside him, whimpering.

"Oh my god, E!" I ran to his side. He groaned as I touched him. "Please be okay. I'm so sorry I left you. You have to be okay."

"I'll be better if you stop prodding me." Elijah cracked his eyes open. His voice was thick, and blood split his lip. He wiped it off on his hand and sniffed.

I pulled him into a hug. He winced but hugged me back.

"Where's Ben?" Joe peered down the length of the corridor before coming into the room.

Elijah spat a glob of blood onto the floor. "Something happened to him. He started gasping and clutching his chest. I don't know."

"Heart attack?" Joe asked.

Elijah shook his head, then groaned and clutched it. "Nah, something magical, I think. He was covered in sparks for a moment."

Had Toby taking Chloe away done that to Ben? Was that Toby's plan all along? It didn't make sense. The power Ben had wrapped around all of us kept us trapped here; I couldn't understand how Toby had got her out.

"Are you okay?" I helped Elijah up into a sitting position.

He leaned against my knees, using them to support himself. "I've been better, that's for sure."

I glanced at Joe. He paced back and forth, his jaw clenched. I could practically hear him grinding his teeth together.

"Where's Ben now?" I asked Elijah.

"He went stumbling off." Elijah closed his eyes and leaned heavily back against me. "Don't know where, don't care."

I smoothed the hair back from his face. His skin was clammy under my touch, and his cheeks had a sunken look.

"How much energy did he take from you?" I asked.

Elijah shook his head, then grimaced again. "Too much. I hit him a couple of times. He can't punch for shit."

"Can you get up?" Joe asked.

"Yeah, but you got anywhere we need to be?" Elijah asked. "Otherwise, I'd rather stay put."

Joe's eyes flicked between us, and suddenly I was scared.

"I think we're going to need to run," he said.

"Run?" The word cut off in my throat. I doubted Elijah could stand, let alone make a break for it. "What do you think he's going to do?" I asked Joe.

He shook his head. "No idea, but everything's unravelling fast. We have to be ready."

A heavy weight grew in my chest.

"Is Chloe... dead?" Was that why Ben's magic had weakened? "Toby wouldn't have..." I couldn't say it.

Joe shook his head. "No, she's..." He hesitated. "I don't know. I think I would feel it if she was hurt."

If I still thought the Geminus connections were real, maybe I could have believed him.

Without meaning to, my hand moved to my stomach, touching the prophecy hidden there. It felt like Joe had a plan he wasn't letting us in on. I hoped saving us was a part of it, and we wouldn't end up collateral damage.

"You can piggyback me, right Cal?" Elijah patted my knee. "Crap goes down, I'll jump on your back and you run like the wind."

I let out a laugh despite myself. "Let's call that plan B."

"Shh!" Joe slashed the air in front of us with his hand. "He's coming." He moved to Elijah's other side, hauling him to his feet. I scrambled up, putting my arm around Elijah's waist.

"Is this the part where we run?" I asked him. I listened for humming, or some other sign, but no siren-like sound guided our way.

Joe shook his head. "Not yet. Just stay calm, and hopefully

we won't have to."

Ben's footsteps echoed in the corridor, slowly coming our way. Then finally, there was humming, but it wasn't the magical kind. It was Ben, a loud, overly jovial song spouting from his lips.

It cut off as he turned into the doorway. He grinned as he saw us, but there was none of the floppy drunkenness from earlier.

"There you all are. Seems my sister's gone a wandering. What do you think team? Feel like a visit home?"

Something inside me seemed to rise up and plummet down at the same time. Home – his home. The school. He was taking us back.

Chapter Fourteen

Toby

I'd like to say that I was calm and rational in that moment. I'd like to say that I took charge and knew exactly what to do about the fact that I'd just kidnapped someone. I mean... of course we had been planning to kidnap someone, but there was a world of difference between grabbing Callie and getting her out of there and grabbing Miss Trager's sister.

A flash of power crackled in the air, followed by an explosion of sparks, and Zo and Asher landed on the stairs, tumbling down the last couple onto the tiled foyer floor. I didn't take my eyes off Chloe.

"No 'are you okay'? No 'welcome back'? Pretty rubbish after..." Zo trailed off as she caught sight of Chloe. "Woah."

"Is that Chloe?" Asher eased himself up and came to stand next to me. "Did we do this?"

I nodded grimly. The three of us stared down at Chloe's crumpled form. Her head was still slumped, her hair falling over her face.

"Is she okay?" Zo crouched down and gently turned Chloe

over. A deep welt ran diagonally across her chest, the skin purple and bleeding in places.

"Is that from Ben's magic?" I asked. What had I done?

Asher crouched down next to Zo. He started a healing spell on Chloe. "I think her ribs are broken."

A crackling pop sounded as his magic found the breaks in the bone. The skin on her chest shifted sickeningly, her ribs slithering back into place. I looked away, nauseous.

"This... this is bad, right?" Asher said. "I mean, we really screwed up."

"*You* screwed up," Zo said. "I'd nearly caught up with Callie when you dragged me back here. I would have got her if she hadn't run away from me."

"You were following a dog when I found you." Asher scoffed.

"Following it to Callie!"

"What are you guys doing?" Julianna padded into the room behind us. She stopped when she saw Chloe. "Woah."

"That's what I said!" Zo said at the same time Asher yelled: "It's not what you think!"

Julianna dragged her eyes away from Chloe to stare at him. What Asher meant by that, I have no idea, because of course it was exactly what it looked like.

Julianna opened her mouth, but no words came out. I felt Zo tense, getting ready to hover and Asher rose, taking a step towards Julianna as if he was going to have to rush in to comfort her, but then Julianna started laughing.

"What the actual...?"

Suddenly we were all laughing. I doubled over, gasping for breath as I tried to calm myself. This was not funny... except it *really* was.

Chloe groaned. The four of us all silenced immediately,

Asher stepped in front of Julianna, and Zo reached for my arm, squeezing it tight.

"She's waking up!" she hissed.

No shit, Sherlock, I heard in my head, almost as if Elijah had been standing next to me.

Chloe groaned again, and we all took a step back. She slowly raised her head, then gasped and clutched her chest. The welt had faded with Asher's intervention, but I bet it still hurt like hell. Asher flicked his hand, and glowing ropes appeared around her, binding her in place. They weren't attached to anything, but I guess they didn't need to be when they were more of a magical barrier than a physical one.

"What the...?" She jerked her head, tossing the hair out of her eyes. "What is this? Who are you people?"

Well, that stumped me. She'd been chasing us for the last six months. We'd crossed paths so many times as we'd fought each other but apparently, she didn't have a clue who we were. Maybe Miss Trager was right, and they really were completely under her brother's control.

She stared around the foyer, recognition seeming to dawn on her. "Am I... home?"

The word hit something inside me. I'd been expecting her to say something like "back at the school" but of course this had been her home first.

Zo step forward. "We're not going to hurt you." She raised her hands, trying to make herself as nonthreatening as possible.

Chloe's eyes darted towards Zo, but then she looked back at the rest of us. She reminded me of a frightened animal. The reality of what we'd done hit me.

I stepped forward, moving up beside Zo. I raised my hands too, placating. "She's right. We're not trying to hurt you. We didn't even mean to bring you here. We were trying to rescue Callie."

"Callie," she repeated. She blinked, scrunching up her eyes, as if trying to clear her head. She opened them again, suddenly. "My sister... Ursula..."

Zo and I looked at each other. Fear clouded Zo's face, and a similar sinking dread filled my stomach.

Strangely, it was Julianna who took charge. "I'll get her. It's okay, she's here." Julianna turned and started to walk up the stairs. After only a few paces Asher followed her.

"I'll come with you."

Chloe was back to staring around at the room. "It's different."

Because half of it's been blown up several times, I nearly said – blown up, flooded, had plants growing through every orifice...

Chloe stretched out a hand, as if she thought she might be able to reach out and touch the walls with her pinkie. She didn't fight against the bonds. In a weird way, she seemed... content. Maybe we had actually done a good thing, getting her out of there. It didn't change the fact that Callie was still trapped, but maybe it wasn't a complete disaster.

Footsteps thundered above us, and I turned to see Miss Trager racing down the stairs, Asher and Julianna behind her.

"Oh my god." Miss Trager clutched a book in her hands, but she dropped it as she saw her sister. She ran down the last few stairs towards Chloe, stopping just short of touching her.

"Ursula!" Chloe broke into something that was halfway between a laugh and tears. She reached up yet again, as if to hug her sister, but was caught by the rope.

"I'm so sorry. I'm so sorry. I should have trusted you." Miss Trager started to cry too. She didn't approach Chloe though it seemed like she wanted to hug her, just as much.

I didn't have siblings. I had no idea what this would be like, but I could see the bond between them. Even after all these years fighting each other, they still really wanted to be together.

Miss Trager stepped back suddenly, her eyes turning wary. "Are you still under his control?"

Chloe hesitated, then nodded slowly. "Not right this second, but yes, if he comes here then I'll be back under his control."

Miss Trager swallowed, then nodded. "Then we'll have to do everything we can to break it before he gets here."

I glanced at Zo. She'd taken half a step back. I wondered if she was thinking the same thing I was. Perhaps we could just try edging slowly out of the room before Miss Trager noticed us. She was happy to see her sister, but I didn't think that was going to cancel out the fact that we'd completely disobeyed her.

Miss Trager glanced at us and shook her head slightly. "How did this... how did you get her here?"

I cleared my throat. "I kind of just..." I made a motion with my hands as if picking something up. "We used the bracelets."

Miss Trager blinked at me as if that was the last answer she'd expected. "I didn't think that was possible," she said quietly to herself. Something flickered in her face, and I wondered if it was guilt. She almost seemed upset that she hadn't tried just picking up her sister and running before.

"It broke her ribs," I told her. "And I don't know what else."

Miss Trager looked back towards Chloe, anxiety and indecision written across her face.

"We don't have long," Chloe said.

Miss Trager nodded. She stepped towards Chloe, tentatively taking her hand. She shook a little, as if that was a hard thing to do. Perhaps it was. From everything she'd told us, they hadn't exactly been the closest of sisters before this all happened, and they must have years of guilt and anger and grief to work through.

Chloe squeezed her hand. "I'm sorry," she said. "But I have to do this."

Miss Trager's eyes shot up, and so did mine. Zo and I both launched forward, but it was too late. A swell of power rose in the room.

"I have to give it back," Chloe said.

The power exploded, throwing her and Miss Trager back. Both their heads hit the floor hard.

Julianna screamed. Zo and I started forward again, rushing to Miss Trager's side, but neither of us made it. A searing pain ripped its way through me. I stumbled to my hands and knees. Zo landed beside me. Neither of us screamed, but Zo's face pulled back as if she would. I felt mine shape into something similar.

"Jules!" Asher yelled. I turned to see Julianna writhing in similar agony.

Miss Trager lay unconscious, and power shimmered over her. There was so much power coming from Chloe, and we were too close to it.

"Zo..." I tried to say, but no sound came out. She turned to face me. It was like she was slipping away from me, getting smaller and smaller as she disappeared into the distance.

Zo let out a whimper. "Toby?"

I reached for her hand, as everything went dark.

Chapter Fifteen

Callie

I stared up at the school. It grew more imposing with every step, but I didn't care. I wanted to run towards it.

This place had never been a home to me, always a prison, but I would have given anything to be safely back inside it. Instead, I was about to be forced to attack.

Ben took his time, his pace unhurried as he approached his former home.

Elijah brushed the back of his hand against mine. "You okay?" he murmured.

I gave a single nod, not daring to look at him. The prophecy was still strapped to my stomach, and I wrapped my arms over it, reassuring myself.

"Do we have a plan?" he asked.

I shook my head. "Look for threads, I guess?" That hadn't exactly worked out for us so far, but what else did we have?

Ben and Joe reached the stairs just ahead of us. My heart thudded at the thought of walking up them, of opening the door at the top.

Suddenly, Joe gasped. Mosby started yipping, panicked

barks calling for our attention. Joe doubled over, clutching at his stomach. Ben stumbled too, his hands flying to his temples. I turned to Elijah, my eyes widening.

"Run?" he mouthed, but Ben was already straightening up.

Ben shook himself and tentatively moved his hands from his face. He'd gone pale, and his eyes flicked back and forth, not settling on anything. "They must have put up a new kind of ward," he said.

Joe was still doubled over, his mouth goldfishing as he tried to suck air in. He leaned heavily against Mosby, the Labrador the only thing keeping him upright.

Ben stepped hesitantly onto the next stair, and then the next. And then he was moving forward again, his pace steady and unhurried. The arrogant confidence of that chilled me.

"Are you okay?" I asked Joe.

Joe nodded, but sweat dripped from his temples and his skin was grey. "Keep walking," he said. He tried to straighten up, but then doubled over again. Mosby licked at Joe's face, anxious to help.

"What's going on?" Elijah asked. "Are you hurt?"

Joe shook his head, but a gasp escaped from his lips even as he did. "Help me stand up," he said, his breathing strained.

Elijah propped Joe's arm around his shoulders. Joe leaned heavily on him and eased himself upright. This was no ward. Joe didn't look like he could stand unaided, let alone walk. Light flickered over his skin, shimmering in a way that made him even paler.

"Elijah..." Joe turned his head, speaking in a low murmur. I caught the word "prophecy" but not much else.

Elijah's face paled and his eyes flicked towards me. I glanced nervously towards Ben. He didn't break his stride, but turned back, frowning as he saw us huddled at the bottom of the stairs.

"Just keep going," Joe said, loud enough for me to hear this time. "Don't let him know anything is wrong."

That I could understand.

Be silent.

Be small.

I slipped my arm around Joe's waist, helping support him, and Mosby squished between our legs, pressing against Joe. We moved forward together. Joe gasped at the movement, and sweat beaded on his forehead, but he didn't cry out. I glanced across him to Elijah, raising my eyebrows. Elijah's skin was still blanched, and his jaw clenched tightly. He stared at me for a long moment, then he slowly started to nod. I frowned. What the hell was that supposed to mean?

Ben unlatched the school door, propping it open for us. We shuffled into the foyer, still holding Joe up.

My breath caught in my throat. Miss Trager, Chloe, Julianna, Zo and Toby all lay on the floor, unconscious. Chloe and Miss Trager's heads were both bleeding. I didn't know what I was expecting, but this wasn't it.

Asher crouched beside Julianna, his eyes wide and panicked. He scrambled to his feet as we entered, moving to stand in front of the group. He spread his hands wide as if he thought he had enough magic to hold us back.

Ben took in the bodies slumped on the ground behind Asher, and something unfamiliar flickered across his face. "What happened? Are they okay?"

Asher shook his head. "What do you care? You did this to them."

"I didn't do this! And of course I care. They're my sisters." Ben strode towards Miss Trager.

Asher sent out a blast of magic. Ben flicked his hand and Asher flew backwards.

"Asher!" Elijah launched forward, leaving me scrambling to hold Joe up.

Asher's head hit the floor. Elijah grabbed him, pulling him upright, but Asher slumped against him.

Asher blinked and his eyes rolled, only barely staying conscious. "You're back," he said to Elijah. Fireflies lit up, marking the broken connection between them.

"Elijah, get away from him!" Ben yelled.

Don't, I wanted to say. Just a moment more and their connection might heal.

But Elijah took a step backwards, almost robotically. Asher slumped down to the floor, holding his head. I reached for Elijah, pulling him close to me and Joe. He didn't look at me, instead staring at Asher. Elijah's breathing was fast, his chest heaving with each inhale.

"Did you just...?" I didn't say it out loud. I *couldn't* say it out loud. A string of fireflies stretched out between him and Asher. I forced myself to look away, not daring to hope.

Ben crouched back down beside Miss Trager. "Hey, little mouse... come on, wake up now."

Miss Trager stirred but didn't wake. Zo, however, opened her eyes, waking. I inhaled, sharply, and Joe squeezed my hand – a warning. I bit my lip, willing myself to stay silent.

Zo was behind Ben, just far enough out of his line of sight that she might be able to ease herself up and get away before he noticed. She slid a hand across the floor, reaching for Toby. He was still unconscious.

Wake up, Toby, I said inside my head. *Wake up, but don't move.* I tried as hard as I could to push the mental picture of what I was seeing to him. If I could just pass it to him, then he could show Zo through their connection.

Ben stroked Miss Trager's hair back from her face, then turned to Chloe. "What did you do, kiddo?" He touched her forehead, and Chloe whimpered. She didn't wake. Energy flowed out of her into him. Too much energy... far too much. This wasn't like with Joe, where she seemed to be voluntarily passing it on. He was taking it from her, killing her.

"Stop!" I yelled.

Ben looked up at my shout. His eyes focused slowly on me, and he frowned. "For a moment, I could have sworn you were your mother."

Anything else I might have said stuck in my throat.

Ben looked around at the foyer, his gaze casual. "Last time I saw this place it was in flames. You remember that, Joe?"

Joe went tense.

Ben's eyes flicked back to me. "Your mother blew herself up right here, Callie. Did you know that?"

Bile turned in my stomach, but I didn't give him the satisfaction of a reaction.

"I figured she stashed her magic first, but now I'm wondering if it all scattered into the walls. It's always been about the school, hasn't it?"

Toby's fingers twitched, and a low hum started in the room. Suddenly, a stream of thoughts flooded into my head – Zo's and Julianna's voices, even Asher's, echoing through the connection now Toby was awake. It was too muffled to make out words. I looked at Elijah. He didn't give any sign that he'd heard it.

"Sammy's magic is gone, Ben." Mr Grandace appeared at the top of the staircase, Miss Caraway behind him. "And it's time for you to let go of everyone else's."

Ben chuckled. "You're all grown up now, aren't you Arthur?"

Mr Grandace straightened, making himself taller as Ben stood and walked up the stairs towards him. Once, I'd seen the headmaster as intimidating, but not now. His stupid cloak was gone, and his devil beard had grown out into a shaggy mess. More than that, he just looked small next to Ben. My captor would crush him if they fought, or rather, Ben would drain the energy out of him.

With sickening clarity, I realised that's exactly what would happen. One by one, Ben would drain us all. His sisters still lay unconscious, perfect targets, and Zo, Toby and Julianna were hardly in a better position. Elijah, Joe and I were all under his control, unable to stop him. This was it. This was how we were all going to die.

Joe shifted, turning his head towards me. "Do you still have it?" he murmured. His eyes flicked to my stomach.

I half raised my hand, wanting to touch the prophecy to reassure myself it was still strapped to me. Instead, I gave the smallest of nods.

He nodded back. "Your mum will tell you what to do."

I frowned. "My mum?"

Joe didn't answer, turning to Elijah instead. "It's the only way to end this."

Elijah nodded.

"Keep him away from her for as long as it takes. Tell the others."

"What are you talking about?" I asked.

Joe turned back to me. He touched my shoulders gently. "I've always been your dad, and I've always loved you."

Guilt rushed through me at his words. I opened my mouth, but he shoved me across the foyer before I could speak.

"Attack!" he yelled.

And Mosby did. The sweet, gentle Labrador launched himself forward, tackling Ben to the ground, and sinking his teeth into Ben's neck.

Chapter Sixteen

Callie

"Oh my god!"

Joe launched himself after Mosby, using his bodyweight to keep Ben down. I gasped, waiting for the rope around my chest to crush me, but the tightening of the magic never came. Elijah grabbed my hand, dragging me towards Toby.

"What the hell is happening?"

"Just get behind Toby and the others."

I tried to pull away. "No! We'll put them in danger."

Elijah didn't answer, instead picking me up and practically throwing me at Toby.

"Callie!" Toby sat up, sparking into life. He grabbed me, swinging me behind him. I clung to him, my fingers digging into his back in a desperate embrace. My cheek pressed against his chest, and I felt his heart fluttering under his skin. It felt like home.

Elijah spun around, sending out a flare of magic, then suddenly Asher was beside him strengthening it.

"What the hell?"

Elijah put his arm around Asher, clapping him on the

shoulder. Asher grinned at him. Their connection. They'd all been silently – frantically – planning while pretending to still be unconscious.

"How did Joe just do that?" I whispered.

An explosion rocked the room before anyone could answer. I stumbled, but Toby grabbed me, keeping me from falling backwards.

The tiled floor of the foyer broke apart, schisms appearing across it. We braced against what remained of the tiles. In the centre of the room, Mr Grandace and Ben fought, swirls of magic crackling in the air above them. Joe and Miss Caraway stood behind Mr Grandace feeding magic into him.

"How is he doing that?" I yelled. Why wasn't Joe under Ben's control anymore? The rope of magic around my chest finally tightened, and I doubled over at the drag of energy as Ben drained me. Elijah groaned, feeling it too. But this time, something felt different.

"No!" I said, and my magic listened. It fought back against Ben's pull. *I* fought back.

"We have to keep Callie safe," Elijah told the others, his voice choked. "Away from Ben's control. She can end this. Joe read it in the prophecy."

Your mother will tell you what to do.

Suddenly, the prophecy was hot against my stomach, burning to be taken out and read. But not here. Not where Ben was close enough to grab it from us.

"Upstairs, the planning room," Asher said. "Mr Grandace put wards around it."

Elijah stooped down, looping his arms under Chloe's shoulders and legs.

"Leave her," Toby said. "She did this to us."

Elijah shook his head. "Joe said to help her." He nodded to Miss Trager. "And her."

"Fine." Asher picked up Miss Trager.

She stirred, waking as he did. "The book..."

"It's okay. I've got it," I told her.

"She gave it back," she murmured, but her eyes were already closing. Blood dribbled down her cheek from the wound on her temple.

"Come on." Toby pulled me to my feet. He, Zo and Julianna surrounded me, rushing me up the stairs. Elijah and Asher followed after us, carrying Miss Trager and Chloe. The stairs shook, knocking me to my knees. I clutched my head. It wasn't just the explosions from Ben, it was the vibrations... that humming. Discordant sounds pressed in around us like we were trapped in the centre of an orchestra tuning their instruments.

Fight back.

I forced myself to stand. Mosby gave a painful yelp, which made me turn back. He ran from Ben, retreating to a corner, tail between his legs.

Toby's arm circled my waist. "Come on, Reactive Girl. Don't stop. You've got this."

At the top of the stairs, he led the way to one of the old classrooms. I paused just inside the door. Pages and pages of red writing lined the walls, all of it swirling, the letters rearranging themselves into new strings of chaos.

"Put Miss Trager and Chloe over here," Zo said. She grabbed a blanket from one of the chairs and laid it out in a corner of the room. She and Julianna helped Asher and Elijah settle Miss Trager and Chloe on it.

The women were both pale, their heads still bleeding, but light shimmered around Miss Trager in the same way it had around Joe. Something had happened. Chloe had done something to them, but whatever it was, it hadn't been for her own benefit.

I glanced over at Chloe. She was so still, her face bloodless. "What happened?" I asked.

Zo shivered, but Julianna stood up taller. She seemed centred somehow, the calmest of all of us in the middle of this chaos. "Chloe arrived back, and like... blasted herself and Miss Trager," she said.

"But why?" Asher asked.

His voice was hoarse, and he seemed to be holding himself back. His eyes were locked on Julianna, like he thought he was going to have to catch her. But she wasn't falling. I could see it in her – a sudden strength and resolve.

"I don't know," Toby said. "Maybe she was trying to weaken us?"

If that was the plan, it didn't seem to have worked. It wasn't just Julianna standing taller. They all were.

"But why did you bring her back here in the first place?" I asked. I felt like I was so close to understanding this, if only the magic would stop flickering around me. There was so much power in the room, all of it trying to draw my attention at once. I couldn't focus on any one thing.

"I didn't mean to. I was trying to grab *you*, but the magic led me to Chloe instead, and—"

An explosion downstairs shook the floor beneath us, sending us all to our knees. Miss Trager gasped, sitting up. She stared straight ahead, her eyes wide but seeing nothing. "She gave it back," she whispered.

And then pain ripped through my chest. I cried out. Toby grabbed me, but I shoved him away, his touch hurting more. I heard a pop as one of my ribs broke. I couldn't fight back against this.

"What the fuck is happening?" Zo screamed.

Bleeding welts opened up on Elijah's shoulder, following the line of the rope of magic. Asher clung to him, pouring healing magic into their connection.

"Enough!" Elijah gasped. "Stop with all this useless shit. Cal, you have to stop this. The prophecy told Joe you can do it. So do it!"

Everyone turned, staring at me. Discordant vibrations sounded as each of their faces turned towards mine, and behind them more and more letters swirled. The pages began to fall from the walls. I clutched my chest, trying to hold my rib cage together.

"I don't know," I said. "There's too many pieces. I don't understand what's going on."

Zo pulled herself up, a fierceness building in her face. "So we lay it out." She picked up one of the sheets of paper from the wall and turned it over. "Ben is stealing magic from us." She wrote that down, with a number one next to it.

Another wave of pain rocked through me, and I whimpered. I couldn't do this. I wasn't strong enough to fight this.

And then Toby's hands were on my face, holding me gently. "It's okay, Reactive Girl," he whispered. "You got this."

I closed my eyes and leaned into him. Slowly, all the other humming notes dropped away, leaving only a soft sound vibrating through the two of us.

"He wants my mother's power back," I said. "His own is unstable. And he said something about side effects of siphoning magic," I said.

"Miss Trager said that too," Zo said. "She was reading a book about it." She and Julianna wrote all of that down.

"Chloe is stealing energy too," I said. "And the magic told you to bring her back here."

Toby shook his head. "I don't know. I think it did? I might have just made a mistake."

"Chloe said she had to give something back," Asher said. "Then she blasted Miss Trager."

Another explosion from downstairs rocked everything. Searing pain rent through my chest, and two more pops. I felt my ribs snap with them.

"I can't," Elijah gasped. He stood slowly, almost robotically.

"Stop him!" I dragged myself up and stumbled towards Elijah. He flung out an arm, shoving me back.

Asher grabbed him, but Elijah threw him off. Power rumbled from Elijah. Chloe lurched upright, barely conscious. If she could have walked, she would have been shambling after him.

"Oh god, Ben's got control of them both." I would be next.

"Calliope…" Ben's voice rang out from downstairs. "Stop fighting me and come join us…"

Pain stabbed through me. Then another pop.

"Let Elijah go," Toby yelled. "Protect Callie."

"No!" I screamed.

But Elijah had already gone, out the door and into Ben's clutches. Chloe stayed where she was for now, but it wouldn't be long until Ben took her. The others crowded around me, pouring healing magic and strength into me. It burned just as much as Ben's power over me, all of it competing and confusing.

"Calliope…" Ben called again. "Come help me find your mother's magic."

Maybe if we just gave it to him, this would be over. Maybe his magic would stabilise, and he could stop this. Let us all go.

I gritted my teeth. He was getting in my head. He would never stop this.

Toby clutched my face again. "Just focus on one thing," he said. "Stay with us."

He brushed my cheeks gently with his thumbs, but I couldn't focus on him. The fireflies around him were too bright. Too much magic that Ben wanted to steal. I stared at Miss Trager instead, at her wide vacant eyes staring back at me from where she sat on the floor.

"The book..." she whispered.

My movements felt slow, but I reached for the prophecy.

Miss Trager shook her head. "The book..."

What did she mean? There were no other books in the room, only sheets and sheets of paper scattered over the floor. There was only one page left on the wall. I stared at it. The red ink swirled, letters rearranging themselves into words.

"She will give back the magic she stole, and they will be powerful enough to stop him," I read aloud.

Miss Trager nodded slowly. Her skin shimmered with the movement. *She gave it back...* Miss Trager hadn't meant the prophecy. Chloe had found a way to reverse the flow of magic. She'd turned it around, pulled it away from Ben, and given Miss Trager and Joe some of their magic back.

Miss Trager shivered, her face pale, but the vacant look dropped from her eyes. Just like Joe she was growing stronger.

"It wasn't just Ben stealing magic, was it? Chloe was always doing it too."

"She didn't know," Miss Trager said. "Don't blame her."

"And today she gave it back."

She'd given Joe and Miss Trager years' worth of power all at once. Somehow that had made Zo, Toby and Julianna collapse and...

"It wasn't just you and Joe she stole from, was it?" I said. "They've been stealing from *all* of us all along."

That's why he got stronger when we used our magic. That's why we could hurt him with force but not power. That's why Joe had trained Mosby to attack.

"It was a spell in a book from the library." Miss Trager rose to her knees, her legs finally steady underneath her. "He burnt it, trying to hide what he'd done, but the magic was too strong."

As if it had heard her, my mother's book lit up. It burned under my shirt until it felt like I would ignite. I ripped it free, throwing it to the ground. Words unravelled from the pages, stretching out to touch all of us. They crawled up my arms like tattoos, then ink began to bleed from them. It burrowed under my skin, until the words were inside me.

They each chose five to siphon from. Two alive, three not yet born.

I could hear my mother's voice in my head, speaking the words of the prophecy aloud.

They shaped the strangers in their minds and siphoned their magic. He wanted to become powerful with their power. But he took too much. He took too much.

"I didn't know," Chloe whispered, her voice cracking with tears. "Ben said it would make me stronger. Strong enough to get away from Dad."

"You siphoned magic from Joe and your sister," I said. "And then Julianna, Zo and Toby. That's why they collapsed too. You started stealing from them before you knew them – before they were even born."

"It was only supposed to be a little. Only what they could spare. They were never supposed to know."

Ben had done the same spell himself. He had taken magic from Mr Grandace and my mother, and then me, Asher and Elijah. But then he had stolen from Chloe too, and all the people she had siphoned from, and it was too much power. He'd taken too much, and it had made him hungry for more.

"Call-i-o-pe..."

The sing-song of Ben's voice made me sick.

"Where did your mother hide her pow-er?"

Ben had stolen so much power already. Why was my mother's so important?

"If he wants your mother's magic so badly, then we have to find it first," Zo said. She put the sheet of paper she'd been writing on aside, turning to me expectantly instead.

They were all turning to me expectantly. "Don't look at me," I wanted to say. She may have been my mother, but my only knowledge of Sammy was through her writing.

Her writing.

The entire room was covered in it – pages of letters copied from her notebook. I knelt down on the floor, picking up the book. The pages were blank. All the words had scattered, crawling off the paper and up over my skin. It was inside me now, words competing with the fireflies and the humming and all the rest of it.

But my mother's power had always been in writing.

I picked up a pen.

Where is Sammy's magic? I wrote.

Drips of ink appeared on my skin like sweat. They ran down my arms, letters forming as they fell. They rearranged themselves on the page, forming handwriting all too familiar to me. My mother's.

I gave it all to you.

Chapter Seventeen

Toby

The rest of us watched as Callie unravelled... the magic and herself. I closed my eyes, trying to follow everything she'd said. Chloe and Ben had done a spell years ago. Chloe had stolen her sister and Joe's magic, and some from me, Julianna and Zo. It shouldn't have been enough for us to ever notice.

"The prophecy told me to follow the threads," Callie mumbled to herself.

Ben had done the spell too. He had taken from Mr Grandace, Callie's mother, Callie, Asher and Elijah. But he had also stolen from Chloe, and thereby everyone she had stolen magic from too.

And somehow, that had tied us all together.

"I thought it meant something," I said.

Zo frowned. She seemed to be the only one listening. "What did?"

"The connections between us."

I'd thought the field of power between us had meant something – that my connections to Zo and Callie were special – but they'd all just been part of Ben's sick plan to make himself stronger. We were random strangers who had enough magic for him to steal from, brought together only because Sammy's prophecy told Mr Grandace where to find us.

Zo's face softened. "They do mean something. The links you made protect us. They're probably the only thing that has."

Miss Trager said that too – that it was the broken connection between Elijah and Callie that had made them vulnerable to him. But would any of this have happened if I hadn't linked us in the first place? He'd been dormant for years, hiding out, controlling Chloe and Joe, and stealing so little magic from us we didn't even notice. When I formed those connections, I must have dampened his ability to siphon from us. I'd forced him to come take more.

Callie moved around the room, shifting people as she did. She ran her hand along imaginary lines in the air, as if tracing the connections between them.

I could hear her thoughts, most of them racing too fast for me to catch, but there was one thing that kept repeating. *She will see the threads, and she will follow them. They will all find the way out when they untangle the web.* That's what she was doing. She was untangling the web.

She moved over to Miss Trager, tracing imaginary lines between her and the rest of us.

"But where does this one go?" she murmured to herself.

Through her mind, I saw the lines of the connections light up. There were so many of them overlapping. She traced one back to herself, then on to the prophecy.

"This one is my mother's," she said. "But then where is mine?"

Her magic... was that what I'd been connected to all those months, or had it always been her mother's? Was that why her connection with Elijah had broken? Too many threads of magic trapped inside her, and something had to give?

I reached out, gently touching the thread of magic that ran between the two of us. She started as I did, and a hum almost like a chime rang out in her mind. She took a slow breath, calming herself. This one wasn't like the rest of the competing sounds in her mind. This one sounded right.

"Guys!" Zo said.

I tore my gaze away from Callie. Zo stood by the doorway, her eyes wide. "Chloe's gone."

I spun around. The blanket where Chloe had been lying was empty. It had gone suspiciously quiet downstairs. Callie's eyes went wide.

"She will see the threads, and she will follow them. They will all find the way out when they untangle the web," she said, her words tripping over each other. "They must break the connections, and it must end in fire."

I froze. She'd heard it in my thoughts – that fragment of the prophecy.

Julianna practically screamed in frustration. "That doesn't make any sense! Our connections are the only thing keeping Ben from getting to us."

"Not those connections," Callie said quietly.

I understood now, why everything sounded so discordant in her head. There were the connections I had built, the ones that helped us. And then there were the ones that Ben and Chloe had made. The ones that Sammy and Miss Trager had snapped.

No, I said inside my head. *You can't.*

Miss Trager looked between me and Callie and shook her head. "No. You can't do that. Breaking those connections is too dangerous."

"You did it!" Zo said.

"But it didn't solve anything! Snapping those connections

stopped him siphoning from me and Arthur but put everyone else at more risk! He just took more power from all of you when he couldn't get to us anymore. And it killed Sammy!"

"The bracelets." Asher fumbled in his pockets, pulling out the bracelets he'd stolen. He doled them out, handing one to each of us. "They protected you last time. Will it work if we only have one each?"

"It will have to," Zo said.

My eyes flicked around the room. Bracelets already circled Zo, Asher and my wrists, but Callie's were bare. She didn't take one when Asher held it out.

"This is madness!" Miss Trager snatched the bracelet, though whether she planned to force it onto Callie's wrist or ban us all from using them, I wasn't sure. "You can't do this, Callie. I won't let you."

Of course, there was another way. I took a slow step back, heading for the door.

"I have my mother's magic. She gave it to me. She must have wanted me to do this!"

"That doesn't make any sense!"

I slipped out of the room, before I could hear the rest of Miss Trager's argument.

I turned at the landing, stopping before the lower set of stairs which led into the foyer. Ben couldn't see me from here, but I could see everything through the banisters. Chaos surrounded him. Chloe and Elijah lay at his feet, their faces disturbingly pale. Mr Grandace fought Ben partly with magic, partly with fists. Joe and Miss Caraway fed energy to Mr Grandace, but it wasn't enough.

I lit a fire in the palm of my hand. *It must end in fire.* If I burnt my connection to Callie – the one that Ben's spell had created – would the others light up too? Would it burn the ropes Ben had bound them with? I imagined the whole web of threads – mine, and Ben's going up like fuses.

But was I far enough away from Callie that it wouldn't burn her?

I raised my palm. I couldn't see the connections the way Callie could, but I could hear them. I could feel that ping in my stomach when the magic was right.

I moved my hand, waiting for the chiming sound. Nothing. And nothing caught fire.

I swallowed, staring at the flickering light in my hand. Images of Miss Trager's fireball from back when we were first training at the school filled my head. I remembered the pain as the flames had erupted over me.

Toby!

Callie's voice sounded in my head, and then there was a woosh. I stumbled backwards as she enveloped me in something that was a combination of bear hug and tackle. She clapped her hand over mine, extinguishing the flame just as she had done when she leapt across the field to save me from the fireball. She clutched the prophecy in her other hand, and she gestured with it, banging it angrily against my chest.

"Don't you dare!" she hissed, then wrapped her arms around me again. "Don't you dare try do this alone! I'm not losing you like that."

I hugged her back, holding her tight. Her reactive magic had brought her to me. I pulled her tighter against me. The humming turned melodious. Callie's magic really was her mother's, except in those moments when her reactive magic broke through. This was all her. This was what I was connected to. I couldn't break it.

She pulled back to look at me. Pings sounded in my stomach, and suddenly I saw everything through her eyes. Strings of fireflies stretched out around us, all of the threads she had been following.

Two of them seemed brighter than all the others.

Callie gasped. "I've never seen it like that before." Her eyes went wide, seeing everything both through her eyes and mine.

She reached out, touching one of those bright threads. It coiled around, anchoring somewhere deep in her stomach. The other end looped back to the prophecy.

"This is what we have to burn," she said. "This is the connection we have to break."

I reached out, taking hold of the other bright thread. It led down the stairs to the foyer. We peered through the banisters, tracing the magic. It ended at the book Miss Trager had dropped. The spell book – the one from the burnt-out library. The book that had started this all.

Chapter Eighteen

Callie

The spell book lay on the ground at the base of the stairs, its cover bent back. We all peered through the banisters at Ben and the others. They were locked in battle, their focus firmly on each other. Mosby cowered in a corner, alive but terrified.

"What's the plan, Reactive Girl?" Toby asked.

"Yeah, I mean if this is all you got, I'm going to be pissed," Zo added.

All around us, I could see the threads of magic. Everything we did, even if it was to fight Ben, it just gave him more unstable power.

Be silent.

Be small.

"No magic," I said. "Just force."

Surprisingly, it was Julianna who nodded first. "He's weak physically. We just have to get close enough."

"No heroes," Miss Trager said. "We only have to distract him long enough for Callie and Toby to get to the book."

Nods passed back and forth between the group. It almost felt like we should all be putting our hands into the circle to give a cheer like before a sporting match. Instead, we silently walked down to the landing.

"Three..." Asher whispered. "Two... one."

The others all ran down the lower set of stairs and out into the foyer screaming. Ben looked up, startled, but he was too drunk on the power he'd just sapped out of Chloe and Elijah to react. Asher reached him first and tackled him to the ground just as Joe had done earlier.

Toby and I ran for the book. I snatched it up when we reached it and clutched it to my chest with the prophecy. The cover was warm, almost as if it would burst into flame. Ash spread from it onto my hands. This had started in flames, and it was how it needed to end.

We scrambled back up the steps, away from Ben.

"Fire," I said to Toby. "Quickly."

He raised his hands, flames lighting in his palms. My heart squeezed at the thought of setting my mother's book alight, but at the same time, I felt her words shifting under my skin, wrapping me in warmth. She would be here, with or without the physical book.

Toby's eyes flicked back and forth between mine. "Are you sure?" he asked.

I nodded, certain. "This is it. This is how we fix this."

Toby took a long, slow breath. "Then let's do it." He placed his hands on the covers of the books.

A small string of smoke rose up, but the pages didn't catch alight. He frowned. "Why isn't it working?"

The spell book had survived the whole library burning down. We had nothing on that. I stared around at the room. Zo had caused enough fires with her magistations, but I doubted she'd be finding much funny right now. Perhaps we had been right the first time – breaking the connections could cause explosions.

"Perhaps it has to be you, Reactive Girl?" Toby held out the book.

I took it from him, reluctantly. Months ago, I'd sat in Zo's garden, willing flames to sprout from my hands and got nothing but rotting sunflowers. What was to say I'd get anything more useful this time?

"Come on, reactive magic," I whispered.

The pages of the spell book whirled open, just like the prophecy had, but no ink spread off the paper this time. The flipping stopped on a page in the middle of the book.

"Side effects of stolen magic..."

I scanned the list, taking in the information as quickly as possible.

Excessive siphoning may cause magic to become volatile... hunger for power... Mood swings... Weakened bone density... Rapid ageing.

All of this was what we were seeing in Ben, but none of it was helpful.

I skipped down to the bottom of the page where there was a list of warnings.

Never siphon from more than three people from each generation...

Never siphon from reactive magic users...

Well, that explained a lot. No wonder this had gone so wrong for Ben. I froze at the last item on the list.

In the event of death of one of the magic-users you are siphoning from, all power must be absorbed by the siphoner immediately to avoid risk of explosive instability. Avoid allowing posthumous magic to connect with other siphonees.

"Oh my god."

Ben hadn't absorbed my mother's magic, because she'd given it to me. I looked up. I met Elijah's eye across the room.

He lay on the floor, so pale and barely moving.

"What is it?" Toby tried to take the book back from me. "Did it tell you something?"

I slammed the book closed. I turned towards him, clutching it and the prophecy to my chest.

"Callie?"

I pulled him towards me, kissing him. He hesitated, then his mouth moved against mine, kissing me back.

I pulled away slightly, leaving my forehead pressed against his. "You know I love you, right?" I whispered.

His eyes widened. *Why are you saying goodbye?* he thought.

I turned, jumping off the top step. A second later I landed across the room, next to Elijah. He sucked in a breath and pulled himself upright.

"Callie!" Toby screamed from the other side of the room. He started to run, but it was too late.

"We gotta try one last time," I told Elijah. The threads of my magic– or rather, Sammy's magic – reached out trying to connect with Elijah's. This was why it had worked with Toby and not him. Because Toby had connected to my magic, but Elijah had been coming into contact with my mother's posthumous power – exactly what the book warned against.

Ben's eyes locked on mine. He took a step towards me, but six bodies converged on him pummelling him with fists and kicks. All force, no magic. Even Mosby left the corner, once more growling and gnashing his teeth. Zo grabbed hold of his collar, and then pushed a silver bracelet over his tail. I let out a breath. Good. He needed to be protected too.

I turned back to Elijah. Either he would be able to connect to my magic, and we would be strong enough to shut Ben out, or... he would connect to Sammy's and I would erupt in flames, taking the books with me.

Elijah frowned. Then his eyes flicked to the books in my

arms. He shouldn't have been able to read my thoughts, but somehow he always seemed to be able to.

"One more try," he said.

He grabbed my arms and the threads of magic wrapped around us, trying to regrow our connection. At the same time, they forced us apart. Elijah wrapped his arms around my waist, refusing to let go.

"No!" I tried to push him away. "You'll burn. It's just supposed to be me."

Energy built between us, pulsing around the books. Elijah moved his head, bringing his lips close to my ear. "If I had to be stuck with anyone," he whispered, "I'm glad it was you."

"No," I said again. But his arms just locked tighter around me.

There was more I should say. He had kept me safe all these months. He had loved me, even when I couldn't reciprocate. And now we were going to die together, to save our friends.

My hands burst into flame. Searing pain erupted over my skin.

"You have to run," I told Elijah.

He shook his head. "Not until it's done."

I clutched the books, watching the pages ignite. It spread out down Ben's connections. This was it. My mother's power poured out of me, spilling out into the books.

"Stop!" Ben screamed. "What are you doing?"

Flames spewed up as Sammy's magic came into contact with Elijah's.

"It's going to explode. You have to run, E!"

A strange half smile crossed his face. "Joe told me I'd die saving you. I didn't believe him."

I went cold. "What?"

"Get her out of here," Elijah yelled.

I started to turn, but Joe grabbed me before I could stop

him. He snatched the burning books and threw me sideways. His and Elijah's eyes met, and then everything erupted into flames.

Epilogue

Ursula

My brother didn't die in the fire. He should have perhaps, but I couldn't let it happen. I slipped a silver bracelet onto his wrist during the fight. I hadn't known what was going to happen, but I had figured better safe than sorry.

When he woke, a few days after everything had settled, he had no power. None whatsoever, and he was trapped in the body he had created for himself, excruciatingly old before his time. I set him up in what had once been the sick bay, surrounded by copious plants and flowers. My mother would have been proud, though maybe jealous that my plants never wilted, zapped of energy, in the way hers always had.

I tried to persuade Chloe to stay, but she said she had to leave. She would be back, though, she promised. Once she'd figured out who she was now she was free from Ben's control. I needed to do the same.

Perhaps we all should have left. Continuing in a school where so many people had died was kind of macabre. But the new Principal had insisted. She said creating something new here would be a way to fix everything that had been broken in the magic.

I stood outside the classroom on the first day, watching.

"We should carve our names into the desk," Julianna said.

I smiled, remembering the A.G. and U.T. carved into the desk. I wondered who had added the heart around them. Even now, it made me blush a little. It had never been like that between me and Arthur, but then again, there had never been time. Who knew what life would hold now there was no prophecy marking a cryptic path for us to follow.

"Yeah, sure. Let's be a high school cliché," Zo said.

I smiled. Zo had always been my favourite.

"We should add their names too," Callie said softly.

The others went quiet. Mosby nudged at Callie's hand, as if sensing her sadness. Elijah and Joe had sacrificed themselves to save us, as had Sammy all those years before. Carving their names was the least we could do to remember them.

Toby put his arm around Callie, pulling her into his side. He kissed her forehead gently. If I didn't look at him, I could almost imagine she was Sammy, standing with Joe's arm around her.

"You might have to do it for me, though." Callie held up her hands, still bandaged from the burns.

Toby grimaced. I could tell he desperately wanted to heal her hands for her, but she was determined to do it herself... once she learned how, that was. I admired her for that. And she might actually have a chance at it now Sammy's magic wasn't competing with her own. It would just be a case of her learning to feel safe enough to use her power. So far, she could only do that with Toby, but with time she would find a way to feel safe taking risks – allowing herself to make noise.

Zo pulled out a pen knife. "Come on then. Better do this before the teacher gets here, or we'll all get detention."

I laughed at the thought. I still didn't know what magic school was going to look like this time around, but I couldn't see myself holding any of these kids in detention after what we'd been through together.

"I think we can do better than a knife." Asher closed his eyes and ran his finger over the surface of the desk. His name appeared, carving itself into the wood.

One by one, they added their names followed by the names of the people who had died here. Joe. Sammy. Elijah. At some point, I would ask them if it was okay to add the names of my parents too. But not now. This moment was for them.

I felt a hand on my shoulder, and I jumped.

Miss Caraway smiled. "Sorry, I didn't mean to frighten you."

"It's okay."

"Are you ready for this?" she asked.

I nodded, though could I ever be ready for this? She smiled again, then strode into the room. I trailed after her, enjoying watching her in action.

"All right, children," she said, her voice rich with power.

Everyone scattered, going back to their own desks. They eyed their carved tribute nervously as if they really thought I would punish them for it.

"As you know, my name is Miss Caraway, and I am the new Principal of the school."

I still couldn't believe Arthur had handed over the reins so easily. He'd insisted on taking up a new position – school librarian. Who was I to refuse?

"In the coming months, other instructors will arrive to teach you in the traditional subjects, but for now we are focused on rebuilding your confidence and control with magic, after the ordeal you have been through."

I let out a breath. *After.* It felt amazing to finally be able to say that our "ordeal" as she put it was over.

My gaze wandered over the students. Callie's eyes traced over the names carved into the desk. Sadness flickered behind her eyes, but she also seemed more peaceful than she had ever been. Both her parents and Elijah had sacrificed themselves to save her, and I think she finally understood how much she had always been loved.

Toby shuffled his desk closer to hers. She looked up, and he put his arm around her. I had a feeling those two were going to cause me trouble.

Zo made a face, poking her finger down her throat. Toby rolled his eyes and mouthed the words "deal with it". Zo looked towards Asher and Julianna, the two of them equally full of hormones and puppy love. Zo gave an even bigger eye-roll, but I had a feeling she was finally happy for them. I didn't need magical connections to know what any of them were thinking, most of the time. Nor did they, really.

I would need to start recruiting for more students soon, though. I didn't want to leave Zo as the fifth wheel for too long.

Miss Caraway started to write on the whiteboard, drawing a flow chart explaining the different types of magic. I almost wanted to sit down in the back of the classroom and play student myself. With everything that had happened, my own magical instruction had been haphazard at best.

"You're ready, Reactive Girl," Toby whispered to Callie.

She nodded and glanced at her bandaged hands. "No shit, Sherlock," she whispered back, causing laughter around the room. "Let's learn some magic."

440

Helen Vivienne Fletcher is a children's and young adult author, spoken word poet and award-winning playwright. She has won and been shortlisted for numerous writing competitions including winning the Out-standing New Playwright Award at the Wellington Theatre Awards, making the shortlist for the Storylines Joy Cowley Award, and the finalist list for the Ngaio Marsh Best First Book Award.

Helen has worked in many jobs, doing everything from theatre stage management to phone counselling. She discovered her passion for writing for young people while working as a youth support worker, and now helps children find their own passion for storytelling through her work as a creative writing tutor.

She lives in Wellington with her disability assistance dog, Bindi – a five-year-old, playful Labrador who loves soft toys, cuddles, and can fit three tennis balls in her mouth at once.

Overall, Helen just loves telling stories and is always excited when people want to read or hear them.

Also by Helen

Reactive Magic Series
Reactive
Magnetic
Volatile
Explosive

Familiar Magic Series
Familiars and Foes
Accidents and Apparitions (published in Jingle Spells)
Curses and Cousins

Young Adult Books
Broken Silence
Underwater
We All Fall

Children's Books
The Trespassers Club
There's No Such Thing As Humans
Aunt Kelly's Dog
Jenny No-Knickers
Do Fruit Worry About Getting Fat?

Short Stories
Symbolic Death

Find out more at www.helenvfletcher.com

9 781991 198013